CONFESSIONS OF A
CLUELESS
REBEL

TOM CORBETT

Selected Praise for the Author's Non-Fiction Works

"…I found "Ouch. Now I Remember" to be a witty yet edifying read, riddled with some funny moments… with many of them making me laugh out loud. I enjoy his writing style, it was comforting yet candid, like listening to a respected relative recount their own life with unabashed honesty."

—Pacific Book Review

"…throughout the memoir, Corbett's prose remains engaging, consistently mixing insight with the familiar jokes that one would from a close friend. A thoughtful memoir about life and politics told in a (n} … endearing style."

—Kirkus Review

"…the emergence of Corbett's humanistic world view…gives Ouch, Now I Remember intellectual gravitas. Corbett imparts an enormous amount of wisdom and humanity."

—Clarion Review

"If you truly want to understand how public policy works, read this book. Corbett's descriptions about how laws and programs are developed gives readers a real take away—genuine insight into the discipline of public policy."

—Mary Fairchild, Senior Fellow
National Conference of State Legislatures

"Corbett's stories from the front lines of policymaking, like *All Quiet On The Western Front*, provide great insight into the way the world actually works, not what the generals or policy planners think is happening."

—Matt Stagner, Ph.D. Policy Fellow
Mathematica Policy Research, Inc.

"Tom Corbett's The Boat Captain's Conundrum is a winning performance."

—Forward Clarion Book Review

"Corbett takes a topic often shrouded in numbers and dense writing and turns it into an intellectual, yet conversational memoir."

—U.S. Review of Books

"Corbett's reflections, woven together with great insight and humor, transforms public policy from a class that is boring and mundane to a career that can be engaging and germane

—Karen Bogenschneider, Ph.D.
University of Wisconsin-Madison

Reviews of the authors fictional works:

"Palpable Passions delivers a compelling story arc infused with historical fact that should appeal to readers…"

Blue Ink Reviews

The book…feels like a screenplay; its dialogue is abundant and punchy, its landscapes well defined, and its characters have significant bonds. Palpable Passions uses bright, earnest characters to show that a microcosm can be as complicated as the big picture."

Foreword Book Review

"…Tenuous Tendrils, by Tom Corbett, is a compelling journey from exile to redemption. Like its characters, the book is quite clever and features an abundance of humor. Many heavy scenes are punctuated by conversations about the futility of war and the humanitarian failings of government also feature omniscient narrative wit that keeps the text from being bogged down by sentiment and allows the character's personalities to shine."

Clarion Review

"Corbett has created a captivating novel. The book title perfectly describes the fragile thread that spirals around each individual…to create an enthralling story that anyone will love to read."

U.S. Review of Books

Amazon Reader Reviews for Tenuous Tendrils.

"A penetrating look into the human soul and the fragility of relationships."

"Tenuous Tendrils is a conversational and meditative look back on a man's life. I really like the depth of detail that the author brought to these characters."

"This book was incredibly personal on so many levels. Overall, I found this to be an extremely touching and educational read."

"I personally loved this book. It was refreshing and thoughtful."

"The overall story is incredibly genuine, realistic to the time limits it covers and thoughtful. Each time I put down the book I found it moderately difficult since I wanted to know what would happen next."

CONFESSIONS OF A
CLUELESS
REBEL

TOM CORBETT

Other Books by the Author

Confessions of a Wayward Academic (Hancock Press, 2018)

Palpable Passions (Papertown Press, 2017)

Tenuous Tendrils (Xlibris Press, 2017)

The Boat Captain's Conundrum (Xlibris Press, 2016)

Ouch, Now I Remember (Xlibris Press, 2015)

Browsing through My Candy Store (Xlibris Press, 2014)

Return to the Other Side of the World with Mary Jo Clark, Michael Simmonds, Katherine Sohn, and Hayward Turrentine (Strategic Press, 2013)

The Other Side of the World with Mary Jo Cark, Michael Simonds, and Hayward Turrentine (Strategic Press, 2011)

Evidence-Based Policymaking with Karen Bogenschneider (Taylor and Francis Publishing, 2010)

Policy into Action with Mary Clare Lennon (Urban Institute Press, 2003)

I don't know where I am going but I am on the way.
—Voltaire

The planet does not need more successful people.
The planet desperately needs more peacemakers,
restorers, story tellers, and lovers of all kinds.
—The Dalai Lama

History repeats itself, first as tragedy, second as farce.
—Karl Marx

Additional Copies:

www.amazon.com
www.barnesandnoble.com

Published in the United States of America

ISBN hardcover: 9781948000215
ISBN softcover: 9781948000208

This work is dedicated to my long-suffering mother and father, Jane (Spiglanin) Corbett and Jeremiah "Tom" Corbett. I am sure that all new parents are excited with their newborns and cannot wait to see how their offspring will mature and contribute to society. I am confident that my folks took one look at me and concluded that they were not going to make the same mistake a second time. Thus, I am an only child. Please note that any and all shortcomings I evidenced as an adult are my responsibility alone. No blame or fault should be attributable to these good people. God knows, they tried.

I also want to take a moment to thank Mike Middleton and the others at Hancock Press for pushing me to redo and republish my earlier memoirs. If you are going to tell your story, you might as well get it right.

CONTENTS

PROLOGUE

If you want to keep your memories, you first have to live them.
—Bob Dylan

Ouch, Now I Remember was the title of my original personal memoir published in 2015. That title was a no-brainer. This expression of surprise mixed with a touch of regret was a common response to memories retrieved from the detritus of a long life. Peering back into the mists of time and the fog of long-ago events can be a perilous undertaking, sometimes evoking moments of pain, regret, and embarrassment. Ouch surely was a common refrain. As I reworked the original manuscript for republication, though, I recognized a deeper underlying theme. I was a rebel of sorts, pushing back against my rearing, my culture, my expected destiny, my professional norms, and the larger society about me. My resistance was seldom overt and never quite intentional. It more or less just happened, as if it was meant to be and I was the innocent bystander. In effect, I was clueless, an attribute that has defined much of my life.

In the very beginning, I started out to write a single memoir. After a faulty start, that original plan was abandoned. More than one tome would be necessary. Best to torture people in small doses; after all, I am not a sadist. I decided to focus first on my professional life and later return to write about my earlier years, at least for the most part. Now. I have been given an opportunity to update and tweak both works. ***Browsing through My Candy Store*** has become ***Confessions of a Wayward Academic*** while ***Ouch, Now I Remember*** is being rereleased as ***Confessions of a Clueless Rebel***. The closely aligned titles reflect their intimate connection.

When I first considered this project, recollections cascaded and tumbled through my head with raucous intensity and velocity. They did so in a random rush, in much in the same way I compose my more scholarly works, or at least what passes as scholarship for me. I express a thought or two and suddenly others pour forth with abandon. Most gush out rather effortlessly as if the first few were a knot that, once loosened, unleashed the remainder from an involuntary incarceration in some secluded recess of my brain. Some recollections, however, do require a bit of excavation work, particularly if they are buried deep under layers of accumulated nonsense. It is as if they don't want to see the light of day. When they do emerge, it is obvious why they might have preferred to remain hidden.

Reactions to these buried nuggets from the past vary considerably. The more deeply hidden treasures sometimes bring an "oh yeah" or even a "wow!" response. Others, too many others, bring a dreaded "oh crap" response. That one was painful, or embarrassing at the very least. It must be one of those false memories planted by someone out to do me harm, not that I am paranoid or anything. Still, it is obvious that George W. Bush did not get all the "evildoers" in the world, as he liked to call them, even with his fondness for guns and bombs and waterboarding. After all, Dick Cheney survived his administration. Though Dick did graduate studies at the University of Wisconsin, where I spent my professional career, he left that fine institution before I arrived. So, I doubt he ever harbored any personal animosity toward me though one cannot be too careful.

Why attempt a memoir if the process is uncomfortable? The answer is simple. If I don't, who will? No one cares about the path I trod more than I, except for Rascal, my dear Shih Tzu puppy. Then again, he has been bribed with copious blobs of Wisconsin cheese. Even then, he mostly ignores me. Apparently, my charms are decidedly limited. I remain one of the legions of average folk who trod through life the best they can, seeking to make lemonade out of lemons but more often doing the exact reverse.

If there is an organizing principle or theme to this labor of love, it is a 'breaking away' theme. I look upon my earliest pictures. How ordinary and sad was this urchin, the only child in a Catholic, working class family where larger broods of children were a source of pride; Always one of the last kids to be picked for the neighborhood athletic contests; So slow in elementary school that

I was segregated with the other slow kids; Sufficiently unwanted at home that my parents would constantly move when I was out to play and leave no forwarding address. Yet, this utterly ordinary child slowly managed to erect his own world view and path in life, one that could never have been predicted from those humble beginnings when the smart money was on my early demise through sheer incompetence.

While a bit surprising, my life trajectory was not a unique journey. It did, however, have its moments. I have shared aspects of my Peace Corps in earlier works which remain in print...*The Other Side of the World* and *Return to the Other Side of the World*. I recommend them highly...I could use the royalties. Still, much remains to be said. After all, every personal journey is replete with untold triumphs and tragedies, successes and failures, joys and sorrows yet to be told. Every journey is stuffed with endless epiphanies and insights that, though seldom unique, enrich each of us immeasurably. Some may even strike others as moderately profound or, in my case, profoundly inane. My journey is no exception.

I have done a number of semi-interesting things, to me at least. During my journey I have studied for the priesthood, joined a radical organization during my college years, taught social policy at the University of Wisconsin, participated in union negotiations, helped develop President Clinton's welfare reform proposal, worked the 11-7 shift in a major hospital and as a night watchman for a city sewer system (where no sewers went missing on my watch I might add), testified before a Congressional committee, helped run a major university-based research institute, worked with troubled kids in a distressed neighborhood, and served on a National Academy of Sciences expert panel. I also worked as a ticket taker at a movie theater, a role that helped my social popularity soar. And that is just what I recall at this moment.

There have been moments of humor such as the time I was grilled by military intelligence as a threat to the country. There were several moments of total fear such as when I was surrounded by rabid rednecks in Texas, by outraged patriots in my hometown of Worcester Mass., and by Wisconsin social workers bent on avoiding paperwork. There have been moments of wonder, like the time I was seduced (or did the seducing?) by a female Peace Corps staffer under the stars of Rajasthan the night before going to my rural village for a two-year stint. And there have been moments of black despair when I truly thought that an addiction to alcohol was destined to destroy me. We will get to all that and more in time, but clearly there were many bends and bumps in the road on my way to the golden years.

The point is that nearly everyone's life is interesting. We all have adventures, big and small, worth a bit of reflection. We have all survived challenges and learned lessons from which others might profit. How does the old bromide go . . . a life not reflected on is a life not worth living? I chose not to pass on my genes to future generations, for which generous thanks are expected. Thus, these ruminations might well represent my only contribution to our evolution as a species, admittedly a rather meager contribution indeed! However, I remain convinced these reflections will contribute more to society than a bunch of little Tommy Corbett's being foisted on an innocent and unsuspecting world.

The steps to this memoir . . .

This memoir was not the product of a singular conscious decision. No, it grew out of smaller, incremental steps. The first was a gathering of former India-44 Peace Corps volunteers in May 2009. This was the volunteer group I trained with in Wisconsin and served with in Rajasthan, a rather bleak province located in the northwest corner of India bordering on Pakistan. It was the first reunion of any kind I ever attended, that I ever considered attending. It never occurred to me that I would enjoy revisiting ancient times or that I could make small talk with people I barely recalled from four decades earlier. I was wrong, as I often am.

The India-44 gathering proved an emotional experience for all of us, including me. Toward the end of our time together, we could sense a bittersweet aftertaste, that unpleasant residue that emanates from something that remains incomplete. We wanted to know more about one another and at a deeper level. Some half-century earlier, when we trained for the rigors of India, we were absorbed in ourselves, whether we would make the cut and whether we would survive two years in harsh and lonely conditions.

At times, the selection process pitted us against our fellow trainees where we were asked to rate our own peers, a tasteless exercise. In the end, the perception that we were engaged in a zero-sum game made any real bonding just a bit more difficult.

Upon surviving a hard training, we would then be tested by two tough years in rural India battling isolation, disease, doubt, and our own incompetence. During our service, we buried our own insecurities within ourselves, perhaps afraid that revelation might allow our fragile and incomplete selves to unravel. We surely embraced one another considering our common struggle but never really got much beyond a surface understanding of our fellow sufferers. Now, several decades later, we sat around in a living room in Oakland, California, and openly shared our failures, most of us for the first time. For me, it was a bit like the Alcoholics Anonymous meeting I attended for a while. Experiences and feelings that you thought were yours alone turned out to be commonplace, group emotions shared by all. Failures that were deemed personal were discovered to be distributed broadly like some outbreak of the flu. That pervasive sense of not doing enough, of being an imposter, turned out not to be yours alone but rather a common response to a shared challenge.

As my fellow volunteers talked about what they brought back from India and what they did with their subsequent lives, it was clear this was an exceptional group that had accomplished much. True, there were no members of the top 1 percent of the income distribution among us. Then again, no one embraced such an ordinary ambition…to simply accumulate money and trinkets. We seemed to focus on different forms of achievement. A disproportionate number went on to obtain advanced degrees, many from the nation's elite universities, and seemingly everyone contributed to the well-being of their communities and their fellow man. It would seem we had taken a misbegotten adventure and turned it into something quite contributory, if not essential, to our subsequent life trajectories.

Conventional metrics of success, like status and wealth, did not matter to how we saw one another. At our first reunion, one of our members looked around the room and quietly said something along the following lines:

What a great group this is. No one cares if you are rich or poor, successful or not, good looking or not. You just know you are going to be accepted and loved because you were one of a group that had experienced something intense and special together. Some of those who have passed will never be able to join us again. But they will not be forgotten. They were members of India 44. We are members of India 44. We are a band of brothers and sisters with a connection forged half way around the world a lifetime ago and yet which has endured to this day. We are very fortunate indeed.

We finally shared ourselves with one another through two volumes of reflections titled the *Other Side of the World* and *Return to the Other Side of the World*. Through these two vehicles we began to know one another more fully and perhaps even ourselves more deeply. When finished with the Peace Corps reflections, two chapters in edited works hardly seemed sufficient to even touch upon the things I had to say. More was on the way. For better or worse, the spigot had been turned on.

The second step arose when I perused the first draft of a manuscript completed by Mike Simonds, a fellow Peace Corps volunteer from India-44. He recounted his tortuous path through some seventy-five romantic and not-so-romantic relationships, most of them taking place only in cyberspace. These connections were with women he met on a dating site after his marriage fell apart. Mike is my image of everyman. He is a prime example of a guy women ignore at their own peril and loss ... quiet, unassuming, sensitive, and caring.

In my experience, women don't really see the nice guys while expending great energy chasing total losers where a predictably horrendous ending is apparent to all, except for those apparently brain-dead women doing all the chasing. In any case, I found the story of Mike's tragic romantic adventures very entertaining, instructive, and even uplifting. Again, every life story has merit. You do not need fame or notoriety to touch others. Besides, Mike included a description of me that begs sharing as I relate in *Confessions of a Wayward Academic,* my recently released policy memoir:

> *He (Mike) apparently despaired of lucking out with any of the PC gals attending the final going-home party in New Delhi. He feared competition from some of the guys like me whom he described as "Tall and dark, with the rugged good looks of someone who could adorn the cover of a romance novel." Of course, this was just before it was discovered he had a detached retina and was whisked off to a U. S. Military base in Germany for emergency surgery.*

Upon completing the two Peace Corps volumes and Mike's draft, memories that might constitute a more complete personal memoir kept wandering through my head. It was clear these musings would not let me alone until I did something with them. Still, it wasn't until I turned that eventful 7-0 in May of 2014 that I sat down to write something just about me and not an edited volume of group reflections or an academic book. Even that step was predicated on an unexpected, perhaps serendipitous, turn of events.

The policy memoir . . .

My wife, Mary Rider, and I intended to do a lot of traveling the summer of 2014. Instead, we brought a new puppy into the house. We had lost our dear Cavalier King Charles spaniel, Ernie, in September 2013. The need to replace Ernie became overwhelming by the next spring, at least on my spouse's part. Ernie had been our first dog after many cats. He had big brown eyes, floppy ears, and the sweetest disposition imaginable. My absolute, firm decision to wait several years before getting a replacement dog wilted. Besides, in household decision-making, only one vote counts. I will give you one clue: it is not mine. Thus, Rascal entered our lives, a frisky devilish pup that loves to steal my shoes, socks, underwear, and anything else that might contain pungent odors associated with yours truly. I must possess pheromones that only attract dogs. I suppose all I can really say is that they do not attract women. Without travel to keep me from mischief, step three kicked in and my word processor beckoned.

For the first week or so, I wandered between a personal memoir and a set of reflections on my policy career. Then I finally decided I would focus on my professional life. After discarding much of what I had written up to that point, the recollections tumbled forth faster than I could type. Some nights I would jerk awake at 2:00 or 3:00 AM with vignettes randomly floating in my head. Should I jump up and write them down. Could I trust myself to wait until the morning? How many might be lost in the vain effort to get a decent night's sleep. Worst of all, were they real recollections or half-baked images concocted in that penumbra between sleep and consciousness? Still, despite constant vigilance over a pup that was determined to poop on the rug and not in the great outdoors, I had completed a draft of some 125,000 plus words in about six weeks. The number of words could have been much higher but that total, to me at least, pretty much bumped up against the tolerable length for a readable work, a self-imposed limit I since have abandoned.

As a kid, all the other boys in the neighborhood dreamt of being cowboys or soldiers or space cadets or athletes (no one in my poor neighborhood fantasized about being a captain of industry). I would dream about being a writer. Not sure where that came from since I did not exactly grow up in a literary household. At best, my father read Perry Mason mysteries and Reader's Digest condensed books. Certainly, the neighborhood kids I hung around with read little more than whatever was printed on that morning's breakfast cereal box and maybe the daily sports page.

Below is a passage from a letter I sent to my college sweetheart from India sometime in 1968 most likely:

The book you sent several months ago finally arrived the other day. I suspect I may enjoy it very much. In school I tended to concentrate on psycho-social and political questions much to the exclusion of more artistic and literary works. Now that I have time to rectify that oversight, I don't have access to very good literature. I have a compulsion to pour through several diverse authors including Camus, Hemingway, Kierkegaard, Dostoevsky, Proust, Fitzgerald, Joyce, Sartre, Updike, etc. as well as poets such as Cummings, MacLeish, and Alden.

As I believe I mentioned previously, I'd really like to do some writing myself. I haven't done anything serious

since my seminary days. The old need is welling up again.
I can feel it, but it takes a bit of courage to tackle something
of this nature honestly.

I guess I've always wanted to write. As a young
boy I even started two 'novels' which fortunately never
progressed beyond the first chapter. Yet, until now this
desire or need, while rather effectively buried beneath
the insecurity of my own perhaps realistically appraised
commonness, remained annoyingly there in a persistently
conscious and restless latency. It occasionally emerged,
briefly at the seminary where I somewhat immersed
myself in contemporary philosophy while wrestling with
the enigma of self-definition, and during my last semester
at Clark where socio-political problems captured my
attention. Yet, for the most part Clark did little more
than devitalize this 'poetic expressive necessity' through
a kind of scientific rigidity and intellectual sterility . . .
It had become gauche to equivocate about concepts using
ambiguous artistic expressiveness. And of course, it did
not help that I remained as ill-defined as ever and just as
insecure. Now this need is as compelling as ever and, what
the hell, there are plenty of lonely hours to fill.

I recall coming across an article about my father one day,
written when he was in high school in the early 1930s. It was
mostly about his contributions to his high school's basketball team,

but one line caught my attention. When asked what he wanted to do when he became an adult, he mentioned becoming a journalist, a newspaper writer.

A journalist! I never knew he had such dreams. He had adventures as a young man flirting on the edge of the mob in Worcester Massachusetts and working in Bingo parlors along the East coast when these were profit-making operations. But he settled for a life working at various factory jobs until a worn-out body forced him into a custodial position at the public library. He was, as I recall, a very smart man with numerous talents. He had a quick wit, was a good storyteller, and possessed the skills of a deft graphic artist. I believe he had many of those classic Irish gifts of quixotic expression in good measure, along with a few ethnic curses as well. He was also devilishly handsome with a great head of hair, which somehow eluded me.

I now wonder if he thought he had settled in life, if he ever regretted not pursuing some path deemed beyond his reach as a young man coming of age during the Great Depression. Having been touched by a similar muse to express myself on the written page, I have considered whether my life in the university and doing public policy was also a kind of settling for second best. I know I had fun doing what I did, but was it really what I was meant to do? Though I don't engage in much second-guessing or "what might have been," this is a question that has lingered. Such musing made another literary adventure unavoidable. Okay, that is an overstatement since more worthwhile endeavors competed for my time and attention. I could have turned my considerable talents to cleaning the toilets and picking up the dog poop deposited by Rascal. But when faced with a choice of doing something useful and wasting time, I always go with frivolous nonsense.

Rebelling or surviving…?

This literary adventure will fill in the spaces of my early years and what events and influences brought me close to the halls of power and scholarship. I touch upon my professional experiences again but from a more interpretive and contextual perspective. Here, I want to tackle some of the bigger questions we all ask from time to time. The one question we probably all ask ourselves in later life is how we got to this point in our personal journey. It has always been a source of amazement to me that I did as well as I have. Trust me when I say I am totally inept in the details of everyday living. One example will suffice for now while others will surely follow in the subsequent chapters.

I recall going into the basement one day to retrieve something or other. I noticed a rubber tube extending from the water softener and lying on the floor. "Hmmm," I said to myself, "that does not look right." I picked up the unattached end and looked all over the machine for a place where it might fit. Seeing none, I concluded that this was a problem that needed professional attention. In the meantime, I placed the loose end of the rubber tube into a nearby basin where any discharge might harmlessly go down the drain.

Satisfied that I had responded intelligently to an emerging disaster, I went upstairs to call an expert.

The water softener guy arrived in due course. I accompanied him down to the basement where I explained the "problem" and informed him of my temporary solution. Immediately, I got the look, the look that says, "Oh my god, I am dealing with another cretin." My body began to shrivel with embarrassment even though I yet had no idea what dumb-ass thing I had done now. The technician calmly explained that I was correct to put the unattached end of the tube into the basin since it was, after all, a drainage tube. Why didn't the earth ever swallow me up when such a fate was needed and desperately desired?

When he prepared the bill for his house call, he wrote in the space under services provided the words "explained operating procedures." I am sure he shared many a laugh with his colleagues as he regaled them with tales about the numb nut who could not recognize a drainage tube. There are service technicians all over Madison sharing stories about this moron who really is too stupid to live on his own. I cringe with embarrassment at the thought of it.

As I casually reflect on the arc of my life, it is not clear I enjoyed any sort of cumulative learning path. Understanding might well track in a curvilinear or even an oscillating path, responding to increasingly complex input and influences. Yet, this is precisely why such an expressive and literary adventure so late in life makes sense. You don't really know something until you try to communicate it to others. You cannot "know" your own life until you try to tell your own story. Perhaps meaning is in the telling.

Before starting, let me confess a couple of things. First, there is no way I can write this without repeating vignettes also found in other reflections, my Peace Corps and Professional memoirs. So, don't wrinkle up your nose when you come across something familiar, assuming you have read my earlier works at all. I figure many of my readers are, like me, older than dirt and can barely recall what they ate for breakfast. Just assume it is all new and have a good laugh or cry or nap, whichever reaction hits you most. In any case, they remain hilarious. Second, I don't try to catalogue my entire life. I focus on the early days though I do briefly cover topics that were first introduced in my previous memoirs. I do repeat some of the stories and vignettes but only to remind readers about the quality of those earlier works. It is not too late to go out and buy a full set of these masterpieces to share with those whose friendship with you has run its course.

Also, I will not try for chronological coherence. Recently, I chatted with two colleagues from the University of Wisconsin. We traded secrets on how we go about writing, usually for academic purposes. Even given the formal constraints of that world, we agreed that our better efforts emerged from a certain unstructured approach. Don't constrain yourself to outlines or straightjacket-type conventions, simply let it flow. That certainly seemed true of my many lectures and talks; the better ones were those not overly planned in advance. While I am not a total loose cannon, I would rather just start and see where the muses take me. So, let's give this a shot . . . *A Clueless Rebel.*

Tom Corbett

Madison Wisconsin

May 2018

Clueless Rebel in his prime

CHAPTER 1

DESPAIRING

The only thing worse than being blind
is having sight but no vision.
—*Helen Keller*

I was stepping down both as associate director of the Institute for Research on Poverty at the University of Wisconsin and from my teaching role in the School of Social Work. To mark this milestone, my colleagues threw a party for me. My best guess is that they feared I might change my mind and hang around even longer. Though much loved by many colleagues, in my own mind at least, several had been lusting after my preferred parking space. I could see it in their eyes. Why doesn't that old fossil leave, though I was hardly fossilized by academic standards. It struck me that changing the locks on my office door and the posting that picture of me with instructions to "shoot on sight" would have done the trick. Apparently, however, they thought some added incentives were necessary.

Making sure I left . . .

I had thought that any random phone booth might accommodate all the likely attendees for this soiree. But you can't find those things anymore, so they settled for a nice, big room overlooking majestic Lake Mendota. This expansive body of water abuts the bucolic campus and constitutes one of five lakes that make Madison such a lovely city. The choice of venue proved fortuitous since quite a few people showed up. I was taken aback for a moment. Then it hit me, you needed a big crowd if you were going to pump up the guilt factor. People invested in cards and some even kicked in money. It would be embarrassing were I required to give it all back. I wondered at the time just how much some were paid to show up in person.

My big send-off prizes included green fees for two at a golf course. I initially assumed it would be for nine holes at the local mini-golf course, the kind where you putted the ball through a windmill or between a clown's legs or even into a cardboard alligator's mouth. But I was shocked to discover it was to a top-flight course where the pros were scheduled to play the PGA Championship a couple of years hence. It must have set them back five hundred bucks even then. Wow, they really must have wanted to ramp up the guilt level. Either that or they thought I might never survive a round on such a difficult course. It had been noted that groups of vultures often circled over my head on golf courses.

Apparently, these scavengers assumed that anyone playing as badly as I must be on the verge of kicking the bucket.

Surprisingly, I survived the eighteen holes, and even had a good time. I always get my money's worth on the golf course. It struck me as odd that golfers would pay out all that dough and yet try to take as few shots as possible. I figured I had already plunked down my money, so I should take as many whacks as I could. It is not as if they discount the prices when you take fewer swings at the damn ball. Hey, I had learned a lot from the economists with whom I had worked over the years. They taught me to get my money's worth. And I do, on the golf course that is.

In truth, my spouse and I almost chickened out. We checked into the American Club in Kohler Wisconsin, a many star resort of national repute. The Kohler family owned the town, built several prime golf courses in the area, and made their fortunes by turning your common bathroom into something that looks like a luxurious spa fit for a Maharaja. Then we headed out to the course to see what we would be up against the next day. The guy at the club told us to go out back to watch golfers as they approached the eighteenth green. From our vantage point, it looked like the fairway was comprised of incredibly small landing areas set amidst tall whispery brown stuff you would see on links-style courses in the British Isles. You hit into that crap, and you might as well take up knitting as a hobby because you will be in there forever.

So, we watched these golfers struggling to get to the green or blast their way out of these huge sand traps that might well be confused with the Gobi Desert. I immediately broke out into a cold sweat. We knew that uber-wealthy golfers often flew their private jets in from the East or West coasts just to play at this course. I was certain we would be paired up with hotshots who would audibly groan as I repeatedly launched towering 120-yard drives into Lake Michigan. Then they would complain to the management who would summarily issue a lifetime ban on me. With visions of impending ridicule dancing in my head I turned to Mary and said, "Let's go home and just lie to everyone that we had a great time." Once again, she ignored my sage advice as she had repeatedly during the eight or so decades of our marriage.

Mary prepared some thirty-six balls for the next day's anticipated disaster and still worried if that would be enough. Still, we sucked it up and arrived on what turned out to be a gorgeous fall day. Our caddy, a requirement for this course, took one look at Mary's supply of golf balls and said, "You can take five, maybe six balls." After all, he had to carry two bags and endure the witnessing of excruciatingly bad golf. They did earn their money. Despite all our angst, we were paired with a couple of regular retired guys from Racine Wisconsin and had a great time. I lost only one ball, and no vultures showed up. Mary did not lose a one. Caddies are great! It also helps if you don't hit the ball very far.

But back to my party. The assembled crowd was, in fact, a poignant selection from the past three-plus decades of my life in Madison, Wisconsin. There were the usual suspects from the Institute for Research on Poverty where I had spent the bulk of my professional life. There was a scattering of faculty from the School of Social Work where I had taught for many years, where I had endured the agony of numerous faculty meetings and where I had spent many an hour looking over applications for admission to the MSSW (Master of Social Work) program. I was gratified to see numerous students from the Social Policy practicum course for second year master's students that I taught. There were even some folk from the State of Wisconsin where I began my professional career in 1971. And, of course, there were assorted acquaintances and even strangers who, I suspect, wandered in for the free food.

Peter Albert was there with his lovely wife, Susie. We worked together only briefly for the Wisconsin Department of Family Services (DFS) in the early 1970s. DFS was the state agency that ran welfare and human service programs throughout the state. We managed to bond during that brief time together as people do who face the specter of death together. As I describe more fully in my companion professional memoir, *Confessions of a Wayward Academic*, Peter and I were sent out to train public social workers in Wisconsin how to complete a form I had designed. This ingenious masterpiece captured the total set of services they provided clients on one page. I thought the form very clever indeed, perhaps a work of art. They thought it a travesty conceived in the very bowels of hell. Beauty, after all, is in the eye of the beholder.

At a critical moment in the initial training session, I thought my life in danger. The audience had worked itself up into a boiling rage. Being quick witted and unscrupulous, I deftly shifted all blame to Peter. Hey, I faced almost certain death at the hands of enraged social workers. Spending a few years in jail for malicious indifference to human life seemed a preferable option to being torn apart by hostile bureaucrats being asked to do more paperwork, no matter how justified the request. But we made it through. In the end, Peter did get his revenge. He was best man at my small wedding way back in 1972. Wow, I have been married forever! He grinned maliciously throughout the ceremony. When I asked him why he had stopped by my retirement party of sorts all these decades later, he simply said, "Well, I was there at the beginning and thought I would be there at the end."

Another compelling character from my early state days was Bernard Stumbras and his sweet spouse, Sharon. Bernie had been instrumental in getting one of my favored whacky ideas off the ground during my rather short stint as a real State of Wisconsin employee. Even though I remained a technical retard throughout my life, I was well aware of both the power and necessity of computers from the very beginning. Consequently, I fought hard to automate the management of social welfare programs. It struck a few of us as inevitable that we move from a pen and paper approach to managing welfare and human service programs into the digital age.

When a group of us young Turks at the time started lobbying hard, as only the young and the righteous can, the old guard running things banished us back to our cubicles. Even then we kept meeting in our homes after work and on weekends. It all seemed rather futile until Bernie Stumbras rose high enough in the organization to champion our cause. Wisconsin subsequently led the nation into the computer age of program management. Bernie was to pass away too young, but I will always recall him fondly as a gifted and visionary public servant.

Of course, not everyone from the old state days was there. There was this one Wisconsin state bureaucrat my wife tragically mistook for me one day. At the time she worked in the same State Office Building as I, a place known as 1 W. Wilson. It was one of those older state buildings that looked like a mausoleum built with convict prison labor back in the 1930s. That was probably because it was a mausoleum built in the 1930s though I am not totally sure about the prison labor. In the summer, the building's concrete blocks would heat up during the day. With no air-conditioning back then, I recall the sweat dripping onto whatever papers were on my desk. We were not a coddled bunch.

In any case, my wife had to use the restroom. The closest one was on the floor just above hers. When she emerged from the stairwell, she noticed one lone male leaning over a water fountain, what we call a bubbler in the Midwest. Otherwise, the hallway was empty. Apparently, he was a tall and handsome and sophisticated-looking guy since she thought it was me. Either that, or she forgot to take her eyeglasses. Looking around to make sure no witnesses had appeared, she crept up behind this poor schlep, reached in between his legs, and gave his balls a good love squeeze.

Unfortunately for her, and especially for the poor schlep, he was *not* me. It took the EMTs a good hour to scrap the poor bastard off the ceiling and restart his heart. In truth, we really don't know if he was there or not. While making abject apologies, she fled the scene without getting a good look. Fortunately, this was before we became so sensitized to the evils of sexual harassment in the workplace. I am sure a sneak attack on a man's family jewels is forbidden considering today's stricter standards of personal conduct. Maybe he did show up to get a look at the poor schmuck who remained married to this maniac for all these years.

In any case, I looked over the audience. I must admit, I was a bit proud. I had worked with some very smart and good people, both dedicated public servants and nationally renowned scholars. I had touched many students and affected public policy in innumerable, even important, ways. I even made a few scholarly contributions though I hardly considered myself much of a scholar. It was a rich and full life. The question remains, just how did that happen? There was nothing from my early years to suggest any kind of latter success would be in the cards. As a child I recall lying in bed worrying how I would survive as an adult. It seemed highly improbable that anyone would pay me for anything I might offer the world after my parents threw me out of the nest. I soothed my anxieties by concluding that I could always enlist in the military; they would take anyone. Whether I would last longer than my first failed chin-up is another matter.

One thing was sure, I did not look out on the world with any excess hubris or overconfidence. Was that false modesty operating? Was it a defense mechanism to take the sting out of any future failures? Or was it a calculated and accurate appraisal of my prospects. In quickly reviewing a host of images and memories that flooded through a largely uncluttered brain, evidence mounted supporting the hypothesis that my childhood fears of future failure were well taken. In my tender years, it sure looked as if I were destined to become one of life's more notorious screwups. It was all there if you knew where to look, a series of what I call 'yikes' memories, those that cause a facial grimace that others see as an uncontrollable tick.

This kid needs help . . .

As a child, we lived in what was called a three-decker. These were three apartments, one on top of the other. In those days, the owner often lived in the bottom flat and rented out the two above. In our case, we lived in the first floor flat. The owner was an absentee landlord who owned several buildings. A Worcester firefighter and his family lived on the second floor while my aged grandmother and her unmarried daughter, my aunt, lived on the third.

An early ouch memory involved the young daughter of the second-floor firefighter. We were playing in the backyard when she coyly suggested that she would show me hers if I would show her mine. Now, not being the brightest bulb on the marquee, and being a young tot at the time, I had no freaking idea what she was talking about. Show what, look at what! Females, as we know, mature faster than males and we never seem to catch up. But I got it after a bit and we commenced to do the dirty peeking even though it all seemed a little weird to me at the time. What the hell was I looking at and why?

"What is going on down there," I heard boom from above. For a moment, I thought it was the voice of God. But no, it was a female voice, and we knew back then at least that God was an old man with a flowing beard. Rather, it was the shocked and disapproving words from my matronly, grey-haired old grandmother who was peering down at us from her third-floor back porch. There was a look of disappointment and even disgust on her face. This was not good.

She always struck me as straight out of central casting . . . a somewhat plump lady with a kind face and a saintly demeanor (when she was not cross). She also had a touch of that Irish brogue lingering from her youth in the old country. I spent hours in her flat where she made the greatest eggnogs imaginable and where we played the card game Old Maid. I never quite put it together that our third in this childish game was my aunt who was, in fact, an old maid.

Oh god, I thought, this sin will send me straight to hell. In the Irish pantheon of human transgressions, anything involving one's genitals was clearly beyond the pale. Even the phrase "beyond the pale" had an Irish origin, meaning the barbaric world that lay outside the immediate area surrounding Dublin. You went beyond the civilized world of Dublin if you ventured beyond the "pale" where the English rulers held close control. In truth, though, any place populated by gangs of drunken Irishmen could not be considered civilized. Without doubt, showing my family jewels to the gal upstairs was way beyond every pale imaginable and had to be a mortal sin punishable by pitchforks and brimstone. I could tell that by the shock and disgust in my grandma's voice. Up came my pants and off I scampered, frantically plotting how I might make it on my own at age four or five or whatever I was at the time.

As most Irish lads from my era will attest, our indoctrination into the evils of worldly sexual pleasure began early and occurred often. Sex was sinful, degrading, embarrassing, and those were the good things about it. You surely didn't talk about it. Hell, it was even a sin to think about it. How many times did I tramp into weekly confession as a young teen and start with, "Dear Father, I have had 8,147 bad thoughts in the past week." And then I had to confess the lie I had just told since the real number was much higher. It wasn't until much later that I realized I was totally normal. Boys have sexual thoughts at a rate of one per 7. 7 seconds (or was it 0. 7 seconds) while girls had naughty thoughts at a rate of about one per 7. 7 months. As I think on it, males have some 100 times as much testosterone as females. It is some wonder girls have any erotic thoughts at all. I always wondered what they confessed each week since they obviously were not fantasizing about me or any other male for that matter.

In any case, I don't recall any punishment from this escapade so Nanna (what I called her) must have remained discrete. Maybe she thought that God's wrath would be enough. Still, I scratched out the job of Pope from my list of future life aspirations. She always was the kind person who forgave me. Surely her sweet grandchild had been led into sin by that second-floor vixen.

My bigger problem remained, what might I do in life. My parents would kick me out someday. When that happened, I would have to fend for myself. That looked like a dubious proposition to me. Maybe I could become a cowboy, an astronaut, or a soldier? These were our heroes back in the 1950s. We watched the Lone Ranger, Hopalong Cassidy, and the Cisco Kid with rabid adoration. That looked like fun, riding around while mixing it up with assorted bad guys and always being the hero. A lovely lass would fawn over you though that seemed not much of a draw at that age. Then again, I never ran across a horse in Worcester Massachusetts, my hometown, nor did I ever see a cattle-drive up the middle of Ames

Street where I lived as a tot. Moreover, I had never seen a gun since the takeover of our sanity by the National Rifle Association was decades away. Besides, it occurred to me that the bad guys might shoot back, a prospect that did not sound promising. And once I realized that the few cowboy jobs left paid crap for really hard work, the cowboy option was struck off the list. I was already developing a strong aversion to real work.

Being an astronaut, however, held real promise. That dream was inspired by a popular kid's show of the times known as Tom Corbett Space Cadet. Talk about a favorable omen! Any show named after me had to be a sign of something or other, right? It was more than just a TV show though. There were a series of books, and all kinds of crap you could buy adorned with his picture, from lunch boxes to plastic ray guns. You can easily guess what my nicknames were in those days. These monikers started out all right, but the initial luster faded when "space cadet" was contracted to things like "spacey," clearly more accurate if less appealing. Many years later I realized you had to be good at math and science to get into space. The astronaut prospect immediately became even more improbable than getting to second base with any of the Catholic girls I knew at the time. Okay, another possibility off the list.

TV stardom flickered for a moment. My mother entered my name for consideration by a TV show at the time called *Names the Same*. A contestant with a clever name came on and the celebrity panelists had so many questions to guess what it was. I still recall one contestant with the name Ginger Ale. But there probably were legions of Tom Corbett's out there. As far as I know, they never responded. It was their loss I figured. On another occasion, I recall her dragging me to some traveling audition for characters in either the *Our Gang* comedy series or some spin-off of the same. I was a real tot at the time. My memory of this event is sketchy at best. I cannot recall if we were supposed to do anything besides look cute. What I would have done to display any talent is beyond me. In truth, I did not have any observable advantages, not even one. In any case, despite looking as cute as I could, my obvious star qualities were overlooked once again. Go figure! Celebrity status on the tube clearly would have to wait. Being a movie star looked even more remote. I moved both options down on the list.

Well, I could always become a soldier. World War II and the Korean conflict were still fresh in our memories. With Russia looming as our biggest enemy, war looked like a growth industry. Hey, how many times did we duck and cover under our desks in grade school to protect our skinny behinds from a nuclear blast. Even I, clearly not the straightest arrow in the quiver, wondered how that flimsy desk would protect my ass if the big one was dropped on Worcester. My hope was that Worcester was such a sleepy backwater that not even the Russkies would care enough to bomb it.

It was many a year before I would realize that my aptitude for combat was less than zero and my likely survival time would be calculated in minutes and hours, not weeks or months. Hell, I would probably shoot myself before getting out of basic training. Still, I did not eliminate that option from the list of possible adult vocations right off. After all, the army would take just about anybody. It fell totally off the list much later when I realized I was a dedicated coward and possessed a distinct aversion to the sight of my own blood.

What about a job that demanded academic achievement or cognitive skills like teaching? Here too, the early evidence clearly was not promising. I went to a run-down elementary school near where I grew up. It catered to other working-class kids like myself who, for the most part, were not destined for any kind of intellectual achievement or scholarly success. Staying out of juvenile hall was considered a notable accomplishment. However, I do remember playing the part of King Harold in a reenactment of the Norman invasion of England in 1066. I am sure you all know that Harold lost the battle, the crown, and his life … an arrow purportedly shot through his eye. I died in my grammar school classroom with great drama, clutching an eye and slowly, ever so slowly, dropping to the floor. Perhaps I had discounted an acting career in undue haste.

Immediately, another "yikes" memory crowded in. When I was finishing up the third grade, I was assigned to a special class for the following year. It was special in that it was a dumping ground for the slow kids. Of course, how such decisions were made back then always eluded me. At the end of one year, I recall the teacher telling the whole class which students were being held back (not promoted) for the next year. Only two or three suffered this fate but I do recall one boy who, when so informed, burst into tears. His selection befuddled me totally since he seemed one of the smarter students in the whole class, much smarter than I. But one did not question authority in those days, no matter how arbitrary it was applied. I paid attention to his future academic achievements, which were exemplary as I recall.

But I digress, a fault not easily remedied on my part. I don't have any specific recollections of that year with the slow kids, but a sense of personal failure did settle over me. I thought of myself as no more than average, certainly not smart or talented, but certainly not slow in a school that did not attract particularly bright kids to start with. Fortunately, my tenure among the slow and purportedly hopeless kids lasted only the one year. For my fifth and then final years in grammar school, I was once again returned to a mainstream class.

Funny what sticks with you, I recall a discussion of whether a turkey bone could be used to predict the weather. Apparently, you could intuit the climate to be experienced in the coming season by examining variations in color along the bone. I think the teacher asked why we still need weather experts if all we needed was this amazing tool. That stumped me at the time. I think I figured out the answer later that day and wanted to run back and tell her.

Too late though. Still, it showed my early promise as a first-class suck-up.

I was also made a school patrol guard. I got this white belt that went around my waist and over my shoulder. I monitored the line of kids who went from Upsala Street School up Fairbanks Street to Ames Street and then down to Vernon Street and beyond. I was to keep my eye on the dumb shits under my charge to make sure no one darted out into traffic and got themselves killed. It was my first taste of power and authority. Perhaps there might be a future as a leader of men…a dictator perhaps. However, the little shits barely listened to me. Some were sufficiently bratty that I was tempted to nudge them into the oncoming traffic. Alas, good judgment prevailed, and I shelved any aspirations for world dominion.

Taking incompetence to the next level . . .

At the end of that year, I once again was called into the principal's office. Oh, oh, I worried, had they decided I was too dumb for junior high school? But no, I was told I would be placed in an advanced class at Providence Junior High. Go figure! By this time, I was thoroughly confused. Was I smart or, as I had previously concluded, dumber than dirt? In either case, a life of intellectual pursuits and scholarly endeavors did not seem in the cards. If they were so uncertain what to do with me, I surely could not possess enough talent to survive by my wits and intellect. Fortunately, we would all eventually be proven wrong, but that is a story for a future chapter. It turned out to be easier to fool people than you might think.

Of course, there was always the prospect of becoming a great sports star. What kid did not grow up fantasizing about hitting a game-winning home run to the screams of adoring fans? All of us future hall-of-famers spent untold hours playing every imaginable sport game in the streets and at the nearby public park. Okay, none of the guys tried synchronized swimming, you can imagine why. Mostly, we played in the streets early on. After all, why walk two blocks to the park when you could get a pick-up game in front of your house? Okay, Jackie, you run to the Chevy and break left to the blue Ford and I'll hit you with a pass. The ball would then bounce off the Ford as the pass fell incomplete. A moment later, Jackie would also hit the Ford before slumping into a heap on the street.

Today, someone would rush out of their house screaming at such unruly ruffians. Somehow, no one cared all that much back then. Our parents would kick us out of the house and tell us not to come back until supper was ready. No one worried about perverts or child-nappers or other unspeakable miscreants. Perhaps they realized that no one would want to grab losers like us. Or maybe they simply were hoping we would, in fact, disappear? I did notice that my folks would often move and leave no forwarding address, but I always managed to track them down. For the first half-dozen times or so, I assumed it was just an honest mistake. Later, my mother would encourage me to play in the heavy traffic. At the time, I thought she was hoping I might improve my motor skills as I dodged between the cars. Now, I am not sure about that.

While I did have a few moments of glory on the playing fields of Worcester, it was clear early on that my fame and fortune would not be found in the sports world. In junior high school, I was a pitcher on the baseball team. I recall getting to first base one day. Now, it is true that I was a crafty pitcher and could hit the damn ball on occasion. However, the one attribute essential for athletic glory that I did not possess was speed. In fact, I could only run at three speeds . . . extremely slow, glacially slow, and dead stop. On this day, however, I saw the coach give me the steal sign! The steal sign, what was the idiot thinking!

This had to be a mistake, I thought. But there it was again, the steal sign. He must have noticed the uncomprehending look on my face since he then screamed, "Steal second base, you moron." By then I figured he was serious. So, I summoned up all my resolve, hitched up my pants, and let loose for second base. The pitcher, knowing who was squatting on first base, had hardly looked in my direction to keep me close. There I was, thundering down the baseline with all the grit and determination I could muster. And then I went into a perfect slide as dust and cheers surrounded me. At that moment I waited expectantly for the tag that surely would greet me. But it didn't. There was no tag. I was safe. But how in

God's name could that possibly be? It had to be a mistake. It just had to be!

I stood up brushing the dust off my uniform and trying to think through what went wrong. Surely, I could not have legitimately stolen second base. *I know, I know*, I thought to myself. The batter must have hit a foul ball. That was the *only* explanation that made sense to me. So, budding brainiac that I was, I started trotting back to first base. When the shock wore off the other team, they threw the ball to the second baseman who casually tagged me out to end the inning. For what seemed like an eternity, the world was totally silent. Then sounds emerged, mostly the gleeful cries of our opponents as they danced toward their side of the diamond.

The horror slowly hit me. Yes, I had stolen a base, a boy so slow of foot that his speed was calculated with an hourglass. Then what did I do in response to this moment of glory? I embarrassed everyone who ever played the game by strolling back toward first base and was tagged out to end the inning. Unfortunately, there was no hole in which to bury myself. Neither did God rescue me by striking me dead despite my silent pleas. So much for a merciful God. I was beginning to have serious doubts about His mercy.

Our coach had a very prominent Adam's apple, which I could see bobbing up and down as his face turned crimson. Whatever was coming out of his mouth was probably not suitable for anyone of a tender age, but I wasn't listening in any case. I was still pleading with God to end my misery. Fortunately, someone brought my glove out to me, at least there would be time for his homicidal rage to diminish by the time I was within reach. Okay, I could erase major league baseball player off my list.

Hey, I could always earn a living with my hands, like building stuff or repairing stuff. They did have these vocational classes for boys back then in junior high at least. The gals were off sewing and cooking while the boys did printing and shop and manly stuff like that. Betty Friedan would not have been happy. Once, I helped my dad build a birdhouse. Among other skills, he had a pretty good command of the manual arts. In truth, he built it while I watched. Then he had me submit it to city-wide competition. "My" entry won a ribbon. Well, my dad's entry won a ribbon. Inside, I was ashamed; the work was not mine.

When I took shop in junior high, I thought I might learn some of these wonderful skills. But I struggled. It did not come naturally. My hopes of learning a useful trade drained away one day in a pool of blood. I was sharpening the blade of a plane, a tool used to smooth out the surfaces of wood. I had this useful instrument honed to a razor-sharp edge. Then the instructor called us all over for a lesson. I turned off the grinding lathe and proceeded to take off my protective eyeglasses. You needed them since sparks shot off in all directions during the grinding procedure.

So far so good. Unfortunately, I had forgotten to put down the sharp blade I had been grinding. It went right through my ear as I lifted the goggles over my head. Funny thing, I never felt the blade slicing through my flesh. I joined the outer circle around the teacher as if all was okay. I was just beginning to feel something amiss along the side of my neck when a boy on the other side of the circle looked over at me and pretty much fainted away. It turns out that ears have a lot of vessels and my limited supply of blood was pouring down the side of my neck onto my shoulder. The only other thing I recall is a few girls screaming in the hall as the instructor rushed me to the nurse's station. Gleefully, I told the girls I had cut my ear totally off. I rather enjoyed their screams. I was a jerk from early on! That evening I crossed the manual arts off my rapidly diminishing list of vocational possibilities.

Okay, maybe I was not cut out to be a builder of homes or other magnificent edifices. Perhaps, however, I might earn a living as a car mechanic. After all, lots of boys in the 1950s and '60s tinkered with cars. It was a male thing. Now, I had never been so inclined but with a little training, who knows. Fortunately, I never gave this option any serious consideration. Even I was sufficiently aware of my shortcomings in the practical arts not to dwell on that nonstarter. Good thinking on my part as a vignette from my early adult years later affirms.

One day, as a young man, I decided to simply add oil to our car. This would save money, a decent aspiration for any young couple without much in the bank. I bought a whole case of oil and one of those funnels I had seen used to pour the liquid into wherever it goes. Ah, there was the rub, just where does it go? When I got the hood up, it was not obvious. After I looked around a bit, I found something I thought said oil. I unscrewed the cap and plunged the funnel into the opening so that the oil could seep into the engine. Immediately, however, the oil flowed out and over the top. I had never seen that happen at a gas station. Now I decided to check the manual and soon found I was forcing the liquid into the transmission oil reservoir. Oh bother!

I dragged my fanny into the house to chat with Mary, my partner at the time who would soon be committed to a life-sentence as my spouse. At this moment, I don't believe we were yet married so she might still have been willing to put up with my crap. I asked her to call a garage to inquire if what I had done was a big problem or not. She was to imply that she, a dumb broad, had done this stupid thing. And she did it! She must have still liked me then. My stupidity turned out not to be a problem, but I gave the remainder of the case of oil away and decided to use professionals in the future. In fact, my only do-it-yourself skill is to use a telephone to call an expert to fix whatever needs attention. I am a big fan of the sage advice to *know yourself!*

Perhaps my future lies in the fine arts. In fact, my father was an excellent graphic artist. As a young man, he did superb drawings using colored chalk on fine sandpaper and drew a few cartoons that made it into the local paper. He really did have a deft touch. At one point, he bought a few "starter" books for those interested in learning the basics of that craft. He never pushed, just watched to see if I had any interest or aptitude. I picked the training books up, gave it a little try, and then wandered off to some other pursuit at which I was equally inept. After a while, he gave them away to someone who might appreciate them. He never said a word to me. I don't know if I had failed him once again, but I felt as though I had. My ineptness was becoming more pronounced, if not obvious. One more time, I buried a bit of shame inside where the debris of my youthful disasters was accumulating.

Next it was time to fail my mother. Her ambition for me was to become the next Lawrence Welk. To be accurate, she really had me pegged to be the guy that played the accordion on Lawrence's show. I think his name was Myron Florin or something like that. Even back then, in the pre-Beatles days, there were not too many young guys yearning to become a master accordionist, if that is what they were called. I mean, really, how could you pick up chicks with an accordion, aside from beating them over the head with it and dragging them off to your cave? It was, after all, on the heavy side and might serve as a weapon. But my mother, being Polish, loved dancing polkas to the strident beats that emanated from that infernal instrument. I had been dragged to many polka dances as a young lad and was forced to spin around the floor with a bunch of overweight mothers while the men slunk off to the bar to get drunk. I yearned to be old enough to join them. So, off she sent me to weekly lessons.

Trying to learn that hellish instrument was pure agony. It also was agony for the poor teacher who earned a living listening to talentless schmucks like me every week. I would have shot myself through the head after two weeks, if guns were as readily available then as they are now. I think I lasted two months. In that time, I created nothing that would ever be confused with music. When I told him that I was ending my career as an aspiring accordionist, I saw a tear stream down his face. It was not the loss of income he was grieving, but the restoration of his sanity and the preservation of the dignity of the musical instrument to which he had dedicated his life.

In any case, I was tempted to scratch the arts off my vocational list. But perhaps I was in haste. There was a moment in high school that showed just a glimmer of promise. I was muddling along when, during my sophomore year I believe, our English teacher assigned a composition to the class. We were to write a short story. Okay, this had nothing to do with algebra, Latin, French, science, or any of those classes where you had to know something. This had everything to do with my imagination and my ability to express that imagination. This was in my wheelhouse if I had such a thing. While everyone else groaned, I grinned with anticipation. Somewhere inside, I had an unlimited supply of BS just waiting to escape.

When the teacher asked for volunteers to read their short stories, everyone else sank a little lower in their seats as my hand shot up. Since I was apparently the only willing victim, he gave a resigned sigh and called on me. Apparently, he was not expecting much from someone who had showed so little promise. My little story was clever indeed. Details escape me now, but I do recall that it was rich in evocative language and imagery. It deftly led the listener (or reader) into a world of danger, suspense, and anticipation. I built the tension paragraph by paragraph until my audience was convinced that apocalyptic disaster was about to strike. But the denouement was where my genius lies, the whole story was about a simple neighborhood basketball game and nothing more than the final shot of the match. Oh, such a clever devil was I.

I finished my story, almost afraid to look up. Maybe I was way more impressed with my imagined talents than they would be. But when I did summon the courage to look around me, I saw immediately that it had worked. My classmates seemed awestruck. This total dufus had done something admirable, go figure! I could tell my teacher was both impressed and maybe a little suspicious. Did this loser really craft something that suggested a bit of skill? Wow, maybe I had stumbled on a talent at long last. But what to do with it? Really, how do you translate some modest talent at storytelling into something that paid the bills? I really did enjoy eating every day and having a roof over my head. Therefore, I put that thought on the back burner. But I never forgot how much I enjoyed playing with my imagination or that one moment where I moved others with my words.

Of course, both of my parents had their own vocational plans for me. My father wanted me to be a lawyer, and my mother wanted me to be a doctor. Okay, their aspirations were driven by the vision of me making big bucks. The lawyer thing had no appeal for me whatsoever other than the fact that I had read a few Perry Mason mysteries . . . the fictional defense lawyer who always managed to win for his client by getting the real guilty party to crack in the courtroom. I could not imagine doing that even if I were writing the scripts.

I must admit, though, to being attracted to the healing professions. I had been enamored with Albert Schweitzer working in Africa to save the natives and Tom Dooley, a Catholic doctor who worked in South East Asia as the French were losing their toehold in Vietnam. Dooley battled godless Communism and disease with equal aplomb. Helping the less fortunate through my healing powers certainly held some appeal for a guilt-ridden young Catholic boy like me. After all, I was still wallowing in self-loathing for having some eight thousand bad thoughts each week, or was it each day, which surely could only be exculpated by a bunch of extraordinary acts for good. It was not clear that even saving mankind could save me from eternal brimstone.

Later, in college, I sought employment as an orderly in the Catholic hospital located not that far from our home. I could work the 11-7-night shift and then head off to classes in the morning. At the same time, I could assess whether I had an aptitude for dealing with sick people. The problem with sick people, if the truth be told, is that they are sick. They throw up, sometimes lose their bowels, and even die on you. I can yet recall the first time I walked up to a patient's bed, took one look, and realized this guy was gone. And there was the time I held on to a man's wrist taking his pulse as it faded and stopped. Reality is just so real, not like TV dramas.

Moreover, the night shift in a big hospital is not the best place to become inspired toward a healing profession. Being a Catholic institution, they were cheap. Many nights, there was one nurse, a student nurse, a female aide, and me to run a whole floor. On occasion, there was just a student nurse, the aide, and myself. I cannot fathom how they got away with that, but Catholics ran the city, politically at least, so maybe they were cut some slack. You just hoped that nothing went wrong. You get into this gallows humor thing where you joke about hoping they pass, or pass their bowels, on the next shift and not on yours. But of course, things went wrong all the time, and the next shift did not always arrive in time. And who did they call when shit happened, literally and figuratively? The orderlies.

I guess my favorite ouch moment was the night the nurse's aide and I failed to communicate. She went into one room to give an enema to a female patient at the same time I went into a room to give a male patient the same treatment. Between the two rooms was a shared bathroom that could be locked for privacy of course. Given Murphy's Law, we both finished our enemas at the same moment. Both patients jumped out of bed and raced for the same bathroom from opposite directions. There was, after all, not much time to spare, and they had no way of knowing that another desperate patient was heading for the same destination. Our victims both opened the door at the same moment and stared in disbelief at one another. The man, being a gentleman, told the woman to take the shared toilet while he rushed out of the room and into the nearest available sanctuary. Unfortunately, it turned out to be a female room. The women, not expecting a frantic male to rush in with obvious distress on his face, began screaming in terror.

Oh, just another uneventful night on the ward I thought, as I struck doctor off my vocational wish list.

Running out of time and options . . .

By now I was getting older and running out of possibilities. I was in college, a time when most young people were deciding on the future trajectory of their lives. I, on the other hand, did not have a clue. I chose psychology as a major since that was the strongest department at Clark University, where I ended up pretty much by accident. That, however, is a story for a future chapter. After all, Clark was the place that Sigmund Freud gave his one and only American lectures and the place where the American Psychology Association was founded. Besides, it seemed like a major where I could BS my way through most classes. It was hitting me that cleverness and an expressive communication style might pay off for me. It had better since I had no real skills. Some were becoming confused that I was showing signs of intellectual promise. To further this error in judgment, I laid claim to be a late bloomer? Surely, no one could say I bloomed early.

In fact, by college I was fooling some contemporaries so completely that I was tapped as a future star in the psychology world. One clue is that I was awarded a National Science Foundation (NSF) research award, something given to four or five of the top psych majors that year. You were paid on a full-time basis for eight weeks over the summer during which you designed and carried out an original research experiment. Throughout the process you were mentored by a senior faculty member. The whole purpose was to encourage budding young scholars to devote themselves to a future in the academy where they would teach younger minds at the same time they pursued truth and knowledge.

This sounded better than working for a living, so I was game though, truth be told, I continued to work the graveyard shift at the hospital. Another clue that I had been tapped as one of the gifted few came when I asked my faculty advisor where I should think about applying for graduate school. Without batting an eye, he said Harvard, Yale, and Stanford. For a poor kid from a working-class neighborhood who had scraped through school during his formative years, he might well have said Mars, Venus, and Mercury. I smiled weakly, thanked him, and immediately discarded those suggestions. I was thinking more of a community college.

It is all a bit fuzzy after so many years, but I developed a research design for my NSF summer project that would plumb the mysteries of what we budding scholars termed the 'primacy of early learning' concept. Basically, patterns imprinted early on would last longer and be more difficult to erase than patterns learned later in one's development, at least if one was a rat. And since many humans I knew could easily be confused with rats, I thought my results would have general applicability. Looking back, the topic selected made sense. The early scripts I had absorbed proved extremely hard to erase. Some are still with me and now I am older than dirt.

Anyways, I designed an ingenious maze, bought a whole bunch of rats at different age levels, and used aversive incentives (mild shocks) to train them to do certain things. Then I measured subsequent extinction rates and looked at patterns across age cohorts. That, at least, is what I can recall. Please don't ask me the results, if there were any, after all this time. What I do remember all too well were the number of times I managed to shock myself as opposed to my subjects. I did feel bad for the poor things, so maybe I intentionally hurt myself out of some sense of misplaced empathy. My most compelling memory came at the end of the summer. Somehow it never occurred to me that I would have to dispose of my subjects when it was all over. No one else could use them, and there was no retirement home for lab rats who had finished their tour of duty. I was given a liquid concoction that I injected into the lower segment of their abdomen to send them off to rodent heaven.

I was not looking forward to this. Some had grown large by this point, and it struck me that they somehow knew what awaited them. Besides, I had grown to like them. Some of the younger ones were still cute. But I marched through my onerous task. The only consolation was that death appeared rather painless though several struggled and did not go without a fight. Toward the end, my moment of truth came. As I plunged the needle into a large rodent's squiggling abdomen, the damn thing peed right into my face. He had his revenge, and I struck another line through my growing list of avocations not to be pursued . . . research psychologist.

My list of skills that I would bring to adulthood surely would be in short supply. Worse still, I did not add much to this impoverished skill set during my early adult years. Occasionally, I would stray out of my comfort zone to tackle a practical problem. Why I would do something so profoundly stupid is beyond me. One disaster will suffice at this point. While talking to our neighbor, I noticed a beehive situated in the ivy that crawled up the side of our house. I can handle this I thought (what an idiot). So, I grabbed a rake and approached the hive. Slowly, I raised the rake high overhead and came down upon the hive with a mighty whack! Of course, I was so tense, I missed the hive by two feet. But I did arouse the bees who swarmed at me with considerable outrage. Off I ran through our backyard on day one of the mighty battle between Corbett and the killer bees.

Not to be undone, I came back on day number two. This time I crept slowly to the hive and took better aim. Down came my second whack which, to my glee, struck the hive. But only half of it came off and now the hive's residents were quite pissed off. Once again, I am running through my yard trying to outrun my pursuers. Back I come on day three. My target is smaller, but I am getting better at this, or so I thought. For the third time, I struck at my nemesis with a mighty whack. But this time the damn rake got caught in the vines. For a moment I struggled to disengage my weapon until I realized that a whole swarm of by now totally enraged bees were headed straight for me. I still believe they had an attack plan laid out for me. For a third day, neighbors witnessed this clearly unhinged guy running like a wild man through his yard.

Then it hit me, just call the man. I immediately called Bee B Gone, or some other such business, who came and quickly took care of the problem. Why I had strayed from my basic principle of always using an expert for all practical needs is beyond me. I assume it was a case of temporary insanity. While all ended well my wife was quite curious about that rake hanging from the vines on the side of our house.

My mind snapped back to the University of Wisconsin and my so-called retirement party. The assembled crowd expected me to say something appropriate on this fine occasion. And I did. I thanked the many who were in the room and the many who could not be there that day. I thanked my parents for imparting a valuable lesson by example . . . never take a job that involved heavy lifting. They had these real jobs, all of which looked like work to me, and I saw the toll it took on them. I went on to say how blessed I had been. I literally fell into a great career by accident, one that allowed me never to quite grow up. Basically, I flew around the country working with the best and the brightest on some of society's most vexing social problems. It was hugely challenging, and it was so much fun. And best of all, they paid me to do this. As my cousin's husband always said, is this a great country or what?

Yikes, I was hopeless. Yet, somehow this unremarkable kid from a working-class neighborhood who seemed lost through most of his youth eventually stumbled into this wonderful and fascinating career as policy wonk, manager of a research unit at a top university, and a teacher of young minds. Really, how did that happen? The several ouch memories that flew before me as I stepped to the podium that day brought back just how improbable that journey was. There was an important life lesson here, even the hopeless and the vocationally handicapped can make it. Clearly, this was a land of opportunity, at least it was several decades ago when I started out. Back then, this was a land where even the incomprehensibly incompetent and totally talentless could find some success. Not so much now I fear.

Well, let's go back to the beginning for a while, to a time when I was young enough to still be excited about stuff, perhaps even younger. Undoubtedly, there are lessons there for others who struggle with life's daily tasks.

CHAPTER 2

EMERGING

We must have perseverance and above all confidence in
ourselves. We must believe that we are gifted for something.
—*Marie Curie*

What determines who we are? Is it biology or environment, nature or nurture? Are fundamental traits or dispositions hardwired at birth: liberal or conservative, artist or nerd, extrovert or wallflower, skydiver or couch potato? I have glanced at many of those studies where small samples of identical twins are separated as infants and raised in different environments. This is about as close as we can get to separating out the comparative contributions of genes versus environmental inputs. When tracked down as adults, I am typically astounded by the similarities reported between each set of genetically matched twins. Okay, they obviously look alike and demonstrate similar talents. I can buy that. But when they buy the same brand of toothpaste and squeeze the paste out with identical techniques, I begin looking around to see if Rod Serling from the Twilight Zone is lurking in the background.

On the one hand, it is rather disheartening if the cards we are dealt at birth are so determinate of our fully formed selves. I spent my professional years working on programs designed, in part at least, to alter behaviors in ways that make adults a bit more independent and successful in life. Perhaps I wasted a lot of time if their fates were, in fact, assigned at birth. Fortunately, there also is a ton of evidence to suggest that social inputs do matter. It is just hard to accept that all behavioral tendencies are fully explained by the initial allocation of biogenetic material.

Still, recent research suggests that conservatives and liberals have distinct brain structures. By that, I don't mean that right-wingers have grey matter that screams scumbags while progressives evidence cranial shapes suggesting they are torch bearers of truth and justice. All that is true enough, but I am talking about physiological differences that manifest themselves in subtle, yet persistent patterns. For example, that portion of the brain that picks up on threatening stimuli is bigger in conservatives. That makes them more attentive to new input from the environment. They tend to react negatively to these changes and to respond defensively. Conservatives like constancy and the familiar. Liberals deal better with stimulation and change, or so the argument goes. People who look different are a threat to the right wing, the Communists, or terrorists are everywhere and will take over the world in six weeks unless they are all killed off. This is a bit extreme, but you get the drift.

As a college student at Clark University in Worcester Massachusetts, I was a psychology major. This was not a bad choice for someone who had no idea whatsoever what he wanted to do in life. The Psych department was, by far, the strongest department in the school. Thus, I was fully exposed to the theories of operant conditioning. Give me enough bananas and time and I can teach a chimp to type out Macbeth on a word processor. Of course, it could be that chimps are educable, and humans aren't. The more I hang around people, the likelier this hypothesis appears. Something must explain why otherwise decent folk end up voting for obvious scam artists like Donald Trump or, for that matter, Republicans in general.

Despite my exposure into the secrets of the mind, mysteries remain. Just what does determine who we become? As with most fundamental questions, there probably is no easy answer. It is part nature and part nurture, each contributing something to the final product in some complex interactive way. But why even care? For one good reason! During the space of a few years, I was to go through a radical transformation. How to understand such a dramatic change? Was my adult character determined at birth? Did I somehow respond to environmental stimuli differently than my peers? These are unanswerable conundrums for sure but fun for speculation.

Absent a clean answer, I started looking back to my beginnings of my own life. I doubt this reflective exercise will reveal any penetrating insights. But what the hell, you can only play so much golf in these so-called golden years.

Ethnic input . . .

I come from Irish and Polish stock. My dad was born in south Boston, a kind of Irish ghetto. His folks had emigrated from County Mayo I believe. I now am sorry I never had any curiosity about where my grandparents came from, at least until it was too late. My dad's parents moved to Worcester when he was quite young. I can recall my dad's mom very well and her reprimand of me as the neighbor girl and I peeked at each other's privates is etched in my memory.

As a child, I spent much time with her. She was perfect for the grandmotherly role, a plump matriarch with graying hair and much love to dispense. At the same time, she was not shy about expressing her opinions as an Irish temper lurked behind that kind smile. She likely had doubts about the parental care I was getting early on, which she probably blamed on my mother. Her son was blameless, probably by definition. In her own way, I strongly suspect, she tried to make up for perceived shortcomings. It was a noble, if hopeless, effort.

My father's dad was a mystery to me. He was almost never mentioned though as a child I knew he was alive. Once, I vaguely recall sitting in a car while my father visited him, but I was not allowed to go. I was not clear why at the time. Later, I learned my granddad was in a state mental hospital, the circumstances never made totally clear. Only once did I hear my dad mention his condition, that he would occasionally drift off and simply stare out the window for hours. It sounds like a deep form of depression to my unprofessional eyes. When he fell into that state, those around him would know it was time to take him to the "hospital" for a rest or whatever euphemism they used in those days.

My mother's family emigrated from Poland, I know not what city, but their journey probably happened around the end of World War I. The family name was Spiglanin, which undoubtedly contains about half the syllables of the original version. My aunt Mary, the oldest child, was born in Poland. Piecing together bits and pieces, they apparently arrived in Kenosha, Wisconsin before moving east to Pittsburgh and then on to Worcester. One reason for this migration west to east was that they merely followed employment opportunities in heavy-labor type factories. Another theory, according to my mother, is that they found Wisconsin too damn cold, which it is. Like many immigrants from that time, my grandfather wound up working the steel mills, hard and unforgiving work at relatively modest pay. Still, I am sure it was better than in the old country since they managed to own their own home while raising a decent-size brood of children.

I could not have been much older than three or four, so maybe this was one of my very earliest memories. I don't know whose car we were in, but we pulled up in front of my grandmother's house on Endicott Street. My mother ran inside for some reason. A moment later, she rushed out of the house screaming, an image that has stayed with me to this day. She had found her mother collapsed on the floor. I don't know if she was already dead, but I was never to see her again. You don't forget such things.

From what I can gather, both of my folks were considered "lookers" in their early years. From all accounts, my mother was a heartbreaker when she was young. Apparently, there were many suitors. She later lamented the fact she let guys get away who eventually became rich and successful. Unfortunately, she settled on a good-looking Irish guy with great charm and a suspect reputation. It was a decision of the heart that she revisited many times. But he looked like a catch. He was known as a dark Irishman with black, wavy hair and striking good looks. When they spent time in New York City during their early years, they would occasionally hit the nightclubs. On more than one occasion, as I was later told, other patrons would come up to his table asking for his autograph. Apparently, he would be mistaken for a matinee idol of his era, Tyrone Power or Cornel Wilde or some such luminary lost to us today. Long after the bloom was off the rose, she lamented the fact that she had not listened to her mother who had strong reservations about this slick wise-guy wanna-be.

My mother's peak years were her teens and early twenties when she was attracted many young men under the watchful eye of her dominant mother. While my dad had a more angular face framed by that swath of dark, wavy hair, my mother was fair skinned with a rounder, sweeter look. In social venues, she was vivacious and full of laughter. I assume she would prove very appealing to the young men of the times and that is what the game was all about. You got a man who would then take care of you. Picking the right one was critical. I am quite sure my folks cut a dashing figure in their courting days. Too bad they could not stand one another over the long haul.

They met when my dad worked for an outfit that ran for-profit bingo games, which were viewed as just this side of the illegal rackets. The story is that my mother was told that the good-looking guy calling out the numbers wanted to date her. Her immediate response was that she did not go out with Jewish guys. Why had she jumped to that conclusion? I guess it was his slightly swarthy look under the bingo-hall lights. That reservation brushed aside, he had the bad-boy allure attached to the wise-guy group he hung with that ran Bingo operations before the good Catholics took over. She relented and then had to fight through her mother's objections. Lesson here is to always listen to your mother.

The matriarch of the three Spiglanin sisters, my mother's mother, apparently ran the household with an iron fist. I have the vaguest memory of her, all these elderly Polish ladies back then came across as strong and uncompromising icons that looked as if they had just come in from plowing forty acres with their right hand while fighting off ravenous wolves with their left. They dominated all within their view including these meek men who served as their husbands. As I think on it, my dad's mother certainly looked matronly, but she was equally domineering. She also could be as stubborn as all get out even if she doted on me as the young waif who was woefully neglected by her daughter-in-law.

Okay, I can now look back and see some bad ingredients being thrown into the family stew. We had this Irish-Polish mix. You know, the Celts are kind of dreamers, poets who would rather muse about lost worlds and loves in lush poetry and prose than do real work. The Polish side struck me as practical and iron willed where you broke both the earth and other people to make it in a harsh, unyielding environment. It was an oil and water mix.

Consequently, these two worlds did not blend with any easy charm. I could tell my father had imagination and dreams. In a different world with greater opportunity, he could have achieved much in life. He had smarts, wit, charm, and was a wonderful storyteller. But in his real world, he eked out a marginal living laboring in dull, repetitive jobs that offered little to whatever dreams he might have put away sometime in his youth. Sometimes I would see him play with ideas, like coming up with a better way of making a product at work or finding some pattern in the lottery numbers. For his culture and world, he read an amazing amount of material and thought hard about things.

My mother also had dreams, mostly based on the worn myth that her looks would bring along a charming, handsome prince that would sweep her to a life of leisure and luxury. And when she wound up in a cold water flat, while working in factories or as a waitress, her visions of a pampered existence dissolved into the drudgery of routine and never having enough. Enough, of course, was always dictated by what others had, a home of one's own, nicer cars, trips, clothes, and the best of all things material. A good man was a provider and someone who yet had time to lavish attention on his wife.

What my father did provide my mother was me, at least we will go with the prevailing theory that this is true. I was much taller than either of them so maybe there was a bit of truth about that lanky mailman story. In any case, she might have preferred nice clothes and fancy house to this bratty kid running around the house. Then again, you can't always get what you want. It was during World War II when my mother became pregnant for the one and only time that we can be reasonably certain they had sex. My father was 4-F and thus exempt from service. He escaped the war due to a case of ulcers, which living with my mother would surely exacerbate. It was a medical condition that, as far as I know, never bothered him again. She came to the family way in Wildwood, New Jersey, where my dad ran a Bingo game for an outfit that had sites up and down the east coast. Bingo was much different then, a form of low-level gambling until it was generally outlawed and relegated to a fund-raising scam for churches and other charities.

Anyways, her due date was approaching when my dad was asked to operate a Bingo parlor somewhere in Florida. But my mother wanted to be near her mother for my birth, so they returned to Worcester, never to leave again. Now, a dispute over why they were stuck in cold, dreary Worcester became gist for a continuous fight for the remainder of their lives. She dragged him back, he would contend. No, he didn't have enough ambition and guts to break away, she retorted. Her fault, his fault, a ceaseless exchange of guilt and insults that held them together until my father passed in 1987. Of course, there was always this lingering guilt that they stayed together only for my benefit. They usually murmured something about divorces being too costly, but I often wondered if my presence made them stick it out. That would pile on more guilt for sure.

When I would call them in my adult years, I hated the fact that they both could be on the phone at the same time. The conversation could go well for a few moments before something would get them started. After that I might wander away for a few minutes while they went after each other on some issue that had been in dispute since Eisenhower was in office. Perhaps I should have suggested some advanced conflict-resolution technique like the rock, paper, scissors exercise. The arguments, of course, were never were about the topic *du jour* nor about which one was correct. They were always about the deep unhappiness with their lives, particularly on my mother's part.

I am not sure my father was unhappy with his lot. You could tell he had native intelligence and some imagination but not a lot of assertiveness. Only a couple of times did I hear a faint complaint about what his life had become. He lacked the fire and the will that set apart those who would fight hard for their dreams. But I think somewhere inside the dreams existed, and at some point, he invested them onto me. I began to accumulate a lot of guilt. My birth, along with a bit of misfortune, may have hastened his departure from the fast life of his early years. Later, I was never sure I did enough to let him live his deferred dreams through me.

One day, I recall, he opened the door to his closet. He told me that before he got married he had eight new suits in his closet, now he had one old one. Was he sharing with me his wisdom about the evils of marriage? This might well have been his way of encouraging me to stay unattached without explicitly saying so. Or, maybe he was telling me that his downfall started with me. I sensed some critical piece of advice was being imparted but I am afraid I failed to fully absorb his wisdom. And yet, I nodded as if I knew exactly what he was saying.

Environmental input . . .

During my childhood, we lived on what was called Vernon Hill. Worcester reputedly was built on seven hills, much like Rome. But any comparison ended with the hills, there were no ruins other than a host of dilapidated tenements, no architectural splendors other than an antiquated City Hall and train station, and few historical sites of much significance. No plague or memorial has been erected to signify the spot of my birth. Go figure!

Founding father John Adams did teach school there for one year as a young man but had the good sense to head back to Boston and help lead the revolution for independence. I should point out that early work on the birth control pill took place at a spin-off laboratory from Clark University located just outside the city in Shrewsbury Mass. That pill was a local achievement of great significance to my generation. And yes, Robert Goddard did invent the liquid fuel rocket at the same Clark University. Unfortunately, Robert's wife forgot to take the lens cap off the camera, so the big moment is lost to history. Goddard launched the space age in a farmer's field that would later be turned into the local golf course where I learned that cursed game. One day, while hacking myself around the course, I stumbled across famed scientist Werner Von Braun, along with other dignitaries, as they commemorated a plaque to honor Goddard's historic event.

Worcester in those days was a charmless, industrial city where success was defined as somehow leaving the city for a better place, which usually was defined as just about any place else. The second largest city in New England at one point, it fell into a slow decline during my days there, losing some fifth of the population by 1970. Contrary to the prevailing consensus, my presence in the city probably did very little to accelerate the decline. I struck me as a tired, poor city with few prospects. Yes, there were the WASPs (White Anglo-Saxon Protestants) who populated the city's affluent north side of town, joined by a decent size Jewish community and a growing number of Catholic professionals who had climbed their way out of the ethnic ghettos. They were out there somewhere but way beyond the reach of my world as a kid at least.

My childhood world was to be found in one of the many ethnic enclaves that dotted the city. Waves of immigrants had been absorbed into Worcester's already diverse mosaic a generation or two earlier. Ethnic-based clubs and social networks were formed to assimilate the newcomers, there Polish and Lithuanian clubs on Vernon Hill. They help new arrivals to get jobs or deal with the local government bureaucracy, or learn the language, and provide social welfare help if needed. Not surprisingly, those from the major ethnic clans sought one another out and settled next to one another. Later, when the immigration flow slowed, they evolved into social clubs for those with shared cultural roots.

The Italians were largely found on the east side, along Shrewsbury Street. The Polish and Lithuanians settled on one side of Vernon Hill, the side that sloped down toward Millbury Street. The French were often found in some of the smaller communities like Webster Mass. There was even an identifiable Swedish community in an area known as the Village where the big steel company was located. Of course, we Catholic boys knew the Lutherans were surely headed to hell, but they seemed nice enough. And there were small African-American, Hispanic, and Chinese communities on the periphery of the downtown area. But the biggest tribe of all was the Irish. They dominated several of Worcester's hills . . . Bell and Grafton and much of Vernon.

These ethnic enclaves were hardly prosperous. Yet, they were held together by tradition and social norms. We felt safe and secure. At the bottom of Vernon Hill, in the Polish enclave, was a park. During the summer, they had an excellent basketball league where the best players in the city would strut their stuff. Despite the poverty of the area, no one ever felt unsafe. Players from the Boston Celtics would play an annual game against the league all-stars every summer. We saw Bob Cousy, Bill Sharman, Bill Russell, and the other stars from Boston's early championship years. Can you imagine Lebron James playing against local men at a neighborhood park? I think not.

Back then, knowing your own tribe was essential. It was one of the first and most important lessons of your young life. Growing up in Worcester, Massachusetts, for kids like me, essentially meant coming of age in a very Catholic, very ethnic, and very working-class world. For those needing a translation, cultural relativism was not the norm. This fierce tribalism prevailed. Upon being introduced to someone new, you were likely to be asked, "What are you?" While a reasonable response might be along the lines of "Gee, I am a human being," such sarcasm would generate either a blank stare or a punch to the nose, depending on the size and IQ of the inquirer. Irish, Polish, Italian, or some acceptable mix of the tribes was the response demanded. And from that, you became a known quantity; the questioner could fill in the blanks.

One early memory on being acquainted with my tribe stands out. Some distant relative had a farm outside of the city, which, come to think on it, must have been one of the last half-dozen farms in the state. Anyways, it was a great adventure to go out amidst nature and the animals and fresh air. It cemented my firm belief that these were among things to be avoided at all costs later in life. Work, diet and other such four-letter words were also to be avoided assiduously. It was on one of these visits that I first recall being asked the "big" question by someone "What are you?" Maybe this was a test since everyone presumably knew who I was.

Caught off guard, I still recall freezing at the very moment this Big Question was popped. Pondering over a response, I applied the incisive logic that would later bring me the same level of success I enjoyed in the world of academia....none. I speak English, so I must be English. Not wanting to appear even more retarded than I was, I blurted out that response rather than remain mute. Unfortunately, my logic sucked. To make matters worse, my very Irish father overheard my response and, to say the least, was not amused. I learned much about Celtic-Anglo history and relations over the next several minutes.

Today, most of us tend to forget just how pervasive the sense of tribe was back then. Prejudices were not confined to the simple distinctions such as White or Black, Gentile or Jew, WASP or ethnic though, believe me, they were all alive and well. Your response to the question "what are you" positioned you in a complex mosaic of ethnic, political, and class distinctions. It framed you in a web of status and expectations that went far in defining who you were and how you were to be treated.

The only non-Catholics in my early world were the few Jewish kids sprinkled among the multitude that cavorted over the streets and playgrounds of Vernon Hill. For example, I recall playing ball with Jordan Levy who was my catcher when I pitched during my junior high days. He became a long-serving mayor of Worcester in his adult years. But most of the kids around me were Catholic, white, and living in relatively poor households. Okay, most families probably were not dirt poor, at least as we came to measure poverty more formally in the 1960s. No kid went without food or clothing as far as I know. There were no evictions that I recall. Still, money was scarce, and everyone seemed to be scraping by from paycheck to paycheck with little to spare.

Within our larger working class, white, Catholic tribe were even further divisions. Five Catholic churches could be found on or near Vernon Hill. One would assume that a Catholic church is a Catholic church, right? Hey, it was the same indecipherable Latin mass back then no matter which one you attended. But no, two of the five were considered Irish, one was Polish, one was Lithuanian, and one was French. Many worshipers would walk past the nearest church or two to find "their" church. I never could figure out where the French lived that filled up their church since none seemed to live in the area.

My mother grew up near the area's Polish church, known as St. Mary's by the non-Poles and Our Lady of Chestachowa in the local community. Even into her early adult years she had trouble going to confession in English since the Polish language was used exclusively in most religious functions. By the time I became aware of things, she had long stopped going to confession. As I approached my teen years, I started attending the local Lithuanian Catholic Church since it was closest to our new tenement on Fairfax Road. While the mass was always in Latin, some of the sermons were only given in Lithuanian. You can imagine how moving these rites were for me. I was totally clueless.

Walking the streets back then, you could still find older women out on their stoops, wearing babushkas around their heads, talking to one another in Polish or Lithuanian. The wife of the man who owned the tenement building we lived in on Fairfax Road had lived in Worcester her much of her adult life and could speak virtually no English. If I were reading the newspaper on the front stoop she would rush out with one of the few questions her command of English permitted. "Who die, who die?" I would then scour the obituaries for Lithuanian sounding names. Back then, it was easy to live among your own tribe and never assimilate into the broader society.

This sense of tribal connection also afforded a sense of security. We roamed the streets and backyards with abandon. Only darkness or hunger brought us home. Exiled to outside, we would range over our neighborhood and the nearby playgrounds with abandon. There was little fear of abduction or whack jobs shooting up schools. I can recall visiting a priest at the local Catholic Hospital on Saturday mornings with other very young kids. I have no idea what we talked about other than he gave each of us a candy bar at the end of our visit. Today, suspicions of pedophilia would abound. But I certainly have no memory of anything untoward happening. Was I not cute enough to warrant his attention? In fact, aside from the (mostly) innocuous beatings we gave each other, we were reasonably happy and secure in our little world. Bad things must have happened back then, but the possible existence of perverts, serial killers, and mass murderers never penetrated our consciousness. We were oblivious to danger. Today, you routinely see stories about female teachers seducing their male teenage students. That simply was unheard of in my day. I cannot recall even fantasizing about such a possibility.

Moreover, our world seemed expansive and endless as a child. Today, that same world looks so small and confining. Perspective is a wondrous thing. But what strikes me looking back was that it was so homogenous. We were from different ethnic backgrounds but were virtually all Catholic and surely all white. We were all economically struggling, but no one was truly destitute as far as I know. All the couples seemed to be locked into unhappy, but stable marriages. There were few divorces, and if there were sexual dalliances or abuse or neglect, these things were kept silent and out of our view. I cannot think of any family that looked anything like the Nelsons or the Cleavers or the Andersons, which were the big TV families of the 1950s. No mothers wore tidy, aproned dresses during the day while they flitted from a few household chores to a bridge game or the beauty parlor. The woman seemed tough and gritty and hardened by lives of endless struggle on the edge. The dreams of their youth had been replaced by a hard, unyielding reality.

Still, we had continuity in our lives. We knew our culture, what was expected of us, and what we expected from others. There were few surprises. There were no luxuries and very few amenities. Then again, neither were visible hardships or the lack of basic necessities. Sure, there might not be central heating or hot water at the turn of a tap. You might have an icebox and not a refrigerator. A car and television were things that came later in life for us. I recall my mother washing clothes with a scrub board and a big tub, no washing machine until later in my childhood. Then, you squeezed the water out through a device composed of two motor-driven rotating cylinders through which you fed each item of clothing.

Of course, being the numb nut that I was, I stuck my hand in between the rollers one day to see what would happen. What happened, of course, is that my hand and then my arm were drawn into the rollers as I screamed my bloody head off. I was rescued from my own stupidity before my arm fell off or other permanent damages ensued. Another time I started playing with some household device we used to heat up water for baths and so forth. No one had heard of showers, you cleansed yourself by soaking for a while in your own dirty water. I am not exactly sure what I did, but from the reaction of my folks, I had the distinct impression that I almost blew up the house. Though every effort was made to beat the curiosity out of me, that effort was doomed from the start.

When we did eventually get some "modern" devices, I don't think they were top of the line. I remember a washing machine that seemed to walk across the floor when operated. It shook so badly that the whole apparatus moved in random directions. My job was to keep the infernal device from destroying other pieces of furniture. When we finally had a car of our own, it was rather ancient. Can anyone yet recall what it was like to drive a vehicle that did not have power steering? It ain't easy, let me tell you. I recall one gem that was so rusted out you could look through a gaping hole in the floorboard and see the actual road rushing by. I tried passing it off as permanent air-conditioning but everyone one knew it was just a heap that was falling apart.

Space heaters were another fixture of my early years posing a threat to life and limb. Being the low person on the totem pole, my bedroom always seemed to be the farthest from any source of heat.

Piles of blankets were okay, but your head was still exposed. The condensation that streamed from mouth and nose was a constant reminder that it was damn cold in my bedroom. Deciding to get up to pee in the middle of the night was always a close-run decision. Should I freeze my ass off to relieve myself, or could I make it to morning? No wonder the bed wetting went on until I was thirty-two.

But we knew no better. Sure, it was commonly known that there were the rich families on the other side of town. But they were from a different universe. I can only recall one example of upward mobility from my area, at least in the early years. I had a good friend in grammar school called Mike Jr. His dad, known by all as Big Mike, was a football coach and teacher who went into politics. As Mike Senior moved up the political totem pole, the family suddenly fell into good times. First, Mike Jr. matriculated at a private school. Then, they started driving Cadillacs and not Fords. Soon after that, they moved to a fancy house on the other side of town. It was a classic American success story until Mike Senior was found guilty on many counts of accepting bribes in public office and went off to jail. In those days, a good deal of mischievous political behavior was excused. You really had to be visibly corrupt to pay for your sins in that political environment.

One day, during Big Mike's trial on many extortion and bribery charges, my dad casually mentioned that he was going to be acquitted. I asked how he could possibly know. Without missing a beat, he said the fix was in. I scoffed but sure enough, Big Mike was exonerated of all the charges. But the authorities had so much on Mike that they brought him up on additional charges. This time my dad mentioned that Big Mike was going to jail. But the case hadn't gone to the jury yet, I protested. This jury couldn't be fixed was his response. And sure enough, Big Mike went to off to the slammer. My dad's explanation was that he had gotten too greedy and pissed too many people off. A little graft was okay; Big Mike went too far. I guess there were lines in the sand even among political thieves.

For part of one summer, I caddied for the elite at the Worcester Country Club. I did briefly glimpse into that privileged world as I chased golf balls around their manicured links. But the journey across town by bus was too daunting and that experiment did not last long. All I knew about these alien tribes is that they were different from me and mine. They likely were Protestant and thus on the wrong side of the religious divide. And they were likely Republican and thus on the wrong side of the political divide. And they were rich, thus on the wrong side of the class divide. In some vague way they were the enemy that rigged the rules against us honest working stiffs. It was easy for me to accept these views early on since I did not really know what work was, nor what wealth meant. I just knew that those people had most of the goodies and we did not. And that was just not right.

Our cultural continuity and stability, along with a tight tribal affiliation, gave us things that were better than money. We knew who we were and what was expected of us. More than that, we felt part of a bigger network. I doubt any of the mothers in my neighborhood read Dr. Spock or worried if their kids were being exposed to great literature or science. Staying out of the slammer was good enough. These struggling families stayed together from what I recall and stayed put. I can think of one family on our street where the mother had divorced and remarried.

In one instance, a neighborhood wife and mother ran off with another man. She apparently had an affair with her boss where she worked. One day, while her husband was at work and son at school, she and her paramour ran off to California together. Now that shook up the neighborhood, a mother left her young son behind with just a note saying how much she loved him. Her boy was quite a bit younger than I, so we did not hang out. Eventually, he grew up to be a firefighter like his father and earned some notoriety for bravery in a blaze that took down a factory and killed a number of his fellow firefighters. A book of this event brought the incident to national attention. That was the outlier case. Otherwise, stable, nuclear families were the norm.

We were Catholics, Democrats, ethnic, union members, and hardworking cusses that made this country great. Okay, I wasn't but my folks were. In any case, their hard-work built America into what it had become, the beacon of the free world and the defender of liberty against the godless Communists and atheists and other evil doers who threatened our way of life. It was a simple world, black and white, not in racial terms (though that was a big divide) but in truth versus falsehood. Good and evil were transparent to all. Grey was for confused eggheads and fellow travelers who failed to see what was obvious to the rest of us. Besides, we had God on our side, and the Pope in Rome. Why all those other heathens did not see the obvious truth of our beliefs was simply beyond me. It really was quite simple then.

This was my world up through my early teens. I had little doubt about who I was. Being lazy, I recall going at mass at the Lithuanian Catholic Church around the corner as opposed to the Irish Catholic Church that must have been at least a mile away. I got close to the younger priest who yet spoke with a thick Lithuanian accent. He had escaped his country as the Communist took over after World War II and drove out what remained of religious freedom. He was a hero to me. He had taken risks for the principles and the God in which he believed. It just seemed so easy to identify the heroes and villains in my world at that time, that golden period before everything became so complicated.

Parental inputs . . .

I can't remember how old I was but obviously not old enough to know better. I was angry at something and stormed into my bedroom letting fly with some invective aimed in the general direction of my mother. I think I reached deep into my limited vocabulary of expletives to convey my displeasure. It was an impetuous move, a classic back-forty mistake that you wanted to grab back immediately. The error of my ways was confirmed immediately as I heard my father stomp toward my room, his anger unmistakable. He was not coming to congratulate me on sharing his own private opinion of my mother's character.

There was no escape for me; my plan in this instance had not been well considered. As he came around the corner, his face a brilliant crimson hue, I frantically tried to recollect those words to a perfect act of contrition. Nope, high anxiety always numbed my useless brain at the most inconvenient times. Could I reason with him? After all, I had heard him yell similar things at my mother all the time, and at the same volume level. Apparently, however, there was a double standard here. No reasoned arguments came to my lips. All I had time to do was brace myself before the whack came. I next recall clearing my head from the floor across the room. Wow, I had tapped his Irish temper this time. Put that lesson in the neural filing cabinet for future reference.

Physical discipline happened but not all that often. Good thing since he had a helluva right cross. I guess my parents did the best they could. I have always thought that parenthood was more a privilege than a right. You should be trained, examined, and given a license before being allowed to procreate. Hell, in some places we require people to be licensed to do rather simple tasks like cut hair or board a pet. But anyone is permitted to have a child. What is with that? Without question parenting is *the* most difficult challenge that most people undertake. You are charged with this tiny living being whose fate is totally dependent on what you do. And we let just about any moron do it! Frankly, I am stunned.

Several retired colleagues of mine and I used to meet periodically to talk about issues affecting families and children and society. They were scholars, physicians, lawyers, educators, and other such professionals. We called our little group Wisconsin Cares, a clever if somewhat exaggerated moniker. For a while, we struggled with ways to require new parents to sign a pledge, or some other affirmation, that would demonstrate they were aware of the responsibilities associated with raising a child. It might also identify those who might profit from help early on. Instead, we intervene as a society only after most children are subject to undeniable abuse or neglect or their behavioral issues spill over into society. This is like leaving the corral gate open and being surprised by the fact that the horse is now five miles away and galloping fast. Parenting is not like deciding to go into the Peace Corps or spending a summer in Europe. This is the rest of your life, requiring dedication and skill and deft management of so many things.

Pretty early on in life I decided not to have children. There were a lot of reasons, some of them I will get into more later. For one thing, I was overwhelmed with how all-encompassing parenthood was. This totally vulnerable being was dependent, and

I mean totally dependent, upon you. Really, what could be more demanding, and utterly frightening, than that reality? That kind of all-consuming responsibility was totally beyond me. Later in life, I would help run a nationally known research institute, consult with states and the federal government on some major policy issues affecting millions of people, and mold young minds as they prepared for their futures. All those things came relatively easy to me, or at least did not overwhelm me. But take on parenthood? That task seemed way beyond my meager capabilities. Strangely enough, many people over the years told me I would have been a great dad. I must have fooled them with my humor and blank stare, which they confused with profound wisdom.

Fortunately, I had proof early on I would be childless as an adult, which was a great relief to me. How is that you ask? Teen girls in my era had this surefire test for assessing how many children a guy would eventually sire. They also thought this test could figure out the sex of the offspring. They used this procedure to check out the available stock of future husbands. Their test seemed very scientific at the time. They would attach a needle to a piece of thread and place it against one of the boy's fingers. Slowly they would raise the needle up and carefully observe which way it swung, if at all. One full circle clockwise meant a baby of one gender, a full circle counterclockwise meant a baby of the opposite gender. My needle never moved, no matter how many times they did the test. I felt bad for some of the other poor slobs in the neighborhood who were destined to have a dozen kids or so. I was safe and could romp through life having unprotected sex, which I was stupid enough to do on occasion but not often.

I have always been just a bit shocked by the cavalier fashion in which young people make the parenting decision, what I think is the most important of their lives. It sure strikes me as more important than marriage. There, you are dealing with another adult, well we hope so at least. And if you pick a loser, you can dump them unless you buy into that "until death do you part" thing. But many girls entered pregnancy to "keep" some loser, or gain short-term attention, or have something to love. Yikes, get a dog, not have a kid! It struck me that my folks would have failed any parenting test at the time they sired me though it was not like I was aware of much in those early years. What I did sense was that I was a profound inconvenience for them. I cramped their style. And yet, I recall the later arguments between my aunts and my mother about who really raised me in those early years. They wanted credit, how was that possible? My wife would laugh at these squabbles; they are fighting to take credit for this guy? What is with that!

As I did emerge into the conscious world, I was aware of being dumped a lot, which was good preparation for my pathetic attempts to seduce girls. I spent a lot of time with my grandmother (dad's mother) who lived upstairs from us, with one aunt (dad's sister) and uncle who lived up the street, and with another aunt (mom's sister) and uncle who lived around the corner. At other times, I recall being taken to card games where my parent's played poker and drank as I snuggled among the coats on some bed. This is probably where I developed my skill of sleeping through just about anything.

My parents were still players in their younger years. They enjoyed nightclubs and gambling and drinking and other frivolities of that generation. I yet wonder if I would have turned out okay if my mom had not drunk and smoked her way through her pregnancy with me. Anyways, when I became more cognizant of things, that strong feeling of being a nuisance pushed me to seek comfort and attention with nearby relatives.

My aunt Ag and uncle Bill were my favorites. I spent a lot of time at their place which was located only one long block away from us, very near the big neighborhood park. They were sweet, gentle people. Bill had a college education, the only member of my extended family to achieve that status. He worked as a salesperson for Nabisco products and I think rose to be regional sales manager or something like that. They came closest to the "Leave it to Beaver" image of the 1950s American family except they had no children. What I most loved about their home was the sense of love and calm that prevailed. So, I became their surrogate child.

It is not as if I did not spend time with my mother's sister, the other aunt who lived nearby during early childhood. I did. Aunt Mary had two daughters who loved using me as their live doll, one you could dress up and push around the neighborhood, down steep hills, into the path of oncoming traffic, and so forth. Apparently, I was marginally more lifelike and amusing than the plastic dolls with which they would normally entertain themselves. Clearly, my difficulties in life started early on. It would only get worse.

Once I recall these two cousins gave me a doll for Christmas just when I was old enough to know this was offensive to my manhood. Of course, being who I was, I manned up and cried like a baby at the insult. Then they took it back, and I cried some more. On another occasion, the older sister was playing grown up and serving coffee to the adults one day. I still have this memory that she spilled some of this hot coffee on me, an allegation she denies to this day. I can't push my claim too hard though, my wife loves this cousin as the sister she never had. If they did engage in a little torture from time to time, it probably was warranted. I recall once getting mad while at their house and kicking through their screen door in a fit of anger. Come to think on it, I sometimes would lay down in stores and throw a fit if I did not get what I wanted. Who was that brat? No wonder I did not want to sire a little Tommy Jr.

But it was Ag and Bill that served as my ideal parents in the early years, particularly after Nana went to a nursing home. They gave me the love and attention I craved. They were both calm, affectionate, and sweet where my folks were volatile and preoccupied. My uncle would let me sit on his slap as he drove his car, and my aunt even taught me how to knit. I wonder if I had some gender identity issues. They had books for me to look at and seemed to care about how I was doing. One book I can still recall. It was titled *Tommy on the Train*. There were inserts that you could move back and forth to give some animation and movement to the story line. But it was the sense of serenity and love in their home that I recall. I needed that desperately.

I came back home from their house one day. I probably had spent most of day at their place. There was a suitcase outside and the door was locked. I recall banging on the door and wailing away. When my parents finally let me in they told me that perhaps I should move in permanently with Ag and Bill. Again, I cried. Apparently, I cried a lot. It was just a little joke on their part, at least I think it was. But maybe I should have considered the offer more seriously or at least negotiated a better deal like no more liver and onions.

There were a few warm moments that come to mind. I do recall my mother sitting with me as I went through my Baltimore Catechism as a young boy going to religious instruction. If you had the audacity to go to public school, which I did through the eighth grade, you were required to attend religion classes at the local parish each weekend. No way would the Catholic hierarchy let the forces of secularism poison young minds. I recall sitting by either a wood or coal stove on cold winter nights going through the Q. and A. format. It was a nice, if isolated, expression of maternal concern.

Our primitive way of heating the flat in the early days did bring the family together. You did not want to get too far from the space heaters or stove on winter nights. Eventually, we secured a gas heater I believe. One day my dad and I were watching TV. Men, as women will tell you repeatedly without being asked, are clueless. In truth, we do seem to miss a lot around us. I do remember my dad saying, "Do you smell something?" "No, I don't think so," I replied sniffing in the air. A moment later my mother came screaming into the room as a coat she had draped over a chair went up in flames. Disaster was averted, but it was an early clue that my olfactory sense was a bit lacking in acuity.

My dad occasionally would do dad things with me as a young kid. He was known to throw a ball on occasion. In truth, I only have one memory of us doing that. I even have one memory of him on the golf course with me. How did that happen? Sometimes we might listen to a ball game on the radio or watch a big prize fight on TV. The Friday night fights were a big thing in that era. I think they were sponsored by Gillette razors…*look sharp, feel sharp, be sharp.* The jingle has stayed with me all these years. In general, though, he was not into those dad things when I was a young urchin. I am sure he seldom held me or changed a diaper or gave me a bath. He was very fastidious, always finding hair in his food or a stain on his shirt. I am sure I was way too messy for him.

Once, in my teen years, I came down with a bad infection in my foot. I had worn a new pair of ill-fitting shoes during my shift at the public library and had hobbled home in severe pain. As my mother pried my shoe and sock off my swollen, ugly-looking foot, she screamed. My dad screamed too, but only because I was wearing a pair of his socks. It was his firm belief that a man could not have too much underwear and socks. After the screaming died down, they took me to a doctor, the only time that happened other than my tonsil crisis and when my appendix burst. On this occasion, the doc said it was the worst infection he had seen that did not require hospitalization. My dad continued to grumble about his lost sock, which now was stained with ugly puss from my foot wound. Good thing he had his priorities right.

I believe they both got into the parenting thing a little better as I got older. It really is hard to theorize accurately about your own childhood. You are too close to it and yet estranged as well. The emotions and embedded scripts keep you from being overly analytical and objective. Still, as I evolved and grew, I undoubtedly became less of an inconvenience to them. At the same time, they also evolved in their lifestyle. They never did totally give up what they considered the good life, but they pursued it now with less vigor. They began to settle into more of a routine. Though they never gave up on the poker games, the nightclubs, and parties with friends, they probably were just a little more worn down by the demands of everyday life.

In any case, I think they started paying more attention to me. I was slowly becoming a focus, really the focus, of his life. In a perverse way, that increased the pressure and the guilt. My best guess is that they each began to see me in a different way. For my mother, I was a commodity she could use in the constant negotiation with others about the quality of her life. For her, possessions and the status that comes from material things were extremely important. She competed with her sisters and others in her world for prestige. Most of them had homes of their own; she did not. Some of them had new cars. She always had used cars of dubious quality. Others always had nicer clothes and jewelry and more expensive furniture. She had none of these things, at least in her eyes.

But she had me and maybe I could be an asset in her efforts to solicit status, if not praise, from her friends. This did not turn out to be a good thing from my point of view. I became the object of a constant stream of criticism. My hair was never combed right. I was never clean enough. I was never polite enough. I was never deferential enough. There were these ever-changing standards that I could never, ever satisfy no matter what. My error, of course, was thinking that I could. So, failure was guaranteed and a constant reminder of my shortcomings. I was missing the big point and would miss it for many, many years. The goal of satisfying her was elastic and would always be just beyond my grasp.

I did experience an epiphany on the subtleties of parenting one day. I recall being at my friend Andy's house. We were probably ten or so at the time. I always thought his mom very sweet and nice. On that day, she told him to go into the bathroom and wash up. He grumbled a bit and she started to scold him gently. Before she could go further in her admonition he cried out, "I know, I know!

Why can't I be more like Tommy Corbett?" What! That is what my mother always said to me. Why couldn't I be more like Andy or Ritchie, or David or whomever? It hit me at that moment. All parents were frauds. They all used the same techniques to belittle and embarrass us. The other kids were always perfect while we were abject failures! It was so obvious, why hadn't I seen this earlier?

Still, my mother took the various belittling technique to a whole new level. She was literally consumed with what others thought. It paralyzed her. I did not get any true insight until after her passing. She kept me away from some family members because she thought my wife and I were not living up to some ideal image. Mary kept her own maiden name and did not wear a wedding ring. We thought such a symbol conveyed ownership at the time, among other sins. But we did manage to reestablish contact with the extended family on our own and became very close to Ag and Bill along with my older cousin, Carol. This was the one who pushed me around in a baby carriage and into oncoming traffic when I was a baby. As mentioned, my wife came to think of her as the sister she never had.

One day we were driving through northern New England with Carol and her husband Jack when my cousin asked Mary (my long-suffering spouse) if she made some unbelievable amount of money in her job. Now, Mary made a very good salary as a high official for the State Supreme Court, considerably more than me, but this amount was outrageously high. It was way more than the Governor made. Carol went on to tell us that this is what my mother was telling everyone. Apparently, she would brag about me and Mary constantly, about how successful we were and how much money we made and the great house we had. My cousin went on to say that this is how it had always been, her Tommy was perfect. Her Tommy was smart. Her Tommy was successful. Her Tommy was rich beyond measure and famous to boot. Mary, whom she tried to hide from the relatives, was also a raging professional success. When I was growing up, though, all I ever heard was criticism and my failures as a son. Believe me, that is not what you needed to hear if your ego is not very strong in the first place.

My dad also began to project his hopes on to me but in a slightly less damaging way. He began to see in me all the things that he could never be. I would get an education, become a professional, and make a name for myself. He was less concerned that I would make money or acquire fancy things; they never held control over him as they did my mother. But I think he hoped I would become a person of significance, something that eluded him. He had been good in sports, I never was. He was talented with his hands as an artist and maker of things. I can barely tie my shoes without aid. He was funny and charming. Okay, I did inherit some of that . . . Thank god!

I always thought I had failed them early on. If there was one dominant sense of self that consumed my early years, it was a feeling of failure. I did not measure up. I was not good enough. I was an embarrassment. My parents wanted me to be all manner of things that I would never become. My mother wanted me to be filthy rich and perfect in ways that were impossible to satisfy. I think, in the end, my father might have been relatively satisfied with what I became in later years. For my mother, the story is different. It was not until I became an old (older) man that I hit upon that essential truth, the bar of success would always keep being raised. I simply could not satisfy her needs. In the end, that realization made things easier, but nothing could erase the pain completely.

My father may have passed-on to me one of his gifts to me. As I matured, I proved to be rather quick of wit, imaginative, clever, and a decent storyteller. Perhaps I had inherited just a few of the traditional Celtic gifts that many Irish possess, along with a curse or two. But it would be many years before I realized I had such gifts. The most precious gift from my dad was an ability to make people laugh. I never told conventional jokes but had this inherent, dry wit that was just there. It was as much a part of me as the ability to breathe. Like the story-telling ability, God put it in inside me, a talent that I treasure beyond measure.

I can't say there is much evidence here to explain my development to adulthood. I desperately wanted to be good, do the right thing, to please my parents. I had not yet realized that was impossible. I had bought into my culture and all that entailed though, in my head and heart, I argued with several the premises that everyone else seemed to accept as givens. Very early I was disturbed by scenes of racial segregation and hatred throughout the land, I was affected by a sense of suffering and lack of opportunity around the world, and I could not readily accept some of the foundational beliefs of my faith. Other than those feelings, kept within myself, I probably looked average, if somewhat clueless.

My childhood was not ideal, but neither was it extraordinary in any way. In childhood, none of us seemed abused or willfully neglected as far as I know. Besides, we all had an extended family in the neighborhood, others who did seem to care about us and look after us. And there was an extended family beyond the neighborhood to care about me as well. Still, if I were a betting man, like my father, I would have wagered on a future life trajectory that was totally uneventful and predictable. There was little to suggest I would break away from my culture and a destiny within my Catholic, working-class world.

So, let us start looking at what did happen.

CHAPTER 3

REMEMBERING

Reality leaves a lot to the imagination.

—John Lennon

Not that long ago, my wife and I visited Ames Street in Worcester, Massachusetts, the site of my early years and the source of my earliest memories. It looked pretty much the same after all these years except that everything appeared cramped, a bit smaller, and perhaps more worn by time and struggle. Why did my universe seem so expansive and exciting back in my childhood? The innocence and exuberance of youth, I suppose. In any case, after wandering the streets and reminiscing for a bit, I called some old friends we were going to meet later that day.

"You're on Ames Street?" they asked in shock. "You can't walk around there, it is too dangerous. They had a murder near there just the other day." I looked around again. It struck me as the same comfortable cocoon in which I had grown so many decades ago. Still, there were some changes. One of the three-deckers was gone.

The street was now one-way. Just how did we navigate this narrow corridor back then? Otherwise, it looked like the working-class neighborhood it always had been. Even in my day, it had been a bit shabbier than many of the other nearby streets, too many kids and too much mayhem. Back then, though, no one thought about murderous miscreants lurking about nor did anyone worry about their safety. As far as I recall, I was the only danger the mothers on the street warned their kids about, "stay away from that weird Corbett boy, you hear!"

Where was the problem? How could a place that looked so familiar and innocent harbor evil or imminent death? Then again, the street was empty. I could not see the faces that lived in the surrounding apartments. Were they still Irish working-class families struggling from week to week, perhaps with an occasional Polish, Lithuanian, or Jewish family thrown into the mix? Or were the families now headed by single parents, darker of color, more desperate economically? There were few clues in the empty street. As I kept looking at the familiar scene around me my mind wandered, as it is wont to do.

A lifetime ago . . .

An early, primordial image suddenly came back to me. I walk through driving snow illuminated in the dark night by a string of hushed streetlights. Looking up, flakes emerge from the blackness to sweep past as if I were journeying through the billions upon billions of galaxies that make up our universe. As each one twists and turns and finds its own path, I am taken with the depth, breadth, and the individuality of the spectacle. Each flake is unique and yet, as a collective, represents something far more than small particles of moisture congealed about specks of dirt. To me, the spectacle embraces something beyond the building blocks of one of those fierce winter storms I can still vividly recall from my childhood. The driving snow is nothing less than the cosmos brought down to a human scale and to my childhood world.

We seemed to have a lot of wintry storms back then in the late 1940s and early 1950s. The younger I was, the bigger appeared the stage on which I ran and played and dreamt of things beyond my tiny world. The summer storms were fierce and frightening. One swept through the city when I was barely nine years old. This rare tornado left about one hundred dead and a path of destruction in its wake. The winter blasts were also special. They could paralyze the city and turn our local streets into wondrous playgrounds replete with ice castles and snow forts and stranded, useless cars. When nothing moved, we would use our sleds to careen down Worcester's hills using city side streets as our personal playgrounds.

I can still recall huge icicles hanging from the eaves of the third-floor roofs. I was convinced that one would snap off one day and pierce my skull, which would at least get me some parental attention and maybe even time off from school. Oh, the glory of it! That is, if I were not struck dead as a result. Years later, I would be incredulous when the local news would report that the most recent snowfall had set some new record. Surely, those huge drifts of white stuff surrounding me as a child were massive compared to the pedestrian storms of recent days. Perhaps, though, everything just seemed bigger and more significant back then.

In those early years, even the simple act of walking through falling snow somehow was transformed from a mundane moment into a great journey. I would no longer be little Tommy Corbett. Now I was a space explorer. I was destined to be a great adventurer, sliding effortlessly through space toward galaxies and experiences that can only be dimly imagined back on earth. The boundaries of my life would never be on the grimy streets of Vernon Hill in Worcester, Massachusetts. Oh no, they would be found somewhere out there, somewhere beyond the known and the familiar.

Decades later, I would resonate to the story told by twin sisters from a poor, working class family who were raised in Chicago. This is a vignette I have used elsewhere since I find it so compelling and instructive. Even better, their story resonates faintly with my own. As very young girls, they both recall looking out on their surrounding world through the front window of the upper-level tenement in which they were raised. The street below was a magical place for them . . . one that teemed with all sorts of sights and sounds and magical delights of their Irish neighborhood. Much later, as adults, they discovered a startling difference about what they were seeing in those early years. One sister did, in fact, concentrate on the street scene below. That was as far as her gaze needed to wander to satisfy any need for adventure and stimulation. The other, however, was inevitable drawn to what was down the street and what might be beyond where her attentive eyes could take her. Just what delights were around that corner and out of sight, in those places where only a vivid imagination could see? Just what did the wider world promise?

It turned out that their childhood interests predicted their adult paths quite well. The sister who focused on the street below stayed in Chicago the rest of her life, married, and essentially spent her time raising a family. Her more curious sister left Chicago early, sought a doctorate in Russian Studies at Georgetown, and spent her life as a political operative, public official, and consultant in Washington. For a time, she served as a top staff person to Senator Ted Kennedy. I would gaze out from the 3rd floor tenement flat we lived in for a while. I could see all the way to Holy Cross College and would wonder about the kids that would get to go there and lead exciting lives. All that seemed beyond my reach, but I would dream.

It might just be that the need to "fly from the proverbial nest" is hardwired in some way. Some of us evidence a "need" to strike out and discover new worlds for ourselves, both figuratively and literally. We need the excitement that comes from novelty, from testing ourselves, from embracing change . . . even when those challenges are tarnished by a touch of the absurd and perhaps more than a little futility. And we need to believe in things beyond ourselves and outside our own provincial worlds, in visions of a better world that we can help erect.

Perhaps that is the first and most important epiphany of my life, one I did not fully appreciate for some time. I suspect most others do not see the world in the same vivid and imaginative way as I, at least I don't believe they do. Others often do not make connections across disparate phenomena nor see deeply beyond the surface of things. Looking at the world with imagination and originality is a gift, a wonderful gift. Some people see the trees and others the forest, while a few can see both the trees and the forest. Perhaps this gift of imparting significance onto big and small and seemingly unrelated things is a blessing of my inherited gene pool or perhaps it is partly an accident of the times.

After all, I came of age when an action hero named Tom Corbett-Space Cadet was very popular among us urchins. There were books, a TV series, space guns, lunch boxes, and all manner of diversions that might be fobbed off on the gullible kids of the time. He was no Davy Crockett among my childhood peers, but this Junior Space Cadet was a pretty big thing at the time. And they named him after me, how cool was that. All of us kids watched his adventures on our 12-inch TVs as long as the vacuum tubes had not burned out or the horizontal and vertical controls did not fail. Then all we saw were crooked lines or rapidly moving images. Even watching TV back then was not for the faint of heart.

The show was clearly before the high-tech special effects of George Lucas. You watched Tom and his sidekick, Roger Manning, on a grainy screen as they tackled one adventure after another in the depths of space. When they were dodging an asteroid storm, the actors would run from one side of the spaceship (read studio set) to the other as the camera swung back and forth and the music revved to a high pitch. No digital recreation of space back then. A cardboard cutout of a rocket moved across a black background painted with stars. Still, could life get any more exciting than this?

Sure, corny and primitive by today's standards but gripping to us kids at the time. Of course, just as Tom and Roger were about to vanquish some interstellar foe, the anticipated disaster would strike. The picture twisted sideways or rapidly flipped up or down. This was accompanied by a lot of cursing and taking vacuum tubes to the TV store to be checked out. Despite the occasional technical problems, I felt blessed to have the same name as a real, live action hero. You might not be totally surprised that I came to be called "spacey" which, unfortunately, had absolutely nothing to do with our astronaut hero.

The nickname spacey nailed me as the clueless kid in the area. As a small boy, my mother would tell me to put the garbage out in the can adjacent to the house. This meant lugging a bundle of refuse wrapped in the day's newspaper a few feet and dropping it in the appropriate container. Somehow, I would get lost in that short journey from our tenement flat...an arduous journey of twenty, maybe thirty, feet. Most mortals of average competence, even young kids, could handle the task. And yet, my imagination immediately would take me on some wonderful journey from which I would suddenly awaken while walking up the street carrying this load of garbage. I would quickly glance around hoping that no one had noticed. Still, I could see the snickers among the ever-present witnesses. It was not an auspicious start to life. I am sure many a neighbor commented on that silly kid walking aimlessly up the street carrying the family's daily refuse. His poor parents surely have a hard life with such an addled boy to care for. Perhaps he is just a little slow!

The street . . .

Ames Street was the canvas upon which I painted my early life. Back then, it seemed more like a wall mural literally teeming with possibilities. There were kids everywhere—the Clancys, the Pellerins, the Monahans, the Perrys, and the Luceys. This was the era when large Catholic families were more the norm, before they simply started ignoring the birth control promulgations from Rome. My folks ignored Rome from the beginning, I was an only child. Either that, or they took a vow of celibacy immediately upon producing me.

The street offered endless opportunities for amusement where we played cowboys and Indians, war, football, and a kind of ad-hoc baseball. With World War II a recent event, endless battles were reenacted where we once again crushed the forces of evil. It is a good thing I don't recall any German kids on the block, and certainly no Japanese kids. All this took place on a narrow way that could barely accommodate one-way vehicular traffic. Sure, there was a huge seventy-five-acre public park a long block away but why journey that far when so much adventure beckoned right outside your front door?

Few of our activities were organized or supervised back then. Today, kids are chauffeured from one highly organized activity to another highly organized activity. A colleague of mine would tell me how she was always taking her daughter to a dance performance in Chicago or even Florida. The next week, she seems to be taking her son to a ski competition in Colorado or a rowing competition in Georgia. My adventures involved shorter trips. My mother just yelled, "Get the hell out of the house and don't come back until supper time." You then wandered out into the street and simply screamed, "Hey, Ritchie," or Davie or Jackie or whomever, "can you come out and play?" If maybe five other kids responded to your screaming, you might do a little football. The sidelines were marked by the street gutters and the end zone might be the blue Ford parked up the block.

As I think on this, I am amazed. Back then, we seemed to maraud around the neighborhood with impunity getting into whatever mischief we could conjure up. Of course, no one supervised us. No kid wore a helmet while riding a bike. We would fire BBs or arrows (with rubber tips) at one another without fear of injury or death. We would pelt each other with ice-covered snowballs and simulate football games without any protection whatsoever. Somehow, we all survived. Perhaps we were a hardier generation. Of course, all the hard knocks from unprotected football and war games might explain how I turned out later in life. But we won't go there right now.

We would burst out of the house onto the street and just start yelling, more like screaming. Assorted child inmates from other apartments would soon materialize, usually with their mothers yelling, "And don't come back until supper time." Now, it might be time for a little street baseball even though our beloved Red Sox had already drifted down to the middle of the league. Ah yes, the Red Sox! How any young Sox fan managed to make it to adulthood absent some severe psychosis while rooting for those bums is beyond me?

Back to street baseball. Oh, you don't know what street baseball is? It was very ad hoc game that could be played by as few as two kids and one tennis ball. One player would bounce the ball off the steps leading down from the three-decker across the street from where I lived. If he hit the step just right, the ball might soar over the bush separating my front yard and the sidewalk. That would be a home run. If the "hitter," the person bouncing the ball off the step, used a slightly skewed angle, the trajectory of the balls flight might be too high or low. If the fielder, who was stationed across the street, fielded the ball cleanly, the so-called batter was in trouble. However, if the "fielder" missed the ball and it landed in the bush, it would be a double. A missed grounder would be a single. Any caught fly would be an immediate out, as would a fielded grounder where the ball was accurately thrown back to the steps from which it was originally launched. If the batter were so far off as to bounce the ball up into the second-floor porch of the adjacent three-decker, he lost his turn for that inning plus risked getting a noogie on the arm.

Such simple games amused us for hours. There were no X boxes or computer games and social networks. Even the telephone was a party line, at least early on. Surely, few under sixty years of age recall what a party line is. You shared a telephone line with several other households. If you lifted the receiver off the cradle with care, you could listen to ongoing conversations from others sharing your line though nothing of interest ever seemed to be said. I never heard one crime being plotted or tryst being arranged. If you really had to make a call, you begged the other person to get off the line. Obviously, a kid chatting with his friends was not considered important, so you just did not do it. You met face-to-face and talked. Yes, that's right, you had actual conversations.

One of my first memories was playing a baseball game in our side yard next to our tenement building. I cannot recall what we used for bases but the 'field of play' seemed huge at the time. As an adult the yard, in truth, turned out to be tiny. Ames Street, where we played so many games, likewise was little more than an oversized alley. Today, even the one-way traffic has difficulty getting by cars parked on the one side where it is permitted. Back then, there were fewer cars. However, traffic was two-way, and parking was permitted on both sides. Navigating one's way up and down the street must have taken great skill, particularly in winter when the snow piled up. Then again, maybe the cars were narrower in the early 1950s, but I don't think so.

The so-called parking 'war' after winter storms could be intense and bitterly fought. You dug out "your" space, since everyone parked on the street, and then placed on it a chair or some other piece of large furniture to tell others that this territory had been rightfully claimed. Heaven forbid anyone might throw your chair aside and assume ownership over this precious piece of real estate. Much yelling and a few raised fists would surely result. As I think back on it, this system for parceling out precious parking spaces worked reasonably well. There were simply unwritten codes of conduct that you violated at your own peril. Surprisingly, peace and accord usually prevailed. An unexpressed compact existed acknowledging that we were neighbors and that we were all in the same boat. Today, we are moving toward a society where everyone would be packing heat and there would be shootouts in the street.

Of course, my folks did not have to worry about parking and navigating tight spaces in my earliest years. We had no car and took a bus everywhere. Public transportation, how quaint! I still recall how almost everyone on the bus would make a sign of the cross as we passed the church at the bottom of Vernon Street. In my young world, everyone seemed Catholic and pretty much just like me. And I still recall the day I, for some unfathomable reason, refused to give up my seat for an elderly woman as my father was ordering me to do. I should have taken note of his Irish temper surfacing but I was dumb as dirt from the get go. Perhaps this was an early effort to stake out my break from parental control. It was, all in all, one of my first "back forty" ideas . . . a stupid idea of the first-class order for which I was to pay dearly. There are stupid ideas, really stupid ideas, and "back forty" ideas. The last were so over the top and self-destructive that you ought to be taken out to the back forty and shot. You were, by definition, too stupid to live. When my father got me to our house, I discovered just how foolish my stubborn behavior was.

The small side yard next to our three-decker opened into a rather large backyard that seemed to extend to the back quite some long ways. This expanse permitted large hordes of unwashed kids to play out fantasies of being brave Americans knocking off dastardly Nazis or Japs or, in the 1950s, the Chinese. At other times, we were hunters on safari or explorers seeking out new lands. Or we might be pioneers clearing the west for brave settlers. The only limits to our sense of exploration were our imaginations. It was only later that I realized we had inflicted genocide on many Native American tribes and more recently supported the most awful dictators who pretended to agree with us. But in those innocent days, the good guys were easily identified, always wore white hats, and fortunately looked exactly like me. How convenient!

No one had the least concern about kids roaming the streets unsupervised. I cannot recall a single warning to be on the lookout for sexual predators or perverts. We had no "be wary of strangers" talks. Did evil people not exist back then? That is hard to believe. But, of course, you never seemed to be alone very often. Perhaps the very social fabric of our neighborhoods had a built-in form of protection. My sense is that terrible things happened but went unreported out of shame or, with no 24/7 breathless news cycle, remained known only to those involved. Clearly, there were no Amber Alerts in those days. Caught up in the world of war or sports heroes, I oft would be dragged back home only by the sound of my mother's scream that dinnertime had arrived. Sometimes, she would summon me with a whistle. I thought that clever until I realized it was a dog whistle whose pitch was beyond the scale of human hearing. The fact that I could hear it when none of the other kids could gave me pause.

Anyways, given my mother's limited interest and skill in the culinary arts, the prospect of dinner was not much of an inducement. Perhaps abduction by some miscreant would be referable. The threat of a good whack across the bottom if I did not return promptly proved most effective, and apparently, I never proved attractive to the neighbor sex perverts, if there were any. If I walked into the house to the smell of liver and onions, I wanted to rush back out and volunteer for a suicide mission. Death was far preferable. I still cannot tolerate the smell of liver being fried. Everything seemed fried back in those days with mashed potatoes and a stringy vegetable out of a can. There even was Franco-American spaghetti from a can. What was that all about? At least call it Italian-American stuff, it would not make it taste any better, but you might think it came from the correct country. Let's face it! No one goes to either Ireland or Poland, my ancestral homes, for the food. Kielbasa and "Pigs in a Blanket" or forty varieties of potato do not make for enticing dishes. But I survived.

It was, all in all, a very average childhood. We had little money though I was not aware of that at the time. We were one of the last houses on the block to get a TV, I yet recall waiting anxiously for the twelve-inch Fada (I think that is what it was called) to arrive. I desperately hoped it would arrive before the scheduled time for the Lone Ranger that day. Through most of my early years, there was no central heating in the tenement flat, no car for transportation, no refrigeration to keep things fresh, and no hot running water. For a bath, at least in the early years, I recall my mother heating up big pans of water to at least take the chill off the cold water used to fill up the tub. All of that seemed normal and not a hardship.

We even had an ice box that had to be replenished daily with the frozen stuff. The ice man would arrive each day, pincer a block of ice, and carry it to "box" where our perishable food items were kept on the back porch. Of course, any neighbor kids who wanted some milk could easily treat themselves. It is amazing we did not die from tainted food. Then again, we often bought our meats from Arby Siff, the Jewish guy who had a small store just up the street. I can recall my mother asking if a piece of meat was fresh, he would hold it up to his nose, sniff it, and pronounce it fit for human consumption. On hot days we kids would chase the ice man or the milk man who also used blocks of ice. Chips of ice would fall off their trucks. They might be a little dirt covered, but hey, the cubes of frozen moisture were cool to the lips on hot summer days.

Come to think of it, street life pulsed with vendors who livened up daily life. There were milkmen, coal men, ice men, peddlers of various kinds. Now, just the thought of some of these jobs strikes me as horrendous. Back then, not so much. Since trucks could not get to where the coal was to be stored, the three-deckers being too close to one another, the coal man would have to deliver the goods on his back in what looked like large leather sacks. He would hoist load after load walk up the narrow passage between houses and dump the coal through a small cellar window into a shoot that descended to the coal bin. To my child's eyes, some of these labors seemed to be kind of cool. You could get dirty on purpose. I did not remain so enamored for long.

I did not think much about this at the time, but someone would have to keep the furnace stoked and blazing if there was to be heat in the coal-fueled houses. All I can recall in our place on Ames Street was some heat thrown off from the kitchen stove which never worked all that well. In the winter months, my bedroom was farthest from any source of warmth. I could see the condensation from my lips on cold winter nights as I snuggled under all the blankets I could find.

I was always on the outlook for future occupational possibilities. There were some jobs that seemed a little less taxing and, more importantly, within my skill set. Occasionally, I would see a rag man or someone who would sharpen knives and perform other useful services. There were fruit and vegetable peddlers who pushed wagons piled with offerings up the street in my earliest years. I can even recall an itinerant photographer who took a picture of me sitting on a pony. In days when personal transportation was a luxury, entrepreneurs came to you. A man in a suit would stop by the house from time to time to collect insurance premiums. Now that seems bizarre. But I always had the feeling that most of these itinerant occupations were reserved for those truly on the edges of society except for the guy collecting money. After all, he wore a white shirt and tie.

The police walked the beat back then, symbols of authority and figures to be held in just a bit of awe, if not fear. There were "call" boxes located on corners throughout the city. The patrol cop, if he needed assistance, would have to run to one of these and call in for help or to report a riot or that he had been shot. I suspect that the odds were in favor of various scofflaws in those days with communications being so primitive. By the time the beat cop ran to a call box, got his key out to unlock it, and then called in his report, the crook likely had sold his purloined goods to a fence and was enjoying his ill-gotten booty at a resort in Mexico.

On the other hand, everyone looked out for everyone else. I don't recall instances of crime, assaults, rapes, or any kind of everyday mayhem that dominate today's news. It must have happened. Worcester was not populated by saints as I recall. But mayhem seemed to happen outside of our world or at least our attention span. Since it is hard to imagine that all evil in the world did not emerge in the 1960s along with birth control pills, I assume a lot of bad things were happening that we simply did not know about or at least people did not talk about. Guilt and secrecy were dominant back then. The Irish were known for not disclosing dirty laundry. If a kid was doing 30 days in Juvenile Hall, everyone was told that he was at summer camp though no one from my neighborhood ever went to summer camp. And no one was an alcoholic even though drinking was an ethnic passion and vice of choice.

Years later, after I had returned from two years in rural India, I spent some time with my folks before heading off to graduate school in Wisconsin. I casually mentioned one night that I was going for a walk. My mother asked me where, obviously worried. When I told her, she blurted out, "You can't go there." I was incredulous and argued I had always felt safe in our neighborhood. "That was then, it is all changed now." It seemed inconceivable to me that a couple of years could transform the world so completely.

Safe, working-class neighborhoods were now too dangerous for a strapping young man who had just spent two years on the edge of the Rajasthan desert. *Wow*, I thought, deciding to keep her happy by staying home.

Some struggles . . .

Growing up, I really had no idea that we were poor. In truth, we likely were not poor in an official way. We had no recognized poverty line back in my childhood. Besides, my parents always worked. My father toiled as a factory worker and my mother as a waitress, mostly slinging drinks in bars or nightclubs though she did do some factory work for a time. Once I recall she accepted a position as a matron in the city jail but quit after a few days when she realized what kind of lowlifes she would be required to handle. Our family income probably was typical for our neighborhood of working-class families. Our problem was that what came in flowed out just as fast for alcohol and good times. As a result, there were constant squabbles over money. Then again, everyone seemed to squabble over money.

I don't recall any physical wants; there was always food and clothing and shelter. But I do recall those fights over money very vividly, a constant bickering about there not being enough. My mother had married with high expectations and never forgave my dad for failing to deliver. And if it were not money, there were many other excuses for arguing. Despite the apparent hostility, I can see why she was attracted to him in the beginning. He had been quite handsome and roguish in his youth. He ran with the fast crowd with weekend poker games and other, edgier, activities. Many evenings at local nightclubs were the norm. When my mother met him, he worked for a Bingo outfit that was for profit in those days, a low-level form of legal gambling.

My dad was a classic bad boy for his day, just the kind of guy to attract a young, Polish girl looking for adventure and maybe a little danger. Her mother was a grand matriarch who ran the family with an iron fist and what better way to seek independence than to date a young man who was totally unsuitable. Okay, he was Catholic, but he was Irish and smooth and ran around with the wrong crowd…guys who gambled a lot. We are probably not talking Al Capone here, but you did pay what you owed.

One of his early claims to fame was that he ran this football pool. It was illegal of course but gambling was part of the local culture's DNA. There were no points back then so picking winners was not as hard. It turns out that one Friday a local sportswriter picked every winning team on my dad's slate of college games for the next day. Too many guys would merely mimic the sportswriter, which skewed the betting terribly. You can guess the rest. He and his partner owed money to all these winners, money they did not have. I heard this story from my dad, his sister, and others. He first went to his own kind, the Irish, to see if they would bail him out. No deal. So, he had to go to the Italians. They did, but he was out of the business, which I assumed meant that they took over his illegal operation. But he managed to stay alive, which was a good thing for me I think. He told me that when the word went out that his obligations would be paid, a line formed out the door of a certain Worcester bar that stretched all the way down the street and around the next corner. It was the end of his career as a small-time wise guy.

Still, he must have looked good to my mom, and she probably had high hopes for an exciting life. The back and forth baiting of one another was a kind of constant background noise to my early years. All the early promise, and danger, diminished and disappeared as he took safe jobs such as a machinist in one of Worcester's many factories, Crompton and Knowles. They originally made looms for the factories that made clothing when we actually made such things in this country. With time, he no longer seemed so exciting, and the life she envisioned never came to pass. I once visited him at his place of employment. It had a certain Dickensian look of the early industrial revolution. I made a vow that I would not end up in a similar place.

I doubt that she ever forgave him this so-called failure to be exciting and, more importantly, rich. That was what defined a good man in those days and he had failed. Unfortunately, she never let his failure go and the consequent sparring was endless. It seemed unceasing to me, no escape seemed possible. Many a night I cried myself to sleep as they fought in the next room. As an adult, I would call home. They would get on different extensions and soon would be going at it again. I could put the phone down, make myself a sandwich, and pick up the conversation/argument ten minutes later without missing a beat.

In retrospect, it is now obvious that scarce money resulted in some basics being overlooked. I never recall seeing a doctor back then until I got very sick on occasion. At four or five years old, it turned out that my tonsils needed to be removed. I can still recall the old-fashioned way they knocked me out. They covered my mouth and nose with some cloth or a strainer-type contraption and slowly dripped something on it. Slowly I faded into oblivion. I later recall being rather sick as a dog, but they gave me ice cream, which I thought rather a treat. The procedure seemed to improve my appetite. I went from a skinny kid who looked like a refugee from a concentration camp to a pleasantly chubby urchin, an unfortunate sign of things to come. I wonder if I can get some tonsils reattached at this point in life, I could stand to lose a few pounds.

The Worcester grammar school system came to the rescue for me and the other less affluent kids in the neighborhood. Occasionally, we would be marched to the Lamartine Street School to have our teeth cleaned and our eyes checked. I doubt they did this in the rich areas of town. During one of the eyesight checks, I read the chart with my left eye covered. Then the nurse switched eyes to test the one on the left. I saw nothing, a blur. Hmmm, maybe that was why I was such a dummy in class. Unfortunately, being able to see at long last helped but did not solve all my academic performance problems. But you must start somewhere.

Some charms were associated with our economic challenges. In our Ames Street flat, there was a stove that could be fired up to give off heat in the kitchen. My mother and I would huddle around it in the winter as I studied my Catholic Catechism. Q. Who made us? A. God made us. Q. Why did God make us? A. To worship and serve Him. Q. How do we worship and serve him? This series of questions inevitably led us to the immutable truths of my early years . . . you were saved if you believed in the one, true, universal and apostolic church and damned if you didn't. Even as I absorbed these immutable truths, something in the recesses of my mind rebelled. What about some poor kid growing up in China? The system seemed awfully unfair to him or her. I should have realized early on that I was doomed to eternal brimstone.

An early kitchen stove had what looked to me like a cavernous place where you could burn coal (I think) or maybe it was wood. You could pry the lid off and toast your bread over the open flame. That was fun. The same source of heat was used to give some warmth to the cold water that came out of the tap for my bath. Preparation for that ablution took forever to get ready, and still I made do with tepid bath water. One learned not to linger long in the tub during the winter months. In any case, who needed to bathe more than once a month? After all, in medieval Europe they only bathed once a year.

All in all, I don't recall spending much time in the house, certainly before getting a TV and later discovering books. We kids were always outside. We would play our fake baseball game by using a tennis ball on the stoops in front of the three-deckers. Disasters would ensue regularly. The ball might shoot upward landing in the second-floor front porch of the adjacent three-decker. That would mean tramping up the stairs, ringing the doorbell to ask if we could retrieve our lost treasure just one more time. Our desperate hope was that we had not woken anyone up from his nap which, if so, might earn us a quick kick to the backside. Of course, if we had knocked over someone's treasured potted plant, the kick was probably a certainty unless we decided to shift to football on the spot. We really were pains in the backside and thus were the recipients of many well-placed backside kicks.

Another game we played endlessly involved chestnuts, or what Ohioans call Buckeyes. These hard nuts can be drilled through the center and a shoelace inserted to make a weapon of sorts. You had a long string with a hard nut on the end with which you could go around hitting another kid's nuts, though not his real ones of course. Rather, we had an elaborate game where you took turns whacking each other's carefully crafted nut. Still sounds dirty, doesn't it? If your nut broke, you lost. If a guy's nut survived so many battles, it was retired to the nut hall of fame. Yes, a young man could get quite attached to his nuts, so to speak. This falls a little short of the computer games of today, but it kept us occupied.

Though mischievous and loud and undoubtedly irritating, we were not bad kids as I recall. Once a group of us started rummaging around in the basement of the three-decker across the street from my place. In one storage area we found some neat stuff. I have no idea what it was, but the word *neat* suffices to describe this loot. We were dividing the treasure up when the owner happened upon us. We scattered as he sent poorly aimed kicks toward our backsides. We got good at dodging kicks, lots of practice. For days after, I lived in agonizing fear of the knock at the door when the law would drag me off to my just punishment. In the end, nothing happened.

I went to grammar school in an ancient, run-down building in a working-class neighborhood. Even without major competition from middle or upper-class kids, I managed to be average at best. I can't imagine how dumb you had to look (or perhaps be) not to excel at Upsala Street Grammar School. Surely, there was nothing in those early years to suggest I would spend most of the rest of my life in school and by that I don't mean because I was kept back for several decades. My educational tenure surely did not start out with a bang. I recall my first day of kindergarten. I started crying as my mother dropped me off and did not stop for weeks. I certainly wasn't into any adventure just yet. But I did get into the milk and cookies they gave us during kindergarten along with the afternoon naps. I still like cookies and milk while naps remain my specialty.

We were all so innocent back then. Someone wrote "Carmody is a bum" in chalk on the red brick side of this turn of the century edifice. Miss Carmody was my teacher at the time and a tough disciplinarian. She had a perpetual scowl as I recall. Still, any expression of disrespect was beyond the pale in those days. The natural assumption was that one of my classmates was the culprit. I recall sitting for what seemed like hours while the principal prodded and pleaded for the guilty party to confess. We all stared at one another wondering which of our peers had the courage to say what we all felt in private. After a while our curiosity switched. Now we wondered why the evildoers did not have the guts to own up to their own misdeed. In any case, it turned out that someone who graduated a couple of years earlier had done the dirty deed. The miscreant was paraded into the class and made to apologize to us all and, of course, to Miss Carmody. With the crime solved, learning, such as it was, could continue.

Looking back, I probably did learn something in school, but don't ask me what. I need not emphasize that my grammar school drew from neighborhoods that were far from affluent. My older cousin insists that we received an excellent education there. Perhaps she did, we are not so sure about me. The reality was that many families in this area were struggling. Yet, marriage was still the norm. I cannot recall any of my peers being raised in a single-parent household though a few were on partner number two. Not that all these marriages were made in heaven, far from it.

I am reminded of the Clancy clan from across the street. Joe Clancy worked as a bellhop at the city's major downtown hotel. With a slew of kids to support, I am sure money was tight. Yet, he always seemed to come home each night well on the other side of tipsy. As he staggered off the bus and up to his flat, I often would be sitting on our front stoop with friends. We considered his homecoming a great spectator sport. First, we would speculate on whether he would make it all the way in a vertical condition. If successful in that regard, the betting would be on whether he would survive his arrival home. As he entered his three-decker and started up the stairs to his second floor flat we would initiate our countdown . . . Ten, nine, eight, seven, and so on. Our anticipation soon would reach a fever pitch.

Somewhere close to zero we would hear the gentle words of Gert, his wife, as she sweetly greeted the arrival of her husband home from his day's labors. "You drunken SOB, where the hell have you been?" Of course, the evidence of where he had been being obvious. It was where he had been every other evening, but I will assume the question was rhetorical. Her sweet words of endearment usually were accompanied by some crashing and other like sounds as available objects were hurled in Joe's general direction. Yet, they remained together and probably had some affection for one another, if the size of their brood was any indication.

Games . . .

As the years passed, we slowly abandoned the streets in front of our houses for the large public park close by. There always seemed to be gangs of kids available for pick-up games of baseball, basketball, or touch football. The "sides" for these competitions were picked with great scientific accuracy. Two "captains" were selected. These were the two best athletes present on that day and pretty much everyone knew who they were. Needless to say, I was never a "captain."

With the captain issue decided, baseball teams were determined in the following manner. A bat was thrown in the air by one captain and grabbed by the other captain somewhere on the barrel. Then they alternated clasping the bat with a hand up toward where it narrowed. The one who could last clasp the hitting instrument got first pick of the assembled talent. Then they alternated picks until the teams were complete or the available talent was exhausted, whichever came first. For other sports, the odd-even or rock-paper-scissors exercises might be employed to determining the which captain would get to pick first. The NFL draft had nothing on us.

There was another, slightly less politically correct, method for deciding the composition of teams where a bat might not be available. It involved the eenie, meenie, miney, moe chant where you went around the circle pointing at the next participant with the utterance of the next word. I won't go into detail since the chant included extremely racist words that now embarrass the hell out of me. Then, I gave it not a second thought.

The remainder of this team-selection exercise proved an accurate, if humiliating for me at least, barometer of where you stood in the neighborhood pecking order. Someone like me knew that I would not be a high pick. That was ok. But soon they would be down to the dregs . . . the poor kid on crutches, someone's sister, and a neighborhood mutt. When they looked at me, grimaced, and then picked some kid with a full cast on his left leg, I would feel like disappearing in some hole under the turf. When picked, I would be sent out to right field, the graveyard for the terminally challenged in athletics. It would have been kinder to just shoot me. I am sure that option was discussed on occasion.

Okay, perhaps I exaggerate somewhat, but only a little. I did play Little League baseball during my last year of eligibility. The team was supported by Standard Foundry, which threw in money for uniforms and equipment. We were terrible. In my first game, attended by my parents of course, I let a ground ball roll through my legs for an error. I burned with humiliation. I was still burning when I came to bat in the next inning. I can still recall a pitch coming toward the plate chest high. I was in that special zone that only the great athletes can experience. The ball appeared to float toward the plate in slow motion. I put everything I had into that swing and looked up to see the ball arcing toward center field for a home run. You never forget those moments. After all, for someone like me they were quite rare.

I was a big kid for my age and managed to swat several home-runs that year while hitting something over 400, which was pretty darn good. Perhaps I was a late bloomer, and there was hope for me after all. But then I would look at Davie, the real athlete on our block. He was built like a Mack truck, strong as a bull. If I recall correctly, he hit something like 22 or 24 home runs in 18 games, a prodigious feat that I am sure yet stands in the annals of Little League mythology. As a pitcher, he once hit an opposing batter in the head and panicked that he had killed the poor kid. He refused to pitch for the remainder of the season he was so shaken.

Dave and I were neighbors and constantly played sports together, he at a slightly elevated level. In one basketball game I recall losing my head for a moment and taking a swing at him. Immediately, I knew that was a back-forty idea. This was worse than that, a decision so stupid that you should be put out of your misery on the spot since you were way too stupid to continue breathing on your own. After my one ill-considered punch the world stood still, just like the time I threw a hanging curve ball to Davie with a game on the line. It was one of those pitches that just seemed to stop cold right in his wheelhouse so that he could get every inch of his powerful frame into the swing. That ball circled the earth for about a decade, being confused with Sputnik on more than one occasion.

On this occasion, though, I caught a glimpse of the other kids doing a sign of the cross, convinced they were about to witness a homicide. But he liked me and took pity on me. He only gave me a quick punch to the stomach from which I crumpled to the ground in a breathless heap. I may have passed out since I recall watching some pretty stars for a bit. Upon coming to, I recall several kids peering at me to see if I was still alive. Even Davie was concerned, he really was a softy at heart. With my continued existence among the living affirmed, they all started giving me that "what the hell is wrong with you" look. It had been a suicidal move on my part. Have I mentioned I was awfully slow as a kid?

Back then, your futility and outright incompetence would be documented in the local paper. They included box scores and short write-ups of the previous evening's big events. It is hard to imagine they sent reporters out to cover us kids, so parents must have phoned in these big stories. My one moment of fame came when I was called in as a relief pitcher in at a crucial moment in the game. We were ahead by one run in the last inning. Our opponents loaded the bases and their clean-up hitter strode to the plate. It was all on the line. Tension ran through the crowd, which was of decent size. People found this stuff entertaining in the 1950s.

Our manager went to the mound to talk to our ace pitcher, and my best friend, Jerry Petraitis. After a quick conversation, I was called in from first base to get the last out. Jerry handed me the ball and gave me his usual look of confidence. "Oh, god, not

Corbett," his eyes said. Then he whispered something like "Screw this up and you will be eating dirt for supper tonight." I worked the count to two balls and two strikes. Then, as I reared back for my next pitch, it was as if all was in slow motion again. I went into that athlete's special place, what they call the 'zone.' I recall thinking, this is it! Just throw the damn thing as hard as you can. And that is just what I did, straight down the middle of the plate. The batter swung with all his might. If he had connected, that ball would have needed a visa as it headed for Cuba, and I would have dined on dirt that evening. But he missed, and we won. The next day, in the Worcester Telegram sports pages, there was a big print headline leading in to the Little League box scores that read "Corbett plays perfect fireman's role." Relief pitchers were referred as firemen in those days since they "put out fires," so to speak.

We urchins, with boundless energy and no computer games, tried our hand at other games such as football and basketball. Touch football was big since it did not require much equipment and minimized the danger of severe brain injuries though something must explain my dismal performance though life. Too many football concussions would do nicely. When we could, though, we would scrape enough equipment together to play some "real" football matches against kids from other neighborhoods. This was the era when helmets were of little use and real faceguards were an innovation of the future. The only other protection would be shoulder pads. We liked the pads because they made us look like real football stars. That was it. Besides, only sissies would have used anything more. We were tough guys. We would beat on each other for a while and then drag our sorry asses back home for dinner.

During a football game one day, a guy pulled up with a camera and posed us in various action shots. He was from the local paper. One such pose had the hero, not me, lying on the ground hugging the pigskin after scoring a touchdown. Three of us had holds on various parts of his anatomy in our futile attempt to prevent the score. I think I was smiling broadly as I gouged out one of his eyes. Sure enough, there was a big feature of us kids playing sandlot football in Vernon Hill Park the very next morning. Somehow, amid this real sports action, we were all looking at the camera. I was beginning to think there just might be fame and fortune with this sports thing,

In those early years, the only basketball court, if you could call it that, were two hoops hung on either end of what we called the "grand stand." This was an edifice built of large boulders situated at the top of a steep incline in the public park. Presumably, in the World War II era a band used to play from this structure for the entertainment of the listeners enjoying the serenity of the park. This, however, must have been before my time since I cannot recall it used for that purpose even once. Rather, it was our round ball court.

I doubt the hoops reached the standard ten feet in height. In fact, one basket may have been shorter than the other since they were just appended to whatever support was available. Neither were there ever any nets. But none of this mattered. As young kids, the height of the baskets seemed proportional to our short statures. And we had fun. We managed raucous games that vaguely resembled basketball until misfortune struck. This occurred when an errant pass or shot bounded over the railing and down the sharp incline toward a wading pool some two or three hundred yards away. An argument would then ensue over who was at fault though blame usually would be assigned to the kid lowest on the totem pole. And off I would go to retrieve the wayward ball.

Perhaps our favorite game was a variant of stickball, a make-do game made famous by baseball great Willie Mays on the streets of New York. All you needed was a tennis ball and the long wooden handle of a broomstick. You also required a place to play. We used the nearby tennis courts. Why they had built a tennis court before they built a regulation basketball court is a good question. No one I knew played tennis. I can never recall anyone actually playing tennis on these courts. That was a sissy game. Eventually, the nets disappeared and our "ballpark" was perfect. The fence at one end of the court was a backstop. You flung the tennis ball toward the hypothetical plate, usually outlined in chalk on the black concrete surface, while the batter wielded a sawed-off broomstick as a bat. Any fielded grounder or fly ball was an out, along with strikeouts of course. A ball hit off the opposite fence of the "court" was an extra base hit while a grounder reaching the fence was a single.

Anything hit over the opposite fence was a home run. We all pretended to be our Red Sox heroes putting the hated Yankees in their place.

I can remember being late for my paper route one day. But they begged me to stay since it was the final inning and the game was on the line. We needed one run to win the game. Davie, my pugilistic nemesis, was pitching. I could hardly see the ball when he pitched, never mind hit it. But I got in a zone for that one moment, focusing all my limited faculties. Bat, well broom stick, met ball, and the sphere streaked on a line drive still rising as it cleared the fence by a foot…a walk-off home run. I just dropped the bat and nonchalantly sauntered-away to deliver my papers. Another unforgettable moment.

On hot summer days we would plunge into the wading pool with some seven thousand other kids and a smattering of adults. As far as I recall, there were no lifeguards or hygienic treatments to cleanse the pool. One can only imagine hordes of teeming bacteria and other micro-organisms swarming around us. But we would splash about with abandon, dunking one another, and undoubtedly gulping down copious amounts of toxic water. It would have been instructive to have taken pictures of our intestinal tracks for medical research. They could have been compared with similar pictures from third world countries, sort of like what my intestinal track probably looked like after two years of well water in India. In the end, no one died.

We also seemed to have unlimited energy back then. Even at a pretty young age, I would literally walk miles dragging the set of golf clubs my uncle gave me. After climbing this monstrous hill, I would finally arrive at this run-down nine-hole course. We then would play all day for a buck before trudging all those miles back home. No one ever checked on my well-being or that of my buddies. We were gone from daybreak to nightfall. One might think that heat stroke and collapse was a possibility on hot summer days. In addition, any of us could have been kidnapped and taken several states away before anyone noticed our absence. But then again, there seemed to be no pedophiles back then or at least we never heard about them. And surely there was no risk of kidnapping for ransom, unless the miscreants would be satisfied with a six pack of beer. But I disappointed my parents and kept returning home every evening.

A sanctuary . . .

I did have one personal sanctuary that was mine alone. When I wasn't damaging neighbor's cars with a football or breaking their windows with a baseball, I would saunter the two miles or so to the nearest library, not a popular destination among my friends. Most of them could read of course, but it was prudent not to brag about that fact. For me, though, books were fodder for that imagination which, from the earliest days, never ceased to be active and rewarding. Perhaps it just part of me, perhaps it had something to do with being an only child who still had lots of time by himself.

After all, you could not be roaming the streets 24-7. But I did love the written word and worlds that those words would open for me. I would avidly consume the Readers Digest Condensed books my father received.

I cannot speak to where this love for the written word came from. I cannot think of any friends who evidenced the least interest in books or literature. No one ever asked what I was reading or wanted to swap their latest favorite. This love of the written word was a solitary romance but one for which I am so desperately thankful. Perhaps my imagination was fueled by the great old radio shows . . . *The Shadow*, the *Inner Sanctum*, *Dragnet*, the *X Factor*, the *Adventures of Sherlock Holmes*, several Westerns, and (of course) *Tom Corbett Space Cadet*. One inestimable advantage of these old radio greats was that you had to fill in the blanks. With suggestive audio effects, you created the scene in your imagination . . . no HD pictures to stare at blankly or video games where people exploded in gory heaps of bloodied flesh. Years later, when I subscribed to XM radio, I would listen to these shows once again. I was reminded by how these shows invited your imagination in to be part of the production. We should bring these back in some fashion for the kids of today.

Perhaps that is what I most take away from those early years. So much was left to our imaginations. We made up our own games, we filled in the contexts of the radio shows to which we listened, and there were whole series of books like the Hardy Boys, which fed our thirst for adventure and excitement. Even our typical rough and tumble boys' games of war or cowboys and Indians demanded that we role play in imaginative ways. If you were already disposed to create worlds in your own mind, this was fertile ground indeed. And all that solitude that came with being an only child further stirred my imagination.

My childhood was not totally ideal. It was not the stuff of a 1950s *Leave It to Beaver* household, not by any means. Money always seemed to be scarce, something that hung over the house creating insecurity and friction. There were constant arguments and even threats of imminent divorce. Many a night I wept as they went at it in the adjacent room. I can yet recall my father breaking the window to the door in a rage and, on occasion, whacking me upside the side of the head but usually when I deserved it. But all in all, it was average stuff for my time and place.

I looked around Ames Street one more time. It really did not look all that different to me. It still looked like the wonderful place of my early dreams and adventures. How could such a place be dangerous? Where was all this evil that people feared? Perhaps, as the old saying goes, you can't go home again. I sighed. Then we got in our car and left.

CHAPTER 4

LEARNING

In a good bookroom you feel in some mysterious way that
you are absorbing the wisdom contained in all the books
through your skin, without even opening them.

—Mark Twain

It was 1979. I took several months off from my position as a researcher at the Institute for Research on Poverty at the University of Wisconsin-Madison to finish up the predissertation requirements for my doctorate. As was my wont, I had applied myself to earning this advanced degree with less than the required diligence. Thus, as the year 1979 dawned, I found myself facing several incompletes and the dreaded preliminary examination. Apparently, you can take the boy out of Worcester, but you can't take Worcester out of the boy. Why work when you can play, which in my case meant getting involved in several complex social policy challenges? And why actually do what you are supposed to do until you are really up against it? For me, it was even more nonsensical.

Was I out having a good time? No! I was tilting my lance at a few impossible policy issues like reforming Wisconsin's welfare system. Can you say the second coming of Don Quixote?

In those days, unlike now, the preliminary examination for a Ph. D. in social welfare was a big deal. You needed to pass this obstacle before beginning your dissertation, the final hurdle. You confronted five questions, one developed by each member of your committee, and had three hours to respond to each one. That came to fifteen hours over three days to test whether you had a command over all knowledge in your disciplinary field.

To make matters more interesting, I chose a committee that was considered, hands down, the toughest that one might put together at that time. They were known in the School of Social Work as the "Poverty Boys," the top researchers at the Institute for Research on Poverty (IRP), the major national think-tank on the topic. While I saw them more as colleagues than as my professors, most of my fellow doctoral candidates in the program saw them as the equivalent of academic hell. My fellow doctoral candidates looked at me if I had lost what remained of my sanity by putting this committee together. Truth be told, my link to common sense was never strong.

In the end, I wound up taking time off from my ongoing projects at the Poverty Institute to apply myself to the task at hand. I almost choke at the writing of this sentence. It is not easy for me to get out of character by doing the right thing. However, I can if pressed. I can even be nice but only for very short periods of time before I start to hyperventilate. Discipline and focus just are not my strong suits. In this instance, though, I was doubly motivated to do the right thing for once in my life. Sure, no doctoral candidate ever wants to look like a failure, but I had long been accustomed to lackluster performances. I was motivated in a different way, however. I did not feel like a typical student. I looked upon my committee as peers with whom I had been working before entering the program. I was not supposed to fail. In some ways, I was already a member of their club though with a very minor-league status. Screwing up now would really reveal me to be the fraud I felt myself to be inside. It would be like letting down family, in this case a family that I kind of liked.

It is one thing to do the normal progression, move from bachelors to masters to doctorate with no real breaks in between. Each stage then is another rite of passage to the elite world of academia. But I had been doing relatively high-level state policy work and then running a complex research project at the university before sliding back into the doctoral program. Even then, I eased back only a little on my ongoing work at the Institute. At one point, the powers-that-be caught up with me to inform me that I could not hold a nearly full-time appointment at the university and be a full-time student simultaneously. It was against some rule. I seldom bothered to read any rules assuming it was easier to say I was sorry than to ask permission in the first place. For me, school was just a sideline thing. Problem was that I am clever but not that clever. It was not always easy to juggle a rather full research schedule and be a full-time doctoral candidate simultaneously. This just might explain the several incompletes that I accumulated. Also, it does not help when your favorite animal is the sloth.

I think the faculty had some trouble figuring out how to treat me and I them. I recall the husband of a gal with whom I worked with during my first real job as a research analyst with the State of Wisconsin. Steven was studying under the mentorship of an acclaimed scholar of the Federalist period in early American history, Merrill Jensen. Poor Steven talked about Merrill as if he were a minor deity. He both worshiped the man and feared him. Steven was always on the lookout for any real or imagined transgression on his part that would put his hopes for a terminal degree in harm's way. Maybe somebody at a party would smoke pot and somehow Merrill would find out. Maybe he would slip up and utter some witticism that Merrill found offensive. Maybe he would wear the wrong clothes to seminar one day. It was always Doctor or Professor Jensen and total deference. He would never consider addressing Merrill with any familiarity until he had earned his own doctorate. Steven went through the program walking on egg shells.

I greeted my committee members as Irv, Mike, or Sheldon and treated them as badly as I treated everyone else. When it came to my sharp wit, I take no prisoners. When two of my good colleagues rose sequentially to be the Dean of the U. W. College at Letters and Sciences in recent years, I told each in turn that I would not let their new position affect how I treated them. I would treat them like shit as I always had. Both appreciated my honesty.

But that is neither here nor there. I must have been one of the few Ph. D. students who enjoyed the prelim process. Yes, I was that weird and demented. Many back then told me that I really did need to get a life. Even more tell me that now. In any case, I surrounded myself with books and articles and spent day after day absorbing all I could. It was fun. There were no work deadlines to fret about or people to manage or problems to solve. I could while away my days reading stuff and pondering great thoughts. *This is great!* I thought. This academic crap is better than working for a living.

It turns out that I love pondering great thoughts, struggling with incomprehensible conundrums. There is, after all, a singular joy to the act of learning. Understanding the world about me, at least parts of that world, had always held a fascination for me. I never cared about how practical things worked but the machinations of society and the interplay of people and concepts of social justice entertained me to no end. Moreover, the conundrums on which I chose to focus would provide endless intellectual twists and turns. It was not as if someone would come along and solve these societal issues. I had a lifetime of puzzles to ponder. Besides, this affirmed what I had always thought. Doing this so-called academic stuff was nothing like getting a real job. And, if you got lucky, someone might pay you for doing it. What a scam!

The current Republican Governors of Florida and Wisconsin have made points about education that I find particularly repellent. Rick Scott, in arguing for reforms in Florida's approach to higher education, stressed that the basic purpose of college is to make more money, period. That is why he went to college, to get credentials that would help him become rich. Scott Walker, in his 2015 budget bill, slashed funding for the University of Wisconsin by amounts that were shocking even by Republican standards. More amazingly, he excised language in the University of Wisconsin mission statement that got to the heart of what is known as the Wisconsin Idea, that the university should pursue truth in the service of resolving public issues. The backlash was immediate. Undeterred, Walker next went after tenure. Why protect well-known leftists or ask the experts for help with the public's business when wealthy political donors will be telling you what to do in the first place? The university's primary mission is to serve the needs of private sector employers in his mind, period. Why educate the next generation at all? He dropped out of college, or was kicked out depending what story you believe, while earning a mere 2.3 G.P.A. Then he went out to systematically wreck Wisconsin's finest public institutions. Who needs to think logically about stuff?

Such money-grubbing, anti-intellectual sentiments fill me with great sadness. It reminds me of one of my mother's obsession with not having enough money, constantly belittling my dad's failure as a provider. As a result, she endured a rather bitter, unfulfilled life, always comparing her lot with those who had more. It never occurred to her that there would always be those with a little bit more. That is a labored analogy but that is the beauty of analogies, they only must make sense to the person who is creating them in the first instance.

Like these short-sighted Republican governors, my mother saw my pursuit of an education as being only about money. How rich could I become? She harped on the money thing to such an extent, and so constantly, that I vowed the pursuit of wealth would be the very last thing to motivate me in life. I made many vows as a youngster, most of them totally absurd like building a body like the one Charles Atlas had on his workout commercials. However, one vow was made more often than others, and with more fervor. I would never let the pursuit of riches dominate my life. There is a lesson here . . . always pick ambitions that are easy to keep.

At some point, learning became a thing in itself, its own reward. It ceased to be utilitarian but rather a process to be embraced and enjoyed. And most of all, eventually I would be proved correct all along. A lifetime dedicated to pursuing knowledge beats the hell out of working for a living. And it certainly beats the mindless pursuit of wealth, by far. Real work, like manual labor, always was a loser from the start. Avoiding that needs little in the way of explanation. Avoiding riches is less obvious, perhaps a comment on that is warranted. As I saw it, you can have too much money. Sure, I wanted to eat and have a roof over my head. But after the basics are secured, the chase becomes rather meaningless. On the other hand, the seduction of most intellectual challenges is irresistible. There is always another conundrum or complex puzzle to command your attention and energy. Acquiring knowledge and understanding sustains you forever. Solving society's challenges, or trying to at least, never gets old.

Grammar school . . .

The pursuit of knowledge started out slowly for me to say the least. For a long time, a very long time, I cannot recall demonstrating any cognitive talents that might suggest a future in the academy. The real question was whether I would make it through school at all. This school crap did not impress me at the start though the kindergarten naps and the snacks were great. That took the edge off. But the rest seemed foreign and even scary.

Most of my grammar school experience is rather a blur, but I do recall not feeling any particular affinity for either school or learning. It was something I did until I was sprung at the end of the day to maraud through the neighborhood harassing the good people of Ames Street and beyond. Oddly enough, I recall missing the first day we started working on arithmetic or basic numbers. What a tragedy! After that, I never caught up. Years later, I would stare blankly at those puzzles where the boat was going one way at twenty miles an hour and the river was flowing the other direction at ten miles per hour, so how long did it take the boat captain to eat his lunch. If only I had not missed that first day whey when we started numbers!

I really don't know if I learned anything of substance during those early years or not. Clearly my teachers were confused, assigning me to a slow class for one year in grammar school and then to an accelerated class when I transitioned to junior high school. During those early years in school, I never had any sense of doing well or poorly. You were graded or assessed on both deportment, basically behavior or not being a dedicated delinquent, and academic performance. My grades in real subjects are lost to me. The behavioral ratings focused on such things as "gets along with others" and "applies himself" and "doesn't pick his nose in class." I typically did pretty good but not stellar. I would have scored better on deportment had I not wiped my nose treasures on my shirt. Undoubtedly, using the kid's shirt next to me on occasion really tanked my grade.

In those long-ago days, they would give you what they called U-warnings, *U* standing for unsatisfactory. I distinctly remember getting a few of those, more than one for penmanship. In truth, my penmanship did suck. It still sucks but that matters less now. If anything, I sensed being very average in most areas. I tried sucking up, like volunteering to be the ink-well filler, remember pens that you kept refilling with ink? I am not saying I am old, but my school had just graduated from using quills with which to write only a couple of years before I arrived. In any case, I am certain my teachers considered me as an excellent candidate for a totally undistinguished life. If I had become president and they scurried back to find out what I was like back in my early days, the response would have been "Tom who?"

My sense is that I was considered a good, obedient kid who generally tried hard but was rather dull and hopeless. Certainly, no one confused me with any kind of intellectual prodigy, even in this run-down grammar school on the wrong side of town. There was no sign, none whatsoever, that one day I would be taking my doctoral exams at a top research university. If you told this to my teachers back then, they would have looked for a sky full of pigs in full flight once they had arisen from the floor while laughing hysterically. Okay, I think I have made my point here.

But here I was, many years later, doing just that. I finally managed to clean up those pesky incompletes and take my prelims. I recall staring at the first question. You were permitted to take books and notes into the exam. Very briefly, I tried looking a couple of things up, then took a big breath, and said screw it. If I didn't know something by know, it did not count. After that, I simply let everything flow and flow it did. Out poured tons of ideas and facts and analysis I had accumulated both inside the classroom and while out in the world doing policy work.

Upon finishing, my wife and I went on an extended trip through Yugoslavia (before the breakup into Serbia and all those other

Balkan countries) and Greece. It was a great trip that included a precarious drive along the Adriatic Sea several hundred feet above the water. Our pleasure, and anxiety, was heightened by German tourists rushing past us as we made or way down this winding, narrow road. I stopped thinking about my prelim performance since I probably would plunge to my death any moment now. Academic credentials would be useless as my decomposing body washed about in the sea's currents. Despite a paralyzing fear of my demise, Yugoslavia was great. Dubrovnik was an unforgettable gem. One small village, Primostin, is etched in my head. It is an old town that rises out of the sea connected to land by a small isthmus. In a photo I caught the outline of the ancient town in the evening's amber hue. That picture yet takes my breath away. So many civilizations had fought over this area with each leaving their unique imprint. It was history unfolding before us.

Upon returning to the States, my prelim concerns returned with full force. I was sure my results would be available. Had I passed? Had I failed? Did I make a complete fool of myself? Would I have to change my identity and run off with a traveling circus? Did the circus still exist? What about the French Foreign Legion? I prepared myself for any outcome but there was nothing, nothing official or unofficial like a congratulatory note or a sympathy card. Not only that but no one on my committee said anything, not a word. Well, they asked about my trip and other sundry things but said nothing about my academic career being over. While everyone seemed polite and all, and no one avoided eye contact, neither did anyone give any sign of hope, not even my committee chair.

I tried to be nonchalant. Hey, I never let this doctoral process take up much of my life in the first place. Why should I start acting like all the other paranoid, anxiety-ridden students at this late date? But I was not made of total stone. Eventually, curiosity did get the better of me. So, I wandered up to Piliavin one day, sucked up my tattered pride, and asked straight away, "Okay, is anyone going to tell me how I did?" In his usual calm and measured way, Irv broke into a profane-laden rant, "You mean those blankety-blank idiots over in Social Work never sent you the results," which was followed by a string of further expletives. Irv was not a man to hide his feelings. He was a generous, smart, and loving man but you did not want to be on the bad side of his ire. To the best of my knowledge, Social Work never did manage to get me any official results. Hey, it is an organization run by social work types after all.

It turned out that all was well . . . better than well. Over the weeks that followed I picked up from several sources that my prelim answers were considered exceptional indeed, a model for other students. I had approached my course work pretty much as I had dealt with school in general over the years. I did just enough to be able to continue, but I never let my formal studies get in the way of my education. While some learning for me did take place in the classroom, most was found outside the structured curriculum.

I did apply myself to my prelims, however, and it apparently paid off. Then again, I found the process fun. That was key, as always. I could apply myself if I was having fun. The prelim ordeal was not a rite of passage or a trial by fire for me. It was totally different, a time when I could just sit on my fat ass and think. How great is that! I yet remember a comment from one member of my committee, Irv Garfinkel. Now, Irv was someone with whom I did much work later in my career, and who was considered accomplished as a scholar and quite demanding of others. He is now a Professor at Columbia University. One day, he remarked that I was the smartest student he had ever seen come through the Wisconsin Social Welfare program. Then he paused for a moment, thought about it again, and then reaffirmed his conclusion. "Yes, the best." I was rather stunned. Sure, I was clever enough but the best? I was never the best in any school, anywhere, at any time. I think I was above average in Kindergarten napping but that was, far and away, my moment in the academic sun.

How did I make that journey from a neighborhood scamp who wasted his days marauding through the streets causing mayhem and who demonstrated absolutely no promise whatsoever to someone who would spend his professional life in the academy? And not just in the academy but in a special corner of the academy that so many colleagues considered the absolutely best place to be if you were interested in social policy questions. I can say one thing, it was not planned.

Junior high school...

Eventually my lackluster years at Upsala Street grammar school came to an undistinguished end. Next, I was to spend two years at another undistinguished citadel of learning, Providence Street Junior High School. My tenure at this less than prestigious institution turned out to be an extension of my lackluster grammar school days. There was one difference however. Instead of being placed with the dummies I was now placed with the smart kids in the advanced class, or what passed for above average at "Prov" Junior High. I promptly rewarded the trust my grammar school teachers had in me by once-again returning to my desultory academic ways. We had something like twenty-five students in this advanced class, five boys and some twenty girls. Even back then, when girls were being groomed to be future wives and mothers, they were pulling ahead of us boys academically. Then again, we guys were not setting the bar very high.

Of course, it could be that the five boys in this class were the only youthful males from the area who managed to avoid trouble with the local authorities. Girls, after all, were more mature and better behaved at this age, or any age for that matter. Boys approaching puberty had lost all remaining reason and surely any and all self-control. When you spend virtually all your waking hours thinking about the unspeakable things you would like to do to cute little Suzie sitting two rows over, not much time is left for scholarly concentration. Now that I think on it, boys never really catch up.

We start out as losers and keep falling further back. It is a total mystery to me why girls ever paid any attention to us whatsoever. Boys, as the girls soon discover upon closer examination, really are disgusting. The twenty girls in my class pretty much ignored me altogether. It only took them a day or two to figure out I was not worth any effort on their behalf.

I cannot recall at all how I stacked up against the girls academically; I cannot recall a single one of them, by name or appearance. They might as well have been from Mars. My very strong suspicion is that virtually all of them outperformed me in the classroom. Given my awful performance, they must have. It would not have been very much of a challenge. The boys I remember very well. There was Kenney, Andy, Eddie, John, and yours truly. Each of us knew where we stood within this little male group. Kenney was by far the brightest with Andy just a tad behind. Eddie and I were about equal, and John brought up the rear. It is not like we competed outright, no one expected much from the students of Providence Junior High other than not burning the school down. As far as I recall we never compared grades or anything like that. You just sensed where you stood.

I lost track of Eddie and John soon after leaving for high school, but I managed to keep track of Andy and Kenney. I had spent a lot of time with Andy. He lived relatively close and we were the only two Upsala boys to make it into this so-called advanced group. He had a childhood condition that left him with a severe scar on his leg and a very noticeable limp. His father worked as a mortician in a funeral parlor, so I liked going over to his three-decker flat just in case there was a dead body being worked on. This fascination would have been great material for a child psychologist, but no one had heard of such a thing in my neighborhood. Andy's bad leg never slowed him up all that much, and he was always in high spirits. Eventually, as I learned later, he received an engineering degree from Worcester Polytechnic Institute, a fine engineering college. Perhaps he went on for even higher degrees but by then I had lost track.

Kenney, on the other hand, had problems in later years. I always thought he might become a doctor; he seemed to love science and certainly had an amazing mind. One day he sat me down to fill me in on details about the facts of life, my own parents skipped over that topic and there was no internet filled with free porn back then. He drew out the anatomical parts with chalk on a sidewalk and gave me an amazing biology lesson including a sex education class that corrected many myths. No, the longer you were inside a woman did not determine the sex of the child as I heard several girls hypothesize.

He seemed rather remarkable to me. As I recall, he was from a lone-parent household, just about the only early acquaintance who faced that challenge. His family was quite poor, perhaps less well off than mine. He lived in a three-decker that was located on a busy street adjacent to the railroad tracks. I can no longer recall the specifics, but I recall feeling that his challenges were greater than for the rest of us. Still, I really thought that if anyone, in a literal sense, would make it off Vernon Hill, it would be Kenney. He had the right stuff; you sense such things even at a young age. What you cannot know is how the game of life will play itself out.

I ran into Kenney a quarter-century or so later when he was in his late thirties or so. It was clear his early promise remained unfulfilled. He was working as a technician at the city run hospital taking blood samples. We chatted from time to time, but I could never ask him what went wrong. It was not merely a case of unbounded talent unfulfilled but of a life thrown away. By this time, he was quickly drifting into the advanced stages of alcoholism. The differences between dreams realized and dreams deferred and ultimately lost are not apparent at the beginning of the race. Why do some break away and others not. Maybe if we had stayed in touch I would have worked up the courage to ask these questions. Looking at him, I would not have been surprised if he were dead within a decade or less. Then again, I almost succumbed to a similar fate but that is a story for another chapter.

Compared to my academic experiences in college and beyond, I felt my academic preparation demanding in a few classes at least. There was Miss Harney, the French teacher. She was dedicated and tried to cram a foreign language into our heads. It probably was hopeless except for Kenney and some of the girls. What can I say? I crossed U. N. interpreter off the list. But we did a whole play in

French. I had one line, "Je n'ai pas de femme," or "I do not have a wife." But I can also recall another teacher, for history or geography, who literally did nothing for the semester. We were assigned some independent writing project, which I basically copied from an encyclopedia. Didn't they have lesson plans back then?

High school . . .

By the time I was ready for high school, all my early vocational dreams were losing traction. It was clear that I was not going to become a cowboy or astronaut or movie star or athlete or any of the other vocations that promised adventure, fame, and fortune. It struck me that perhaps I had better seriously reconsider a plan B, which I had occasionally entertained and always quickly dismissed. I might have to get a real job someday. To do that, maybe I needed to develop some academic-type skills, whatever the hell they might be.

It was inconceivable to me that I enjoyed any skills that some future employer might conceivably want. When I looked at the sad sack that peered back at me in the bathroom mirror, any career possibility of worth seemed beyond my reach. Really, I didn't know anything, nor could I do anything. The military, in the end, remained my backup plan. We were in a death struggle with the horrible Communists after all. They would need all the cannon fodder available. In the army, I would get to eat three meals a day and have a place to sleep, until I got myself shot that is.

Sometimes a wave of panic would wash over me. It would occur to me that I better knuckle down and learn something. Even then, I had an intuition that physical labor was out of the question. I watched my father do that kind of work. My sole visit to his place of manual labor affirmed my suspicion that his job was difficult, tedious, dirty, and unrewarding. Nor did it pay all that well. At times he worked two jobs which should have made us comfortable financially had my folks not drank most of it away. It struck me that his life was consumed with real work, which is not a four-letter word without just cause.

While real work was a fate to be avoided at all costs, the jobs that seemed at least acceptable to me demanded a good education. I was not all that interested in money. I surely did not want to go down that bitter road of mindless acquisition that fed on my mother and so many of her friends. It seemed that all the fine ethnic, working class folk from Worcester were always obsessed with "the deal." Where could they scam something for nothing or real cheaply and then brag about it forever. To this day, I ignore deals. When I want something, which is rare, I just go and get it. I am sure that retailers think of me as a complete and total schmuck.

I always thought to myself, never get obsessed with material things. I started out saying never own more stuff than you can carry with you. That evolved into never own more than you can stuff in your car, then cars, then a small van, and finally a semi-truck or two. My intentions regarding the accumulation of crap continued to slide. Somehow with two homes (for a while at least), a country club membership, and a bunch of adult toys I drifted a bit from my early commitment. But my intentions were honorable. And I can say with some pride that I dumped the second home. That is a small step in the right direction though we did rent a seaside place when Madison gets cold in the winter. Perhaps my bragging is not totally warranted.

At some level it struck me that jobs that did not involve real work were premised on advanced degrees. If you were going to get paid for sitting on your derriere all day, you had to fool people that you had talents worth a salary even as you sat around all day. Now that would be great work if you could get it. That secret formula to fool others into paying me for sitting around all day was not my charm or wits or good looks, all of which I possessed in woefully short supply. Yup, I just might need to learn something, develop a skill. It was time to suck it up and get serious.

So, I embarked on this new, if somewhat hopeless, plan to prepare for adulthood. I took the exam for St. John's Prep as it was called at the time. This was an all-boys Catholic school that was rated the best, at least among biased Catholics, in central Massachusetts. It was taught by the Xaverian Brothers who brought their unique brand of discipline to the teaching profession. You broke a rule and you would get whacked upside the head. You complained to your parents about getting hit by one of the Brothers and they would whack you up the other side of your head.

In addition, suit coats and ties were required. They were dedicated to preparing you as men of letters and men of God. That meant focusing on character as well as intellect. I would try telling them I already was a character, but they probably would just whack me upside the head.

But I did not worry about all that at the time. Hell, I probably would not pass the exam anyways. My memory is that only a minority of the applicants made the cut in those years. I cannot recall what the exam was like all these years later, but I recall being dismayed at the number taking the test. I left the huge hall with little hope of a favorable outcome. Hell, I probably hovered toward the bottom of my junior high class, albeit in a so-called advanced class, and there I was only competing against other working-class kids. On that day, I was up against kids who came from the upwardly mobile and successful Catholic families. These were the sons of lawyers, doctors, and businessmen. I left the exam hall without much hope.

Weeks later, I still remember my mother opening the all-important letter informing me of my fate. I watched her face as she broke into a smile. It turns out that she would have something to crow about to her family and friends. Perhaps her son was not brain damaged after all, as many had long surmised. Just how did I do so well? Maybe they mixed up my exam with some kid who really was smart? Not only did I get in, but I did well enough to make it into the top class. Some 120 students were accepted into the freshman class to be apportioned into three separate classes of forty each, with the smartest assigned to the top class (A) and the least able (according to the entry examination) to the bottom class (C). I cannot recall where I specifically ranked among all test takers, but I believe it was somewhere in the top fifteen or twenty of the four hundred or so who took the exam. That really stunned me. My self-image was as a plodder, someone who could get by with a little effort, had received a mighty blow. I might have shown a small sign of cleverness on occasion, but I never stood out, not at all.

On the plus side, this was a small piece of evidence that I would not be an embarrassment to my family. After all, I had stayed out of juvenile hall. On the down side, no empirical evidence supported a bright future where I might earn a living while avoiding physical labor. Not doing awful things is not the same as doing great things. I always sensed I was a disappointment to my parents. They never said so outright, but I could see it in their eyes. They didn't seem all that eager to have a kid in their younger days. What they got was not much to write home about.

Until my senior year, St. Johns was located in a rundown part of Worcester. It was located on Temple Street, not far from downtown and next to some railroad tracks. The buildings were old, one dating back to the previous century, or was it the 17th century. In that venerable structure some upper floors had already been condemned. When walking between buildings, you kept an eye skyward to look for falling bricks. I recall that my freshman classroom was in a basement with no windows. Pipes ran across the room just under ceilings. These clanged and shook from time to time during the winter months so I assume they had something to do with heating the building. If they did, they did not do a very good job. There was no science equipment nor any other amenities such as AV labs or the learning tools that grace contemporary, suburban schools. There was not even an indoor cafeteria. At lunchtime, we ate outside except when there was a raging blizzard going on. Nourishment was supplied by a local vendor called Mike's Lunch Wagon. Mike would pull a truck laden with food and drink into the school yard.

Lunch could be quite brutal during the ravages of mid-winter. The headmaster, Brother Chad, would walk around as the temperature hovered between 10–20 degrees sporting a big smile. He never wore a coat himself, just the long cassock that was the uniform of the Brothers. And he never, ever, signaled that the cold had gotten to him. It might well have been 70 degrees, not 17 degrees, from his demeanor. While our teeth chattered uncontrollably as we downed hot coffee for relief, he would flash that wide smile and acclaim, "Great day, is it not, gentleman?" That smirk would never leave his face as he passed his private little torture on to the next group.

"Yes, Brother Chad," we responded as a chorus, "you miserable SOB" when he was out of earshot. We were convinced he had gotten his headmaster training at the Heinrich Himmler School for Sadists. I suspect the prevailing philosophy was that a little pain helped develop character. That place, I suspect, would be shut down for fostering cruel and unusual punishment in today's environment where protecting our precious, spoiled darlings from all inconveniences is seen as a parental virtue. Damn kids today get away with way too much. And yet, they seem useless nonetheless. When I tell the kids of today about the mound of coal I shoveled into the family furnace at the crack of dawn and then milking some forty cows before walking six miles to school in a raging snowstorm, they merely yawn. No heated buses for us, damn it! Okay, no coal or cows but the walk was probably three miles.

Back then, we were treated like real men. We were young Catholics being prepared for life in a world run by Protestants or worse. We had to be tough and smart. There were also no electives. You took a straight course of difficult subjects under the iron rule of the brothers. The common core curriculum included math, science, history, English, French, Latin, and theology (Catholic indoctrination). You sat in the same room all day as the teaching brothers rotated from class to class. This was their life. I think they went back to their congregate housing at the end of the day and plotted ways to make our lives miserable the next morning. And if they didn't plot during the evening, that only meant they had their tactics down cold.

Some of these men were unforgettable. One of them had been around so long that he had actually taught Babe Ruth when the young slugger had been sent to a vocational school for troubled youngsters that the Xaverian Brothers ran in Baltimore. His face was angular and etched, looking as old as Father Time himself. Our Latin teacher was a gnomish little man with a squeaky voice and a facial expression that suggested he was in eternal pain. If I were trying to teach us Latin, I would have been in eternal pain for sure. He would start each term with the question, "Why do we study Latin, gentlemen?" And being smart asses, we would say in unison, "So that we can have a conversation with Julius Caesar if we meet him in the street, Brother." He would then shout "No," his grimace even more pronounced. Then he proceeded to give his standard rationale why Latin was still relevant in the twentieth century which, of course, was and is a bunch of bull-hockey. We did not appreciate a word he said, and most of us, including me, struggled mightily with the nightly translations.

I also struggled with all things mathematical. It was always apparent I was a verbal guy. Algebraic notations simply were beyond me. Decades later, I was working with a colleague at Wisconsin who, though in the School of Social Work, was initially trained in physics. He loved numbers and was a strong empiricist. We were struggling with some concept and he said, "Oh, I get it," and began scribbling equations on the board. He more easily saw concepts when expressed mathematically. I would then have to translate everything back into English to understand. I envy those who are comfortable with rigorous representations of reality. Their ability to see things more precisely is such a gift. Still, I argued that I saw the world in a more complete way, a manner that was less linear and which embraced more nuanced complexity. We all rationalize away our deficits.

My point is this, people see the world differently, and in the end, you must know who you are. After finishing one high school algebra exam, I realized I was in deep doo-doo. To lighten the mood, I scrawled *Veni, Vidi, Flunki* across the top of the page . . . a play on Caesars note to Rome after conquering the Gauls. His pithy message merely said, "I came, I saw, I conquered," with the word *Vici* being substituted for my witty *Flunki*. Perhaps he would give me a couple of points for excessive wit. My teacher confirmed my fears when he scratched next to my clever Latin . . . almost! Apparently, excessive wit counted for nothing in algebra. If you read this vignette elsewhere, my apologies. Obviously, I was scarred by my mathematical failings.

Every graduate from St. Johns, by God, went on to college, virtually every graduate at least. I can only recall one who did not, a neighbor of mine from Ames Street who brought up the bottom of his class. He did later become the top sheriff of Worcester County, so he acquitted himself rather well in any case. And despite myself, I did learn quite a bit. The competition seemed tough. Both my wife (who went to a similar girl's Catholic school in Minnesota) and I found high school to be the most challenging educational level in our academic careers, and we both spent much time in academia. She earned a master's degree and later graduated from the U.W. Law School with honors. The two of us still go back to high school as the place where we tried the hardest and still did not excel. Admittedly, she did better than I, but then again, I set the bar quite low.

Times were different back then. On average, less than 20 percent of high school students received an A grade compared to over half in 2013. It is estimated that half of all high school students had six hours of homework per week while less than one-third are given that much work today. The Xaverian Brothers, as you might imagine, gave us much more than that. It seemed as if we had six hours per night though that might be a small exaggeration. There were no computer games and smart phones to distract us. We read tough texts that did not have a lot of pictures and had to write essays. Though I finally began to blossom academically around my senior year, I never cracked the top-quarter of my class. The average SAT scores in 1962, the year I graduated, were the highest they would be in decades, maybe ever, probably because fewer took the test back then with a lot of self-selection going on. I did fine on the verbal side but marginally above average on the quantitative side of things.

I suspect the iron fist approach to discipline in the classroom helped though it struck us, on occasion at least, as rather oppressive.

Still, classes were orderly and obedient for the most part. Of course, this was the late 1950s and early '60s. The notion of student rights occurred to no one. Physical discipline surely was not an everyday event but occurred often enough to keep you awake. A hard whack across the face might even lead to a bloody nose. The parents were on board with a healthy dose of corporal punishment, that is for sure. Today, parents rush to the defense of little Johnny or Sally, even after they open up a stand selling Meth in the school cafeteria. Not back then, we might get whacked for looking cross-eyed at one of the brothers. Order, discipline, and good behavior were demanded as virtues expected of Catholic gentlemen.

It was hard not to learn something in this milieu, even if it was only how to avoid getting a bloody nose while still getting away with some nefarious transgression. I still remember the day when I was taking Latin in my senior year. Our original gnomish teacher had been replaced by a Brother who stood over six feet and looked like a college linebacker. On one occasion, I was trying to cheat on my Latin translation with what was known as a trot, an English version of the Latin text. He spotted my terrible sin and charged down the aisle, hovering over me as he quivered with rage. I desperately tried recalling the perfect Act of Contrition but that failed me as well. But he liked me and just said something about how disappointed he was. I think that hurt more than the whack I was expecting.

High standards, a rigorous curriculum, hard competition, and few diversions all helped in our academic preparation. We did have great sports teams, though. Our football squad was undefeated for about three of the four years I was there. The basketball team almost won the New England Catholic championship one year, losing in the finals in the last second. But there was not much else going on except for a few academic clubs like chess and debate. There were no other activities on which to waste time. It probably helped that there were no females around. Given how frustrated we all were and how hopeless it was making any headway with the fairer sex in that day, it is amazing our testicles did not settle into a permanent shade of deep blue or even purple, the infamous blue balls syndrome. Maybe I should take another look, as I think on it, they are rather sad-looking at times.

A fortunate generation . . .

Other things were going on. Though we did not fully realize it at the time, we were a fortunate generation. The post–World War II period saw a dramatic rise in real median incomes in the U.S. and a sharp decline in income inequality. All quintiles in the income distribution were participating equally as the economic pie expanded. This meant that opportunities for young people like me were expanding. We would not have to scramble to survive as required of our Great Depression–shaped parents. We could envision new dreams and consider careers and life trajectories unimaginable to most in the generation before us.

Based on oral histories of the 1950s and 1960s, the labor market was much more benign than today. Jobs were there and even many factory positions paid a living wage. Few college kids in the 1960s claimed they were going to school only to make more money. That figure rose to about half in the mid-1970s and to almost 70 percent in 2005. In 1966, only 42 percent said that being financially well off was their primary life goal, a figure that rose to 75 percent by 2005. Some 86 percent of high school students back then claimed that developing a meaningful philosophy of life was very important, a sentiment expressed by less than half of that population in recent years. Finally, measures of empathy have dropped some 40 percentage points in some polls over the intervening half century or so. We are becoming a nation of self-absorbed narcissists.

Looking back, I suspect two impediments hindered me from doing better in high school. Few of the courses were stimulating. I always disliked math, languages were fine but largely a kind of rote learning, as were the sciences such as chemistry and biology. I did respond to history and English (when it focused on literature). I craved ideas and intellectual stimulation but there was not enough of it.

The other problem was that I was not a happy camper during this time. I remember thinking that life did not hold much promise. School, study, work, and a home life full of conflict, criticism, and tension. Okay, I did have friends but early on there were no girls nor any promise of romance. I played sports but not well enough to bring any adulation in my direction. Scorn, yes, adulation, no! There was nothing awful going on, but life seemed tedious and repetitious. I kept wondering what the point of it all was. What really bothered me at the time is the oft repeated claim by my mother that her teens were the best years of her life. The best years, oh my god! If that turned out to be true for me I would put a bullet through my head right now. Fortunately, she was wrong, completely wrong!

Things did get a bit better toward the end of high school. For my last year, I was scheduled to take calculus. After my struggles with algebra and geometry and such I looked upon this prospect with distinct dismay. Fortunately, things were beginning to change at St. Johns. They hired the first lay teacher around 1960. Now I suspect that only the school administrator and perhaps theology teachers are Xaverian Brothers. They also permitted us to take one elective in my senior year; it was economics. And most striking of all, they moved out of the decaying inner city campus in Worcester to a brand-new suburban campus. Unfortunately, as they moved they changed the name from St. John's Preparatory School to St. John's High on the lame excuse that too many people confused us with another Xaverian run school of the same name located near Boston. I personally think they should have changed their name.

I jumped on the chance to get out of calculus. Besides, economics sounded interesting while another math course promised more agony. However, I felt so guilty about doing this that I signed up for an extra class that took up all in-school study time. This additional class was third year Latin. Those four or five of us from the top class that did not take calculus were bumped down into the next class level, from group A to group B. Remember, you were assigned to a class based on how well you did on the entrance exam. By our senior year, three classes of forty students each were down to two such classes. We clearly had many casualties along the way.

Even with the extra load and my work schedule at the time, dropping down to the less challenging class was a remarkable experience. For once in my life, I did well in school and without trying all that hard. I wondered what it would have been like going to a regular high school that was not all that selective. I found I liked doing well in the classroom after all. Still, my excellent grades in senior year, while moving me up the class rankings, still left me one spot out of the coveted top quarter of the class by the time I graduated.

As I said earlier, everyone went to college from St. John's. It did not even seem like a choice back then when college was not yet a common path, particularly for kids from my neighborhood. I can only recall a couple of local neighborhood kids who went on to four-year schools. On the other hand, for kids from St. John's, the choices were simple. You either went to a Catholic liberal arts college like Holy Cross, Boston College, Assumption College, Providence College, or you went to a secular but technical school like Worcester Polytechnic Institute. What you did *not* do was matriculate at a secular liberal arts college, even Ivy League schools. They, both the St. John's administrators and all Catholic parents, were set against their kids going to any institution where their core beliefs might be challenged. End of story!

Okay, I did know one kid who went to Dartmouth, but he was an extraordinary athlete. Odds are I would have gone to Holy Cross if fate had not intervened. And what was that intervening fate? It was my need to find some significance in my life. Given what kids like me were all about in that era, significance involved entering the Seminary to study for the Priesthood. I will not go into my personal journey to God and back here, that story will come in later chapters. I will, however, briefly talk about my brief stop at a Catholic Seminary from an intellectual development perspective. It turned out to be a very consequential move.

The seminary . . .

Maryknoll Seminary was located in Glen Ellyn, Illinois. It was the so-called minor seminary, the college level preparation for those who would then go onto the major seminary in Ossining, New York to do their final preparation for the Priesthood. In case you are not fully conversant in all things Catholic, the Maryknoll order was devoted to foreign missionary work where new souls would be brought into the one, true, holy, and apostolic church. Members of the order, at that time, could be found in Asia, Africa, and Central and South America. For idealistic young Catholic boys of the early 1960s, it was Peace Corps with a religious bent. You could save souls and maybe even some bodies of those enduring poverty, disease, and political oppression.

But I am here to talk about Maryknoll as a place of study. In that regard it was considered a fine institution academically for a place whose primary mission was to lead young men closer to God. The faculty were all members of the order as I recall. As with high school, there were no options, the curriculum was set. In addition to regular academic subjects, there were add-ons like theology and Gregorian Chant and something like oral interpretation, which I recall was to make us better public speakers or at least able to deliver a decent sermon.

Of course, this was a seminary, so it differed from a regular college in so many ways. You started each day with prayers and a mass. You had a fixed daily schedule of classes, work assignments, more classes, study periods, physical exercise periods, more classes and more prayer, and congregate meals. There were long periods of enforced silence that were not always complied with as I recall. The important thing was that this was a way of life that did not permit much frivolity. I had come a long way from my carefree days roaming Ames Street.

There were only two periods of real free time each week. On Wednesday and Saturday afternoons you could leave the campus, but you could not go very far. We could walk to a shopping mall not too far away where we could at least eat at a regular restaurant.

And of course, there were no girls or beer or drugs or rock and roll. However, I do recall that several upper classmen (those who you could wear a cassock and were called something different, perhaps a postulate) disappeared suddenly. Word eventually leaked that they had met some girls on one of these afternoon free times and did something that was unforgivable. Whatever it was, the consequences were immediate and final.

The upshot of this schedule is there was not much else to do but study. You could not pull all-nighters; it was lights out at 10:30 or something since you had to be up for prayers and mass by some ungodly hour like 5:30 AM. But that was okay. I liked some of the courses. I think I got into Eugene O'Neill, the great American playwright, during an English class there. In oral interpretation, I recall once doing a dramatic reading from the *Iceman Cometh*, an O'Neill classic. The instructor was a Maryknoller who had connections with the theater crowd in Chicago. He was surrounded by autographed pictures of actors that even I recognized. I suppose they needed to be saved as much as tribal members in Africa. I recall finishing my reading, and he exclaimed loudly, "Now *that* is oral interpretation." Had I already struck acting off my list of possible vocations? Perhaps it was time to reconsider.

Presumably, I was now doing college-level work. After so many years of undistinguished academic work, how would I fare in the big time, if this really was the big time? Soon, I began to realize that I was doing well, very well indeed. But I had no way of putting my sudden success into context. This was a little like my good performance in my last year of high school. It was gratifying, but I could explain it away. During that last high school year, after all, I was competing with kids who were not the best in the school. My performance now could be explained by the simple fact that I was in a seminary, not a real college. There was always a good explanation to discount any success that came my way.

Now, there were some less than outstanding performances. I think we got one credit for enduring Gregorian chant. I cannot recall how they graded us; maybe it was pass-fail. Maybe you got the credit if you somehow did not die before the semester ended. In any case, I was awful, terrible. I croaked rather than sang. Still, Gregorian chant, when sung in a church with good acoustics can be breathtaking but only if I mouthed the words and did not utter any sound.

Overall, though, I did well enough that first year to be placed in the honors track for my sophomore year. Wow, didn't they know who I was? This gave me the opportunity to take Greek and be assigned to classes with the better students. If I had continued, and done well, I am not sure what doors might have opened for me. In addition to advanced Latin, so I could converse with Virgil, I was now taking Greek, so I could converse with Socrates. Perhaps I would have been permitted to continue my education as opposed to going overseas. Maybe I would have ended up with a career in the Vatican amongst the most celebrated bureaucrats in the world or teaching in a seminary if any were left.

Who knows, but that was not to be. For reasons I will relate later, I was to leave Maryknoll in the fall of my second year. Still, I was grateful for the educational experience I received. I doubt many Bible Studies Colleges expose their students to rigorous courses. The atmosphere did not encourage free and open inquiry per se, but neither was a straightjacket imposed on your intellectual development. This was far from a lost year.

I left with one thought. Maybe I was not as dumb as I thought I was. Could I really do well at this level? It was not out of the question. But I would need more evidence. My stay in the seminary did one other thing for me. If I had gone right on to college from high school, I would have gone to Holy Cross or some other Catholic institution. It would have been an extension of the cultural milieu in which I had spent my entire life. It is hard to believe I would have exploded in growth as I was about to do. When I looked about what to do next, I found out that Holy Cross did not take midterm applicants. That minor inconvenience pushed me in a different direction and opened new worlds to me.

Here was a kid with little to no self-worth about to enter what he considered a real college. I did so with excitement and a great deal of foreboding. Would it be here that they would discover I was a fraud? In any case, the factory where my father work was located not that far away, perhaps I could wander down there to look for work when my limitations caught up with me? Then I shuddered. Such a fate would demand I do the manual labor I had long sought to avoid.

There had to be a better plan. But let us first go on to a more inviting topic for a bit . . . women!

CHAPTER 5

RELATING

The lunatic, the lover, and the poet are
of imagination all compact.
—Shakespeare

My initial title for this chapter was "sex," which struck me
as more appealing to male readers at least. Let's be honest, what
are men after? They are after release of tension, finding some gal
who might want them physically or at least be willing to service
them while faking the requisite display of desire. This is not rocket
science after all! But then I realized that such an appellation would
have been disingenuous. There is virtually no sex in this darn
chapter. I wish there were. But here I focus on my early years as a
would-be lothario. Sex was way beyond my reach in those years.
It was for most of us poor Catholic boys coming of age in that era
and maybe even for the more advantaged boys from across town.
Those guys, however, were not loaded down with our baggage, plus
they had money, so I suspect they did okay, damn them. In any

case I went with honesty and a title that might at least appeal to those of the female persuasion. They tend to go big time for all that relationship crap.

Consider the following. A male, as we know, has a gazillion times more testosterone as his female counterpart. Since this hormone drives sexual desire, it is safe to say that men are more likely to be just a bit hornier than the distaff half of the population. Rule number one for women, then, is to beware of any man who is conscious and beyond puberty. The conscious part, fortunately, does not occur as often in males as you would think. Rule number two for women is never believe anything a man says. They will promise anything to get what they want. Those promises of love and commitment, puhleeze. This is just men in training for careers as used car salesmen or as televangelists. Hell, I would even trust a Republican way more than a male teenager and you can well guess how much I trust those with an affinity for the dark side. Rule number three is never forget the first two rules.

Simply watch men and women walking along the street. Women keep their gaze on some distant point in the far horizon (or now their cell phone while texting) while men eye every available female between the ages of sixteen and sixty. I myself suffered severe brain trauma as a teen while walking into light poles, trees, doors, glass windows, fire hydrants, and other sundry immovable objects while checking out passing members of the fair sex. Based on my knowledge of male dispositions and behavior, I would wear a burka if I were female and carry large amounts of mace and/or pepper spray at the ready.

As mentioned, young men think about something other than sex at least twice a day, whether they want to or not. The remainder of the conscious hours is devoted to disgusting erotic fantasies. Your typical Catholic young woman of the 1950s and early '60s might permit a sensual fantasy or two biannually and then rush off to confession? Whatever the real gap, we can say that the "men are from Mars" and "women are from Venus." While seemingly incontrovertible, that cute bromide may understate the actual chasm. How about "men are from Mars" and "women are from Alpha Centauri." Nope, not even that distance captures the separation between men and women in matters of romance and lust. Let us just agree that they are far apart.

Crossing into manhood, in a manner of speaking . . .

I am embarrassed to admit that I was virtually in my dotage before I finally lost my virginity. Yup, it was a long and frustrating road before lust overcame virtue, or should I say guilt. There had been opportunities, of course, but I remained a total numb nut for a long time. Let me define a numb nut for you, a man without any redeeming qualities, and certainly no common sense, whatsoever. Now, it is very difficult for me to admit that I was such a loser when it came to women. Sitting here, writing these words, I writhe in disbelief that I might have turned women away, females who indicated an interest in some form of erotic congress. What kind of total moron was I? A total and complete moron . . . that is what I was!

These ouch recollections are clearly among the most painful still retrievable from a largely misspent youth. Admittedly, the number of females pursuing me was never overwhelming but the number was greater than one, perhaps measurably greater. I recall women lamenting the fact that they had been a loose woman earlier in life, a confession laden with guilt. When they provided specifics, however, their alleged promiscuity never amounted to much. Their number of lovers would be the same as some of my normal male buddies on a typical weekend. My regrets go in the opposite direction. I now realize that I need many more erotic memories for my nursing home days when I am too old to chase the female nurses with my walker.

On the other hand, I can legitimately claim that the big moment arrived in a rather unexpected and memorable manner, or at least in an exotic location. I was in India, just having been sworn in as a Peace Corps Volunteer at the end of a long, arduous training period. The next day, we were to be sent off to our sites for two years of what, in our mind, surely would be enforced celibacy. On that long-ago day, I would have bet the mortgage that I would hit senility before reaching the promised land of sexual bliss.

But first, there was to be one last fete at the Lake Palace in Udaipur. The Lake Palace is a moderately famous site, a former palace belonging to what had been the local royalty. It later became a glamorous hotel. As you can infer from its name, it is situated in the middle of a lake Pichola and is only accessible by boat. Jackie Kennedy, among other celebrities, had stayed there and the James Bond movie *Octopussy* used it as a prime location for that film. I would often see it pictured in tourist advertisements put out internationally by the Indian government. In fact, my colleagues from the University claim that it has become one of the most acclaimed luxury hotels in the world. I believe they stayed there.

One of the Peace Corp staff members was tall, slender, attractive, and smart. Indian herself, she attended college in the States where she graduated from the prestigious Smith College located in western Massachusetts. She was, as the saying goes, a stone-cold fox though considered to be off-limits since she was engaged to be married to another volunteer who would soon be finishing up his tour of duty. Normally, I would think my odds of scoring with such a woman to be somewhat lower than winning the Nobel Prize in physics. Somewhat lower! Let me be honest here. I would have put my odds at somewhere below zero, a mathematical impossibility yet still an accurate estimation of my chances. Hell, I think the last time I had employed my patented move, a coat rack shot me down. In my defense, the lighting was poor.

Thinking back, I don't recall spending much time with her that night. In a picture surviving from that evening I am chatting with my two favorite language instructors, Amar and Usha. I loved Amar's personality and thought Usha way too cute. But I never even considered either in a romantic way. I would not risk two good friendships. Indian gals could be friendly, but you just knew they would knee you in the nuts if you got frisky. Well, probably not, but I have always been attached to the family jewels and prefer not to put them in harm's way. Somehow, though, this staffer and I were crowded next to each other in the taxi taking us back to our training camp. We likely were relaxed from that rather strong Indian beer consumed that night. A one-liter bottle of that stuff put you on your way to a good buzz.

The intervening decades mute the sharpness of surviving memories but there must have been some electricity between us. I only recall that our hands met in the dark safety of the crowded taxi. She must have sought out my hand since I guarantee you the reverse would never have happened. Could she have been lusting after me all these past weeks? Doubtful, but I was terrible at reading women. As the old saying goes, I would have trouble getting laid in a woman's prison with a fistful of pardons. In any case, we hung back as the others drifted off to their rooms. Without words, we discretely wandered off to a secluded place under the stars. There, we literally tore each other's clothes off before sinking into the lush grass, limbs intertwined and need finding its ultimate expression.

If I had had a chance to think, I undoubtedly would have talked my way out of yet another opportunity, simpleton that I was back then. But maybe it was in the stars. After all, it was a typical lush, Indian night and there was that canopy of those very stars overhead. The night sky in the rural parts of India, by the way, seems brilliant if not breathtaking. Here you might see a sprinkling of stars. There, you often saw dense fields of prickly lights. Or perhaps I had grown totally weary of being the last numb nut of my generation. After a bit, we dressed and snuck off to her room where the lovemaking could continue in a bit more comfort.

My most vivid memory from that night (okay, just one of the most vivid) was her exclamation at one point that I was "a real man." Excuse me! She must have been fantasizing about someone else at the moment. How could I be a "real" man, whatever the hell that was! How could someone oppressed by many years of Catholic guilt do so well the first time sliding into home base? I could hardly figure out where home base was, the thought of crossing it was on par with discovering a cure for cancer or coming up with a general theory that explained all the forces of nature. That goal, by the way, had eluded Einstein during his lifetime. She must have been dynamite at faking orgasms.

How could this be taking place? I recall thinking at the time. It was not like I had not been drunk with other women who seemed willing in the moment, though the Catholic girls of my acquaintance universally had been ambivalent on the topic of sex. By ambivalent, I mean they were either dead set against it under any circumstances or they were desperately dead set against it with me. On the other hand, perhaps Catholic girls already knew that three-fourths of women would never achieve orgasm through intercourse alone. Males, they intuited, were far less essential than a well-charged vibrator. In any case, it was a bleak era indeed in which to grow up. Let me be more accurate here. It was a bleak period to grow up if you were Catholic, ridden with guilt, and too stupid to breathe on your own.

But now the dirty deed was finally done. I was shocked to discover that I was not struck down by God. The earth did not open, nor was I caste into a bottomless pit of hellfire. What happened was that I had a great time. Hmm, I promptly concluded that this sex stuff was worth pursuing with greater purpose. And I did, though India is not fertile ground, no pun intended, for uncovering many sensual opportunities. They may have given us the *Kama Sutra* but that is where their generosity in this matter ends. I must say that, once I started, I did make up for lost time. If the better survey data is to be believed, I wound up enjoying considerably more sexual partners than the typical male. I will have some explaining to do to St. Peter when the time comes.

You surely will go blind . . .

Today, teen girls aggressively seek out boys, or so I am told. They indulge in sexting where they send explicit pictures and texts to their selected sex object for the week. In my youth, I had a greater chance of becoming the first man on the moon than seeing a gal's breasts. Young Catholic girls still worshipped divine personages with names like St. Theresa of the Uncorrupted Corporal Vessel whose path to the pantheon of the holy Saints was predicated on choosing a vat of boiling oil over sex.

That did not seem strange at all to the Catholic boys I knew and grew up with. It was taken for granted that females were asexual, if not anti-sexual. And that probably was understating the case. Hell, it seemed to us that all the girls in our neighborhood would have chosen martyrdom over sex, no matter how horrific the end. As young kids, we would watch these Saturday morning movies where some villain would be threatening the young damsel with unspeakable things. I think it cost us a quarter for the two movies, a cartoon, and an adventure serial, which made you come back the following Saturday. Throw in another quarter and you got a big bag of popcorn and a drink. Surely you knew the damsel faced unspeakable things since it was obvious that Black Bart wanted more than an innocent kiss though I am not sure we all had figured out exactly what Bart was after. When all looked hopeless, our desperate damsel would roll her eyes and say, "I will do anything, anything, to save the farm and my dear old grandpa."

What could be so terrible we wondered? Early on, we thought that meant giving in to Black Bart's demand for a kiss. Eventually, even a moron like me figured out that she would do the worst thing imaginable, have sex, to save what was most dear to her. While I was not sure what all was entailed in this deed, it never looked like an easy choice for her. You could just see her calculating the cost-benefit ratio. Hell, the old man doesn't have much time left anyways and this farm really sucks. And I would have to have yucky sex to save that stuff, I don't know. But then she would be saved from having to decide. Mr. Right would ride in on a white horse, dispatch Black Bart, and sweep the damsel into his arms sans the kiss. It turns out Mr. Right was a numb nut as well.

With real sex a total nonstarter we Catholic boys were left with masturbation. That should have done the trick except that it also was a sin. Worse, it was a bad sin, one that blackened part, most, or all your soul . . . we were never sure. Non-Catholics probably are unaware of the milk bottle. The milk bottle is a metaphor for your soul. If you commit a venial sin, one of less consequence, a small blotch appears in the milk. If you commit several venial sins, the milk becomes blotchy with black stains as if the corrupting virus has spread. But if you committed even one mortal sin, the milk container is either empty or the milk has turned all black. At this point, I cannot recall which it was, empty or black. Needless to say, one big sin and you were in for it. No white stuff left in the bottle and an eternity of fire and brimstone.

One thing was clear to us boys: pleasure was bad. Sexual pleasure was even worse than bad. It was the big sin, the old empty milk bottle! You did not want to go there, no way! There were these widespread, though always spoken of in hushed terms, rumors that your hands would break out into hideous warts if you touched yourself in those places. Do it too often and surely you would go blind! Satan had special places in hell for boys that enjoyed such acts, places where hideous tortures awaited dastardly miscreants who allowed themselves to be entrapped in the tentacles of lust. I spent hours trying to calculate what constituted too much and how much I could enjoy the pleasure before my hands fell off or I was struck down blind or worse. Yikes!

On the other hand, I never saw any classmates walking around with white canes or using service dogs. Eventually, I figured out that the going blind thing was crap. No question that my male buddies were doing the dirty deed unless I was the only boy in the world afflicted by God with the lust affliction. I felt like Job being beset with erotic temptations. It was sadly certain that all the guys were in the same miserable boat. And yet not one had been struck down by a vengeful God. I was dumb but not that dumb. No, our hell on earth was being surrounded by attractive gals who had no interest whatsoever in sex or in us. They looked upon me with moderate to extreme indifference or disgust. I was experiencing that version of Hell where God puts you on the best golf-course in the world but does not allow you a golf ball.

The Catholic message about sex was alarming if not downright frightening. Our freshman religion teacher in high school told us a story one day. A young Catholic boy and girl decided to go parking to make out. They had been virtuous and had dutifully obeyed all commandments up until that moment. As they necked by the side of the road, passion overcame them, and they enjoyed each other's bodies just a little too much. Exactly what they did he never explained, but it was something you had never done, that was damn certain. Recoiling in horror they were about to stop and say a perfect act of contrition when a sixteen-wheel truck came over the hill and dispatched them into eternity. One mistake, and it was hell forever.

"What?" I said to myself. You mean these two innocent kids fall into the pits of hell for all eternity because of one lousy lapse of judgment? I doubt that story had the intended effect. It probably got me thinking that a deity that arbitrary was probably not worth much devotion on the first place. That, however, is a story for a different chapter. And yet, that is the only lesson from first-year religion class that has stayed with me all these years. I could never make out with a girl in a car after that without experiencing a serious anxiety disorder.

The Worcester Airport was a favorite necking place. It was located on a hill for some reason. That bizarre choice of location for a municipal airfield made it difficult for planes to land in foggy weather and that damn place was often socked in. On clear nights, however, you could see the city lights flickering in the distance below. Given this poor planning, the facility was undersubscribed for its basic purpose. In fact, I cannot recall any night flights coming or going so there was zero chance of being hit by an off-course plane, never mind a sixteen-wheeler truck, and sent to eternal damnation. In effect, you had a nice view of the city lights and much privacy. Still, I remained vigilant, occasionally peeking out the back window for big trucks.

A steady stream of propaganda drummed into us the notion that girls did not like sex though they might use sex for other purposes. Given the girls we knew, that hypothesis seemed beyond dispute. They would exploit your excess testosterone to secure affection, emotional attachment, protection, social approval, simple companionship, and most of all, money or money substitutes like good food or movies. At a minimum, it gave them stuff to laugh about with their girlfriends. I would have added exciting dates to the list, but none of us guys had enough money for that and, surely, our personalities were not a draw. Oh yes, and sex was necessary for procreation for those so inclined. Catholic girls having sex for pleasure, however, simply was implausible, beyond the pale. Who would believe that? Maybe a few Protestant and Jewish girls liked it, but they were going to hell anyways and, besides, we didn't know any of them.

For the longest time I was stuck in this recurring script. I was horny, but I knew that, in the same way Tea Party types know that Obama is a secret Muslim, the girl was not horny and nothing I could do would change that. But she might put out for some other reward. Unfortunately, I did not have money so that meant using one of these softer bargaining chips . . . emotional support or social approval or one of those things we boys could never understand because we were, after all, clueless boys. You could always profess undying love or, when a bit older, make a real commitment but who was *that* horny.

This put me and all young guys like me in a difficult quandary. If a young gal seemed physically responsive, I would immediately be suspicious. What does she really want? Just how is she manipulating me? My defensive shields would be on high alert. Just what is the *quid pro quo* here? It always came down to a little bit of pleasure stacked up against a lot of future grief. It was, oh my god, sex for love! Even I knew a bad bargain when I saw one.

I recall being with a nursing student from the hospital in which I worked at the time. I don't recall this being a date, but we were by a lovely lake on a warm summer night. She was very attractive, and magic was in the air as the romanticists would say. I suddenly did something out of character for me. I leaned over and kissed her gently on the lips. As I did so, I fully expected subtle or not so subtle resistance, something like a knee to the balls, which would immediately put me into a catatonic state. But she yielded to the kiss quite warmly. I can still recall pulling back and asking her why she let me kiss her. She mumbled something about how romantic the mood was but, of course, I had just ruined that. I had somehow made her feel like a woman of easy virtue. Way to go numb nut! Clearly, I could not get laid if I had a bucketful of dough and a private jet.

High school clearly was the lost era for me when it came to girls. I went to an all-boys school, and there were few available females in my home neighborhood. The ones that were there stayed out of sight from what I can recall. On the other hand, perhaps there was some secret, early warning system where my presence in the street sent them scurrying underground. The gals of that era were quite crafty I must admit. When out and about, they would prowl in packs. It was hard to separate out one from the herd. And it was nearly impossible for someone as damaged as I to ask one out on a date if it had to be done in full view of her pack. I could envision the burning shame when she laughed in my face. "Go out with you, ha, ha, ha. I would rather eat worms." That would send me off to look for that serrated knife to use on my wrists, a blade I desperately wished I had remembered to bring in the first place.

Later, I would be surrounded by females. In college they were in my classes, all around the campus, and hung out with me during endless bull sessions. I also met a steady stream of women while working the night shift at a Catholic hospital. Get this, there were young nursing students, always in their final year of study, who were assigned to the ward where I worked. Every week, a fresh woman would rotate through my assigned floor. It was like working in a candy store. And I still did not get laid. How pathetic is that? Of course, the nursing students were Catholic, it being a Catholic hospital. Still, with the sheer numbers in my favor, I would not say sex was totally out of the question. My performance remained pathetic, with many aerial dogfights of an erotic nature and no scores. Corbett is shot down again!

In my defense, I must say that my old scripts were reinforced regularly. I was not a total psychotic. When you are dealing with sickness, pain, and even death in the middle of the night, the usual barriers fall. You get to know people in ways you would not ordinarily. So, I got to know some of these soon-to-be real nurses quite well indeed. While the faces and bodies changed, the story never did as far as I could see. Basically, they were always angling to land a guy by the time they graduated from nursing school. They were going for the RN and MRS at the same time. The rules were strict back then. If you got pregnant before graduating you were out, no nursing degree for you. If you got married, you were out. I don't believe they checked to see if the hymen was still intact before graduation, but I bet that was discussed. So, the almost universal goal was to have an engagement ring by the time you graduated. Then you would work awhile until you and the schmuck had earned enough to buy a house and start a family. Work would be suspended until the kids were old enough. Nurses, they believed, could always get work, which pretty much turned out to be true.

But while marriage was their universal goal, many of them indeed seemed highly ambivalent about sex. I recall many 2:00 and 3:00 AM conversations when all might be quiet on the ward or the coffee discussions in the morning when the night shift ended. During these intimate and rather open conversations, many of these young women betrayed a disturbing secret. They might like some guy that they had snagged, or hoped to snag, but looked upon the prospect of intercourse more as an obligation than any kind of hoped-for pleasure. It was something that had to be done to get the rest of the package. Perhaps this is not surprising given the crap dropped on them from birth to forego intercourse. Okay, after this marriage ceremony you can turn the switch on now. Now, you can enjoy sex but only for procreation. I don't think so.

Even I let my guard down on occasion and spent mildly erotic time with a few of these gals. I was not made of total stone. They had some weird protocols to protect their virtue which each constructed according to their own tastes. You could take only certain articles of clothing off. Or you could only fondle or touch above the waist. The more adventurous ones would let you explore at will, but the panties would remain on at *all* times. They typically approached what should have been a sensuous experience as a duty, saying the rosary throughout. I wonder if they sat around their dorm talking about these rules.

They probably had special rules for me. I found out at some point that the word in the nursing dormitory was to be careful with me. I was designated as a "player," or whatever a dangerous male was called back then. That was hysterical but apparently true. My best guess is that they listened to what I said about commitment and marriage and love and all the stuff I considered total nonsense at the time. In truth, I was the most harmless guy they would meet, and the most honest. So, let me unequivocally assert that honesty is *not* the best policy.

What was clear is that the prospect of pregnancy was viewed as beyond any conceivable pale. We guys still used phrases such as "doing the right thing" and "jail bait" for younger girls and "shotgun weddings." I never actually heard of a real shotgun being used during the ceremony though a few .22 caliber hunting rifles might have been sported about on occasion. In most cases, family and cultural pressure could be just as effective as any firearm. For these Catholic girls, early pregnancy would have been the end of the world. There would be no nursing degree, much family shame, and a reputation shot. Some undoubtedly would have been shunned by their own parents. If I were them, I would have avoided all males like the plague. Oddly enough, I was the safest of men. I was willing to spend time with gals, listen to them, and expect absolutely nothing in return.

Until I hooked up with a few, very few, steady gals, I hardly dated. Thus, my early teen years were continuously painful, like being in a state of perpetual tension without any possibility of release. Everyone has heard the expression blue balls, not to be confused with the Blue Man Group in Vegas. The guys I knew walked around with a case of blue balls all the time. Now that I look at my shriveled excuse for testicles, they have never lost that distinct bluish-purple hue. I should check out other guys to see just how common this is. Maybe this condition only pertains to Catholic guys of a certain age. When I face St. Peter, my argument is that I already have spent my time in purgatory. After all, I grew up Catholic during the 1950s and early '60s. Case closed!

As you know, from the introduction to this chapter, even a schmuck like me eventually gets lucky. Once I did get going on that magical night under the canopy of stars in Rajasthan, I have no reason to complain. There were times when the sex was really great, the kind of "tear off each other's clothes and go at it before you even got to the bed" kind of sex. Not only that, but women seemed to enjoy the experience, many of them anyways. I was shocked by that. It struck me that their orgasms, though somewhat harder to achieve, were more intense than ours. But there was one odd thing, maybe not so odd, that I discovered after I finally got around to spreading my so-called charm among the ladies. Good sex and liking specific women, including love, were not related, not at all.

I am not going to talk about any of the women that I knew in a biblical sense. For one thing, they probably would be mortified at being exposed as stupid enough to fall for one of Tom Corbett's lines. But more to the point, they likely are lawyered up and waiting to pounce with a libel suit or is it a slander suit. I confuse which is which. Can you imagine some poor woman explaining me to a friend who replies with incredulity, "You slept with him? Yuck, what the hell were you thinking?" That assessment would be followed up with how inexpensive personal vibrators had become. Hmmm, I bet many women would pay handsomely to preserve their reputation even if it were a long-ago violation of their standards. There is no statute of limitations on bad taste.

Back to my point though. Intimacy, caring, and communication have little or nothing to do with sex. You probably have heard the old saying that men seek out women for sex and wind up enjoying the relationship. Meanwhile, women seek relationships and end up enjoying the sex. When people look at gay and lesbian interactions, the differences jump at you. Gay men can be in monogamous relationships, but casual hookups are more the norm. Lesbians tend to seek out a partner for a monogamous relationship though many do exhibit patterns of serial monogamy. That is, the stereotypical gender differences appear real.

I suspect men always find the cliché-ridden interaction that occurs when they are found cheating just a bit amusing, unless they are the one involved. The offended woman asks with outrage, "Do you love her?" In most cases, the man answers honestly, "NO, it was just a casual thing!" Of course, she does not believe him. She could not envision sex with another absent some emotional connection. For a man, sex by itself is basically friction followed by release. He slept with her because he could; the same reason Sir Edmund Hillary climbed Mt. Everest because it was there. For the female it typically is far more nuanced and complicated. You know, women need a reason to have sex; men just need a place. With no common experience on which to base effective communication, these interchanges seldom go anywhere other than the emergency room or divorce court. The guy is basically toast.

But there is another thing about men that is surprising. They are more likely than women to fall in love at first sight. True, men are hard to pin down, to get to commit unless they are struck with that special lightening. I recall listening to several coeds talk about their relationships one day while doing some yard work for my wife and me. They were raising money for their sorority. One talked about how her boyfriend had a problem with commitment. I was sitting in my upstairs home office, listening to their conversation through my window. Literally, I doubled over in laughter. "Oh my," I wanted to explain to her, "he had absolutely no problem, sister. He knows exactly what he wants, and it is not to be tied down." That is a primordial male instinct, to remain free. She had the problem in that she had not found a way to rope him in yet.

Despite this male instinct, they fall hard when they do, and it is often immediate. I cannot tell you how many men have said they saw their wife to be from across a crowded room and just knew. There was the guy who worked with my wife in the Wisconsin court system. After being divorced for a while, he was at a social event and saw a woman across the room. He turned to the guy next to him and said simply that woman would be his next wife. He had never seen her before and did not know her name. His companion just laughed but sure enough, he married the woman within a year.

Mary and I were at a wedding not that long ago, and the groom's dad told us he saw his future wife for the first time and knew she was the one before he knew her name. This is a common refrain. It is as if there is there is an archetypal image inside the male brain that floods the cranial cavity with mind-numbing dopamine when a representation of that image walks into view. Women, on the other hand, take more time. They invest more in relationships, and they expect more out of them. Thus, they assess likely partners more fully before making their stupid choice. Surely, they scope out the guy's net worth and job prospects. When all the evidence is scrutinized, neither approach seems to work all that well.

All my early relationships were platonic but enjoyable and fulfilling. Each gal had similar qualities . . . quick minds, a sharp tongue, biting wit, and independent spirits. They seemed like equals to me, and very much like friends. All had expressive eyes, good looks, and dark hair. Most of all, I really enjoyed talking to all of them, sparring with them and, in all cases, sharing thoughts and feelings that typically remained hidden from my male counterparts at the risk of unending ridicule. This is where women are unique. Many will listen without judgment. Males, on the other hand, quickly fall into a macho one-upmanship game, but females will absorb your personal nonsense with quiet understanding. How they do not burst into laughter is beyond me.

Nothing compares to the early relationships in our lives. They remain the most intense and illuminating. I have thought on this point and cannot attest to the reasons for it. It could be that we are like blank canvasses early on and every intimate brush stroke creates colors and forms that seem magical at the time. Later, when the canvas is filled, new women can only dabble around the edges. They might be masters at what they do as women but the possibilities by then are extremely limited. So, I am going back in time to talk about women. These are gals that made a difference in my life in high school and college and helped shape my sorry ass as a representative of the male species.

Maribeth . . .

During my high school years, my first girlfriend was Maribeth. During my high school years, my longest lasting relationship was with Maribeth. During my high school years, my *only* real girlfriend was Maribeth.

In case you are not getting the picture, high school was not only barren in the sex department, it was barren in the romance department. But I did have this relationship with Maribeth. We worked in the same public library during our high school years, the main downtown branch. She, however, worked in another part of the building so I only knew her by sight, perhaps to say hello. She was cute, way out of my league, I thought. Then again, I thought they were all out of my league. In any case, I would have been too shy to go much beyond a casual hi even though she had the dark hair and dancing eyes that typically weakened my defenses.

Fate then intervened. I was at a "sock hop" one Friday night that was sponsored by one of the Catholic churches near where she lived, though I did not know that fact at the time. This church was the athletic archrival to my own high school, which did not sponsor such frivolous social events. I suspect the good Xaverian Brothers had concluded that women were the root of all evil and best keep their aspiring Catholic gentlemen away from temptation. All in all, a wise plan that was doomed to failure. These sock hops were harmless affairs. Mostly the girls stood around trying to look disinterested in the boys and boys stood around trying to look cool. The girls did a heck of a job at looking disinterested and the guys really sucked at looking cool. Their excessive drooling gave them away.

Dancing did occur but always under the strictest supervision. You were supposed to keep enough room between you and your partner for the Holy Spirit. Being a nitpicker, I figured the Holy Spirit was incorporeal (without substance) so you could get as close as the girl would permit. But they had a monitor, in police uniform if I recall correctly, who would tap smooth operators like me (joke!) on the shoulder, "Not so close, buddy." If the gendarme did not interrupt your amorous advance, the girl usually kept backing up as you moved in. Suddenly, the two of you would crash into a wall to the snickers of all around you. There had to be a better way. You had a better shot at eroticism by looking at the patent leather shoes the girls wore to see any reflection up into the mysterious nether-land we all hoped to explore someday.

Anyways, I spotted Maribeth across the dance floor at this sock hop. I no longer recall why we called them that since everyone wore shoes. There she was...this gal about whom I fantasized from afar in the library. Okay, there is no way I would approach an unknown girl but maybe this might be worth a shot. Undoubtedly, it took me forever to make my move. I probably circled her for hours trying to work up my courage. Assuming she recognized me at all, I concluded her initial reaction probably would involve calling security followed up with a restraining order. Maybe, though, she would feel obliged to be nice due to our library connection. I pinned my hopes on that.

I suddenly realized time was running out as I stood there running through one horrendous scenario after another. It hit me that she must have recognized this numb nut hovering in the vicinity obviously waiting to make his move. I could just imagine what was going through her mind. Oh, no, that klutz from the library is going to pounce. She was probably plotting some way she might bolt for the door. But before she could execute her escape, I sucked it up, wandered over, and asked for a dance. I prayed she would not break out into hysterical laughter and suddenly decide that her dog needed to be groomed at that very moment.

I was shocked. She was rather nice to me, no hysterical laughter or calls for security. We danced, we talked, and I even walked her home. I still recall her father waiting for her to arrive home. He must not have been pleased that she was in the company of some lecherous male. By definition, teen males are lecherous. By the way, stereotypes that are true are not stereotypes. They are facts. I do not know what I would do if I had daughters to raise. I am thinking I would keep them under lock and key until they are age 25 or so.

Maribeth would turn out to be only gal I dated with any regularity in high school. She was pert, attractive, and had an infectious smile. She wore geeky glasses and, probably by the standards of even that era, was a geek to the core. I started a lifelong pattern from the start, only getting serious with whip-smart gals. Undoubtedly, she was at the top of her class. It would be years before I recognized that she had the basic qualities that drew me to women. I loved women who were quick, inquisitive, witty, just a bit snarky, but with a sensitive and caring side. A little bit of vulnerability did not hurt either. Those qualities, she had in spades.

It never occurred to me to get sexual. You could climb any mountain, ford every stream, scale any obstacle, and you were still not going to get laid. So, you settled for a little making out, or a lot of making out, long talks, and a few laughs. It was with Maribeth that I first found what made women so valuable. You could talk with them about real things. They listened or pretended to listen. Then again, I suppose if you were talking you were not trying to get into their pants or dress back then. Perhaps that is why they all seemed like such great conversationalists and such attentive listeners.

She was like me in many ways. She was from a working-class, Irish family where the kids were upwardly mobile. She lived in a neighborhood that was already on a downward spiral. But her older brother would go to Holy Cross College and then Georgetown Law School. Maribeth would go to a rather exclusive girl's school near Philadelphia for college, likely on scholarship since her folks were of quite modest means. I think her school had one of those comforting names like Chestnut Hills or Spreading Oaks or something similar. It sounds like a finishing school, but I assume the academics were just fine. Eventually I understand that she earned a doctorate in literature at Boston College. Her girlfriends from the neighborhood had none of the same smarts or ambition that she did, and you could see them quickly drifting apart. It was the same in all these neighborhoods, a handful moved up and out while most remained behind.

We stayed in touch through part of our college years when I would see her occasionally during the summers. We even spent time together during the one summer I was home from the seminary. Perhaps that was a clue my devotion to the celibate life, though technically safe, was not to endure forever. One of the last times I saw her was during the summer when I was at Clark. It must have been toward my senior year since I was living in my own apartment with a couple of other guys. During high school our relationship had been so chaste. Once I tried unbuttoning her bra. She did not say no but asked me what I was doing in such a way that I beat a hasty retreat. Women have several looks and this look said, "If you go any further, I will separate your family jewels from where they are attached to your body." Home plate was way out of reach.

By the time we both were finishing college, it appeared she was a little more comfortable with her body. On occasion, we even simulated sex. I sensed that her body was awakening. It was clear that she still liked me in a special way. She might have been opening to exploring things not comfortable for girls of her era and upbringing. But it would not be with me. Perhaps she was no longer a virgin by then but that seemed unlikely. In any case, I thought it would be better if she opened herself up with someone who wanted the same kind of traditional life she wanted. But I did like her a lot. It would be great to catch up after all these years. When I look at her in those old pictures, a tug is still there.

Maureen . . .

In college there were more casual dates, many nurses or students or other women who passed by in the kaleidoscope of life. One young nurse did break through my general rule against dating Catholic girls after I had reached college. Her name was Maureen. Unlike the others, I don't believe that Maureen ever went on for a doctorate in anything. Still, it was the same old story in many other ways. She was cute, quick as the dickens, witty, bright, with an infectious laugh and personality. Her Irish eyes literally sparkled. You could not help but like her. As I recall her features were not classically pretty, but I thought she effused an undeniable beauty. Besides, she radiated a warmth and affection that just drew you in. She was a genuinely nice gal and had that dark hair along with eyes that danced.

I don't recall how we met. As I recall, she did not have anything to do with the nursing program at the hospital where I worked. I am not sure we had that many actual dates. But we hung out a lot. And I distinctly recall we laughed a lot. She had a way of lighting up a room. I took a summer class with her brother at Assumption College in Worcester. We were studying French. Why, I have no idea. These stupid ideas just popped into my head. I think I just had some Calvinistic sentiment about never wasting a moment, which in retrospect seems way out of character for me. In fact, in my master's program a few years later I organized the LOB society, which is a British word for someone of no worth to society whatsoever. The members of my group were dedicated to sloth and gluttony.

Maureen was way too funny, which I found irresistible. I recall the three of us (her brother, she, and I) stayed up all night at their folk's apartment laughing ourselves silly until we heard the alarm go off in her dad's room. He had to go to work. I snuck out the door quickly. God, I wonder if the poor guy got any sleep. Still, I look back to that night as emblematic of many. We really fit together so easily and well. I can recall going out for New Year's Eve with her once. But mostly we simply enjoyed each other's company.

We just were damn good friends. We did make out every once in a great while, but there was never anything serious. Those moments were more affectionate than erotic. I was just comfortable with her; she was a good friend. I remember her saying once that I was the one boy with whom she might have wanted to have sex. Not that she would have had sex with me but just the fact that I moved her in that way made me feel very special. I suspect she trusted me totally. That was better than sex. It was a great way of relating, as friends and confidants. We would talk for hours.

Once, I recall, we were alone at my folk's apartment. She kept tickling me and playing around until, seemingly by accident, we fell on to the bed. We were half intertwined with one another waiting for the other to make the next move. Frankly, I was conflicted. I did not know what to do next, but was saved by the telephone ringing. I had this sense she wanted to go further with me. I, however, could not escape the feeling that she needed someone who fully shared her world view, her values. Yes, I am a numb nut.

I assume she went on to marriage, a nursing career, and children. She would have been good, very good at all of that. I am sure she made some man a wonderful wife and a sweet and loving mother to any children she might have had. I can still remember her smile and her laugh. Like I said, she had that great Irish laugh and those endearing Irish eyes.

Carol . . .

Carol was a serious college girlfriend, not in any serious "we might get married" sense, but we spent enough time together to be considered a couple. She was rather perfect for me in the usual ways. She was smart, attractive, inquisitive, and very talented. I recall that for a Christmas season show, she sang the lead female part, which was very demanding. They hired a professional singer from New York for the male part. Carol could do it all.

Best of all, though, she was engaged to someone who had somehow gotten himself drafted and was stationed in Alaska of all places. We were a couple without being a real couple. I could not ask for anything better. Besides, she had the dark hair that drew me in. She probably deviated from the norm in one way, maybe two now that I think on it. First, she was not as lighthearted as the others. She had a sense of humor but was more serious and focused. You knew she was going places. She made up for that lack of easy wit, assuming it is a deficit, by being totally engaging intellectually. I must have thought at the time that smarts could be absorbed by close association or intimate physical contact. It was a theory that did not pan out though my fieldwork to explore that theory was worth it.

Second, she appeared to enjoy sensual contact. Unlike the Catholic girls before her, she seemed to respond positively to my body right from the start—a female quality that has never ceased to amaze me on those rare occasions it surfaced. I can still recall that I walked her back to her place from a faculty party (yes, Clark was intimate enough that select undergraduates might be invited to such a party of graduate students and faculty). We were already hanging around a lot but had kept it at arm's length to this point since she was, after all, engaged to this other guy.

We all have experienced those times when there is electricity in the moment. This was one of those times. I knew we would attack one another when we got to her place. She knew that would happen. The pope in Rome probably knew it would happen and was crossing my name off the list of good Catholic boys. We barely got inside the entrance to her "three-decker" when we literally fell into each other's arms with our bodies flailing in all directions. Let me say it might have been wiser to first get to her flat. A flight of stairs is not the most comfortable place for any form of physical intimacy. But we did make it to her place before any permanent injury was done.

Wow, I remember thinking. She is not like all those Catholic girls from my youth paying homage to female saints who chose martyrdom over sex. Once, she openly asked me if I was willing to disrobe so that we could rub against one another. At that very moment, I just knew I was no longer in Catholic girl hell any longer. There would be many mutual masturbation exercises that somehow never culminated in actual intercourse. God help me, I was a total numb nut. She clearly wanted more, and I put her off.

What was I thinking? What a schmuck! Have I ever mentioned that I was a total moron? Why am I using the past tense here?

I can recall when she and I first met. We recognized each other from our common psychology classes and probably had exchanged brief words on occasion but never had a real conversation. Heaven forbid, that would have taken an ounce of courage on my part. As fate would have it, one day we bumped into each other in the main stairwell of Jonas Clark Hall, the original building of this fine old institution of higher learning. The stairs were hollowed out in the center from decades upon decades of students tramping up and down. We started chatting though it is way more likely that she initiated a conversation with me, probably about some class issue. Our chat started off simply enough but then we talked and talked and talked, one subject moving on to the next. Eventually we moved somewhere where we could talk more easily. And that was that, we just started spending a lot of time together. Nothing was decided I guess. It just happened. Damn good thing I did not have to ask her out on a date. I would have simply assumed there was no chance whatsoever. What would a class act like her want with a schmuck like me?

Like all the gals to whom I responded emotionally, Carol was really, really smart. As I recall, she ranked first in our class at Clark. I was always struck by how organized she was while I vainly wandered about trying to locate class notes and course assignments. On the other hand, she had them organized and cross-referenced in several ways. Later in life, I decided to co-author all my more academic works with females. I always had an abundance of ideas but needed someone organized to keep me on track. It must have been somewhat humiliating for her to be seen with a goof like me. I could see her gal friends now. Why are you hanging around with Corbett? You could do so much better.

We took several classes together. When I called her one evening just before final exams to ask about the exam schedule, she screamed, "How could you NOT know the schedule?" Did I mention that she was just a tad bit more organized than I? Just about everyone was a tad bit more organized than I. One day, in class, I raised my hand and made some observation, the details escape me of course. Out of the corner of my eye, I could see her looking at me with this expression of incredulity on her face. "That was brilliant," she exclaimed as if in shock, "I would have sworn you were asleep."

Carol probably knew I had a lot of native intelligence. I was just undisciplined and disorganized and intellectually selfish. If I liked a class, I could be insightful and even brilliant on occasion, probably quite often. If I got bored it was another matter. Perhaps if circumstances were a little different, we might have gotten serious. Carol was Jewish, though. I can still recall my mother almost choking when she asked if it were true that Carol was a daughter of Israel though she phrased it differently. We Catholics admired them for their drive and academic success. For my family, however, they were not our kind. For one thing, most were comparatively affluent. For another, they were not Catholic. In any case, I blandly smiled and replied that I believed she was. I could see my anguished mother trying to figure out how she was going to tell the family. Poor woman, she was so paranoid and paralyzed by what people would think. In a perverse way, I enjoyed the moment.

Carol and I did a lot of fun things together. We went to lectures and museums and studied as a couple. I think I really did expect that during our passionate groping sessions some of her knowledge and brilliance would pass to me through an osmotic process of sorts. We drove out to Tanglewood in the western part of Massachusetts, truly a pastoral and idyllic setting, to listen to a symphony performance under the stars. She asked me to accompany her and another Jewish gal to see a movie, *The Pawnbroker*. It was a searing story about a holocaust survivor who finally finds a way to feel his emotions again. She did not think she could watch it alone. We attended Vietnam anti-war speeches and marched when few others realized how bad the situation was there. I enjoyed her intellect, her broad command of so many topics, her sophistication, and even her sensuality. She was good for me.

Carol asked me to visit her and her family one Christmas break. I demurred, that might have signaled a seriousness that was not there on my part. But I really liked her. We drifted apart a bit when I met Lee (discussed in a future chapter). But like all the women that were special to me, there was no end as such. I drove her to her application interview at Harvard where she would do her graduate work and earn her doctorate in education. I visited her during her time in Cambridge but then lost touch when I went off to India. She eventually became dean of the School of Education at Rutgers University, married, and had a family.

She did not marry the guy she was engaged to at the time I knew her though. I later got to know Arlene, the sister of that guy to which Carol was betrothed during our relationship. Arlene, in fact, would end up marrying perhaps my best friend at Clark. I ran across them a few years ago on Cape Cod where they had a lovely home after long careers in academia. As we sat around chatting about the great times at Clark in the old days, Arlene started to speak very highly of Carol and wished the relationship between her brother and Carol had worked out. It was a funny moment for me. I only confessed that Carol and I were good friends. But I do understand why Arlene felt as she did. Carol was a special and unique woman. As with the others, I would love to catch up with her again.

Women, can't live with them and can't live without them . . .

Exactly what is the story with this strange species called females? Damned if I know. Over seventy years of experience in life taught me one thing, I am clueless. If they strive to be mysterious they have succeeded admirably. I recall so many times where I would have bet the mortgage that a particular female found me attractive. All the signs were there. They would look into my eyes with extended stares, play with their hair, put their hand on my arm or knee, and sometimes even express how lonely they were. Everything screamed that they were flirting with me, only God knows why! I would finally screw up my courage (mostly I would not) and make a pass only to be shot down with a withering "why would you think I would be interested in you" as if I were just above the slug on the evolutionary pecking order.

Then there would be the other group of women, smaller in number for sure. They would ignore me as if I were the original carrier of the Bubonic Plague. There was no eye contact, desultory responses to my sparkling conversation, blank reactions to my lightening quick wit. I would bet the mortgage that any pass on my part would result in a death spiral of my erotic hopes. Why would I set myself up to be shot down one more time? I would pass on the opportunity for more pain only to find out later from some friend that the indifferent woman "had the hots for me," as we said back then at least. No way! I would have bet the mortgage that this woman would have preferred a date with Hagar the Horrible over spending five minutes with me. "No," the intermediary would go on. "You blew it. She was really disappointed you were not interested in her. She was considering ripping her clothes off to get you to notice her." What! Go figure!

Based on a lifetime of futility, I would go with the numbers game if I were to do it all over again. I would make passes at lots of women and simply enjoy the few successes I would have. The trick is not to take the 95 percent failure rate seriously. The rest of me would not change. I generally was kind, open, and honest. All boys knew that the key to the kingdom was to promise undying love. You did not believe it, and you assumed that the girl (hopefully) did not believe it, but it gave cover to all when potential erotic deeds were in the wind. Again, girls could not admit to carnal interests so needed an excuse. I never strayed down that path of disingenuous flattery. I respected them too much. The price of honesty, however, is perpetual frustration. But my integrity is intact. Again, what a schmuck!

The thing is, I liked women. As I started out saying early in the chapter, they strike me as being smarter, more interesting, and capable of greater emotional range and insight than most guys. And I did spend a great deal of time with women after high school. I became a richer, more deeply developed man because of those experiences. They were, after all, more mature and focused than the average male who, at that age, exhibits all the maturity of a slightly out-of-control baboon. At the least, I got to know myself so much better through them.

In the end, my most meaningful relationships with women, at least early on, had little to do with sex. They were about friendship. They were about communicating and sharing and exploring the inner self. I could talk freely with these gals and with the many others whom I never considered romantic partners. By my college years, I hung around with a few women without thought of anything more than they were great companions. I always felt I could be more honest and sensitive without the macho push back you feared from other males. These were, after all, the tender years when we all were seeking out identities and our directions. You could only risk being laughed at and ridiculed so often before you began to believe the negative barbs.

At the same time, celibacy is way overrated, way, way overrated. Everyone belittles prostitution which, as it operates today, is worth belittling. Fundamentally, though, paying for sex makes great sense. After all, the underlying exchange that is the foundation of the sexual act would then be transparent and calculable. The price would be set by some market place. Both sides would be treated fairly in such an open exchange. It is when you confuse sex with all these unstated bartering interactions that we complicate things dramatically.

When I was coming of age, I knew some great women. I never had "real" sex with any of them. But I would not have given up a moment of these relationships for any price. Each enriched me immeasurably and the enduring memories are yet sweet. In my ideal world women would offer recreational sex for a negotiated price while saving real relationships for asexual commitments. Just saying! Besides, in my case it also would have been nice to get laid before my hair started turning grey. Of course, it has occurred to me that maybe I was the *only* guy of my generation who succumbed to the onslaught of guilt imposed by church and culture. Maybe everyone else was going crazy and having a lot of fun while I endured years of, well, nothing! That would be the ultimate irony if it were not so damn sad.

CHAPTER 6

WORKING

Choose a job you love, and you will never
have to work a day of your life.
—*Confucius*

I would never be a captain of industry. That was clear from my earliest days. In fact, as a child I seriously doubted my ability to support myself. My earliest attempts to make money were failures for the most part. Okay, my initial attempts were no more than petty larceny, sneaking through my folks' stuff to hijack a few coins. I never recall getting a regular allowance, so I was usually short of cash and rather desperate.

When pilfering change from a pocket book or wallet, you face a classic tradeoff. Do you take enough to make the theft worthwhile but then risk being exposed? Coin evaporation will become obvious if greed takes over. On the other hand, being too cautious leaves you without the means to procure the essential goods of life. How was I going to get the full Red Sox lineup if I could not afford enough bubble gum baseball cards? Not that the Sox were any good in those years, they generally sucked. But they were my sucky Sox, and I loved them to death.

Early labors . . .

Eventually I went legit. Legal efforts to earn my keep started with odd jobs such as mowing lawns, shoveling snow, and selling various drinks on street corners. None proved to be lucrative ventures. The available yards were postage size lots between these huge three-deckers. Besides, I did not have a lawn mower. I would borrow some ancient push mower whose blades had last been sharpened during the Boer war. Snow shoveling worked but without the ability to create artificial white stuff, the income stream was spotty at best. The lemonade and cool-aide stand idea also had its drawbacks. Car traffic on our narrow street was limited. Foot traffic was episodic, usually heavy at the end of the day when the guys were coming home from work. By then, though, I pretty much had drunk most of my own product and likely all my profits.

Cleary, I needed something more stable or at least predictable. An older boy was giving up his paper route. I jumped at the chance. I can't quite recall how one earned the right to a given route, but I believe it was pretty informal. A bribe might have been involved though the whole process back then seemed based on who you knew, much like the way all jobs in tight-knit ethnic communities were distributed. Today, everything is probably transparent. You likely apply for a paper delivery job and supply a resume, pee in a cup for a drug test, get fingerprinted, and endure a lie detector screening. Back then you just begged the older kid for the opportunity or maybe beat the crap out of him.

In those days a lot went on directly through the delivery boy. I don't recall any girls then. You asked for a certain number of papers. They would be dropped off on a given corner at a specific time each day. I think you had an opportunity to give back unused papers should you have too many for some reason, but I cannot be sure of that. What was clear is that you had to collect enough from your customers to pay for the papers you picked up each day and did not return. In effect, you were buying the papers and took all the risks.

Collection day was once a week and a guy from the paper would show up on the paper drop corner to collect from each delivery boy. The difference between what you were charged and the cost of the paper to each customer was your profit. Sounds easy, right! Not even I could screw this up! Ah, but I could. Today, they make it too easy. You call the newspaper and established an account. The paper bills you directly, and you pay them as agreed upon. No payment, no paper.

A numb nut like me, however, probably could not make a profit selling pardons to millionaire Ponzi scam artists and criminal bankers doing serious time at Club Fed. Making money on my paper route turned out to be a nightmare. In fact, I may have been the only kid to lose money while delivering papers. How is that possible you ask? This was not an affluent neighborhood to be sure. I would make my rounds once a week to collect so I could pay the guy who would soon show up for the money. I believe he was accompanied by a large Italian gentleman named Bruno who sat in the car cracking his knuckles. It was amazing. People I would see all week long never seemed to be around on collection day. The lights would go out inside as you knocked on the door. So, you keep circling back to try again. But persistence never worked. I would notice furtive glances through windows to see if I had left for good.

I got it. Money was tight, but it is not like I was collecting for a new Cadillac or something. This was the freaking paper for crying out loud. What was it, like fifty cents per week back then, maybe seventy-five cents if the Sunday edition were thrown in? Making a profit was always a close-run thing for me. Some weeks I am not sure I covered my costs. Maybe I should have borrowed a Rottweiler to bring with me on collection day. For some unfathomable reason, I kept at it for a long time but clearly this was proof my future did not lie in the private sector.

I did not mind the work itself. I rather liked the discipline that having a paper route demanded. People depended on me, and I did not want to disappoint. Like mail carriers, I would meet my appointed round through storm and dark of night even though some of the bastards shorted me at the end of the week. Still, I took pride in doing a good job. I came from a working-class family, and I expected to earn my keep. After all, some would pay on time and even throw in an extra nickel or dime as a tip.

Delivering papers posed quite a few challenges. Yeah, there were dogs to avoid but there also were logistical issues that needed solving. Many customers were on the second and third floors of these three-deckers. That meant there was a lot of scampering up and down these stairs. On hot summer days, this could get tiresome and certainly slow you up. Speed was essential. You see, there was always an informal competition among delivery boys to finish their route in the shortest time. If finished with celerity, you might be able to get in another game of the athletic contest *du jour* before dinnertime. To be that efficient, however, you had to minimize the vertical climbs. The solution was simple. We would fold the newspapers in a way that they became missiles that might be lofted onto the third-floor back porches.

That may sound easy enough. However, these porches were not as easy to hit as you might imagine. Most were accessed through relatively small openings to the outside world, which gave the residents access to a clothesline. What is that you ask? A clothesline is what you hang your freshly done washed clothes on to dry in the fresh air. Who had automatic dryers back then? People used nature. You used four or five concentric lines of rope that circled in a pentagonal shape. The apparatus was constructed so that you could rotate the lines in a way that each side could be brought close to the porch opening in a sequential fashion.

Therefore, you could use the whole circumference to hang your clothing to dry. You then kept rotating and hanging or unhanging as the case may be. As the drying process proceeded, you could rotate the apparatus to check on whether the clothes had dried and remove if ready. Otherwise, you might frantically unload a semi-dry wash if the weather suddenly changed for the worse. It was all very ingenious. Of course, those sudden rainstorms could always ruin the best-laid plans so the days when clothes lines were ubiquitous were already numbered.

As we went from house to house, we could easily flip the papers onto the first and second floors. That was not too bad. The third-floor throw, however, required real skill. It was, after all, a long throw, a long vertical throw. In addition, you had to navigate around the clothesline, which on many days was full of hanging garments. On other days, someone might have partially closed the opening to the porch, probably just to cheese me off. Finally, there was wind and weather to account for along with other miscellaneous items like plants being posed on the ledge for the afternoon sun or, more likely, simply to cheese me off.

We are talking real skill here. The paper had to be folded just right so it became a missile. You did not want the damn thing coming undone as it passed the second floor. Then you might see the sports page flying one direction and the classifieds in another. It was okay if you lost the world news section, no one gave a damn about current events anyways. But don't lose the funnies. That would be a disaster. It sometimes took two or three throws to find success. When the paper disappeared into the porch, you waited a moment. Was there sound of broken glass, perhaps the scream of a wounded resident, or the epithet of an irate customer whose priceless Chin dynasty vase had just been smashed? Hearing nothing, you moved on. Hearing something, situation probably not good and you moved on even faster.

Getting closer to books . . .

At some point, two things happened. I grew tired of working for little or no money. The other thing is that I became old enough to take a real job without violating existing child labor laws. There aren't that many openings for a fourteen-year-old high school freshman with no observable skills. I eventually found that there was one such job, as a page in the public library. I have no idea where the title came from, other than some apocryphal medieval source, but you did menial jobs and served as a lackey to the professional library staff. I suspect that in olden times pages were youthful gophers for a nobleman's entourage. Despite this tainted title, the work was indoors, did not seem onerous, and I would get paid on a regular basis. Moreover, I would be around books. I liked books, the way they felt and even smelled. It was a private fetish and not one to be shared with the other guys. Even I could not screw this up, or so I thought at the time.

How to get such a position though? Well, I could have filled out an application and mailed it in. Who knows, I might even have been hired. But this was Worcester Mass; politics were powerful. My father grew up with the Irish mafia who ran the city. By run the city I meant they controlled the important positions like city mayor, the city manager, most of the city council, and many top executive positions. Most city leaders came from certain Irish neighborhoods back then. Politics was a traditional way out of the Irish ghettos and on to the American dream of home ownership. My father made some calls and one fine day I was ushered into the office of the city manager, Francis McGrath. He asked about my father and where I went to school. When I told him that I attended St. Johns, the deal was sealed. An obviously clean-cut Irish boy attending St. John's could do no wrong. He picked up his phone, made a call, and that was it. I had a job. I wonder what the unconnected kids did. Don't you just love corruption?

My new supervisor at the library was not that pleased, however. She thought it rather scandalous that I was given a job when other deserving kids had applied in the usual way. What was wrong with her, this was Worcester? I had thought that was how everyone got a job at the library or any other public position. I guess not. To make matters worse, I was always late to work. St. John's let out later than the public schools. I could walk to work in about twenty minutes or so, perhaps fifteen if I ran my fanny off through downtown Worcester dodging the traffic. However, I did not get out until my shift was about to start. I would hustle as fast as I could, but I could not defy the laws of physics. I was always ten or more minutes late. That was strike two against me. But I worked hard, was always polite, and never managed to burn the place down. Eventually, she forgave me though remained rather frosty throughout. I eventually realized she was not Ms. Sunshine to anyone. If I, with my surplus of wit and a devilish smile, could not charm her then she was beyond reach.

The main library was built in 1788, I think. Probably not quite that far back, but it was very old and decrepit. Some of the books were stone tablets etched in hieroglyphics. I recall the elevator in particular. It was not motor powered. Nope, it worked with some clever arrangement of ropes and pulleys and weights designed by the same Egyptian engineers that put together the ancient pyramids. It probably was ingeniously constructed and safe, but I always wondered about the safety of any device that went back further in time than the oldest sequoias found in California. But I would get in, give the frayed rope that came as original equipment a mighty tug or two, and slowly the damn thing would rise or lower as required.

My tasks were not onerous once you had a command over the Dewey Decimal System, an ingenious system for determining where books were to be located on the shelves. The daily drill involved book stacking or placing returned works into their assigned place. I would keep the public areas tidy and straighten the books on shelves, so the place looked neat and inviting. To this day, I am bothered by rows of books that look disorderly, where each book is not positioned right at the edge of the shelf.

A couple of girls from the local girl's Catholic high school would stop by and chat on occasion. I probably came across as a total catch. I had a job after all, probably looked sufficiently like a schmuck so as not to pose any danger to them and evinced that slightly clueless manner. Their devotions to St. Virginius could not possibly be threatened by this obvious klutz. I remained rather indifferent to them, totally aware of how utterly hopeless the pursuit of Catholic girls would be.

I do recall one gal who briefly worked with me. She was black and a senior in high school when I first started and left for college within a year of my arrival. She was the first black person with whom I ever actually conversed. I was struck by how sophisticated and middle class she was. Though I had resisted the more corrosive aspects of racism while growing up, I could not pretend to be free of all stereotypes. I approached her with extreme caution, as if she were an alien being. In addition to her race, she also was a female. It is a wonder I talked with her at all, but we did work together in adjoining sections of the library.

I recall her mentioning that her brother had attended St. John's for a year but found the religious atmosphere stifling. Her family was not Catholic, which must have been a problem. I frankly cannot recall any Protestants at St. John's during my tenure there. His family must really have wanted him to get a fine education or were punishing him for some awful sin. It also must have been very hard on him being the only black face. An all-boys school was not the place to be if you stood out in any way and a black face in the 1950s really would have stood out. I wish I had the courage back then to ask her more questions about what he had experienced or what she experienced as a black female in a city with few minorities at the time. Now when I see the St. John's school alumnae magazine, there are a sprinkling of black faces to be found.

Admittedly, the job was monotonous. At least, however, I managed to make money, unlike with my paper route. I finally was headed in the right direction career-wise. I do recall that the library put on some events during the summer at the common space behind City Hall. Eastern cities liked to have common space or parks in the center of town. Boston Commons and Central Park are famous examples. Worcester had one, but it was not so famous though another city green space, Elm Park, purportedly was the first municipal park in the country. Earlier, I think these places had been communal areas where cows and sheep belonging to several local farmers could roam.

In any case, I suspect these events were part of an outreach campaign to encourage people to read and use the libraries services. Worcester never struck me as a place where the literacy rate was particularly high, but I probably am overly harsh in that regard. There were several colleges located there though that did not totally offset the working class feel of the place. I was put in charge of the music, which meant selecting records to play over the loudspeaker system. I loved a selection called Victory at Sea. It was the music that accompanied a popular TV show during that era that showed clips of our brave WWII sailors and marines defeating the Japanese. It was stirring music, and I played it way too often I suspect. I kept waiting for an outraged public to complain but no one did. Perhaps they liked it as well.

My tenure at the library ended when I went off to the seminary after high school. By the end, my awkward start of being thrust upon them as a political hire had long been forgotten. They liked me. Years later, when my dad's health deteriorated to the point that he could no longer work in a factory, he used his same political connections to get a job as a library custodian. By then they were in a brand-new building on the opposite side of City Hall. I think they were just beginning to move as I ended my days there. I faintly recall helping pack books for relocation. Anyways, many of the same staff were still there and my dad told me they recalled me with considerable fondness. He probably lied to save what was left of my ego, but it might have been true. You never know, do you?

A job down under . . .

My next job of note was with the Worcester Department of Sewers. I needed something temporary right after I returned from the seminary and before starting college. I cannot recall the hiring process here but the same kind of politics, or at least an inside connection, might have been involved. My best friend's mother worked in a clerical position for the department and perhaps she pulled a string or two. On starting, I remember thinking that this could not be very hard. The position was for a night watchman. Just how challenging can looking after a bunch of sewers be? I mean, where would they go after all?

It turned out that I had a few more responsibilities. There was a lot of equipment to monitor and protect from vandalism or theft. More importantly, if anyone was to call because their toilets were overflowing with the detritus from the city sewer system, I would send out my "partner" to determine who was responsible—the city or the home owner. If the city, I would call out a repair crew. If not, the poor citizen had better find some wading boots quick. In a way, you might say that I stood guard defending the good citizens of Worcester from a lot of crap. This was contrary to my usual role as the source of a lot of crap.

I worked the 11-7-night shift except for weekends and holidays when I might be assigned other shifts. My partner and I had a small TV that we could watch until about 1:00 AM when the final station signed off for the night. Then my partner went to sleep on a small cot. I would only wake him if someone called to complain about a sewer malfunction that was sending crap back up into their bathroom. Fortunately, this did not occur all that often. I generally spent the rest of the night reading. About every hour or so, I had to tour the facilities and turn a key in devices located throughout my route. If I failed to do so, I would get a call from some remote monitoring point asking if all was okay. I think I was called a couple of times when I dozed off. This was another job I could handle unless I died of boredom, which was a possibility.

I was working there when President John F. Kennedy was killed. For some reason I had the day shift that weekend. The nation, surely everyone in Massachusetts, was glued to every moment of televised coverage. My friend Gerry Petraitis stopped by the sewer department office to watch the coverage with me. I don't think any of us wanted to be alone. We still liked politicians back then, some of them at least. Kennedy was revered in Catholic families. We could not even feign the cool indifference that is mandatory for younger males. I can still be moved to tears by some of his speeches and his *Ich bin ein Berliner*" speech is unforgettable. Years later I walked through the Kennedy Museum and just the voices of John and Bobby would still bring tears to my eyes. Politicians today bring tears to my eyes but for an entirely different reason.

I first heard of Kennedy's assassination from Gerry. I had taken a long walk that day. I was feeling very restless and unsettled. Something struck me as foreboding and a bit surreal, a premonition perhaps? All seemed way too quiet as I started back home. As I approached our three-decker, that sense of impending doom overwhelmed me again, something was wrong. I just knew it. Maybe it was that the streets were so empty or maybe it was simply a sixth sense of imminent disaster. In any case, at the last minute I veered off and went to his house. I could see agony on his face when he opened the door. I was stunned by the news. I knew something was terribly out of place but nothing this horrendous.

We watched TV in total shock for a while and then went to pick up his mother at work. They were letting the staff out early, and she was crying uncontrollably. As boys, we were not allowed to cry but there were tears in our eyes. I can yet remember a picture in the newspaper of young delivery boys sitting with a stack of papers at their feet waiting to be delivered. The Kennedy assassination headline was clearly visible. The two boys clearly were crying without any evidence of self-consciousness. No one of my generation and background forgets where he or she was on that awful day. Gerry and I watched the coverage that Sunday at the sewer department. It was the day that Oswald would be moved to a more secure location. I remember telling Gerry, you better watch this since they are bringing Oswald out now. He started to move to where he could see the television screen when the shot rang out. Again, that sinking feeling of being caught in a continuing nightmare swept over us.

Then again it was the '60s. So many cataclysmic events were to follow . . . civil rights and Vietnam and urban riots and feminism and the counter culture and more assassinations and the Beatles and drugs. There were even rumors about free love and space aliens landing at Roswell, New Mexico. Only the flying saucer rumor seemed plausible. But the day Kennedy died stood above all else. It was the onset of so much more to come and an end to innocence. It was a defining moment for my generation.

Then, one night a little more than a month later I had an opportunity to be a hero. It came on a cold New Year's Eve as I worked my usual 11-7 shift. My "partner" had been celebrating the New Year early and showed up for work dead drunk. Heaven forbid if anyone had a shit problem that night. I hoped desperately for an uneventful shift. It was not to be, however. Shortly after starting, I smelled smoke, so I toured the building and then the yard where the heavy equipment was kept. No problem was evident, but the smell did not go away. I did another round right away but nothing. Finally, I saw a house on fire in the distance and heard fire trucks. Ah, mystery explained, and I could relax.

But the smell persisted and intensified. It seemed inconceivable that anything so strong was coming from that distance. So off I went on another round. This time, in a small kitchen area, I found a fire spreading up the wall behind a refrigerator. Like any hero I instantly sprang into action with no regard for my personal safety. I dashed around like an idiot cursing that I had never bothered to locate the fire extinguishers in advance. But I found one and started spraying the rapidly spreading flames.

Then I looked more closely at the extinguisher and noticed the caution label saying, "do not use on electrical fires." This surely was an electrical fire. Now what! Would there be a huge explosion and mushroom cloud? But nothing happened. I would have used it in any case, desperation overcoming any concern I had about conforming to cautionary instructions. What a sense of relief when the flames were extinguished. I was a hero! But even I knew that not seeing actual flames did not mean that the fire was totally out. It might be waiting to break out again or, worse, spreading throughout the walls hidden from my view.

I knew I had to call the bosses and the fire department. That was not so bad, but what was I to do with my "partner." He was still passed out on a cot in a drunken stupor. When I say he was out, I mean he was out. As the fire department and the big bosses headed to the building, I did everything I could to get John upright—pushing and pulling and slapping and yelling. I would finally get him propped up against the wall and down he would slide to the floor. As I recall, I did get him sufficiently erect to possibly pass any check out by the authorities. That would only work if they did not talk to him or he did not say anything himself. It did look hopeless. He was rather precariously propped against a wall, and I worried that he would collapse in a heap at any moment. They had to see he was incapacitated, but I don't recall that he suffered any consequences. He must have had connections, as they say.

I have always been proud of my service to Worcester's sewers—not a single sewer went missing on my watch. Still, I recall I ended my sewer career around the time I started at Clark or not that long thereafter. In retrospect, I am not sure why. Other than the fact that it was not conveniently located, I could have plenty of time to study at night. But I left this career path nevertheless. I figured I could only go up from there, up from the sewers that is. Besides, I wanted work with more social significance, where I could contribute to my fellow man. On second thought, saving the good citizens of Worcester from creeping crap was a momentous social contribution but its full contribution to humanity escaped me back then.

Healing the sick . . .

My next job was as an orderly in St. Vincent's Hospital, a Catholic institution of healing within walking distance of my home. Of course, back then I would walk great distances without a second thought. Having experienced enough heroics in defending sewers, my attention would now focus on the sick and dying, plenty of opportunity for heroics there. Once again, I secured a job working the 11-7 shift. I must have had a thing for nocturnal employment. Perhaps that explains my attraction to blood and the fact that I have no reflection in a mirror.

I had a complete physical as a condition of my hire by St. Vs, which is what everyone called it. The attending nurse shocked me by asking if I had been there several years earlier for an emergency appendectomy. For a moment I thought she had some record of the event in front of her. It turned out that she really did remember me. I was stunned. Surely it was not my charm or goods looks that were memorable. When I asked, she merely smiled and said that some cases are hard to forget.

In fact, my demise was a close-run thing. One afternoon I had been playing football with a group of kids. We used the park that day rather than the streets as a playing field. My best guess is the location of the game depended on the number of players. Once we got to five or more on each team we needed more space. Too many players and the probability of running into a parked car became all too real. All was fine until I returned home. I was not hungry and went to bed early. My condition quickly deteriorated. Flu like symptoms got worse, a bad fever broke out, and the pain in my stomach became intense. My parents never called doctors in those days, not many did. It was not like anyone had health insurance or anything and doctors cost money they did not have. Usually I was simply given copious amounts of cod liver oil or milk of magnesia, the cure-alls of those days. Good thing they didn't go for the home remedies, the milk of magnesia would have killed me for sure.

Doctors made home visits back then. This was like the third day since the onset of symptoms when they broke down and called one. I really must have looked like shit. Beside the money, they would miss the gang at the local bar where they hung out daily. By the time the doc arrived at our house, the pain had subsided. Maybe I was cured?

But no, after a lot of probing around my tummy and groin area, he asked for the phone. He called St. Vincent's hospital and told them that he was bringing a kid over and to have the operating room ready. I was helped down the stairs and into the car by my mother and aunt. After that it becomes a blur, but I do know I was rushed right into surgery. Apparently, the fact the pain subsided signaled the point when I was in the greatest danger. That was when my appendix had ruptured, and toxins were spreading through my system. I later learned that it had been a very close-run thing, very close indeed.

I remember being in the hospital for quite a while. They kept draining crap, a medical technical term, from my stomach. Even after I went home I had to return to the doctor's office every few days. At the bottom of my surgery scar, they had left a small hole that was covered with surgical dressing of course. During these office doctor visits, he would probe through that hole and squeeze out even more crap. How much poison could a little appendix produce? I still have an ugly scar on my stomach to remind me of the operation and the aftermath. The long, ugly reminder of my near-death experience ends with a roundish blob where they would force out the remaining poisons during the office visits.

Now that I think on it, I likely would have earned a heavenly reward if I had passed at the time. It was pre-puberty, and I was still spiritually pure at the time though my milk bottle likely was spotty from other transgressions. Everything seemed like a sin back then. But only one transgression comes to mind. We had a dog named Fritz, a miniature German shepherd probably mixed with Rottweiler. He was a mean cuss but was totally loyal to the family. I would bring friends home and ask them to pose as if they were about to assault me. Usually, they were perplexed at my request, but I was persuasive. When my victim would raise their hand as if to strike, Fritz immediately would attack the poor schmuck. The kid would scramble out the door and down the street. I would watch kid and dog disappear as I doubled over in laughter. Okay, a small sign of early sadism and an early sign of my anti-social tendencies.

In any case, the hospital seemed happy to get me as an orderly. I think they had trouble staffing the place at night. After some cursory training, almost none that I recall, I was ready to exercise my healing powers. Basically, I was simply given a floor to which I was expected to show up. It was on-the-job learning after that. It soon hit me that they might have difficulty getting help for this late shift and would have hired Vlad the Impaler (Dracula) had he applied for the position.

Being a Catholic hospital, they did not pay well. This was the night shift, after all, and most young men might want to do other things at night. In fact, almost all the other male orderlies on the 11-7 shift were Jamaican immigrants. They attended some Seventh Day Adventist (I believe) institution located just outside the city. I think the school bussed them in for work and picked them up in the mornings. They were nice young men, very courteous and polite, who would try to reconvert me to a belief in God. I enjoyed sparring with them but remained the agnostic I had become by this time.

The regulatory environment must have been weak in those days since on many nights there would be just a senior nursing student, a nurse's aide, and myself to look after an entire floor of patients. In those days hospitals were generally packed. Patients having surgery would stay for extended periods of time after most procedures. Now they kick you out some four hours after quadruple bypass surgery *and* a lobotomy. Really, who can afford more than four hours in a hospital today? And who wants to survive in any case after being sucked dry of all their money? On the plus side, medical interventions are much less invasive, and the healing time has been greatly reduced. We had to work hard to keep patients alive back then. Make no mistake, we were heroes.

Hard to look back and not wonder how we managed not to kill off more patients than I can recall. As noted above, we had many patients to look after and were chronically short staffed. If there were no emergencies, deaths, or admissions, we could handle the routine stuff easily, and I could still find time to flirt with the student nurses or study a bit. As far as I know, I did not hasten the passing of any patient in our care though that might be wishful thinking on my part.

My most serious crime, at least as I recall, involved giving an enema to the wrong patient. It was easy to do, most rooms had four patients and you could easily mistake bed 3 for 4, particularly if you were suffering from sleep deprivation. I should have picked up on the clue when the patient insisted that the doctor had not told him about any enema. But who listens to the customer, right? Still, even these minor transgressions were a strong clue that any ambitions to becoming the next Albert Schweitzer may have been a bit of a stretch.

The night shift at an urban hospital proved an irreplaceable learning experience filled with unforgettable moments. I would get called to wherever problems broke out requiring me to subdue disoriented patients who wanted to go home at 3:00 AM. I still remember one night getting called down to the emergency room to prop up a guy who kept fainting. As I looked at the seal of St. Vincent's above the ER door, which proudly proclaimed that God Is Charity, the nun in charge kept screaming at the poor man during his brief, noncomatose moments. "Do you have health insurance?" Perhaps He is charity, but St. V's fell just a bit short in that regard. Later, I would learn that America had one of the most indefensible healthcare financing system on the planet, the worst among rich nations by far.

The work proved mostly pleasant and the people generally grateful for any help received, even from an idiot like me. There were bumps of course. If the doctors had ordered it, you had to wake patients up to take their temperature or blood pressure. Now they have these whizz bang instruments that take vital signs from six feet away it seems. We had to take temps the old-fashioned way, by mouth or, if so instructed, anally. Some patients would swear at me that they had finally dozed off after taking a sleeping pill and I waltz in to wake them up a half-hour later. I felt like those Germans on trial at Nuremberg as I told them, "I am just following orders." It sounded weak even to me. But occasionally, I would find a very weak pulse, or a blood pressure reading that was out of whack, or a soaring temp and sound the alarm. That made the aggravation worthwhile.

There were some unique wrinkles to working in a Catholic hospital. For one thing, you had to get people ready for communion in the morning, perhaps it was only on Sunday. It was marked somewhere who desired to receive the communion wafer. You had to make sure they were awake and sitting over the side of the bed if they were able. The other patients were closed off with a curtain, so the priest knew which bed or beds to go to in each room. I thought all this a bit of an inconvenience for nonbelievers but there was no arguing with God or, in this case, whichever nun was in charge that night. "Oh, the patient in bed 3 is dying. Well, he would have to wait to die until Father finishes giving out communion in that room."

Early one day, two guys were up and talking. One says to the other, "Harry, are you taking communion this morning?" "Sure, why not," Harry responds. It sounded like an innocent exchange, but something was amiss in the way Harry responded so I checked out his records. Sure enough, Harry was not Catholic. I cannot recall what he was now, other than that he was doomed. One thing was sure, he was not a member of the One, True, Holy, and

Apostolic faith. For a moment I thought about intervening. But then I thought, what the hell. It can't hurt, so I set him up to receive. Who knows, maybe it turned out to be a life-changing epiphany for him.

Most patients are lost to memory, of course, though a handful stay with me. We had one elderly Jewish patient I recall. For him, we had special instructions. He was permitted to ask for one drink of his favorite alcoholic beverage during the night. The booze was stored at the nurse's station. Amazingly, there was no overnight evaporation. He would buzz me and ask for his drink, not every night but often enough. I wondered how he managed to negotiate this special privilege. Perhaps he made a big contribution to the hospital, the nuns in charge could be bought if you knew their price.

Then there was the eighty-year-old Italian grandmother who kept screaming at me that I should fuck her. That was the best offer I got during my college years. In addition, there were a host of patients who would become fuzzy during the night and would hallucinate about where they were. I got whacked and kicked on several occasions. I still remember one gentleman arguing with me. He was convinced he was on Vernon Street and could see his house a short distance away. I doubt I was terribly persuasive convincing him that he was at St. Vincent's as he flailed away at me. I always felt bad when we had to restrain patients by tying their wrists and legs to the iron railings on the side of the beds. I felt like crap doing it, but it was necessary at times. Drugs, illness, quiet, and darkness in an unfamiliar place can be a challenge to anyone.

One man was there forever, or so it seemed. He had escaped from Communist control somewhere in Eastern Europe and still spoke with an accent. He had terminal cancer but hung on for quite a while. He had such a wonderful smile and never complained no matter his suffering. I tried hard to do whatever I could for him, but there was so little I could do. I felt for him. It is not always good to have such a will to live. I hope we have better options when I reach my end days, being kept alive as one wastes away is a terrible curse no one should endure.

I got to chat with many of the doctors, particularly the interns and residents who were on call at night. You would be surprised at the gallows humor that prevailed. There would be little side comments about "Well, at least we didn't manage to kill that one." One resident-in-training noticed my textbook as he was filling out charts and asked what I was reading. I mentioned it was a famous play, a classic drama, for an English lit course. I have a faint memory that it was one of Ibsen's memorable works. He smiled and said that would be good training if I ever decided to pursue a medical career. There was plenty of acting that went on in medicine.

My own acting surely was involved in fooling others that you know what you are doing even when you were clueless. More than once I was asked to do something I knew little about, but I did it with gusto and confidence. On occasion, though, I might wind up asking the patient, "Just how did the last guy do this?" As I mentioned, I really don't recall much training in the duties I was expected to perform. Perhaps there were fewer lawsuits back then for shoddy medical work, it was probably a mortal sin to sue the Church in those days. In the end, most of us did care about what we were doing. There was, though, a prevalent attitude that if bad shit was going to happen, it would be far better if it happened on the next shift. Just let us get through ours.

Death was particularly inconvenient. I recall finding patients who had passed with no one noticing. On other occasions, I was with them as they passed or cleaned them up after death, which could be a rather messy affair. Other times, you might be dealing with distressed relatives. If they were there in the middle of the night, it was not good news. I recall a family walking to the waiting room in front of me and the teenage boy passing out. Fortunately, I saw him buckle and caught him before he hit the floor and suffered any harm.

One night we had high drama. I heard loud crashes and unusual sounds. I really got concerned as I noticed flashing lights out the window. In the street below were just about every fire engine in the City of Worcester. A wave of panic washed over me. What if we had to get everyone out? We had no drills to prepare us for that kind of thing. It turned out to be a small fire that was quickly extinguished. When any alarm went out from a hospital, it turns out, just about every station in the city responded just in case.

The two co-workers I got to know the best were the nurse's aides who worked on my floor. They were on the other side of middle aged, worn down by life, and doing their best to raise their families on low wages and little sleep. Neither was particularly ambitious in the sense of learning more than demanded by the basics of their job. But they worked hard and were very good people. I have always been angry when the elite castigate the less well off as takers in life. These were not takers. They faced very difficult challenges and generally met them without complaint. Already, I was becoming aware of the advantages I started out with in life.

The nurses and nursing students were mostly younger, the students at least, and it could be fun working with them. Mostly, I stayed clear of any involvement since they were, after all, the dreaded Catholic girls. Alas, on occasion I let my guard slip. On very rare occasions, very rare indeed, one of the older nurses would say something or give me a look that appeared seductive. As you know, I long had concluded that getting laid was impossible, so I always found a way to discount such real or imagined signals. Still, some comments were quite suggestive. I recall asking one for a favor, something trivial. She turned and in a come-hither voice said something like "You can ask me for anything, just anything." I about crapped in my pants but went on as if nothing had happened. Now I look back on those moments and kick myself. Have I mentioned before that I was a total schmuck?

I left St. V's before finishing up at Clark. For years afterward, I would dream about making some big mistake and everyone was mad at me. Over the years, I would make St. V's a regular stop on my sentimental tour of Worcester. Then, one day, not all that long ago, we were in Worcester and I had to make a sentimental tour of the old haunts. I drove by St. V's and found it mostly torn down. I was shocked. It had only gone up around 1960 or so. Was it obsolete so soon? I believe they rebuilt it downtown, but I have not checked that out. For the first time in memory, Vernon Hill does not have a hospital. The only wing still partially standing was the one in which I had worked. Perhaps they were saving it in anticipation of my coming fame.

Saving delinquents . . .

My next job was as a youth worker in a community action agency. The neighborhood it served was located at the foot of Vernon Hill where I had grown up. The area had taken a turn for the worse and was designated as distressed by the powers that be. It probably was distressed when I was growing up, but I never noticed. Over the past decade, the number of minorities had increased dramatically.

I was motivated by the same altruistic impulses that pushed me toward the hospital work that few others wanted. At the Center, I first worked with the younger kids since I thought they would be easier. Another back-forty notion. In case you haven't noticed, I have many of these irretrievably stupid ideas. These young kids came from homes where parenting skills were shaky at best, where resources were nonexistent, and where violence or the threat of violence was ever present. We had a recreation program set up for them at a local church, a place they could go after school. Basically, we tried to keep them off the streets and out of trouble. But it was more than that. We hoped that many of the kids that showed up at our recreation program might learn a few basic skills for use later in life. That was our hope at least.

Theory and reality are often worlds apart. These kids would come roaring into our gym after being cooped up in school all day. I cannot recall much of how I tried to turn these wild things into passable human beings. Whatever I did was undoubtedly insufficient. Not much seemed to work very well but, as I found out later as a college professor, you never really know. I do recall trying to organize basketball games but some basic understandings about human interactions were missing. No one wanted to pass the ball to anyone else since they could not believe they would get the ball back. Trust is a learned attribute that requires reinforcing exchanges with other trusting persons. It becomes harder to inculcate when no one trusts anyone else. I would cajole and beg and threaten just to get one kid to pass the damn ball to another kid. I think we wound up with a lot of 0 to 0 games with no shots at the basket taken.

Some kids were off the needy scale though all appeared needy to me. The bad ones were totally starved for attention or any form of human contact. Some would literally grab onto me and would not let go. I wondered if anyone had ever hugged them before. I would try to give them as much attention as I could, but it was impossible to meet their needs, which were simply overwhelming. At times, simply walking from one side of the gym to the other would be quite a challenge as two small urchins would cling to my legs as if I were their life raft. You sensed they felt letting go would suck them under some emotional quicksand from which there was no escape.

Some of the kids seemed to improve, at least in my eyes they had. They were learning to trust just a little and feel just a little bit better about themselves. But then some little event would set off a regression. I recall having to expel a young kid from the gym because he was basically out of control. He was on one side of the door trying to get it open and I on the other trying to keep it closed. It was a standoff, and I was beside myself. I had to establish limits and stick with them. Otherwise I had no leverage in trying to establish boundaries. But these kids saw the place as a lifeline, a real sanctuary. If it were taken from them, they were lost. I would tell him he could back tomorrow or whatever, but words were never believed. They were lied to all the time. I truly felt helpless and lost at times, most of the time.

Still, my boss thought I was doing a great job. We had beers after work one day. He encouraged me to become a social worker. He thought I had the empathy and compassion and communication skills to be a good one. I was flabbergasted. I was trying hard with these kids, but this was tough stuff. It was the toughest stuff I had ever done up to that point, certainly tougher than protecting Worcester's sewers from theft. I was not sure about this social work thing, but I was more convinced than ever that kids were out of the question for me. I had always seen parenthood as a hard job, perhaps an impossible job. Now I was convinced that my assessment of the difficulties was not over stated. Besides, I could never get past the worry that my kids would rebel and become Republicans. I would never recover from that.

I also worked with the older kids for a while. It was a racially mixed group and there were some tensions. In truth, some of these teens were rough around the edges. Still, they seemed like decent kids to me once you got to know them. The bleak prospects they faced in the future were not fully apparent to us at that time. While they might have found jobs in a host of heavy manufacturing firms that made the Worcester economy hum, such opportunities were already slipping away. Over the next decade or so, those jobs would start disappearing at an ever-faster clip. My own father was a casualty when his factory closed and moved to North Carolina to escape the unions and to slash labor costs. For the teens I worked with, their prospects for a living wage would evaporate along with the hope of raising a family with what they might earn. Oh, they still impregnated their girlfriends, but they had few possibilities of being real fathers. Again, I was reminded of the opportunities that I had and that they would never, ever see.

Research and community service . . .

After my Community Action days, it was off to India and the Peace Corps for a couple of years, which I talk about at length later. After Peace Corps I returned Milwaukee where I pursued a master's degree. I earned my way mostly by being a research assistant for Warner "Bud" Bloomberg, the chair of the Urban Affairs program at the University of Wisconsin–Milwaukee. I cannot recall making great contributions to our understanding of urban problems, but the position did give me my own office, or at least a shared office, with a great view of the surrounding area. I thought having an office great at the time and hoped to get another one sometime in the future.

Finally, I had the outline of a vocational goal for my life. I wanted a job that would give me an office just like this one. Yes, this academic thing looked good. It was indoor work, did not involve heavy lifting, and paid above minimum wage. Since I talk about my days in academia elsewhere I will move on quickly to one of my favorite jobs of all time.

Toward the end of my student days in Milwaukee, my friend had a job as a ticket taker at the Downer Theater. This was an artsy kind of place located in the tony East Side of town just south of the campus. He suggested that I take his place, a real honor and a heartwarming display of personal trust in me. I cannot recall why he gave up such a highly sought-after position though he had just secured a sales job at a major retail outlet. I am not sure I would have bought anything from him. He was a charming cuss but always stoned. Once, he quizzed me on my life to date and then used it to pick up a dazzling blond in the bar that night. How come my life never worked for me? Anyways, it must be fun to go through life in a perpetual haze.

Okay, I thought, why not become a ticket taker? I could make some money and see movies for free. I am proud to say I have seen the Woody Allen movie Bananas some 732 times. Even toward the end of this string, I still would laugh at some of the scenes. Then again, what strikes me as funny is a bit odd. In later years, my wife would catch me laughing away at Rocky and Bullwinkle cartoons. She would shake her head, "But you are supposed to be so smart, how can you watch that drivel?" Drivel! Why, Rocky was insightful and a penetrating commentary on our times. But I had the last laugh when a good friend, and the Dean of Letters and Sciences at the University of Wisconsin at the time, informed her he had bought the entire set of Rocky and his Friends. That shut her up for a few minutes.

But the important thing is that back at the Downer Theater, the manager let me run the place on Thursday evenings. We never sold many tickets on Thursdays but, depending on what was showing, the theater might be quite full. I finally was a very popular guy. I recall one week we had a movie featuring the Rolling Stones. Few tickets were sold that Thursday, but we had a lot of patrons. I am still shocked the damn place did not levitate given the overwhelming smell of weed drifting through the theater.

Besides my soaring popularity, I could eat all the popcorn I could stand. It turned out that I could stand quite a bit of the stuff. Now, this was not a high-pressure job but there was a high note or two. One day I was dozing off at my post early in the evening. I heard someone say excuse me and I turned around to look into someone's chest. I was six feet one inches tall, so this did not happen often. It turned out to be Lew Alcinder, the great basketball player who would soon become Kareem Abdul Jabaar. He was playing for the Bucks at the time and would lead them to their only NBA championship ever. The poor guy must have wondered what he had done wrong to be exiled to such a backwater hick town.

There was a low side as well. I must admit I engaged in a small bit of larceny though I suspect all ticket takers did the same. I would palm an occasional ticket, by that I mean not tear it up. Then I could hand it back to the gal who sold tickets in the booth, and she would resell the ticket a second time. We then would share the ill-gotten proceeds from this second sale. It was never very much and served as a small supplement to our meager wages. But I still never felt good about it; that Catholic guilt stays with you forever. Gee, I hope there is a statute of limitations on petty larceny.

I knew it was time to move on to a real job when ticket taking became a dangerous undertaking. There broke out a rash (well, two or three) robberies of movie theaters in Milwaukee. One night the manager pulled me aside. "We need a plan in case we get robbed," he said earnestly. "Okay, what's your plan?" I asked, just as earnest. "Well," he went on, "I am going to keep the receipts in the office and lock the door. If someone has a gun and forces you upstairs (where the office was), you will use a secret knock." He continued in dead seriousness as my jaw began to drop. "I will then know not to open the door and will call the police."

I looked at him for moment. "Let me see if I have this right. You will be on one side of the door and I will be on the other, being held captive by some criminal with a loaded gun. This is your plan?" He looked at me blankly for a moment. "I have a plan B," I said. "You open the damn door and give the guy all the money. How does that sound?" He agreed with the unassailability of my logic, but I knew it was time to move on.

My days of patching together jobs to keep body and soul together were coming to an end. Probably the only social contributions I had made was to let my poor student friends see a free movie on Thursday nights. It was time to become an adult, or at least more of an adult. I had reservations about this, and as it turned out, my life in the so-called real world would be relatively brief. I would run back to the comforting bosom of the academy in a few short years. In the meantime, I would get my first real job. It was totally by accident. But it set me off on a career that was to be challenging and delightful. But that story can wait just a bit as well. We have other adventures to explore first.

Mom and dad when courting during WWII

Uncle Tim, Grandpa, and Dad in 1943

Dad as a young man

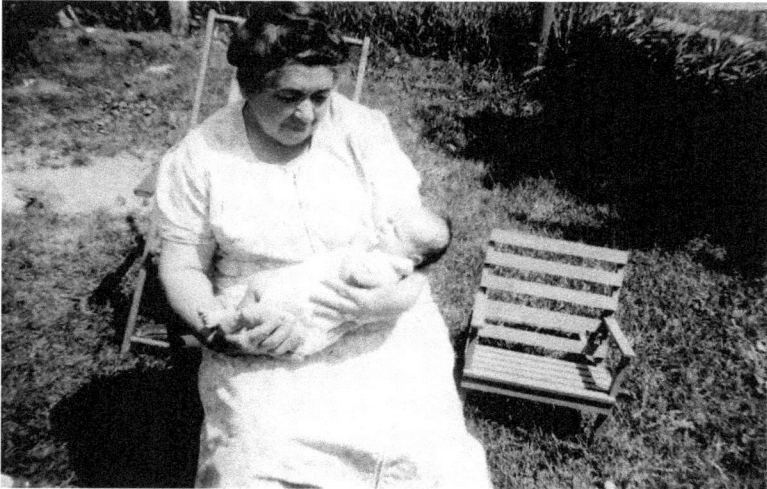

Me as newborn with Nana in 1944

Me, as toddler, with girl from upstairs

My now favorite cousin Carol and I

Endless games on Ames Street

Cousins Paul (left) and Bobbi (right) from our playing days

CHAPTER 7

DEVELOPING

Imagination is everything. It is the preview
of life's coming attractions.
—Einstein

Jonas Cark opened a graduate school on Main Street in Worcester Massachusetts in 1887. It would cater to scholars searching for additional learning opportunities after achieving a Baccalaureate degree in their field of study. Whereas four years of college were sufficient to prepare young gentlemen in earlier years, knowledge was now accumulating at an exponentially faster rate. Four years was no longer enough to master a field of study. Jonas, copying the example first established at Johns Hopkins University, built a place where College graduates could pursue more advanced and specialized learning. He also was an eminently practical man. If his graduate school idea failed, the building he had erected might easily be converted into a shoe factory.

To keep the institution afloat, he next opened its doors to undergraduates as well. Soon, Clark was on firm footing. Its contributions to the world as an institute of higher learning have exceeded anything it might have accomplished as yet another shoe factory, most of which eventually would migrate from New England in search for a cheaper and more compliant labor force. They typically ended-up in the non-union south or the sweatshops of foreign countries.

The intellectual development of this institution was not linear by any means. This small school developed strong faculties in several fields but always remained vulnerable to raids by larger and more affluent institutions. In the 1920s, for example, Columbia University swooped in to raid the strong anthropology department including the eminent Franz Boas. That department never recovered. By the 1960s, however, Clark had developed a decent reputation as an intellectual oasis where free and open inquiry was encouraged. It was not on the stature of iconic small liberal arts schools like Williams or Swarthmore, but it was a very respectable school indeed. It had very strong psychology and geography departments.

I arrived home from the Maryknoll Seminary in the fall of 1963 after a circuitous route through Detroit and Washington, D.C. Perhaps I was delaying the looks of friends and family back home whom I feared might give me that "you screwed up again, Corbett" sneer. We all know that look. They feign concern and wish you the best but just behind that façade is the "so, you couldn't hack it, could you" look. On the way home I visited Don, a hulking but gentle Polish young man I met at Maryknoll, who had left just before me. His folks owned a funeral parlor in the Polish section of town. I helped by directing guests using a few words of Polish I hastily learned. In D.C., I visited Jerry, an old St. John's friend who now was at Georgetown. Oddly enough, Jerry would be there when I arrived at Logan Airport in Boston on my return from Peace Corps some six years in the future, the last time I would see him. This trip, though, would be my first trip to our nation's capital, a city where I would spend so much time in the future.

When I finally arrived home, I looked around for a place to pick up my educational career. My academic success at Maryknoll gave me hope that I just might be able to escape a future that involved real labor. The question was where to look and how to afford it. Going away to the seminary for my college education was quite feasible, it cost my folks nothing. Going away to a real college was something else. They had little to nothing to contribute financially so the cost of an away institution was probably out of the question. Remember, I was not exactly known as an intellectual prodigy early on so full scholarships were not likely to be showered on me. I needed a local place. To complicate matters, the local Catholic colleges did not take spring admissions. But that place across town that almost became a shoe factory did. So, I decided to take a closer look over there.

A den of iniquity . . .

There was one problem with Clark, at least in my world. It was known as a den of Communists and atheists among the Catholic community. Go there and you would lose your faith, your political righteousness and, worst of all, possibly your virginity. Across the street from Clark was St. Peter's Catholic Church, which also ran a high school at that time and which was my school's archenemy on the athletic field. Several times a year the parish priest at St. Peters would rail against the godless intellectuals who had set up shop right across the street. The good pastor would excoriate his parishioners about how good Catholic boys and girls had to be protected against a Satan who employed his wiles on naive youngsters too easily seduced by the sin of intellectualism. Satan was to Catholics like Communists were to the far right, omnipotent and capable of using anything and everything to achieve nefarious ends. Your mind was just another opportunity for evil to play havoc with your soul. There really was no place to hide.

The Catholic view of the place was so dark that I know of not a single St. John's graduate at the time who matriculated at Clark and, as I said, virtually every graduate from my high school went on to college back then. As far as I recall, no Catholic teen who attended any sectarian high school matriculated at Clark during this era. I am not even sure the idea would even occur to them. I certainly never heard any of my high school classmates entertain Clark as a possible college. I doubt that any Catholic high school administrator would submit grade reports or other essential documents to this known den of iniquity, at least not without some protest. This is not to say Clark had no Catholics. It did. They all, however, had come from public high schools. This was further proof that Catholic youth could not be trusted outside of the bosom of mother church. After all, they might start thinking for themselves.

Suddenly, however, that very seditious thought was crowding into my head. Perhaps I should take a shot at attending this lair of sin and temptation. After all, I was reluctant to wait until the following fall to get back to school. But it was more than that. The very prospect of getting out of my comfort zone intrigued me. Why not stretch myself, confront new ways of looking at the world? Maybe that is the way to grow. Besides, that losing one's virginity thing sounded pretty good to me though such a goal yet seemed beyond my reach no matter the school. In any event, the mere prospect of meeting girls who had not dedicated their lives and bodies to St. Virginus of the Uncorrupted Physical Presence was very appealing. St. Virginus, in case you do not keep up with such trivia, is the patron saint of the female body as a holy chalice of the Virgin Mary's pure body or some such nonsense.

My parents were surprisingly supportive. If they did not have to kick in any money, they were ecstatic that I would not be lounging around the house all day. Concerns about the fate of my soul were not among their top worries. They were not exactly strong Catholics. Getting serious about religion would necessitate doing something about their hangovers on Sunday mornings. But I wonder if the more religious members of the family had doubts or concerns. If they did, my mother would have to explain why she was letting her precious little Tommy near Satan's lair. It might have helped that the wife of my dad's brother worked at Clark in a secretarial position. Perhaps that provided some cover. In any case, such concerns never reached my ears, so I went ahead and applied. In fact, I can't recall applying anywhere else. It seemed the only game in town.

The only thing I recall about the application process was an interview with an admissions officer. It now strikes me that they probably did not personally interview all applicants for admission, so what was that all about? Perhaps they did these in-person checks for midterm applicants or because I was in town anyways or maybe I was not a shoo-in for acceptance. I have no idea. The interview itself was low-key and relaxed. What was I interested in studying? Why Clark? What were my favorite books? Was I, hopefully, smarter than I looked? I believe he commented on my College Boards which were decent but lopsided. Not surprising, my verbal score was excellent while my math score was just a little above average. By the end, any concern about my admission had evaporated. He might even have told me at the time, but I can no longer recall

After the fact, another thought struck me. It is very possible that they were thrilled beyond words at breaking through the Catholic Church glass ceiling so to speak. If they got me into their clutches, and I did not sprout horns and a tail right away, perhaps others would follow in my footsteps. After all, I had graduated from one of the top high schools in the area, if not the best, and Clark itself was a fine institution of higher learning located right there in Worcester. They should be getting a steady stream of students from St. Johns; it seemed only natural. They just needed to prime the pump a little. It hit me at some point that they probably would have accepted me if I had been drooling during the personal interview and had told them my favorite book was *Run, Spot, Run.* I should have negotiated a better deal.

As it was, I was able to cobble together enough in scholarships, student loans, and work to pay for an education at a private college. I look at what Clark costs now, and I cannot imagine climbing that mountain today. Of course, I did live at home except for a year at the end when I joined a couple of other guys in a place just off campus. I do recall, however, getting some help from my parents. It was not that much and only for one semester. I can yet recall my mother's hand shaking as she wrote out the check. I am sure she thought this was wasted money, which could have been spent more judiciously for beer, cigarettes, and clothes for herself.

Still, on some undoubtedly cold day in January of 1964, I matriculated at Clark University. I went from about nineteen years within the full embrace of my Catholic, conservative, and working-class culture into a radical new world of ideas and perspectives. I was not overly self-conscious at the time, but I did consider the prospect that my religious beliefs, such as they were, might rub against the secularism, which this institution represented. I looked about for signs of outright apostasy and challenge to my core beliefs at that point in my life. But there was nothing there, nothing overt that is.

No professor railed against God nor did the other students seem to care one way or the other. Occasionally, a professor might ask us to ponder the causality of some observed outcome. "Why did X happen?" When this query was met with silence, at least one frustrated scholar was known to utter, "Did God cause it to happen." Given the topic under discussion that response might not even have sufficed in seminary. It surely was not going to work here so we had to think through the conundrum on our own. But the casual way that the efficacy of divine intervention was played down subtly undermined the foundations of whatever faith I had left.

In the end, I think my religious allegiances simply eroded and washed away. I was not even aware of it. There was no crisis, no late night existential turmoil. I cannot even recall being aware that it was happening. It just seemed gone one day. Perhaps if someone, anyone, had actually pressed me on the topic, I might have argued in favor of a personal deity for a bit. But no one did and that proved an effective way to undo all my prior cultural indoctrination. A lifetime of belief evaporated without resistance or even awareness. It is not unlike those of the Jewish persuasion. When persecuted, one's affiliation and commitment to their roots remained unassailable. But when the external threat disappeared, suddenly interfaith marriage, or at least serious relationships, became possible. Many of my Jewish friends at Clark faced this very issue as their parents questioned their close dalliances with non-Jews of the opposite gender.

The substance of my first semester courses escapes me. I do know they only accepted some of my credits from the seminary. For some unfathomable reason, they were not taken with theology, Gregorian chant, oral interpretation, and the like. I was not yet a sophomore when I started. I did, however, sign up as a psychology major. When rootless and clueless about life, why not take on the strongest department at your institution. In pursuing this discipline, I was convinced that nothing would be learned that would lead to an actual job. Perhaps I could postpone real work indefinitely. Besides, I was a bit taken with the question of what made me tick. For some silly reason, I thought the discipline of psychology might afford some insight into that question. It didn't, just in case you were curious.

What I do recall was a return of my imposter syndrome, big time. Many people suffer from this malady. You don't feel you belong. You are not good enough. Someone is going to come along and figure out you are a fraud. "What are you doing here, kid?

Don't you belong at the remedial school across town?" I was certain each professor would look down his class roster until they came across my name. Their brow would furrow, a small scowl would cross their face, and they would bellow, "Corbett, out!" I would sheepishly pick up my books and slink out of the room.

But it never happened. Days and weeks went by. I even summoned up the courage to speak up in class. Since I did not embarrass myself to tears, I was emboldened to keep at it. At some point, I probably became a pest, trying to slow up those professors who preferred to simply lecture as opposed to engaging the students. I loved the give and take of a more Socratic process. One of my favorite moments, probably not from my first year, involved a professor by the name of Mort Weiner. He walked in with the primary text in his hand. The first thing he did was fling the book across the room. We all jumped in our chairs as it skidded along the floor and bumped up against the wall.

"You are all smart," he started, "so you can read the text on your own. What I want to do in this class is help you think. To do that we will engage in a discussion about some of the bigger issues in Psychology." Wow, this was an intellectual nirvana. I had escaped the tedium and rote learning that had dominated my education up to this moment with exceptions here and there. In my past you pretty much absorbed material, committed it to memory, and regurgitated it back on exams. I could do it well enough, but the process was mind-numbing. I was seldom engaged or excited or stimulated. What we did most of the time did not appear to be real learning. It was a performance that some chimps could emulate though not quite at the same level. On the other hand, some of the brighter chimps might well have put me to shame.

Taking intellectual flight . . .

I particularly loved the give and take that was possible in the smaller classes. Fortunately, Clark was a university of very modest size, no larger than many urban high schools if you only considered the undergraduates. Consequently, most classes were of the small to medium size variety. There were a very few introductory courses that were taught as large lecture-type classes, but mostly I recall classes of very manageable size.

It was even possible to know professors. The scale of the place made many approachable. I could feel something stirring inside me, a growing sense that learning was an adventure. I was overwhelmed with the excitement that the intellectual quest ultimately involved grappling with wicked theoretical conundrums and complex practical questions. The most wicked intellectual challenges were those where no consensus existed respecting the causes, theory, empirical data, and resolutions of whatever puzzle captured you in that moment. For me, this was not an onerous undertaking. This was something to embrace. Soon, the kid who cried so hard on his first day in school fell in love with learning.

During those first months at Clark I remained cautious about my prospects. Okay, no one exposed me as an imposter, but the real test would be when I received my first set of grades. Did the guy who scraped by for so many years belong in a real college? Was my rather surprising academic performance in the seminary a fluke, a simple artifact of who selected themselves into such a place to begin with even though my fellow seminarians certainly struck me as smart enough? Soon, though I did not feel totally out of place, I remained uneasy. It would take a while for me to develop friends and a network to really get some sense of whether I was like the others. We always have angst about belonging in new situations and this was no different.

When I finally saw my first grades, I was stunned. I had to look two or three times, and then check out the name at the top of the page to be sure it was mine. Not only had I done well, I did very well indeed. Between the grades imported from the seminary and those earned during my first semester at Clark, I had soared very high on the class list. I have this memory that I was in the top 10 but it was, after all, not that big of a class. Then it hit me, I can do this work. Perhaps I do belong. Old scripts die hard, they die very hard. I would keep looking for ways to explain away any apparent success for a long time. Moreover, doing so well right out of the gate was not an unambiguous positive. Yes, it confirmed that I belonged in college, even though residual doubts persisted. On the other hand, I began to relax. I can do this stuff. I would never rank that high again but at least I knew I could if I tried.

For me grades were never all that important. Don't get me wrong, I wanted to do reasonably well, so that future options would be open. By future options I meant possibly staying in school to avoid any job that involved heavy lifting. But good grades were never the end all and be all for me. Unlike those who argue that college is about credentials or that it is merely a higher-level vocational school, what I found at Clark was something quite different and special. It was like opening Pandora's box except what poured out were not the evils of the world, depending upon your perspective, but many of its wonders.

Up to this point my mind had wandered around a tiny portion of the world's inscrutable wonders. There were nooks and corners where I had been warned not to look, where evil apparently lurked waiting to snatch up the souls of curious Catholic boys. At Clark, I started to peer into those corners and, guess what, nothing much happened. And what did happen was rather exciting. Rather than evil I found wonder, the rush that comes with peering insides the mysteries of the world. And when you start doing that, old truths come into question.

Some change occurs without notice while others can be traced back to specific events or turning points. I recall taking a political science course in which we covered a series of recent political events, though not so recent anymore. In a matter of fact way, I discovered that the U. S. had intervened in the sovereignty of other countries when we deemed it necessary to our interests and where they were too weak to protest. For example, we might send in the CIA to knock off some popularly elected leader who, heavens forbid, decided to protect a natural resource from exploitation by an American or British fortune 500 company. How dare they? I think what got me is that these events were simply made available as curriculum material in a history or political science class. Such facts were not shared to swing me toward a new point of view. But for me a light went on, again and again. Soon, I was disoriented by the pulsating flashes inside my head. Oh, we are not pure of heart. We do things that we criticize in others. Is this not a double standard? What gives us the right to act one way while damning others for the very same acts. For sure, the devil was making inroads into my neat little world.

Fissures in my childhood culture . . .

Other epiphanies could be traced to an event or some eureka moment. Further on in my Clark career I spent a summer doing a National Science Foundation (NSF) research project, the one, as you may recall that ended with me executing my subject rats and abandoning research psychology as a future avocation. One of the brightest psychology students in the school, named David, also was doing a project. He was very liberal while I was yet struggling a bit with my emerging sense of outrage against atrocities like the Vietnam War. One day we started chatting about the Nam issue, a subject of growing debate among us all. Unlike religion, shedding my ingrained political affinities proved more difficult.

These godless Communists had to be stopped and who else but we pure and selfless Americans could do it.

I kept bringing up arguments to defend our actions there though it was not as if I did not have doubts by this time. I did. But my childhood scripts that we were the good guys fighting evil were deeply rooted and hard to expel. They were almost part of my DNA. I can still remember reading *Masters of Deceit*, a book ostensibly written by J. Edgar Hoover. It laid out in graphic detail the intricate tentacles of the Communist menace as it wound its way into every crevice of American life. I also had been taken with stories of savagery from the Korean War whose images remained somewhat fresh and compelling. There was one vignette that yet gave me nightmares. According to this apocryphal story, some U. S. prisoners of war had glass tubes inserted into their penises and then smashed into small pieces. I could not pee without squirming for weeks after that one.

And there was Dr. Tom Dooley, a Catholic doctor and Notre Dame grad who worked alongside the French in Vietnam as that evil Ho Chi Minh struggled to take his country back from their benevolent foreign overlords...the French. Dooley gave spell-binding speeches at Catholic colleges back in the U.S. depicting the cruel atrocities being committed by the godless Commies on our good Christian, I mean Catholic, brethren. It was no contest, pure good versus pure evil. So, I gave a defense of American foreign policy my best shot.

But I was entering this seminal debate with one hand tied behind my back. By the time I initiated my verbal dual with Dave, I no longer lived in a world of white and black. Issues were becoming fuzzy around the edges, but there were yet parts of my belief system I wanted to keep, perhaps stubbornly so. Perhaps I was afraid to let go of everything all at once. We went at it for a long time, back and forth. I might have an exaggerated memory of that day, but it seems like we did very little work on our respective projects. Science would just have to wait while we resolved this epic issue of our era.

Maybe I struggled so stubbornly because losing would mean giving up a core part of my childhood culture. Maybe I dug in so hard because I did not want to admit that my debate adversary was smarter than I. Maybe I fought to keep my beliefs simply because I was just a stubborn Irishman. But after a while, I knew I was losing. I think I realized that going in. At the end of the day, we agreed to disagree, but I recall going home saying to myself that he was right, and that I had been wrong, dead wrong. Though I needed a bit of time to absorb and fully admit what was happening, I would never again defend the war. In fact, I began to read feverishly on the issue and soon became an early anti-war activist.

Later, I wrote an article for the Clark student newspaper. It was a polemical piece attacking the justifications that President Johnson was using to escalate the conflict. I cannot recall the specifics, but I recall being impressed with my own rhetorical excess. My piece was compelling if I say so myself. In any case, David sought me out in the school cafeteria where I spent half of my college days. It was there that I whiled away many an hour debating the great philosophical and political issues of our time. David, interestingly, was not a regular in our group of philosophers and revolutionaries. He was already married, to a black woman, which was quite radical at the time, he being white and all. Unlike me, he also tended to study and probably attend all his classes. Perhaps this explains the fact that he went on immediately to earn a doctorate in psychology from Harvard. But he sought me out that day and praised my article lavishly. *Wow*, I thought, *I do have a gift with the written word?* His adulation, which he did not distribute freely, meant a lot to me.

Here I was, enjoying a college known for free thinking and spirited intellectual debate in the 1960s where everything was coming under intense scrutiny. My head was beginning to explode with ideas and new perspectives, all crowding in at once looking for space in a finite area. Some things would have to be jettisoned to make room for the new. I loved it, the challenge and the ongoing dialogue and the free and uninhibited exchange of ideas. What impressed me about my good fortune was that those who had gone a more conventional direction were not experiencing the same sense of discovery.

On occasion, I would bring an old high school friend to one of our ongoing bull sessions at Clark, someone who had gone on to

Holy Cross for example. They would mention how much they loved the intellectual feel of Clark. Yes, Holy Cross was a rigorous college with high standards, most likely tougher than Clark back then. But as an all-male institution, the culture at that time was suffocating or so my friends who went there told me. Most conversations were about sports or sex. On occasion, of course, they might reverse the order and debate sex and sports. They wondered what it might be like to talk with and about girls as real people rather than as objects of sexual fascination. That possibility seemed beyond reach for them, however, existing in a male-centered world as they did. They also missed the opportunity to engage in vigorous discussions of the controversial topics of the day. Sure, it happened but just not often.

Once, I visited some old high school buddies at Holy Cross, and we stopped at a bar just off their campus. The owner of the establishment came over to check IDs. As he did, he asked me where I went to school. I said Clark which, apparently, was fine. He then asked the boy next to me who said Holy Cross and that was it. We were informed that they did not serve students who attended that esteemed Jesuit institution. The fine Catholic gentleman who studied there were judged to be little more than caged animals who would ravage the neighborhood establishments if given the slightest opportunity. I was rather taken back by the experience but not shocked.

One Clark gal, Rosalie, took part in an early experiment. Holy Cross and Clark entered into an agreement where students might take an occasional class at the other institution. Perhaps Holy Cross was beginning to think about going coed and wanted to see what might happen if females were brought within reach of their Catholic gentlemen. Better to sacrifice a female Clark student or two than an impressionable young Catholic girl some trusting parents had sent into your care. That might lead to a lawsuit and Catholics, after all, were nothing if not cheap. After her first class or two, she came back laughing. None of the boys would sit next to her. It was as if she were an alien species foisted upon them whose very touch would cause their private parts to wither and drop off. She surely was Satan incarnate, temptation in disguise. As I listened to her, I thanked my good fortune for bringing me to Clark. Oddly enough, Rosalie married a Holy Cross man who was doing graduate work at Clark. She and I are now Facebook friends.

Drifting left . . .

My education at Clark thus sprang from much more than what went on within a classroom. Sure, I learned stuff in my formal classes. The real intellectual skills and dispositions that would carry me through life were taken from the unceasing dialogue outside of the formal curriculum. That is where I refined my analytical skills. That is where I learned to question and probe, to poke at given assumptions and to make sure I could connect the dots on the theoretical frameworks around which I was restructuring the conceptual givens of my life.

Still, not every day brought me a life-changing epiphany. There were the usual high and low moments of any college career. I had one high moment early on. I took this course that covered contemporary events. It was a political science course. The professor was rigid and old school; he still wore bow ties to class and would lecture with a distinct professorial attitude, quite imperious in manner and tone. He was also demanding and a very tough grader. Anyone who got an A on the midterm would be allowed to write a paper in lieu of the final exam. You had demonstrated competence in his eyes and warranted this freedom to do higher level work. He did not give many top marks.

Well, I did it, aced his midterm. He eyed me suspiciously when I met him to discuss my paper. I must have been the only nonpolitical science major to sneak into the elite group. I was more amazed than he since I continued to struggle with the notion that I could do well academically. Just how was this happening? I would listen as other students talked about their backgrounds growing up in the New York area for example. They might casually mention museums or concerts or lectures or other cultural events they had routinely experienced growing up. Culture! Do afternoons at the local bowling alley count? I had little to share in that regard. I don't believe that hanging around on street corners lying about my sex life to other guys who were lying about their sex lives to me would have impressed them. Hell, these kids surely had real sex lives and didn't need to lie.

Anyways, I decided to investigate why Austria didn't fall to the Communists after the Second World War when so many of their neighbors had. After all, Soviet troops occupied part of the country and they never backed off once they had a toe-hold. It was a question that intrigued me and that typically was my motivation to work hard. I was increasingly fascinated with geo-politics and trying to sort out the ever more complex set of beliefs and feelings swirling around in my head. This was a relatively clean issue. We were not that far removed from the McCarthy era of witch hunts and Red scares. Communism still had this aura of invincibility about it . . . at least that is what the right wing of the time kept telling us. Even my idol, John Kennedy had been as much of a Cold Warrior as any of his Republican adversaries. So just how did the Austrians escape the inevitability of the Communist advance?

I no longer recall what I came up with. But I do know that I was gradually developing a more nuanced grasp of the world. My intellectual bent, once released, was ripe for the subtleties that were part and parcel of the real world, and not the cardboard cutout world of heroes and villains. Communism, it soon struck me, was neither monolithic nor inevitable. The more I read, the more this notion of a universal normative and political system that superseded national affiliation and identities became less compelling. The North Vietnamese were more interested in uniting their nation while throwing out foreign oppressors than any concept of a dictatorship of the proletariat. Juárez, the great French socialist at the beginning of WWI, had fought to unite workers to resist the rush to war. Their common socio-political cause of the worker's struggle, he thought, was the only antidote to nationalistic fervor. He was promptly executed by a rabid nationalist and ten-million soldiers soon slaughtered one another in the cause of nationalistic patriotism. Allegiance to one's soil always seemed to trump adherence to some broader, abstract principle. There was no doubt in my mind that the great evils and real villains associated with the Communist system could not long be sustained by its own internal logic. Our paranoid and aggressive response to all things Red struck me as over the top and a terrible waste of lives and treasure.

It is now hard for me to imagine what it was like being a child of the 1950s. The John Birch society got a lot of press back then, they were like the Tea Party of today but without the political clout that comes from the unlimited bank accounts of the Koch brothers and friends. In fact, the father of the current Koch generation was a founder of the Birchers and a paranoid nut case. After he had made a lot of money working with Joe Stalin in the 1930s he decided that Communism sucked. But he went right past sanity to affirm an equally dangerous form of nationalistic Fascism and a super-free market fantasy world. Anyways, the Birchers were uncovering, or so they claimed, even more Communists than Joe

McCarthy, the alcohol-fueled U. S. senator from Wisconsin. They even had our genial president and war hero Dwight D. Eisenhower in bed with the Reds. Between that and diving under my desk in school to practice what to do when the Russkies dropped the big one, which they were certain to do, I was as paranoid as the next guy during the 1950s.

One day, in junior high, a teacher mentioned that at least they did not have an income tax in Russia. That made me suspicious, and I asked him if he was a Commie. He visibly blanched. I realized that had I complained to someone, he might have gotten into serious trouble. I mean, no less a hallowed icon as J. Edgar Hoover, head of the FBI, was warning us of the omnipresence of the Red Menace. They had planted cells of small groups of children in our country. When they grew up they would look just like real Americans but secretly would be ready to strike when Moscow gave the word. They would infiltrate our key systems and, when unleashed, arise to start the revolution. You could trust no one, not even a poor schmuck who was teaching junior high in my godforsaken, run-down excuse for a school. We all had to be vigilant. In the end, I had been too nice to turn him in. J. Edgar Hoover would have been so disappointed in me.

Bumps in the scholarly road . . .

Not all my time was spent peering into the vagaries of international politics. I did spend some time in the classroom taking real courses with uneven success. I generally did well in the courses where I could BS at will. I loved essay exams since that played into my wheelhouse, I could weave great narratives on just about any topic while knowing little of substance. The courses where you really had to learn something were more of a challenge. Frankly, some of my failures were almost comical. This included anything with numbers or formulae.

Every social science major, for example, had to take at least one statistics course. I had hated all things mathematical ever since high school when we had to solve those simple algebraic problems, simple to everyone but me that is. You remember the problems: the boat is going upstream at twenty miles per hour, the river is flowing in the other direction at ten miles per hour. How long will it take the boat captain to eat his lunch? While I knew there were simple formulae for figuring these stupid things out, my brain always froze. Now, what was X? Besides, who cares? The captain will finish his lunch when it is finished.

Without thinking, I simply signed up for the one offered in psychology. This statistics course was taught by a guy from central casting if you were looking for a classic nerd. His first name was Joachim, who names their kid that? Anyways, he was a young man with a distinct accent, probably from lower Transylvania I think, sporting coke-bottle thick glasses. But that was not the real problem. He was painfully shy. He really could not look at the students he was supposed to teach. He would lecture while writing undecipherable equations on a blackboard about which he had some unholy fixation. On occasion, he would recall that there were scores of lost students behind him. He then would spin around and look at us with terror in his eyes. That would not last long as a look of panic, or was it disgust, would cross his face. Immediately, he would rotate back to his blackboard once more. I was lost, to say the least.

That was not the worst part. The class was scheduled for something like 8:30 AM on Tuesdays, Thursdays and, get this, Saturdays. Yes, the class I hated the most, and which was beyond my grasp, had one session scheduled for the first thing each Saturday morning. And since he could not entice us into the classroom with his seductive lectures, he extorted our attendance with unannounced pop quizzes. Yup, it is true. Every now and then, he would pop a Saturday morning quiz on us as I struggled to revive my addled brain from the previous evening's revelry or work on the graveyard shift at the hospital, no pun intended. How I managed to pass the course remains a mystery to this day. It must have been a very close-run thing.

Then there was the time I shot myself in the foot, not literally of course. One fine day I amused myself with the following bit of illogic. Some of the early pioneers in the psychology world were from Germany and Austria and wrote their master works in German. Therefore, if I were serious about this field, perhaps I should learn to read German. I wonder if I had engaged in this piece of so-called logic while dead drunk. Everything you needed to tackle this field had already been translated into English, moron.

In case you missed it, this is a classic back-forty idea, an exemplar back-forty idea. Let me explain once again what a back-forty idea is, just in case you have forgotten from my 247 earlier such idiocies. If you are taken with an idea that is utterly devoid of any redeeming value whatsoever, it is a back-forty idea. You should immediately be brought out to the back-forty acres of the farm and shot. After all, you would not permit any animal that imbecilic and unproductive to waste more of our precious air. This idea was, without doubt, an indisputable back-forty idea. Still, I could not convince anyone to put me out of my misery. No amount of pleading would convince the authorities that putting me down, as they do with terminally ill pets, would be an act of compassion to me and a blessing for all of society. So, I dutifully went through the course and did miserably.

Biology, or was it botany, was another course where you had to really know something. In any case, it was considered one of the easier courses that social science types like myself could take to meet their science requirements. I guess we did not have a "rocks for jocks" course probably because we did not have many jocks. Jonas, the founder of Clark, prohibited the university from ever having a football team. This was a good thing since it is hard to imagine the schools against which we could compete, perhaps some local high schools or Anna Maria, the all girl's college located nearby.

Back then, the school's nickname was the Scarlets (appropriate for a Communist institution) and its visual, iconic representation was a dorky-looking young boy wearing shorts, carrying a book, and wearing large glasses. This was not a vision to strike fear into the hearts of opponents. Now, they are called the cougars, though still no football team.

I recall doing marginally better in this science class than in stats or German, but I knew I was not Nobel Prize material. That was clear to anyone paying attention to my feeble efforts to master the material, particularly in the lab portion of the class. This part of the course was taught by the teaching assistant. She was a petite Asian lass with a strong accent. Like my statistics teacher, communication was not optimal, not that I would have understood things any better even if I could figure out what the hell she was saying. To put it mildly, I was a total klutz in lab. I could never get my microscope to work properly. My only hope was the Jewish kid from New York next to me. He seemed real smart and knew what was going on.

Naturally, there was a final exam for the lab portion of the class. I approached it with dread, if not abject panic. As I marched to my inevitable fate I saw the little Jewish kid who had labored next to me all semester. I grabbed his shirt in a panic, "Tell me everything you know." But that was silly since it was far too late for any last-minute reprieve. As I recall, the exam had lots of microscopes and other exhibits set up. You moved from one to the next and identified what you were looking at or answered some question about the specimen under observation. I might as well have been looking at items from the far side of the moon. There was absolutely no doubt in my mind that I was a dead man. The only thing left to do was attach a toe tag. Not literally but you know what I mean.

A week or so later, the TA handed back our exams. When she approached me, I thought she had a funny expression on her face. For a moment, panic hit me. "I must have gotten a zero." I really did believe that. I prepared myself for establishing some new level of futility and perhaps setting some record for the worst score ever in the history of this class. The other students could carry me out on their shoulders screaming, "Corbett's number one," in total futility that is. Can you get a minus grade, maybe for spelling your name wrong? But then I looked at my mark. It was like looking at those first semester grades all over again. I looked once, twice, three times. To my utter shock, I had achieved one of the best marks in the class . . . thus her expression of amazement, not disgust. To this day, I have no idea how I did it. I really was guessing most of the time or thought I was. Go figure! One thing was certain, my suspicion that grades were rather arbitrary was reinforced.

I am reminded of the time my wife took a statistics course many years down the road when she thought she needed to beef up her skills in that area. Occasionally, she also would have a back-forty idea, like the one she had in marrying me. Now, she is very smart, graduating from the UW Law School with honors. But she had my phobia about numbers. That really is an epidemic, someone should notify the CDC. In any case, she came into the house after her first test with tears in her eyes. "I am quitting," she announced, "I failed the exam with a mark of 60.64."

What? I thought, grabbing the paper from her, suspecting that something was amiss. I was teaching at the college level by then and that grade sounded fishy if not totally improbable. In truth, she had 60 points out of a possible 64; she had aced the quiz. She expected to fail so she thought she had. We were both liable to let our self-beliefs get in the way of our performances though my performances did, in fact, match my low self-esteem on many an occasion.

Psychology was my major, so I was supposed to do well in those courses. And I generally did. There was one course that was a year-long, two semesters, marathon. I want to say it was child psychology or developmental psychology. This was a typical social science type course in which I was expected to do well. I did my usual amount of preparation of the final exam at the end of the first semester and went in with some degree of confidence. But then grades came back I received a final grade of C+.

What! I could not believe it. I went into the final with a decent grade, so I must have failed or nearly failed the final. Though I had occasional lapses in courses where one had to know something, I always managed to do very well in courses like history, literature, political science, and everything in my major except statistics of course. My aunt, my father's brother's wife, worked at Clark. She was a secretary in the economics department. Somehow, she always got my grades before I did so there was no hiding anywhere. Fortunately, I was making honors most semesters, so all was well. A C+ in my major, how would I explain that away?

Today, most students would be in the professor's office in a flash asking for an explanation and an apology. Back then, we meekly accepted whatever was doled out to us even though I was pretty sure a mistake had been made. Okay, I rationalized, I would make up for this failure in the next semester. My intentions, as usual, were way ahead of my behavior. As the end of the semester approached, I was in my usual position of catching up. Still, I was determined to bear down and do well on the final exam. This time for sure. But the night before the final I had yet to start my usual cramming for a big exam. I frantically pulled all my course material about me, opened my text, and immediately fell asleep.

I awoke the next morning. *What happened?* I thought. When reality set in, I realized that I had dozed off immediately upon beginning to study. First fear and then resignation coursed through me. In despair, I packed up my materials and wandered down to campus. I listened to the others as they threw questions back and forth that they thought might be on the exam. I listened in growing despair. It was hopeless. I was a goner. So, I walked into the exam with that serene sense of calm that those about to die often possess. It turned out to be an essay exam. That was at least one good thing. I looked at the first question, just exhaled, and let fly.

Much as with my science lab exam, I was stunned when I received the results. I don't know the grade on the final. I know I went in with a B or B+ or something like that and came out with an A for the semester. Clearly, I aced it. But how? I had studied for the first semester final and did poorly. I did not study for the second semester final and aced it. What lesson should I draw from that? Of course, I drew the wrong lesson. Preparation was clearly overrated in terms of getting good grades. Obviously, the whole process was capricious and beyond my understanding. God, I had decided by this time, was a malevolent comedian who was always screwing with our minds, just like he did by placing us among gorgeous women starting at the Catholic hospital but with no chance of scoring with any of them. It would be better to rely upon my charm and wit than any scholarly application, along with a touch of my Celtic gift for imaginative storytelling. Why work if all was random.

A stimulating environment . . .

A lot of my learning took place outside of the classroom. I fell in with a very smart crowd of students who were intellectually curious and motivated, a mix of undergraduates and graduate students. Clark was small enough where the typical barriers were not that rigid. Undergraduate and graduate students mixed, as did students and faculty on occasion. We spent hours debating the raging political and intellectual topics of the time, sharpening our analytical skills on one another. It was a crucible of parry and thrust with others as quick as you. Great training indeed!

I spent hours in the food area where students congregated back then. Today, there seems to be many such places at a much bigger Clark but back then we had the one. That made it easier to know where to go to pick up a lively conversation. It was the '60s after all and everything was open for analysis and deconstruction. We did not know that the future held a return of rampant income and opportunity inequality and that free inquiry would someday be considered un-American or that conservatives would try to turn the great universities into higher-level trade schools. We would argue and cajole and push each other to hone our own thinking and to help frame our own foundational beliefs. It was an intellectual firestorm within which our core selves were framed and solidified. Shapeless philosophies and perceptions were sharpened through intense debate and argument.

It was like a movable feast. The cast of characters changed from time to time, sometimes the location, but the sense of inquiry and challenge never died. Like romance, this was the time of life when new ideas seemed fresh and raw. It was like no one else had stumbled upon your own insights. You were breaking new ground. Deep inside you suspected that this was not true. As in love, while your erotic impulses were as old as time itself; the blush of first discovery remained fresh and exciting. We were intense for sure yet approached everything with a fierce risibility. We never lost our ability to smile, to laugh.

Starting in Clark and continuing through Peace Corps and a master's degree in Milwaukee, there were so many late-night bull sessions. Each, or at least many, seemed replete with insights and intellectual breakthroughs that kept us going for hours. You did not want some of these sessions to end. We surely recognized all the structural problems our society faced. We were not blind, not totally naive. We thought, however, that we would have the opportunity to correct those shortfalls in our lifetimes. So maybe we were just a bit naive. Still, we all hungered for more analysis and dialogue. It was better than sex itself. Of course, at Clark I was still waiting to find out what sex was all about but now that failure was mostly in my court.

By the end of this process, I learned to speak out for myself. I probably was wrong more than right, but I began to see that my mind was a subtle and nuanced tool. I could weave clever narratives about what was going on around me in rather compelling ways. People listened to me. They liked what I wrote. This process did not occur overnight but slowly. Years of encrusted self-doubt are not swept away quickly. The embedded scripts are replaced with newer, healthier versions of self-appreciation, but often at a glacial pace. For me, that process started at Clark, but more would be required to sweep all the accreted detritus away.

You picked up some information in classes and many other ideas on your own. Years later, when reading essay exams or serving on a doctoral student's dissertation committee I would get frustrated at those who never ventured into the realm of their own thoughts. Okay, I could see undergraduates being intimidated but graduate students should start thinking for themselves. Too many students today parrot what everyone else says about a topic. Yes, it is essential that you show us you are familiar with the literature. What marks you as a potential member of the academy, however, is what you do with the information you have absorbed. What makes sense, what does not, can you spin things in an ingenious or at least a coherent way?

Sometimes, I would stop a student in the middle of a defense to ask them directly what they personally thought on some topic, not what others have said on the issue. Then I would stare into their panicked, blank face. I would kick myself for torturing them so. I wasn't trying to be mean, I really wanted to give them a chance to shine. I loved that part of the learning experience. Then I would find myself answering my question for them even though I often know very little about the substance of their topic.

When I first arrived at the University of Wisconsin, I would occasionally argue with Irv Piliavin, my mentor who brought me to this hallowed place. Irv had first studied physics before switching to social welfare. He was known as a rigorous empiricist who loved research above all else. He took the position that undergraduates at Wisconsin were fortunate because they were being taught by the best researchers available. That made little sense to me. First, those best researchers were primarily interested in teaching graduate students, particularly doctoral candidates, and only if they got stuck in a classroom at all. Teaching was generally viewed as a waste of time, a task to be performed because people insisted that Universities should do such a thing. How foolish! This was not an issue peculiar to Wisconsin by any means, faculty at all top research universities felt that way. They might have office hours, if they teach a course where teaching assistants cannot be thrust into that role. But the huge gulf between faculty and undergraduates remains intact.

My affection for smaller, liberal arts colleges started at Clark. The faculty was approachable. I assume they were excellent researchers. I know they were in the psych department, which had a superb national reputation. At the same time, teaching remained important to the place. Clark could not rest on its research portfolio against better known and endowed institutions. How the current crop of students viewed the place was important to prospective students. Most of my classes were reasonably small, and I probably was a pest as I interrupted teachers with incessant questions. I always loved the give and take of a class, as I did with my peers in our nonstop bull sessions. From conversations over the years, we all loved the place.

It also helped that it was the 1960s. The old comfortable world order was breaking down and everything was being challenged. That is exactly what I discovered at Clark. I went through that uncertain and private place of doubt and resurrection. I walked in on day one a good Catholic boy, straight from his seminary training. I walked out a few years later with a head full of seditious ideas while having led the leftist organization on campus. In the meantime, I tore down the carefully constructed framework that was my ethnic, Catholic worldview and replaced it with something much more complicated.

There were no simple truths. It is amazing how easy it is to go through life with a bunch of givens. There is a God, and this is what you are supposed to believe and how you are supposed to act. Of course, you soon find out that not even the Bible is much of a guide to the truth. Believers in liberation theology on the far left and rabid segregationists on the far right look to the same text for inspiration. In the end, you must figure things out for yourself.

That is what Clark gave me, or at least gave me an opportunity to develop, an environment in which to figure things out by myself. It was not always easy. When I worked the 11-7 shift at St. Vincent's, I sometimes wondered how I did it all. How did I get across town to school? For a while, I had a girl friend's car. When I did not, maybe I took buses, at least two. But I think I walked a lot. I would get off at 7:00 AM, have some coffee with the nursing students and flirt a bit (Catholic girls, no hope), and then set off. I might just make it to one 8:30 class I recall vividly. It was art appreciation or something like that. The professor often would turn the lights down as he showed slides of ancient classics or renaissance masterpieces.

Perhaps he had a catchy delivery, but I don't believe so. At 8:45, my handwriting would begin to waiver and then slide to an illegible scrawl. It was as if someone had turned a switch off. After a five-to-fifteen-minute snooze, I would pick up again and be good for the rest of the day. I believe I aced that course. After all, it was not statistics. Of course, when I say good that was by my standards. I suspect that others watching this zombie walking around campus were drawing their own conclusions.

I still love walking around the Clark campus. It was a time out of time. A few years ago, I sat down with two fellow students from that era. Both have been around academia all their lives. Yet, the three of us reminisced longingly about our heady days at Clark when we started to become who we are today. I am distraught at those conservatives who would destroy liberal arts colleges in the attempt to trammel independent thinking, turning universities into glorified vocational schools. Education is more than technical skills. It is the capacity to sift and winnow and integrate and blend seemingly disparate concepts into coherent and sensible wholes. It is the ability to construct logical models about how things work. It provided a skill set to make sense out of life, which is exactly what conservatives fear most.

I still find it odd that so many struggle with college. Sure, some enroll in these rip-off, for profit scams that should be shut down. Others probably attend only because of parental or peer pressure and have no interest in being there. A good number matriculate simply to make more money someday. So many kids puzzle me by failing to embrace this opportunity. One of the smarter kids in my high school class, someone who performed far better than I at St. John's, struggled mightily at the next level. I recall he bounced around two or three schools before I lost touch. I don't know if he ever graduated. What possibly could have happened?

College for me was a liberation and an enlightenment. I loved every minute. I must have, I spent most of my adult life in one. My mind continually exploded with new ideas and challenges all the time. If I had approached college as an extension of high school or as a higher-level vocational prep regimen I would have died on the vine. I really wonder if I would have thrived as well at Holy Cross, a good very Jesuit school but not exactly a citadel of free thought and intellectual inquiry.

If there is a God, perhaps he looked down upon me and said, "This poor sap needs a push in a different direction. If he goes on as programmed, he will be bored, unchallenged, and totally predictable. At best, he will either fail in school, probably in life, or manage to endure some white-collar career where he spends part of each day contemplating ways of ending his miserable existence no matter how much money he makes. I guess I better send him off to a seminary to shake things up."

There were plenty of hints that I would have been miserable had I not altered course when I did. My resistance to the prevailing racist and exclusionary norms of my childhood culture probably was clue number one. Those intellectual doubts about the tenets of my faith in high school as I sat in religion class were probably clue number two. My persistent itch to find something in life beyond myself probably was clue number three. I needed that push to get on track though. Trying the seminary was important. Leaving when I did so that I could not matriculate at Holy Cross right away was also important. Taking a chance on an institution that no one else from my world had tried was the most important of all. Clark thrust me in the right direction, it brought out the latent rebel in me. Still, it was only the beginning of the journey. Much more was to come.

CHAPTER 8

LOVING

Love is a serious mental disease.

—Plato

I will be honest here since always being Tom is rather boring (what a terrible witticism). This will look like a love story, but it is not, not really. It is more an exploration of the universal qualities that those first emotional connections store somewhere in the recesses of the heart. There are a few early, intimate connections that shape our understanding of love and all that comes later. They teach us the core lessons about the fragility and the promise of human connections, lessons that can be learned nowhere else. As such, they are fundamental and irreplaceable.

My early connection was with a woman named Lee. We met in college. Yes, there were other women as I described earlier but this is the one relationship that stretched me as an emotional being. While this rather tragic connection certainly was not memorable for either its length or its early intensity, its denouement was instructive and certainly compelling. Eventually, too late, I found things within that I did not know existed. We never consummated the relationship, never came close in fact. But it was a first love and thus a special love. It is such early experiences that teach us so much about those painful, unavoidable afflictions that touch our hearts.

Those first compelling attractions are like our first normative, philosophical, and political epiphanies in college. They overpower you with a bright intensity that stays with you a long time, perhaps forever. It is not that they are always deeper and more meaningful than what comes later, especially commitments to a life partner. Still, they have a special quality that opens you up to new possibilities. They set the standards by which later emotions are judged. I certainly emerged from my early connection with Lee a far different young man than I was at the beginning. So, Lee gets a chapter of her own.

Who is that woman?

I retain an impression, though vague, of the first time I saw Lee. She walked across a room, I cannot recall where. It is a singular image that remained indelibly imprinted in my head. One look and it felt like a punch to the stomach. "Who is she?" I think I asked someone long forgotten followed up by the equally inane inquiry "Where did she come from?" Something primitive had hit me—an attraction so fundamental that a sharp ache replaced the space where my heart had once resided. It was young love, mindless and hopeless. I had never felt it before. Mr. Detached was shattered. Wow, does that feeling suck the big one!

Despite my terrible lack of self-confidence, I decided I would make my patented move immediately. I was determined not to let this vision slip from my grasp. Now was the time! I would do it, really? Several weeks later, or was it months, I was still saying to myself, "Now is the time." Good intentions were not enough to get me beyond my usual paralytic state when it came to the opposite sex. Mr. Feel Nothing could not escape the most primal emotion of all . . . abject fear. To be clear, I was witty, smooth, engaging, smart, and even charming when it came to be relating to females in a general way. As a casual friend, I could make them laugh, inspire them with my brilliance, and soothe them with my ability to listen. Really, I was fine when in any casual setting! I only froze when I had to put my fragile ego on the line, when I had to intimate that I might care.

In any case, my patented move was never anything to brag about. In fact, it is better not discussed at all. But somehow, I managed to suck it up and approach her. I cannot for the life of me recall the circumstances. Yet, in my own stumbling, bumbling way I managed to get out an incoherent request that we do something together, maybe even something like a date. I forget what unique and unforgettable experience I dangled before her as a lure to go out with me. Undoubtedly, it was something a bit more unforgettable than a trip to Paris and a bit more imaginative than "your place or mine."

Of course, she was thrilled at the prospect of a date with me. I think she said *no* before I finished my stuttering request. Oh, there were the usual comforting words about how nice she thought I was, but there was this guy she was sort of seeing and thanks for the offer. At least she did not use the one about needing to bathe the dog. Even I figured out that was lame after the first dozen times it was used. Really, how often do you bathe a damn dog? And besides, they did not allow pets in the dorms. In truth, she might have used it since I never heard much of anything after the word *no*. Funny, a man's life is full of those moments when he is getting shot out of the sky, except for those rich guys of course. Still, you never get quite used to plummeting to earth in that rhetorical flaming plane. You might think that by the four hundredth aerial disaster, getting shot down by a gal would become second nature. It does, by a fraction, as the numbing sensation of the all-too-familiar sets in. But sometimes a sharp pain returns, and this was one of those times.

My self-image at the time competed with the amoeba on the evolutionary scale. I did not see myself as attractive to the opposite sex. Perhaps I was a nice guy, with more than my share of wit and charm and smarts, but not attractive in the physical sense. Her *no* should have been that, the end of any further pursuit. Normally, I would have scuttled off to some corner to lick my wounds and lament the fact that I had once again failed as a member of the male brotherhood. Let's face it, why would any attractive female show interest in a lump like me. And by failed, I mean crashed and burned with no doubt or confusion about any last-minute reprieve.

Lee had struck a chord, however. My reaction had been unsettling, inexplicable, and even frightening. Besides, when she said no there was a hint she would have preferred to say yes. I imagined the tiniest hint of regret in her *no*. Usually, most girls said *no* in a clear and unambiguous manner. "Go out with you, hah, I would rather be buried alive with a thousand venomous snakes!" That would be followed by hints about a restraining order and maybe a vague suggestion that a visit from someone named Vinnie the Enforcer was in my future. But not in this case, her *no* did not seem final or so I rationalized at that moment. I was desperate. That should have been clue one that this woman was different.

I was still hanging around with Carol. Hell, I liked her a lot and could explain away her inexplicable attentions to me. I was merely a harmless fill-in while her true love was away, or so I imagined. I was a space-filler. Yet, that relationship also remained improbable to me, yet hard to fully explain. Carol was beautiful, brilliant, comfortable, physically responsive, and good for sharing ideas. This connection was an inexplicable gift. And yet, all that still was not enough to generate in me that special sense of anxiety that just the sight of Lee did. Yeah, this new set of sensations really sucked the big one.

Unbelievably, I found myself plotting how I would make another run at Lee. This was unprecedented. I typically never returned to the field of play after being shot down. This should have been clue number two that something had really gone wrong here. The guy who had erected an inviolable shell of uncaring, emotional isolation had feelings? Who knew? Damn, they were coming up with miracle drugs for all kinds of personal impairments. Why didn't they have a pill for this? Of course, they did but they were illegal, and I was more into politics than that counterculture thing.

After considering various plots and options, rejecting them all out of paralytic fear, a possibility fell right into my lap. I needed subjects for a class psychology experiment. Other students were fair game in this instance. I could talk to her once again using science as a pretext and pretending that my excess perspiration was a return of that recurring malaria I had contracted in Canada. Maybe I even had some inducement to offer my volunteers like money or candy. I myself recall volunteering for experiments where I got the shit shocked out of me by grad students with vaguely Viennese accents as if recently plucked from central casting for a Freud biopic. My experiment was far less dangerous. I casually, so casually, asked her to help me out. I was stunned when she didn't appear to see right through this obvious ruse. Really, it was awfully transparent. For some unfathomable reason, she agreed.

All went well until I realized the little experiment was coming to an end. It involved learning patterns of random strings of letters under varying conditions, the value to science now long gone. Unless I came up with a plan she was going to walk away and out of my life. What to do? Summoning up my meager courage, I smoothly asked her for coffee after we finished, merely as a reward for helping me out of course. We could then wander over to the student union and chat. Then, we would do a weekend in Boston followed by a Caribbean cruise and a big wedding in Hawaii and a bunch of children. Wait, get real, you moron. I hated the very thought of marriage and would rather face the Viet Cong than sire children!

Then I snapped back to the real world. In truth, I didn't feel very smooth. Rather, I was dying by this time. I was sure that at any moment my plane would burst into flames once again and head for earth in yet another dating death spiral. And this was not even a date. We talked, and she showed no sign of sprinting away or suddenly remembering that dog needing a bath. At some point we must have agreed to get together again because we did. That was even nicer. After all these years, I can yet recall how my heart pumped under my shirt. I could never figure out how girls could look so cool when I was about to drop a load in my pants. She probably was not as cool and detached as I imagined. Over four decades later, she yet recalled a few the nonsense string of letters I asked her to memorize that day. Wow!

Lee and I became a couple. When she mentioned being uncomfortable if I were to continue "seeing" Carol, I gently detached myself from that relationship though the three of us remained good friends. She also saw Lee and me as a natural couple, and after all, she was engaged to this other guy. There were dates, I guess, but you never really dated as such in college. There were many nights drinking beer with a few other cronies at a favorite local bar. We just spent a lot of time together. She had a car, which was great. She would drive me home at night and then, after checking to see if I had a criminal record, just gave me her car to use. I only screwed up once when I parked in the wrong place and had to get it released from the police impound area where it had been towed. She forgave me though she did gently suggest she might separate me from my family jewels if I used her car to pick up other girls. But she said this very sweetly, which is what she was, sweet and innocent but armed with a wicked wit.

There were visits to her home in Peabody, a town north of Boston, and the meeting of the parents, whom I liked a lot. Her extended family was Greek Orthodox except for the dad, who was an Irishman. He and I bonded immediately as two detached outsiders with dry senses of humor surrounded by all these hysterical Greeks. Her mother was very pleasant the first time I met her. The second time I visited Lee's home she rushed toward me and gave me a big hug. Decades later, I finally understood that, to her mom, I looked great compared to the Greek guy who had been pursuing Lee. Anyways, hugging and stuff was not done in my family, not even during sad moments like wakes and weddings. I almost backed up through the wall.

I was invited to the "extended family" dinner celebrating Lee's graduation and other family celebrations like engagement parties for Lee's cousins, surely a strong commitment in the Greek worldview. Her whole family liked me a lot. Lee mentioned decades into the future that her mother made a pitch for me the night before Lee was to get married to her first husband. I have found over time that I do well with mothers. Not so much with the daughters. My guess is that mothers see in me a kind of harmless schmuck that could not possibly be a threat to their daughters while the daughters see right through me.

Lee and I did enjoy a certain physical intimacy, but it was sensual and not sexual. I cannot quite recall the first kiss, but I sensed her responding to me from the start, which surprised me largely because she seemed so inexperienced. It surprised her as well which she mentioned at the time. She had only dated one other man, this somewhat older Greek guy who was really taken with her. This was the guy toward which she felt an obligation when I first asked her out and whom her mother apparently disliked. But it was, as I eventually learned, more a sense of obligation she felt toward him, not attraction. He was persistent and quite devoted to her.

So, I wanted to be gentle and reassuring and anything but assertive. She did not need that. I recall us spending a lot of time cuddling, her head nestled under my chin where I would nibble at her ears (which tickled her) and played along her neck with my lips. It is a good thing I was a master at infinite foreplay that would never go anywhere. If that becomes an Olympic event I am a lock. Through all this, we never had sex.

We only spent one night together, a night where the details remain unclear for me, but the emotions remain diamond hard for both of us. Images and feelings of that night remained with us four-plus decades later when we reconnected via cyber-space. She still called it a magical experience all those years later. We both independently recall lying in bed in the morning, the curtains of her Boston apartment at the time moving in the morning breeze. I can recall it feeling so right. Surely there would be many more such mornings, but no. She remembered the details better than I, asking me questions about it. One of her memories is that she served me the worst meal she ever made for anyone, according to her. I cannot recall the meal at all. I only recall sweet memories. I could not agree more with her assessment that there was magic in our moments together even without sex.

Looking back over the decades, only God remembers what we talked about. Whatever it was, it no longer matters. Though a psychology major, she was much more into science stuff. Indeed, she knew how to use a microscope and eventually would get a doctorate in molecular virology or some such thing. She was much less into politics and social issues than I or Carol. None of that mattered. The laughs and the warmth and the sweetness were what left an immutable mark.

I felt toward Lee feelings that were new and raw. Once, we were driving and came across a family with a stranded car. I stopped to help. Once they were all okay, I recall her looking at me with such warmth and love. I will never forget that look, ever. Another time we had seen some romantic movie called *A Man and a Woman*. "What did you think?" she asked through moistened eyes as we left the theater. I dismissed it with some comment about it being just another chick flick. This sent her storming up the street as I stumbled to catch up. She did have just a bit of an Irish-Greek temper. Then she would turn those doe-like eyes on me and I melted immediately. "Best movie ever made," I intoned immediately. I was slow but not retarded.

Looking at pictures of us at the time, we surely made a wonderful-looking couple. It seemed as if we belonged together. I am sure it would not have surprised anyone if we were to announce that we were going to be married. But that would never happen at that point in my life. Beneath the surface both she and I were members of a select club known as the walking wounded. I could feel myself struggling against falling deeper in love with her. It was a classic battle of head and heart. My head, driven by years of watching my poster parents for dysfunctional marriages told me not to go there. My heart marched right on toward deeper levels of affection.

In the end, it might well have been easier just to run away. I left the country to go to India and the Peace Corps (PC) in the summer of 1967. The reasons going half way around the world were valid and quite altruistic. It fit well within my sense of personal responsibility and commitment to saving mankind. In retrospect, though, there was also a sense of convenience to it all. I did not have to confront the emotional turmoil I felt toward Lee and the inevitable end suggested by such feelings. I ran away from what I could not handle straight on—the fear of really committing myself. The specter of the Vietnam draft was not inconsequential but not the prime reason for service in India since graduate school was still a deferment option at that moment.

The months preceding my departure are now obscured by fading memories and conflicted recollections. She emotionally withdrew from me in the spring of 1967, something she did not recall later, perhaps because I may have approached her with conflicted behaviors and attitudes. I was slated to head to the other side of the world in just a couple of months. It is now virtually impossible to completely resurrect what was in our minds and hearts back then though we tried after reconnecting. My best guess is as follows. I very likely signaled a bunch of my insecurities and uncertainties to Lee probably in a hundred subtle and nuanced ways. She, in turn, retreated into her safe place where I was least likely to reach her. I, in turn, saw her retreat as "evidence" of her indifference toward me. That just confirmed my belief that I was unlovable. After all, even though others saw me as "ruggedly good looking," I had enormous difficulty accepting the fact that Lee was attracted to me. The train that would ultimately wreck our emotional connection was picking up speed.

In retrospect, we may well have been engaged in a push-pull dance where a fundamental attraction was offset by an equal amount of fear generated by passions that might well get the best of us. For reasons I can no longer even fathom, I did not ask her to join me at JFK airport to say good-bye. While India was a lot more than running away from Lee, it allowed me to run away from all my fears of rejection and, more likely, my fears of acceptance. And so, we parted with many unaddressed issues and many more complex feelings. The twelve thousand or so miles were enough miles to escape all that confusion.

About a year after getting to India, I received a Dear Tom letter. The day, the moment, it arrived stands out as clearly as if it happened yesterday. Mail, in India, was the highlight of the average day where excitement was typically defined as watching the water buffalo jump (well, not very high I admit) as an occasional bus whipped by. You have no idea of tedium unless you have been to my spot in the bleak desert of Rajasthan. So, I clutched the letter from Lee with delight. My site partner Randy was babbling on about something while I ripped it open and soon read that, alas, Lee would not be waiting for me. She was getting married.

Now, you must understand, I was *Mr. Never Going to Fall in Love*. Growing up, there was no way I was going to make a commitment or get married or anything of that ilk. I had been raised by parents who patented the "marriage made in hell" board game. Replicating that sorry story was the last thing I wanted to do. And to ensure against any unintended progeny of mine facing a similar fate, I underwent a vasectomy shortly after returning to the States. Amazingly, I was found sane in the psychological work up required before the procedure. And yet, I had been using the word marriage in my letters to Lee, though in rather equivocal, if not ambiguous, language. In retrospect, my firm, unyielding opposition to commitment and marriage clearly was cracking all around me. It cracked just a little too late.

As Randy continued to babble (I no longer heard a word he said) I experienced feelings that I recall to this day, almost fifty years later. It was as if the air had been sucked out of my lungs and there was nothing to fill the vacuum. I held up my hand to stop Randy and told him what happened. I can't recall what we talked about after that, but we did get roaring drunk that night.

Reconnecting . . .

My reconnection with Lee after several decades started by accident and, in truth, did not start as a search at all, at least not as a search for Lee. It started in 2010 as a simple search for a new accessory for my spouse's cell phone. While she looked over the offerings, I naturally gravitated to the new toys for sale. Admittedly,

I am a techno dunce. My VCR still blinks 12:00 AM, or it did until they found a way to get it right remotely. But I like looking. What guy doesn't like looking (oh, we're talking about phones here) and they offered such a great deal, a second free phone and another $100 off for being so gullible. Out I walked with two Motorola Droids. I had a smart phone, how ironic is that. I now can't recall if Mary got her new cover.

Wow, and then I found all these great apps (I could see a picture of my former PC village in India on my phone) including this thing called Facebook. Now, I had never considered using Facebook, Myspace, My-Life, or any of these social networks. Frankly, I hate it when my phone rings. Yet, because it was there, and because I wanted to justify my impulse purchase, I tried it, along with several other useless apps or whatever they call those devilish things designed to enhance your life, at least until that fatal crash as you focus on your phone while doing seventy-five on the expressway. One thing led to another and soon I was scrolling down the Clark class of 1966. Suddenly, up popped Lee.

I literally froze, never expecting to come across her again. It had been over four decades since I had seen her last. Worse, there was a way to message her. It was decision time. For a moment or two, I hesitated. Maybe, just maybe, it would be better to keep on scrolling. A bunch of thoughts crowded my head. Would she remember me? Would she want to remember me? Would her reaction be "Oh god, I thought the nightmare of Tom Corbett was far, far behind me?" An even more menacing thought intruded. Would she be at all the same Lee I recalled from college days, or would those fond memories be shattered by peering into the past? Perhaps my recollections were highly idealized. Perhaps she had changed. Would I now find a fat, toothless, harpy with body odor and sixty-plus grandchildren, most of which were happily ensconced in various institutions dedicated to protecting the public? The hesitation really did not last long, though. After all, in one way or another, Lee had never left my head.

Our last contact of any kind was a set pathetic letters full of self-loathing and narcissistic whining I sent her from India shortly before my return to the States in 1969. Letters that tedious and full of self-pity would certainly be a capital crime in most states, or at least should be. By the time we stopped communicating, she had been married for about a year. Now, it was four decades later, a lifetime. Then I thought, *What the hell!* As May 2010, ended, I typed out a simple message. It went something like, "Hi Lee, this is Tom Corbett, from Clark. Remember me?" I thought she would need a clue to place me, to dredge up some recognition of who this guy was. I am not sure what my expectations were, maybe a polite reply with "Oh, are you still alive?" At best I assumed a few pleasantries, an update on career and family, and that would be that. After hitting the send button, frankly, I really sort of prepared myself for nothing. The Lee of my stored memory seemed more like a fantasy or dream than a living person. Surely, that Lee from the '60s was little more than a hyperbolic mirage.

What did happen surprised me as much as her agreeing to that first date so long ago. She seemed happy to hear from me, perhaps she was confused. Anyways, we started off with the expected polite catching-up exchange. These pleasantries quickly morphed into an intimate journey into our past and into the meaning of "us" back in college. What happened, how did it happen, where did we go wrong, and where were we now? What touched me very deeply was that she had saved old pictures of me and us as well as many of the embarrassing letters I had sent from India. She even saved small notes I had left for her in her dorm room and other assorted junk that seemed trivial beyond belief. Somewhere in her stored memories, I still had a place no matter how tenuous.

The letters gave some texture to recollections tarnished by time. And so, we plowed on, separated by nine hundred miles, trying to put together an emotional canvass of what our world looked like so many decades earlier. Our emerging dialogue reminded me of how alcoholism works. Take a drink after a period of sobriety, even a period of forty-plus years, and you immediately find yourself further along in your disease. Very soon, Lee and I seemed way more open with one another than we had ever been in our youth.

This realization led me to the most surprising element of this so-called reconnection. What hit me, with stunning force, was that this *was* Lee on the other end of cyberspace. With just a few typing conventions (underlines, smiley faces, exclamations, etc.) she managed to convey all the endearing emotions and mannerisms that drew me to her in the first place—sassiness, wit, intelligence, insight, insecurity, a sense of common history, and a shared perspective on many dimensions of life with enough differences remaining to spar with one another over. More than that, I felt I knew the rediscovered Lee with more depth and clarity than at any moment of my youth. I doubt she had changed at all. I think I finally could see things more clearly at last and with far less personal baggage.

On the other end of cyberspace, I could "see" her smiling, glowering at me in mock (or real) frustration, jousting with me with her impish look, pricking my pretensions, and stimulating me with her insights and deep sensitivity. She remained a deep body of water ever undulated and changing color as we peeled back layers of forgotten feelings and memories and began to recall what "us" had meant. I finally saw why I had such a strong attraction to her in my youth, how she penetrated the defenses of the guy who was *never* going to let girly emotions get the better of him. What we discovered back then was all kinds of parallels in our lives and in our perspectives. It was as if we had a mutual resonance on things, a shared cloth from which to weave a common bond.

Of course, you cannot really go back again. We both were in stable, loving relationships. Neither one of us would ever jeopardize our significant others nor cause any harm or hurt. We were committed that our piecing together the past would never interfere with our happy lives at this point. Given this firm mutual understanding, it would be easy to characterize our reconnection as a soppy chick movie. Two people who had loved one another are then fated to be apart forever because personal frailties and insecurities doomed them from the start. Then they find each other again, at least for a while.

We did talk about hearts being absorbent. They could always encompass more love. Maybe this nonsense called love is not a zero-sum game. Maybe we can add to each other's happiness and fulfillment in small ways, simply exchanging thoughts and support and comfort and laughs and memories through this miracle of a cyberspace connection. Is that sufficient? Who knows? As I thought back on things, my closest relationships with women were never sexual. They were about connecting.

We have speculated on what would have happened had we not acted like childish idiots back them. She speculated that we might have escaped a terrible fate. Were we too similar she wondered? I also had long thought that our attraction might have failed under the weight of the insecurities we would have brought to any longer-term relationship. We were very much alike, almost able to finish each other's thoughts and sentences. It was eerie. Our similarities and common histories might have proven to be insurmountable obstacles. If we had made it past those early challenges, a huge if, I could easily envision a shared life of perhaps a few tears but also of many laughs and much love. We will never know since that was never to be.

Letters from the past . . ..

We get too old smart, right. The Peace Corps experience is something you confront alone. You might have a site partner, as I did, but you are living in a culture that provides little emotional and social support as well as an abundance of time to think. I sent many letters to her from the other side of the world and received a few in return. These letters were probably the most personal and meaningful correspondence I ever wrote in my life, at least up until this memoir.

The letters she kept all these years shocked me in many ways. It was amazing to look back on reality rather than whitewashed memories. For example, I thought that I had not mentioned marriage until well into my stay in India and that her dear Tom letter to me crossed paths with my proposal letter to her. That would have been tragic in some romantic, chick-flic sense but it turned out not to be true. I first mentioned marriage in a letter from stateside training, even before I headed overseas. Reading it now, my sense of fatalism is palpable. Somewhere inside, I just knew that, in leaving for India, I would never see her again.

Michael (a fellow trainee I was particularly close to) is really wigging out now. His girl has not written for about a week now. Her husband has probably returned from Viet Nam and, needless to say, the situation is tense all the way around. It is another case of the shifting sands of human emotions, the liquidity and vacuity of which never cease to amaze me. The course of human involvement typically seems to run from the improbable to the absurd. The grasping, hoping, seeking become inevitable frustrations and unfulfilled anticipations. Today's bliss and ecstasy are tomorrow's despair and emptiness. To maintain your purpose and direction, you must love and believe in it. And out of the deepest despair of its reality evolves the highest respect for its necessity and appreciation of its existence.

Partially, one may say that love is illusion, or some form of selective reality, and further, that distance perpetuates these illusions. But the emotional character of love is only the superficial surface. Its real nature lies in the contract made between two people. It is the arrangement between separate individuals to share common excitement and joys and accept each other's burdens and fears. It is the merger of their identities as well as their bodies, an investment of themselves and their trust in the other. It is perhaps the most incredibly difficult goal to accomplish and yet the easiest thing to convince yourself that you are doing. It is something that cannot be manufactured but rather must simply exist. Yet, it cannot be taken for granted but rather nurtured and cultivated with all the strength that can be mustered. As you know, this kind of investment has been particularly difficult for me. The exposure and investment of ourselves to other human beings is a noble aspiration, perhaps ultimately unrealizable yet seemingly the only reality worth pursuing.

In rereading this letter, I have realized that it is extremely ambiguous and unintelligible. It is just so incredibly difficult to verbalize emotions in general, never mind probing one's own thoughts and feelings. Beyond that, these kinds of thoughts are alien to my analytical, pessimistic nature. Perhaps there is some kind of metamorphosis, a maturing which is taking place, and I am neither able to describe it nor analyze its direction.

There is something I want to say now, that I must say or perhaps forever hesitate. I do want to marry you. This is an incredible confession for me and I know it will freak you out. Before you retreat into a shell of self-security, let me assure you that I don't believe it will ever happen. Circumstances, two years, and certain common weaknesses will, in all probability, prevent it. But let me also assure you that I mean it and that if you ever, at any time, feel strong enough to make that arrangement, that contract of identities, let me know.

Both Lee and I were shocked on reading this, and other letters, after so much time. Could this really be the cynical, detached Tom Corbett of our memories waxing on and on about love and relationships? One explanation leaps to mind. Perhaps I was busy with training and had hired someone to write these letters for me. But if I really did express such thoughts or, more importantly, embrace such sentiments, then surely some kind soul could have been persuaded to put me out of my misery. I would have labelled these as back-forty sentiments if expressed by anyone else. Yet, here I was apparently talking about marriage of all things! What the hell was I thinking?

My parents, decent people that they were for the most part, would never be described as an ideal couple. In fact, I cannot recall too many civil words between them and certainly no affection. That, however, seemed rather typical of marriages in my working-class neighborhood where economic tensions and life's struggles promptly eroded any early romantic attachments. I mentioned how, as kids, we often sat on the front stoop of our three-deckers while listening to the screaming matches emanating from the surrounding flats. Unlike my wife's childhood experiences (she never heard either her parents or any of her neighbors argue while growing up, really!), I had few positive role models for marriage. Here I was, in black and white, raising the topic of marriage. Fortunately for her, Lee was smart as a whip. After getting her doctorate, she enjoyed a long career as a research scientist and teacher in academia. She was certainly smart enough to ignore my "offer" and move on when a more promising opportunity presented itself. Still, this was an instructive lesson in how we can reframe our own histories.

Once I got overseas, one reality set in. I really missed that woman. What in the world had I been thinking (or why had I failed to think at all?). But it was too late. I had left without expressing my love in any way that made sense and without making a commitment. Even as I wallowed in loneliness and frustration in the Rajasthan desert, I had a hard time expressing fully what was in my heart. My letters weaved from spasms of self-pity to rather obtuse expressions of possible devotion. Even when the word *marriage* burst forth from time to time, I employed it in ways that would put off most women except for those who would marry any male still breathing. Lee could not be counted among these women.

In truth, as I reread my letters, it struck me that I must have come across as the "lunatic" writing in the desert. Looking closely, one could see a desperation born from the realization that the train was already on the track. I, hopeless moron that I was, could do nothing. I waited for it to continue its journey over my family jewels and on to wherever residual human emotions go to die. In my heart, I knew two years was a long time and yet I had never pulled the emotional trigger with sufficient clarity to keep her wedded to me. It was merely a matter of time before she was gone and all that would remain would be the caboose receding into the distance. Enough with the train metaphors already!

In her Dear Tom letter, she recounted how she had met a post doc at Harvard where she worked. I certainly could understand. We continued to communicate until I left India, for about a year after her marriage. My letters, labored in prose a bit thick with self-pity and self-doubt, tried to be supportive of her decision. In my head, I really did believe it was in her best interests. If she had any second thoughts, my pathetic missives would help her get over them. I finally sucked it up when my tour ended and stopped writing. It seemed the right thing to do though, as I recall, her letters back were more open and affectionate than they had been before her marriage. But I had decided. We were history, end of story! Besides, don't you just hate those restraining orders for being a stalker? I was running out of space to store them.

All things pass, right? That dull ache in my heart would be filled with new experiences. Life would move on with all those new women to replace that emptiness where my heart was once located. There were, after all, many fish in the sea and, in fact, I managed to reel in a number. I was appalled at the totally impoverished judgement evidenced by many women. At some point I threw away all her notes to me, looking for finality to what I thought was a part of my life that was finished. Throw it all out, I thought, hanging on to that kind of crap is just silly.

A series of other women from that period did not help all that much. That sense of loss dissipated but never totally disappeared. I never forgot that first sight of her walking across the room. I could still recall looking into eyes that seemed portals to the soul, liquid pools that could express joy, reproach, affection, vulnerability, and caring all in a matter of moments. I would remember the laughs and the way we would joust with one another. And I can vividly recall the sharp pinches of pain when I "thought" she was rejecting me as well as an ecstasy that accompanied those rare moments when I felt she liked me, I could never accept that she might love me. These are the classic symptoms of young love. Time surely for that back-forty solution I totally deserved but managed to somehow elude.

On occasion, when it made sense, I would describe to others about this gal in college, about how she took my heart the moment I saw her, how that heart shattered, and how the memories of her and of us have never quite faded. It was the classic story of young love and lost opportunity. It was the tragic fairy tale that coursed in a dark, yet inescapable, direction…a conventional tragedy. Right after arriving back in the States, I wrote a couple of notes to Lee. They were set on the beaches of Goa on the west coast of India. In them, we would make poetic, erotic love under the moonlight on pure white sand with the rhythms of our intertwined bodies measuring the beats of the insistent, pounding surf. What nonsense, time to move on I realized. I never mailed them, never kept them.

Years passed, and life did move on. There were downs and ups, marriage and career and a diagnosis of a virulent form of TB, undoubtedly contracted in India but lying dormant for a decade or so. Most lingering thoughts of Lee had long faded; the memories becoming rare, episodic occurrences for sure. But somewhere near my heart, that faint sense of loss never fully vanished. It lurked like a chronic disease with little things triggering brief symptoms after long periods of remission.

One day, somewhere around 1990 I believe, I landed at Logan and picked up my rental. As I recall, I was headed to Vermont to do some work with state officials but also wanted to check in on my mother in Worcester, thus the flight into Boston. As I pulled out of the airport, I could see the highway into town had become a parking lot as it so often does. Instinctively, I headed north with some vague plan of picking up the old route 128 artery, which circled the city. Suddenly, it hit me, and I have no idea why. I would be close to Peabody, Lee's childhood home.

She had grown up on Lynnfield St. I had a vague recollection of what the house looked like and some sense of the address. I even half remembered the directions I used to get there some quarter-century earlier. Take 128 North to the first stop light along the whole route, then turn south to a rotary, then three-quarters around the circle, and then . . .? It immediately struck me that this was completely nuts. Yet, I still stopped at a filling station and asked directions to Lynnfield St. But I couldn't move. I sat in the car for a while. *What could I expect?* I thought to myself. Would I drive past the house, assuming I could find it in the first place, and she would magically walk out the door? In that fantasy, she would recognize me, we would embrace, and everything that had gone wrong before would be righted in that transformational and magical moment. If I had bothered to look, I would have noticed the men in white coats lurking by the gas pumps, brandishing the straight jacket which would be used to whisk me off to my new "home."

On the other hand, maybe I would find her parents who would greet me with open arms. Oh, they would say, Lee has been hoping for years you would get in touch. She desperately wishes she had waited for you. Here is her number, call her! This was not the first time I mused about such a lyrical reconnection. At night, when all things improbable seem real, I would fantasize about contacting her parents. This happened very rarely and usually just before my other favorite fantasy where Hugh Hefner asks me to take over his Playboy empire. In any case, her family thought the world of me, which was not the case with their real son-in-law as I found out. Maybe I could just say I wondered how their daughter was doing. Or, how about using the line that I just wanted to say hello to them, just to wish them all the best?

Oh, she is divorced, really? (Ironically, I found out when we reconnected that she was divorced at that point.) Maybe I could just give her a call, I would volunteer. Perhaps I could cheer her up, I would offer with considerable insouciance. And they would be so grateful to me. On the other hand, I could also envision another reaction. I could see them reacting with a "Who the hell are you?"

reaction and a "Why are you bothering our daughter who now has five kids and is spectacularly happy living in paradise?" That would be followed by another restraining order. I might keep that one in a special place. I did not get many of them from parents.

I cannot recall how long I sat in that filling station, wondering just how a rational man like myself could have fallen into such a state of emotional degeneracy. This was simply stupid beyond recognition. In the end, no call was made and the quixotic search for her childhood home was (thankfully) abandoned. I restarted the car and went on my way to Worcester. It is over, get it dumb shit, over! But as the saying goes, it is "never" over until that fat lady sings. By the way, why can't you ever find a fat lady when you need one?

A sad tale . . .

The known pieces are straightforward. After graduation, Lee went off to Boston and started working at a lab at Harvard. I started training for my Peace Corps assignment and finished up my remaining credits at Clark. Except for the time I was off in the Midwest, we had plenty of time to date, talk, get to know each other even better, and spend more nights together. But we didn't do much of that, and we cannot fathom why we didn't.

As we look back, the actuality of youth seems virtually impossible to comprehend. What could we have been thinking? How could we not have spent those last days in the U. S. with the person whom we probably loved back then? And so, we lost our last opportunity to clarify how we felt about one another. I would never really know whether her occasional remoteness was either an expression of underlying indifference or, ironically, a fear borne of too much attraction. My withdrawals were clearer to me—an incapacitating fear of intimacy and commitment. I could not reach out for what I wanted at the time and would endure some continuing regret for my cowardice.

It would have been a stunning miracle, and poor judgment on her part, had she waited upon my return. Her decision to move on makes perfect sense. She worked in an invigorating environment. She met a man who appeared smart, caring, stable, secure, and (importantly) present to her. In any case, he was a Harvard post-doc and had an academic position waiting for him at Georgia Tech, a real career. Beyond that, he probably had a bunch of other qualities that would make me very jealous if I thought on it too much. Contrast that real person who had a future with a guy who flew off halfway around the world with no discernible prospects and a tenuous grasp on adulthood. It really was no contest. Hell, I certainly would have dumped myself at that time if it were feasible.

Sitting in India, I knew the end was coming, could feel it coming. You could literally see that creeping awareness reflected in a growing desperation and futility that seeped through my correspondence with her. By then, however, there was little I could do. And what I could do, I didn't. I never fully verbalized a commitment to her, never formally proposed marriage except in round about, obtuse ways. The train, long approaching, ran straight over me. There were not enough body parts left for the toe tag. Again, with the train metaphors!

The following passage likely comes from my final letter (or thereabouts) before receiving the infamous "Dear Tom" missive.

> *I heard the music from Zorba the Greek the other day. As usual, it sparked a flood of memories . . . For one thing, it reminded me of Zorba's recommendation that we all must possess a little bit of madness, madness that has placed me here, madness that may never allow us to see each other again, but more importantly the madness by which we dare to hope. But the ultimate madness of them all is the one by which we desperately yearn to survive and, in the face of all this increasing insanity, seek the kinds of futile happiness that our illusive dreams pretend. Yet, maybe, just maybe, we'll make it.*
>
> *Still, I want to say something now, not out of fear or lack of trust in you, but simply to clear up any ambiguity. While I love you and do hope the relationship will endure my service here, the reality of the situation is that we will be separated two years, a little over a year more. I also realize that my irascible moodiness, chronic immaturity, and impractical idealism hardly make me an ideal catch. If you have any doubt, or change your mind, please feel completely uninhibited to communicate this to me. Perhaps,*

given my peculiar Irish pessimism, I anticipate it anyway.
And, of course, if you are insane enough to like me, you are
also allowed to tell me that as well.

Perhaps a quick note on the "Dear Tom" letter is in order. When Lee and I processed the whole thing several years ago, we both were dumbfounded at how stupid we were. We cannot quite recollect how we let things happen the way they did. I found it ironic that the words Lee used to describe her memory of me from our college days were, frankly, totally embarrassing. She remembered me as being extremely handsome, funny, charming, caring, brilliant, sensitive, quick-witted, passionate about causes, articulate, and "a divine kisser, the best." Oh, and she simply loved my self-deprecating personal style.

Now, what is a guy who prides himself on that self-deprecating style going to do with positive feedback like that? It is almost enough to make me like myself . . . almost. It is easier, however, to conclude that she is confusing me with some other boy, but she didn't know many other boys. But if that is me she is talking about, it might have helped had she said something like that back then, not that I would have believed her. I could not hear such sentiments. And if I had I probably would have run for the hills in abject panic. What a basket case! It also might have helped had I been more open, earlier.

Sadly, from everything she revealed after we reconnected, her marriage did not turn out well though it did endure for some two decades before she finally ended it. Perhaps her own family also sensed she was making a mistake right at the start. One of the only things I could recall from the "Dear Tom" letter to me was an observation that her family would really miss me not being a part of Lee's life. Here again, my memory played tricks on me. I thought I wrote only one more letter immediately on getting the "Dear Tom" note to say some of the most obvious things . . . you know, the "I understand and don't worry about me and good luck and have a nice life" kind of sentiments. I am positive I wrote such a letter though it did not survive, which is too bad since I would be most interested in seeing if I was as gracious and noble as my memory suggests. But what shocked me (again with the shock) was that she wrote again. We subsequently picked up our correspondence for the remainder of my tenure in India. Below is a snippet from one of my post "Dear Tom" letter:

> *Your ('Dear Tom') letter must have been an unpleasant experience, one which finally having been done would be difficult to repeat. Writing again was a marvelously brave thing for you to do. I'm not sure it was a wise thing, but it did please me, immeasurably. Thanks.*
>
> *You mentioned that sometimes you burst into tears without reason. Well, I must admit there are times when I become misty-eyed. It is not so much for what might have been but rather for what was. The years that have just passed were, at least for me, extremely pleasant ones. And*

the time we spent together was perhaps the most rewarding of all. There was a certain warmth and comfortableness there, and a sharing and excitement which now seem unique and may never again be duplicated. The days at Donoghues (our favorite local bar) . . . are past now and they will never return.

But we are in no way to blame, for it had to be that way. The times and the people who fill those times do change, inexorably, and without apparent conscious direction and there is little, so damn pitifully little, we can really do about it. It, us, would have changed no matter whether I left or not. And I suspect that what we still may fondly be attached to is not what we were to each other or what we might have been to each other but rather the simple function of a time and place in our lives which is irreplaceable. In my Irish Catholic pessimism, there is no room for happiness.

I can surmise what I was trying to do in that last paragraph. I might well have sensed that she had early doubts about her marital choice. It would take several years, though, before the real unhappiness emerged. Her second marriage, I am happy to say, turned out much better. In any case, I felt compelled to argue that our strong college "connection" was more a function of time and place than anything peculiar to us. Thus, it was not necessarily retrievable even if we wanted to try. That was a noble sentiment on my part, apparently designed to make her feel better about her decision or in general. I look back on it now with a touch of amazement. Whether the sentiments were grounded, they were from a man not generally known for his nobility or sense of self-sacrifice. Besides, I am not at all sure I was being truthful.

A sad ending . . .

Lee was to pass from cancer about two years after we reconnected. We never met; it was not necessary. She still had that same aura of goodness and optimism I recalled so fondly even as her health ebbed. She experienced a couple of episodes of renal failure (and near death) during early chemo treatments. Despite this, she kept insisting how blessed she was and how much she treasured the life she had . . . her husband, her family, the friends around her and even me. That positive, upbeat view of life still puts me to shame. Hell, I bitch for days about duck hooking a golf shot into the damn pond.

Her Caringbridge site, a place where friends and relatives and acquaintances could go to check up on the status of someone very ill, typically dying, accumulated almost six thousand "hits" before she passed on in the spring of 2012. It is so clear from the character of the messages left for her that she had been an inspiration to the many who had made her acquaintance. If I were to have a similar site, I am sure I could reach double figures but only if I liberally employed the services of Rent-A-Friend. My assessment of her personality and character were not unique to me. Though she permitted only a handful to get really close to her, she obviously touched all who were fortunate to come within her orbit. She was a special woman.

In several e-mails, Lee had observed something else that caught my attention. From what she sensed about me today, I had not evolved into a "different" person over the years. Rather, I had become a more complete version of the young man she had known so many years ago and to whom she was so drawn. In her mind, that was a very good thing, all those traits she so admired back then now appeared fully developed and expressed.

The core of what people are, who they are, the qualities that center them, appear as constants in their makeup. A relationship is interrupted and silenced for over four decades. When it resumes, a lifetime of experiences does little to shake what made each of us unique and even appealing in the beginning. That is somehow quite remarkable and something I learned from a bond that was never to fully be. Lee taught me how to love, something that was not part of me in my youth. It was an invaluable lesson I took forward into adulthood. I am gratified at long last to embrace the reality that Lee did love that guy from Clark, and she loved the man he became. Such things are good to know, even if too late.

I don't want to lead readers astray here. I do not tarry long over roads not taken or love lost. Life is what it is. I enjoyed a long, happy, and fulfilling marriage to a wonderful woman. My wife and I embrace values and aspirations that are singular and compatible.

As suggested elsewhere, there have few cross words in the over four decades we have been together. And more to the point, there is no way of knowing what would have happened had Lee and I made different choices way back in the1960s. Alternate choices are called counterfactuals by economists. They are fun to speculate about but remain unknowable paths in the end.

I spent a chapter on my relationship with Lee because it was a first love. I am sure we all have them. They really are special and irreplaceable. At the same time, they are not always right for you even as they do so much to shape your heart and the way you relate to others in the future. She was one of the kindest and most loving persons I ever came across. She left her husband, her adopted family, and all those who cherished her far too soon. I am thankful for having had a chance to affirm how special this relationship was to both of us.

CHAPTER 9

MEANING

God has no religion.
—Gandhi

"And so, my fellow Americans, ask not what your country can do for you, ask what you can do for your country." I came of age when John F. Kennedy uttered those immortal words. So many of us were engaged by his rhetorical skill and mesmerized by this vision of personal sacrifice. We were Americans and we were blessed. We were also being challenged. Kennedy was imploring each of us to reach out to the vulnerable and the less fortunate to create a better world. A whole generation, well quite a few of us at least, tried to do just that in their own idiosyncratic and personal ways.

Can you imagine what most politicians of today would be saying, particularly from the far right? "And so, my fellow Americans, grab what you can for yourselves and screw the other guy. Compassion and caring is for suckers!" For them, that is the American dream and the meaning of personal freedom. As long as those at the top get an ever-bigger share of the pie, all is well with the world. Perhaps it is just me, but I don't find such sentiments as uplifting as Kennedy's message. I do admit, though, such sentiments move Tea Party adherents to joyous tears if not celebratory orgasms.

Even before the Kennedy-inspired vision of Camelot emerged, I was thinking about how I would save the world. I remember getting into an argument with visitors from Virginia when I was about twelve or thirteen. They were related to the older Lithuanian couple that owned our three-decker. The visitors were complaining about the damn Supreme Court telling them how to educate their children. This visit took place not all that long after the *Brown vs. the Board of Education* decision that ended segregation in public schools.

I listened for a while until I could no longer take it and began arguing back even though I was a no-nothing young shit at the time. "Of course, the Court had to right such an injustice. Segregation was a stain on our country, and someone has to protect minorities and the powerless," I argued though probably in my vernacular of the time. Where did all that come from? I cannot imagine anyone in my family or neighborhood having such opinions. It was as if these thoughts and feelings had been injected into my brain via some surreptitious plot, perhaps an alien implant. Well, a lot of people did think that secret Commie cells had infiltrated the country and were poisoning young minds. Maybe they had gotten to me. Maybe I was one of them and they had erased my early memories with that fancy gismo I saw once in a sci-fi movie.

The question for me was how to achieve a life of purpose and meaning. Peace Corps was not yet an option in the late fifties when I first started resonating to themes of social justice and of doing good things. So, I did the next best thing, at least for someone still comfortably ensconced within the Catholic cultural cocoon. I began thinking about becoming a priest. Eventually, this evolved into my decision to enter a Catholic missionary order, as I mentioned earlier. They were in the business of saving souls, and people, all over the world including Asia and Africa and various places in between. Well, it seemed like a good idea at the time. I would follow the footsteps of Schweitzer and Dooley, helping the dispossessed and vulnerable in ways that only the irretrievably innocent can believe makes sense.

But how did I get started down this track in the first instance? My early peers did not fret all that much about the meaning of life or about finding significance and purpose. In fact, they gave that crap not a thought at all. The guys I knew focused on the important things, like getting laid or getting a car so they might have a chance of getting laid. The more ambitious worried about getting a job since that was essential to the prior two goals… getting a car and getting laid. But a few of us were swept along into that vortex that would be the 1960s. According to surveys that have been replicated over time, students back then did believe that formulating sound philosophy of life was very important to one's eventual happiness. Now, happiness is defined as making a boatload of dough and buying crap. How sad!

I have a theory about this. Well, I have a theory on just about everything. As I have touched on earlier, we grew up in a special time. During the post–World War II period, the country witnessed a remarkable period of economic expansion. Income inequality was falling, and all segments òf the income distribution participated in this extraordinary growth of wealth and opportunity. Not surprisingly, a robust middle-class developed that became the envy of the world.

For kids like me, the necessities were not a real issue. Sure, my parents spent most of what they earned on booze and gambling, what they saw as the good times. They never owned their own home, or a new car, or any luxuries of note. As I mentioned, in my early years we did not have minimal amenities such as a TV, a refrigerator, central heating, or even a used car. Yet there was never any fear that the basics would not be there, at least not the paralyzing fear that dominated the previous generation. And more to the point, there was every possibility that things would get better, if only we were not incinerated in a nuclear mushroom cloud.

What this socioeconomic environment did, in my opinion, was liberate the sense of the possible. When I was not suffering from my persistent sense of personal insecurity, I could see some hope of carving out a future that would have been inconceivable to my father. But it was more than that. I was not obsessed with making money. I thought about the larger purposes of life. I thought about such things a lot. Why were we here, just to have fun and buy crap and eat good food and screw around? Okay, a couple of those things sounded kind of interesting but that all struck me as unsatisfying in the end. There had to be more.

God . . .

It is hard to know when I began to drift down this more idealistic path. Earlier, I mused about the importance of how we are hard wired for certain dispositions. Some of us tend to see a black-and-white world where everything is hard edged with a razor fine certainty. Such individuals cannot easily handle nuance, ambiguity, or lack of definition. They see threat everywhere, typically seeking simple answers and closure while being drawn to authority and a defined order to things. It is just the way they are and thus see the world in a clear, defined manner. We cannot all be as refined and enlightened as I am. If everyone were, being enlightened would not be special. Think about that.

Others are different, though, including me. We rather thrive on chaos. If you happen to be so cursed, you will be afflicted with an innate disposition where life's answers are not clear or etched in stone. Does that automatically mean you will you evolve into a do-gooder who inexorably tilts at impossible windmills? Are you then consigned to a fate to forever seek out injustices to attack and causes to pursue? I am not sure. Besides, some do-gooders also pursue their causes from a rigid set of personal beliefs. It is that nature-nurture thing all over again. We do have innate dispositions but surely some contextual dimensions of our personal worlds trigger or support those inclinations. Being curious does not translate automatically to altruism. Ever since my Peace Corps group has reconnected, I have spent more time thinking about such things. It may be that I am getting a little bored with the usual retirement distractions like golf. In truth, I have way too much time to gaze at my navel in self-analysis.

Brushing aside all concerns about excessive narcissism, let me briefly return to my early years. As best I can recall, I was always a pretty good boy. Okay, I would throw a tantrum or two, but still, I never displayed any sign of being a future Jeffrey Dahmer, Ted Bundy, or my favorite...Jack the Ripper. I pretty much obeyed the rules and received decent deportment marks in grammar school, except for penmanship but maybe I knew word processing was around the corner. My academics were average, but I was an obedient kid. Still, that did not exactly set me aside as a future candidate for sainthood. I would still maraud through the neighborhood at will most days.

What I do remember were those peculiar thoughts that set me aside from all the others in my world. I remember instinctively rejecting racism when virtually all around me were prejudiced. I was delighted when schools were desegregated and offended when I heard occasional stories of racial offenses in Worcester. They were all stories, of course, since I never actually knew any minorities growing up. I would think about the strangest things. If I heard that we had excess crops, I would wonder why we did not give our surplus grain away to starving people overseas. Surely that is what Christ would tell us to do. When playmates would fight, as kids do, and ask me to take sides, I would try to be a peacemaker. I always disliked conflict and wanted to bring the combatants together.

I instinctively warmed to the loving part of Christ's message. Reach out to those not like you. Share what you have. Give of yourself. It is not the formal rules that count, it is what you are as a person. A very wise U.U. (Universalist-Unitarian) minister once said that he was always puzzled by the Apostle's Creed. This was a Catholic prayer we all learned as kids that laid out certain fundamental elements of Christ's life. This minister, a graduate of Harvard's Theology School, pointed out that there was only a comma between Christ being "born of the Virgin Mary" and "suffered under Pontius Pilot." Think about that, he admonished us. All of Christ's teachings were reduced to a comma. Something to ponder I guess.

So, what was I beginning to think as the 1960s unfolded? For one thing, I began to take my religious life seriously. Now, let me be clear about this. The rational part of my brain was always pulling me in a different direction. I would sit in my high school theology classes and silently argue with the doctrines being imposed. Birth control, I could never buy that one! Why was heart surgery not thwarting God's plan (since God presumably caused the heart problem in the first instance) but contraception actively thwarting His plan? Of course, you just might be on a rampage to make sure Catholics never would enjoy sex. If so, good job!

But I managed to put those rebellious sentiments somewhere in the back of my mind. What I embraced with increasing enthusiasm was what I considered the positive aspects of Christ's message. I responded to those teachings that stressed reaching out to others, to loving the least lovable and to accepting those different from ourselves. I was attracted to the notion of sacrifice for the greater good, of seeing promise in others, and of doing no harm if I could. This was not the vengeful God of the Old Testament, but someone with a simple message based on sacrifice and giving. This was the essence of Christ's message, charity writ large, and getting away from the harsh, rigid rules he saw in the Judaism of his time. This message of love and embracing the other is what got him killed in the end. His blasphemy against the elite of the time was just a convenient excuse. Wow, I could believe in that stuff.

It was not until many years later, while working with some fellow Peace Corps volunteers on our collective reflections, that I looked hard at this period of my life. Given my early environment, how I managed to drift into my adult avocation became even more perplexing. In any case, toward the end of high school, I began going to mass daily as I searched for ways to pursue a life of meaning. There was a peace and solitude about early morning mass, only a few very old Lithuanian women might be around during the week. Therefore, there was lots of time to think about things.

I cannot recall how I first heard about the Maryknollers. They were the foreign missionary storm troopers of the Catholic Church, working in distant lands to bring the One, True, Holy, and Apostolic church to those that knew no better. After all, I had always doubted the fairness of a deity who would deny entrance to heaven those who did not have a fair shot at hearing His truth. Well, I could at least improve their chances, if only on the margins. I cannot recall considering any other order or of becoming a regular parish priest. I am not sure I would have given the priesthood a shot if the missionary path were not an option. Perhaps that was a clue that I was drawn to the romance of service overseas more than anything else.

Somewhere early on, I ran across a movie titled *The Keys of the Kingdom* with Gregory Peck. Now there was a feel-good movie if there ever was one. Gregory played the part of a simple man of God who had grown up in Scotland and went off to the Orient in the 1910s or so to save souls and bodies in a China often ravaged by civil war and other disasters. His humble demeanor was subtly compared to his childhood friend who had become a bishop in the church and enamored with all the pomp and crap associated with high ecclesiastical office. The Peck character never attained great success except for the love of the people around him and the good he did for the few he touched. I cried every time I saw that movie.

The Maryknollers had a recruiter, a Father Beck, who visited my home and school. He was good at his job. At the time, I could see myself as a young man of God, working in difficult, if not dangerous, conditions to bring light and understanding to those in the shadows. That, at least, was my idealized view of things. When I visited the major seminary in Ossining, New York, I was taken with the beauty of the place. It was located on the Hudson River. Catholics always had a gift for grabbing the prime real estate. I was also taken with the seminarians. They did seem straight out of central casting, young and handsome and dedicated. Well, that is my faded memory. My decision to go that route, in any case, was renewed.

I have looked back on this decision from time to time. As with so many forks in my life trajectory, I cannot recall any defining moment. I was not struck by lightning in the manner of Saul of Tarsus, or St. Paul as we know him. I don't recall seeing any visions, hearing any voices, nor experiencing any transformative epiphanies. The whole process was more akin to molasses cascading over a tabletop. It was a slow-motion event. It was as if I had gone through a set of tiny changes and woke up one day to say, gee, I might as well go out and save the world by becoming priest. It seemed like a good idea at the time. Throughout life, I had many ideas that seemed good at the time and more like back-forty inspirations with hindsight.

My reasons for pursuing a vocation were complex and not all of them honorable. I suspect I was attracted to the attention and respect men of the cloth automatically received, at least before all the pedophilia was revealed. People called you "Father," and you allegedly had this amazing power to transform bread and wine into the body and blood of the Savior. Think of that, you were to be blessed with a special gift or power that few of your peers would enjoy. Most expressed their admiration for me in that special way boys congratulate one another, as if I had just volunteered for a suicide mission. I could see many looking at me with disguised contempt, "Why is he doing that! You can't get laid all that easily as a priest." Anyways, I must have ignored the doubters because I signed on the dotted line.

The thing is, I wanted to believe. It made many things easier in a way, especially to please my parents. My father probably wondered what had gotten into his son. Given his rather wild early days, it appeared I was not a chip off the old block. Moreover, this vocation was a way to satisfy that lust for contributing to the public good, piecing together what was inside me with a life purpose. In the end, it all fell together, and I got on a Greyhound Bus in the late summer of 1962 and headed for Glen Ellyn Illinois and the so-called minor seminary.

My intellectual experience at the seminary I touched on elsewhere. The spiritual and personal effects were something else. I recall there was a kid standing outside with his suitcase at the end of the first day. He said he had already decided it was not for him. That seemed good for the rest of us; the place was overflowing. Some new candidates were sleeping in the hallways of a facility that had just been expanded to accommodate an increasing flood of vocations. Spreading the Catholic word apparently was big business in 1962. On that first day, we could not know that his decision to leave would signal a virtual flood of departures over the next few years.

I tried hard to get into the swing of things. During long hours of prayer and meditation, I sought a connection with the divine on some meaningful level. I searched for a presence and a calling that might mean something special to me and for me. I would take walks over the lovely grounds saying the rosary, seeking what I imagined might be deeper thoughts. At the same time, most of us never kept the long silences demanded of us during the day and evening hours. We all seem to break the smaller rules. But in a larger sense we were serious about what we were doing.

We were college-age kids in the end, full of energy with few opportunities to expend it. We did, therefore, play many sports when feasible and had numerous contests between seminary wings or classes or whatever other natural groups existed. I recall one baseball game. I pitched for my team or wing of the school, the first time since junior high school. Apparently, I had not lost my touch, taking a no hitter into the last inning. Once again, I lost my bid for minor immortality at the last moment. In fact, I don't recall giving up a single hit. We lost the contest through walks and errors. What I recall most was getting up the next morning. My right shoulder and left leg (the one you land on during the pitching motion) were in excruciating pain. I nearly collapsed on the floor while getting up and could barely walk. There may be a lesson here. Don't just go out and pitch a full game after years of inactivity. If you do, at least win the damn game!

One day, we lost some sporting event to the first-year kids on another wing. I recall not the event, but I recall our revenge very well. These contests were taken seriously, a matter of unit pride. Somehow, we gathered together a bunch of empty cans and tied them together with twine. That night, we snuck over to the wing where our enemy slept unawares, creeping along as if on a spy mission. This had to break like seventy-five rules of the place. We carefully placed the cans on the tops of the sinks in the bathroom and tied the whole contraption to the door in some ingenious way. Some poor schmuck would open the door and probably crap in his pants at the resulting clatter. Did I come up with this inane plan? Not sure but I suspect I had a hand in it.

Then we snuck back and lay in our beds eager with anticipation. Sometime in the deep silence of the seminary night we could hear the faint, faraway clatter that was the unmistakable sign of a nefarious plan working to perfection. I almost crapped in my bed I was laughing so hard. I vaguely recall that our culpability did not long remain a secret. We were not punished very hard as I recall; they probably gave some leeway for youthful exuberance. Other transgressions were not easily overlooked. The several older seminarians who somehow met girls during the brief time allowed off grounds each week were shown the door immediately.

There were also special, even spiritual, memories. I will use one to illustrate them all. Just before midnight on the eve of Easter Sunday, we all gathered outside the circular chapel that was situated in the center of this newly expanded facility. Each of us was given a candle, and we filed into the nearly darkened sanctuary where a midnight mass was to be celebrated. At midnight, in a circular fashion, one candle would be used to light the next around and around an altar situated in the center. Soon, the whole place was lit with hundreds of flickering lights. The effect was surreal. The hushed sounds of "He Is Risen" could then be heard, first almost as a whisper and then louder and louder until robust hallelujahs rang out in joy. Chills went down my spine, an inspiring moment.

Eventually, you figure out when something is not right. Even I did. My exit from the seminary and from my vocation was the same molasses-type process as my entrance. There was no agonized night praying in the chapel, no seeking counsel with the priests, and no great internal turmoil for my soul. It was the drip, drip, drip of doubt. We laugh at young people who say they are trying to find themselves. As I have aged, though, that rite of passage makes more and more sense. You do have to figure out what is natural for you. You probably won't figure it out getting stoned every night or becoming a rock band groupie but trying out various things and being honest does help, sometimes a lot.

After a little more than a year, this grand plan for saving the world had encountered a problem I could no longer push aside. It became all too obvious that I did not possess a basic job requirement for being a priest. You had to believe in God, really believe. At some level, I knew that the magnitude of my belief was not at that level. I was more interested in addressing the physical and political needs of the poor, not in harvesting their souls for an entity about which I harbored increasing doubts. My rational side never could accommodate the institutional fidelity that Catholicism, or any absolutist belief system, demanded. I simply could not give myself over to blind faith. Forgoing women for the rest of my life might also have been a factor. Then again, I only knew Catholic girls, which was like taking a vow of celibacy in the first place.

Leftward-ho . . .

My road to what I hoped would be a purpose-driven life picked up speed after leaving the seminary when I enrolled at Clark. As detailed earlier, Clark was widely considered a pinko-leftist school where nice Catholic boys would lose their faith. But I held out against the invidious and corrosive effects of rampant secularism with great bravery and dedication for at least two weeks. Okay, maybe it was just a week.

The Clark experience, as you know, represented a kind of intellectual liberation for me as I discussed in chapter 7. But it was also a normative liberation, helping me break away from the encrusted values of my youthful culture. This was not my usual Catholic, ethnic, working class world. Suddenly, I was exposed to cultures and ways of thinking very diverse from my own. Suddenly, I was expected to think things through on my own. The old scripts were no longer sacred and inviolable.

It was, let us not forget, the sixties. Very early on I became aware of an anti-war debate that was emerging around college campuses. This was the era of teach-ins where extremely smart people dissected our foreign policy. I can recall one such debate where a spokesperson from the State Department tried to justify the war against a small group of critics. It was a mismatch. The academic and student critics demolished his attempts to defend the indefensible. I felt sorry for him. Either evidence supporting our involvement was classified or they had nothing. It would anticipate the weapons of mass destruction fantasy by several decades.

On another occasion, Abbie Hoffman spoke. Abbie was later to earn national fame as one of the co-founders of the notorious Yippie movement, a cross between anti-war activism and the personal anarchy represented by the more culturally oriented Hippie movement. But when he visited Clark, he was still seeking respectability by wearing a suit and tie. He gave a spell-binding talk that linked carpet-bombing tactics in Vietnam to some of the most horrendous bombing raids during WWII. His message was effective. We were destroying a country seeking to free itself from foreign domination. Ho Chi Minh had sought our help early on, but the French used old loyalties and our obsession with Communism to draw us into a horrendous conflict on their side. We wound up supporting an oppressive colonial regime, and not for the first time.

I can still remember the evening that Wayne Morse, the dovish U. S. senator from Oregon spoke at Clark. He gave a spell binding speech that lit up his audience. President Johnson was using a trumped-up incident in the Gulf of Tonkin to launch a major and very questionable war. Someone had to stand up to this impending disaster. That should be me I thought. If you saw a wrong, you had an obligation to at least speak out. I recall a wonderful young man from the seminary who also left around the time I did. The next time I saw him was in one of the national news publications like *Time* or *Newsweek*. He was burning his draft card with several others in front of the Liberty Bell in Philadelphia. This was early enough to warrant national coverage, it would soon become a fad. Recalling his sensitivity and compassion, his symbolic action made perfect sense to me. I could appreciate the journey he had taken and the source of his outrage. I still wonder what price he paid.

Carol, one of my two college girlfriends, and I decided to attend the first anti-war march in Worcester. It followed Senator Morse's fiery speech. I can yet recall our frustration as we searched for where the demonstration was to take place. We knew it was a downtown somewhere near City Hall but were not quite sure where. I can still recall rounding a corner from Elm Street where my old library had been located onto Main Street. There was no mistaking what played out before us. Anti-war sentiments were still tantamount to treason in 1965 or so. The 100 to 150 or so protestors that gathered in front of the center of municipal government and power were surrounded by thousands (it seemed) of home-brewed patriots devoted to sending these Pinko-Commies where all traitors belong. Frustration quickly turned to anxiety and then dread but we sucked it up and plowed ahead.

Once we joined the march, things went from bad to worse. As I looked around, one thought overwhelmed me, I am going to die. My imminent demise turned out to be a rather a close-run thing. Our feeble protest march stopped at one point and I could sense a group of bikers straight out of the Brando movie—*The Wild Ones*—staring at me with undisguised loathing. "Let's kick the shit out of the tall one with glasses," one of them with the steroid-fueled muscles sneered. As far as I could figure out, I was the only tall one with glasses in the vicinity. For the first time in quite a while I searched my memory for that perfect act of contrition. If I could fake sincerity, this just might sneak me into heaven, at least if

St. Peter was napping when I arrived. Fortunately, the line started moving again and all I had to worry about was ducking eggs and beer cans.

Obviously, I did not die on that day, but the simple truths of my childhood were quickly withering as my working-class parents looked on with a mixture of befuddlement and despair. Their one and only child seemed on an inexorable decline and fall toward perdition and, worse still, permanent unemployment. After all, what would the neighbors, relatives, and anyone else that counted say about all these shenanigans? Who would ever hire this brainless twit?

During my seminary tenure, I was ready to enlist in the armed forces during the Cuban missile crisis to help thwart godless Communism. By my junior year at Clark, I was heading the campus leftist organization (which I helped found), leading anti-war marches. I even joined the Students for a Democratic Society (SDS) group, more as an intellectual statement rather than as a revolutionary act at this time. We called our campus leftist group the "Student Action Committee" or SAC. This was a take-off on the Strategic Air Command, those guys that flew 24-7 so the Russkies could not sneak in a quick attack. Our cleverness knew no bounds. Of course, the 24-7 retaliatory bombers would not exactly stop any attack. It would simply enable us to kill as many of them, if not more, than they killed of us. This mutually assured destruction, or MAD, was sold as a form of deterrence. Over time, we did avoid a nuclear holocaust by the skin of our teeth. Arguably, then, it worked.

There were moments, of course, when we could have gone up in that mushroom cloud. During the height of the Cuban missile crisis, a Russian submarine was being pursued by American warships near Cuba. Submerged, absent contact with anyone, depth charges exploding around them, sweating in 120-degree heat, they came within a whisker of launching a nuclear warhead. For all they knew, World War III had already started. Three men had to give permission, and two did. One Russian commander stood up against his peers and likely prevented a nuclear holocaust. On another occasion, in the 1980s, the computer screens where the Soviet command kept watch on us showed incoming American missiles. It looked real. The commander in charge had minutes to decide, launch a retaliatory attack or hope for the best. He guessed the Americans were not that stupid and he was right. It was a computer glitch. Good thing he did not know us well. Some American leaders have been that stupid.

The rhetoric of the time, however, struck me as absurd in the extreme. Arguments raged whether it was better that the handful of nuclear holocaust survivors all be capitalists as opposed to living in an intact world shared with Communists. This was the "better dead than red" position. Apparently, we had as little rational dialogue then as we have now. No wonder I was rushing toward the left and toward what I saw as a last refuge of sane and critical thinking.

I don't recall doing much of significance during my days as the leader of a leftist group on campus. We talked a lot, brought some speakers in, held informational and teaching sessions, and wrote position papers. This was before the students for a Democratic Society became the wing nut group of the left much like the Tea Party and its spin-off groups are now the wing nuts of the right. When I joined, they were yet a cabal of very smart young people debating issues and carving out a personal set of beliefs. As frustration further overwhelmed common sense, some kept moving to the left. Those of us who kept some attachment to reality decided it was wiser to get off that self-destructive train and went in our own direction. Again, with the trains!

Yet, I do recall moments of bitter rage and frustration. I can see how smart and well-meaning young people are driven to acts of irrationality. We were killing hundreds of thousands based on the flimsiest of analogies, the domino theory. If Vietnam went Communist, Southeast Asia would soon follow. After that, the virus would spread west to India or, God forbid, east to Australia and then on around the globe. After New Zealand, could California be far behind? My god, we would all be speaking Russian within a couple of years. The whole premise was absurd. We merely had stumbled into a war of national liberation and then turned it into a vicious civil war of our own making. Now, we had escalated things into part of the wider geo-political struggle between ideologies. Good going.

If we had just supported their nationalist aspirations from the beginning, their first political act probably would have involved opening trade relations with us. The Vietnamese, once free from the domination by the French colonials, would likely revert to their natural inclinations within a generation or so. They are a nation of small business people and entrepreneurs by nature. With a little positive help from us, their kids would soon have been applying to the Wharton School of Business. It is remarkable that they harbor as little ill will against us as they do, at least that is what I hear from tourists who have visited. Our destruction of their country did little to further our national goals and delayed our ability to forge a friendship that would have been a natural outcome of a more sanguine approach. Even from the perspective of another half-century, I remain stunned that I could see things more clearly than the experts with all their inside intelligence. How tragic!

Perhaps my most visible efforts as the head of SAC were to mount protest marches on a few occasions. One time, Hubert Humphrey was to speak at Clark. I loved Hubert. He was a good man who did much for this country. But he had a case of White House fever and had to remain loyal to Lyndon and his war, which he did. I am sure it killed him inside, but he really wanted to be president. Ambition can be a devastating mistress, so we picketed his appearance. I can recall my father mentioning that his fellow workers were talking about taking care of those Commie protesters at Clark. It was his way of expressing his disappointment in me, which affected me deeply. I was letting him down but, as the saying goes, I could do no other. We were divided on this and no quick repair of our split was apparent at the time.

My long-suffering parents did enjoy one consolation. Their decision to stop at one child now appeared prescient. While I can only speculate, they must have looked at what they had wrought and concluded no more of this. But then again, they never did seem to like one another so perhaps there were other explanations. I never quite got over the hurt I may have caused my father. By this time, he really was proud of my success in school and what looked like a life on the right track. Now, I was doing things that must have perplexed him deeply. Yet, there were few fireworks, just an obvious silent disapproval, which really cut deep.

My adventure into left-wing politics probably resulted in a file buried somewhere in the bowels of the FBI. Someone we had never seen around campus suddenly started attending our SAC meetings. He tried to be very helpful but struck me as being a little older and his enthusiasm seemed a bit forced. His language also struck me as scripted, as if he had practiced the rhetoric before showing up. I had no proof that he was a plant from a government agency, but I would bet the mortgage on it. It did not bother me. I assumed that came with the territory. Besides, we were not doing anything all that dangerous or treasonous. My life was an open book, the only danger I represented to others was putting them into a coma with my boring life.

A casual acquaintance had finished law school during this period and taken a position with the FBI. He took me aside one day and advised me of the potential consequences of my activities. It might cost me scholarship opportunities or even jobs someday. He seemed very serious. I pondered whether he was trying to dissuade me from my chosen political activities out of real concern for me as someone he knew or as an FBI agent thwarting the enemy within. I thought the very notion of long-term consequences overblown but did give his prognosis some consideration. Still, I never entertained the thought of stopping. I was young and idealistic and lived in that generation where the future really did seem hopeful and full of opportunity. Wait until my generation came of age, I argued. It would be a different country once we assumed power. Despite all the insanity and violence, America had not yet ceased being a land of opportunity, relatively speaking. That sad day was yet to come.

I was never part of any larger conspiracy. Occasionally, activists from Boston or New York would stop by. Once I attended the New England meeting of SDS that was held at the University of Massachusetts. My long-suffering girlfriend, Lee, drove me out to the Amherst campus. The meeting itself was disappointing in some respects. It was as if all the major issues had been decided, the war was wrong, the economic system bankrupt, the political system beyond repair. There were no longer the fiery debates that set my mind aflame. You could tell that the level of cynicism was running too deep at this point.

With all ideological and political matters settled, it was just a matter of time before the instinctive responses would turn violent. When you see unreasoned violence about you and cannot get people to listen, the level of frustration reaches a blind flash point. There were moments when I approached those limits, but I always held back. It was a point of no return and that is not where I wanted to go. This is not to say I was not tempted, my anger and frustration ran deep. But somewhere inside I was more a pacifist than a revolutionary. The man who first raises his fist in anger is the man who has run out of ideas.

Meaning through service . . .

As I stumbled forward in my normative renaissance, the prospect of the Peace Corps loomed larger. One of my friends at the time was Neil Riordan, a graduate student at Clark whom I had known loosely from the old neighborhood on Vernon Hill. Neil had done a Peace Corps stint in Iran that we talked about at length. Besides, what was a Psychology major with no visible skills (some things never changed) to do as his draft board eyed him with increasing interest?

I weighed two options—graduate school and Peace Corps. My advisor at Clark insisted that I apply to the top schools for graduate studies in psychology...Harvard, Yale, and Stanford. I thanked him politely, exited his office, and asked myself, "What kind of funny

CONFESSIONS OF A CLUELESS REBEL

cigarettes is he smoking?" That plan was a non-starter at the time. Hell, I was a working-class kid who could not even keep his final exam schedule straight. It would take many additional years before I realized I was not quite as dumb as I looked.

In the end, the battle over my next step in life was brief. I read about a Peace Corps program in India in public health. Perfect, I thought. My hospital career of emptying bed pans, giving enemas, and otherwise keeping the crazies at bay during nocturnal full moons certainly gave me a heads up for this program. After all, I could realize my long-held dream of being a contemporary Albert Schweitzer (or Tom Dooley), and in exotic India no less. After all, this was the home of Mahatma Gandhi, a personal hero of mine. It was, as they say, a done deal.

I have this admittedly vague memory (aren't they all?) that there was a conflict between the Graduate Record Exam (the GREs) and a Peace Corps exam with both being given on the same day. In my memory, I signed up for both and later decided which exam to take. I then weighed the relative merits suggested by the hypothetical life trajectory associated with each alternative. The more I reflected the better India and public health looked. But perhaps that is just a convenient memory that lends some drama to the choice—the path not taken and all that. What is certain is that I did not take the GREs until I was in India. I started the Peace Corps process and soon was Milwaukee bound for training in the summer of 1966.

My training for the Peace Corps, it turns out, would be another turning point in my life. Just the location of the training seemed an adventure. For a Worcester boy, Wisconsin was an exotic location. You need to remember that Bostonians believed that civilization ended at route 128, the main artery that circled the city in those days. We Worcester folk were far more sophisticated. For us, civilization extended all the way to the Hudson River. Perhaps you think I exaggerate. But I recall the Worcester train station as a kid, in the days when people still travelled by train. A sign there actually read "Albany NY and *the* West." If it had not been for my brief seminary experience outside of Chicago, I probably would have anticipated that cows would be meandering down Wisconsin city streets and indoor plumbing to be a luxury enjoyed by the wealthy few. Despite these trepidations, it was off to Milwaukee. Little did I know that I was destined to spend my adult life in the Badger State and to fall in love with Madison, the state capital.

I recall being told that it would not be the public health track for me despite all my experience working in a hospital. No, I was to be a poultry expert. I wanted to protest and point out my years of service to the sick and dying. Instead, I hid my disappointment, fear of deselection perhaps and was quickly rewarded by learning skills that I just knew would benefit me in the coming decades—like debeaking a chicken. If you need to ask what that is, you surely must be too citified. To make matters worse, all the gals were assigned to the other program and would be sent to a different province in India. For obvious reasons, this seemed a rather grim prospect, though the gals might have been somewhat relieved. I cannot imagine they would want to be surrounded by a bunch of oversexed young males. In any case, it appears gender profiling was alive and well—the boys were to be chicken farmers and the girls would be healers.

I remember physically preparing for the rigors of the training experience. In my mind the physical preparation would involve heroic challenges such as traversing deep chasms over rushing rivers on a rope. Fortunately, we just ran around the track at the University of Wisconsin–Milwaukee, our training site. That alone was enough to almost kill me. Somehow, drinking a lot of beer in college, while plotting the revolution, failed to shape my body into a finely-honed machine. I made it halfway around the track before collapsing, lungs screaming for mercy. I was trying to keep up with one of the gals, I think she was from Kentucky and had done track in college. As I collapsed to my knees desperately sucking in all available oxygen within a square mile, her trim, athletic body receded down the track. *Well,* I thought, *if this is my last earthly image, it could be worse.*

I remember our first Indian movie. Like all Bollywood productions of the era, it lasted three days, or so it seemed. Even *Gone with the Wind* mercifully ended after eighteen hours. Somewhere around the end of the second day, the male and female leads were running toward each other across an open field. *Yes, this is it*, I thought, as did the male lead. You could tell since he now was drooling. But no, just as they were about to embrace, the ground between them opened and they were separated by an earthquake. We had 7. 4 more crises to go before they were to finally connect, at which time we saw a wonderful ballet of butterflies, a somewhat pathetic proxy for the real thing. I mean, after all, this guy put his life on the line about a dozen times to get the goodies. But it was good preparation for the deprivation in "companionship" we would experience once we got to the subcontinent.

I remember Hindi classes and culture sensitivity classes and the Tuxedo Bar. A few lessons yet resonate. We were pushed to recognize our own prejudices and unexamined assumptions. I recall one of the staff asking if we ever thought about why we call part of the globe the Mideast. It is east of what? Think about that! I remember doing very well in Hindi class and getting puffed up about that. But when we got to India and the real world, I watched the Hindi fluency of a fellow black volunteer soar, while I flatlined. He had graduated from a small southern college and I thought myself intellectually superior. How foolish of me. I also absorbed a lot from the technical content of our poultry training. To this day, I can still distinguish a chicken from a cow. But a lot of the Milwaukee experience remains a blur.

I recognized immediately that I was immersed in another transformative experience. Below is a passage from one of my letters to Lee:

I really don't know where to begin. The past three or four weeks have been filled with exciting experiences, not only in the sense of different or pleasing but rather in the sense of challenge and growth. That growth and challenge emanate from a basic tension which is derived, I believe, from an elementary realization of what you are and what you want to be. The people (here) have forced me (and I them) to articulate and defend some of my most basic assumptions, my most basic sacred cows.

In the articulation of that defense, there inevitably emerges a more meaningful realization of yourself and your relationships with others. It is very difficult to put into words what I feel in my heart. The one thing of which I am certain, however, is that I will not experience this program unchanged. Whether or not I ever become a Peace Corps volunteer or not seems irrelevant. The important thing is that I feel I am changing and growing, in which direction it does not matter. I would have to assign the major responsibility (for this growth) to several staff who have encouraged and inspired an atmosphere of inquiry and questioning.

I remember many little things like walking down the street with Carolyn (Watanabe, then) and Nancy (Simuel). A car with a couple of young Black men screeched to a stop and they asked if this was a protest march of some kind. Seeing a white male walking with an Asian and a black female apparently stood out. Like a lot of places, Milwaukee was seething with racial unrest, some of it organized by an iconic Catholic priest named Father Groppi.

At some point, I recall being at our training director's house during a period where a prominent Milwaukee judge's home was being picketed for belonging to a whites-only social club. Four of us, including a congressional aide who was visiting decided that justice required that we join the protestors. We arrived late, and the National Guard tried to keep us away. The visiting congressional staffer, who had been most reluctant to come in the first place, now totally lost his cool and started screaming about his constitutional rights at some twenty-year-old kid sporting a rifle and looking scared shitless. We got to join the march. Ironically, the judge turned out to be the father of my future wife's best friend, though that piece of information was unknowable to me at the time.

Another vivid training memory involves racial injustice. Part of our training took us to Houston during the Christmas break. One evening, a small group of us went looking for a "private club" where you could join for an hour or so to get a drink. We ran into some others of our group who had just been refused admittance to such a "private" club, ostensibly because one or two of them were black. They can't get away with that, we thought, and back we went. To get "proof" of discrimination, we put some white guys at the front, and they paid the club membership fee and went in. I recall being right next to the first black in our group, though I can no longer recall who it was. The fun really started when our little interracial group reached the front of the line.

Instead of the nominal "membership" fee, the very large man guarding the door pointed to our black member and said, "For you the fee is $10," or some other seemingly outrageous amount for the time. When the guy saw that he was going to pay it, he said, "No, for you, the fee is a million dollars." Then, after a few more words, the pushing and shoving started. The locals were not impressed that we represented the United States Peace Corps. They reacted to that bit of information with a few expletives attached to the less than complimentary attribution that the Peace Corps was nothing but a bunch of Commie-Pinko faggots.

I have a vivid image of a trainee named David, a veteran of civil rights marches in his native Virginia, dropping to the ground in the entranceway. It was a technique he learned protesting racial injustice in his native state. Eventually, we were pushed out to the street and surrounded by a rather large group of menacing-looking rednecks, the size of which has grown in my mind over the intervening years. The term *rednecks* seemed appropriate. On the other hand, I thought their entire heads looked red, not just their necks, the color further brightened I believe by a rapidly growing desire to beat the shit out of us, if not kill us.

For the second time in my life (well, third if you count my one attempt to run around the track at UW-M), I thought I was a dead man. But I saw a police cruiser coming down the street, the cavalry to the rescue. When they pulled up to determine the reason for this rowdy gathering, I asserted with righteous indignation that a violation of the civil rights act had just occurred. I can still recall the look of total incredulity on the cop's face when he said to me, "I don't give a fuck about civil rights." He then rolled up the window and cruised on down the street.

Now, I thought, we are totally dead and went back to work on that damn perfect act of contrition yet again. But we survived and some of us dutifully trooped down to a federal agency (perhaps the FBI) the next day to file some form of complaint. I recall one of the other black trainees not with us that night, laughing at us without any real mirth. "What the hell were you thinking? This is Texas." Whether we knew it or not, some of us white kids were growing up quickly. Playtime seemed to be over.

Two other cross-cultural experiences remain with me. First, we had our Waunakee, Wisconsin, farm experience. You must understand that somewhere during our preparation we were told that India did not need poultry experts. They needed agricultural experts. So, we were to spend some time on a real farm in the quaint town of Waunakee. This rural paradise is located just north of Madison and touts the fact that it is the only Waunakee in the world. This must be true since it is written on a sign visible to visitors as they enter the town. Apparently, no one else in the world has been moved to compete for that singular honor.

While learning to be farmers, we lived in tents and absorbed the unique culture of rural life. Now, I had avoided barbaric rituals like camping out in tents all my life and for good reason. I have a lot of my father in me. He always thought outdoor living was overrated. Even picnics were off limits. If God wanted us to eat outdoors, according to my dad, He would not have created restaurants. Though not an educated man, he had acquired considerable wisdom in life, which he shared generously with me. My favorite T-shirt, which I particularly relish when visiting national parks, was the one proclaiming, "My idea of roughing it is when room service is late." That always evoked a chuckle from the park rangers, but I was serious.

I cannot recall what I learned on the farm, other than it deepened my appreciation for being born and raised in a city. Still, I remember people being very nice to us and the farm family neighbors coming over for a party in our honor. At the party, they sort of looked at us as if they were doing research for a Scientific America article on discovering a new, alien species. My memory is that we could see interstate 94 (the primary Milwaukee to Minneapolis artery) from our tents, and that the place had a sign along the highway saying Henry's Seed Farm, or something like that. Years later, after returning to the area, I thought about stopping to ask if they remembered our little group but then feared that they would. You hate to dredge up painful memories for folk. Over the next several decades, I would pass that sign and strain to see the place I thought our tents had been pitched. Then one day, I realized the sign was gone.

The second was the Indian reservation in South Dakota where we were exposed to a real cross-cultural experience. I always considered most of Indiana as a vast wasteland that even god ignores. Let me tell you, Cherry Creek South Dakota truly is the end of the earth, or was, until I got to my village site in India. On the way there, or maybe the way back, we stopped in Aberdeen South Dakota. Sure enough, we had trouble getting served in a restaurant because one of the dark-skinned Indian PC staff was with us. This just went to prove you could get screwed anywhere in this great land.

It was blazing hot when we arrived on the reservation. We applied our usual cleverness by erecting the tents in an overlapping configuration so that it could serve as a kind of communal shelter. Frank Lloyd Wright would be duly impressed. Once finished, everyone else went off to a swimming hole while I stayed back to keep an eye on things and do what I do best, take a nap. I have always been strong at napping. I keep hoping that they make it an Olympic event someday. Sure enough, a storm blew up, and so did our tents. For five minutes or so, I ran around holding on to tent posts and then said the hell with it and went back to my nap.

The biggest edifice in the town was the kind of community center/church put up by the Mormons. At some point the local boys challenged us to a basketball game at this center. After three minutes, it was clear we were going to get our asses whipped, which is the equivalent of losing badly, very badly. The big difference is that they could run, and we couldn't. I had not made much progress in the stamina department since my aborted run around the UW-M track. So, as I would huff and puff my way to one end of the court, the flow of the game would be going the other way. Death once again stared me in the face as I sought yet again to recover the first line or two of that revered Catholic prayer, the Act of Contrition. Unfortunately, my oxygen-deprived brain was not working. At my last moment of consciousness, someone rushed into the center yelling, "Fire, fire." That's right! I was saved from sure death by a direct act of the same deity I had discarded so casually in college. Go figure!

We rushed out to see a brush fire heading toward our tents. I am sure those conspiracy theorists who argued that it was set deliberately to hasten our departure were wrong. After all, we had to be the best entertainment of the decade. After bravely putting out this raging conflagration, we were congratulating one another when we noticed what looked like another brush fire up on the hill near a house. Off we raced to play the hero one more time. As we were crushing out the last embers, a woman came out of the house and quietly asked why we had put out her fire which she had set, as I recall, to keep snakes away. We gave her a match and sheepishly wound our way back to the camp. For the remainder of the day, though, I worried about what was keeping the snakes away from "our" tents.

There were small lessons and insights everywhere, of course. I recall toward the end of our reservation visit asking a teenager what he was going to do in the future. "I am going to college," he exclaimed. It seemed to me that he had never thought about that possibility before our visit, it was just too far beyond his experience. He probably never went but at least the thought crossed his mind. For a moment at least, he was aware of a wider world.

Looking around, I wondered where inspiration or ambition might be found in this hardscrabble, desolate piece of earth. Even the river that wound through the village betrayed you. Walking into the river, looking for some respite from the summer heat, you would immediately find your legs coated thick with silt pushed along by the current. As modest as my own circumstances had been growing up, they were infinitely advantaged compared to those kids living amid such impoverished isolation. Clearly, anyone who thinks life's starting line is equal has never been to Cherry Creek SD.

It rained the day we were to depart on a bus. Still, quite a few of the villagers gathered to see us off. A great cheer went up as the bus lumbered down the now muddy dirt road. A greater groan erupted as it slid off the road into a gulley. The whole village now joined as one in pushing us back onto the road to make sure we got on our way once again. They made a difficult task look easy. The prospect that our stay might be extended galvanized all into decisive, united action. It is like when mothers lift cars by themselves to save their babies. Desperation allows us to accomplish great feats.

The biggest training surprise had been that India no longer needed poultry experts. At first, we thought that a good thing since we had none of those in our group. India now needed agricultural experts. Bad thing, none of us could fake being one of those very well either. However, I do think a couple of the trainees had seen a farm at one point in their young lives. On the other hand, we all had eaten chicken at one time or another. No matter, we had enough hubris, and ignorance, to believe that we could make a positive contribution despite the lack of skills, experience, or knowledge. We were wrong.

In the summer of 1967, stateside training was over, and we were bound for India. So many shiny, hopeful faces that started out on the Peace Corps journey were now gone. Someone estimated that only one-quarter of those starting on day one remained at the finish of our two-year stint. Many had decided on other paths during training, others left when the reality of India became undeniable, but a number had been deselected...bureaucratize for being involuntarily cut from the program. I had gotten close to one gal who was deselected, I believe at the end of the first summer. I could not for the life of me see how she differed from the rest of us. Hell, I couldn't even run around the damn track, not even when chasing an attractive female. I questioned the training director but, of course, he could not talk about it. In truth, I did not protest all that much

In India, I would face the bigger challenges in my search for meaning and a path in life.

High school prom with Maribeth

The clueless rebel in college figuring things out.

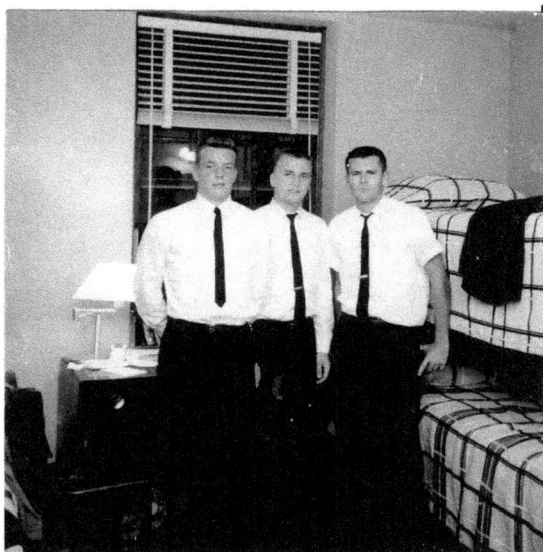

Me, on the right, with Seminary room mates

Carol at Clark

My graduation picture

Lee on graduation day

CHAPTER 10

SERVING

It's really a wonder that I have not dropped all my
ideals because they seem so absurd and impossible to
carry out. Yet I keep them, because in spite of everything,
I still believe that people are really good at heart.

—Anne Frank

Our chartered Peace Corps flight from London to India stopped in Beirut. You could see a strong military presence along with scars from the most recent outbreak of civil strife. Then, after a stop in Tehran to let off other Peace Corps groups, it was on to Delhi. As we crossed into India, we had a sign of things to come. The cowling covering one of the engines simply crumpled and fell off. This got everyone's attention including the Air India flight crew. Our near-death experience did rate a minor piece on the front page of the *India Times* the next day. The good volunteers of India-44, however, had been spared to wreak havoc on the subcontinent for the next two years.

In some respects, we were well trained. They told us India would be hot, and it was. In many other respects, we were not. They had tried to prepare us for many of those divides that separate our two cultures. In the end, that simply is not possible. For example, you can be told there is a difference in how time is calculated, and you even can appreciate that difference as an abstract piece of knowledge. But when someone tells you the bus "is just now coming," you are simply grounded in a Western expectation to look for the bus. The fact that "now" might mean five seconds or five minutes or five hours or even five days is beyond us. Time is more than an abstract concept, it is a culturally defined phenomenon. It is a construct that shapes how our minds and even our bodies work. And that is just one obvious example.

But I get ahead of myself as is my wont. The in-country experience started with, guess what, more training. I struggle now, over four decades later, to recall what I learned about cutting-edge agriculture. But frankly, I draw a total blank. One inescapable lesson taken from our experience is that you cannot turn a bunch of urban bred and raised kids into farmers in a few weeks. Farming is very much a craft, a complex vocation where experience and aptitude play key roles. Some master its complexities through a lifetime of exposure and hands-on training. Others study it in our colleges and universities where the intricate interplay of soils and fertilizers and ecological interactions are investigated in detail.

We got a smattering of preparation amidst intense training in language, cultural nuances, and so much more.

The Peace Corps staff members were a committed bunch, and the program invested lots in us (okay, too much in things we would never do). Moreover, the staff were top notch despite working with the terminally uneducable. I still remember Usha and Amar, two of our India-based language instructors, with great fondness. Both were advanced university students in Delhi and became good friends to a few of us. Two other volunteers and I enjoyed visiting Amar's family over in the Radio Colony section of Delhi. Later, the three of us were invited to the wedding of her brother up in the Punjab. It was a lavish affair and an unforgettable cultural experience.

As we neared the goal line of our endless training, I recall a couple of isolated images. We briefly stayed at some school, likely a dormitory for a local Udaipur college. Each night, when we returned to our room, the biggest rats I ever met would greet us, and I do mean of the rodent variety. We would chase them around the room, finally realizing that some would take refuge in the drainage pipes that dumped excess water out into a courtyard. With vengeance in mind, we poured near boiling water down the pipes. This proved a temporary defeat for the rat kingdom since there were always more to terrorize us the next day. Still, our small act of revenge felt good. Those rats were huge, surely able to devour a city bus or any smaller volunteer who strayed within reach.

I recall a conversation with several students, probably at the same school. "So, what do you eat in America?" one asked. We were always getting such intellectually provocative queries. Upon running out of meats whose Hindi equivalent I could recall, I threw beef into the list. This comes back to me as a classic ouch memory. It was a word thrown out that could not be retrieved. The student's faces twisted with horror; cows being sacred to most Indians then and probably now. I immediately realized two things. It is very hard to explain a concept like cultural relativity with a sixth-grade command of the local language. And second, for almost two years, there would be no such thing as a casual conversation.

But really, what I most remember about those final training days were the basketball games. Somehow, the American Peace Corps all-stars wound up playing a brief series of games against the local boys from Udaipur University. This quickly became a popular event with local spectators supporting the home team and the PC family cheering for the stalwart Americans. Hah, Naismith (the creator of the game), would have been proud of the way we demonstrated the superiority of U.S. round ball skills. Then again, showing up the local youth may not have been our smartest move.

One day we arrived for a scheduled match, but the opposing team had been switched. In place of the local kids was a military team, or so we were told. Perhaps they were the police, they were big and tough in any case. As I think about it, they might have been lifers from the local prison. I don't know how the rest of our team fared, but every time I moved to the basket, or tried for a rebound, my midsection would be rearranged by an opponent's fist. The locals in the crowd enjoyed the mauling, perhaps our one contribution to improving US-Indian relations. I can still recall our mild-mannered agriculture instructor from some Western state screaming at the officials to call a foul, just once. Visions of the headline "Peace Corps group ejected from country after basketball brawl" danced in my head.

Our local university opponents must have forgiven us since they asked three of us to join the regional team to help represent Udaipur at the all-India tournament in Jaipur. We eagerly accepted. After all, how many points would we score for Peace Corps and America if we brought basketball glory back to our home area? There was one problem with this plan, though. Udaipur was a basketball backwater. Most of the other teams participating in the tournament could play the game, which I thought put us at a disadvantage. While my conditioning had vastly improved since our debacle on the South Dakota reservation and my aborted marathon around the track during training, we were soundly defeated in our first game. It was not even close. We played one more game against some other losers and were quite competitive as I recall. I believe we may even have won, though no discoverable record of our overall performance remains. Our days of athletic glory were over, but the trip was great fun.

Eventually the day of reckoning arrived. After a seemingly endless period of preparation, and one final celebration at the Lake Palace, we were to be dumped off at our sites one fine morning. The Lake Palace, by the way, is a very romantic hotel, a former playground of the last local Raj of pre-independence India, situated in the middle of (you will never guess) a lake. Many celebrities have stayed there, like Jackie Kennedy, and at least one James Bond movie extensively used it as a background site. Oddly enough, I believe it was recently chosen by experts in such matters as the best luxury hotel in the world. That's right, in the world! In retrospect, this last party had all the trappings of the condemned man's last meal.

Salumbar . . .

My site partner and I were scheduled to head to a place called Salumbar, a decent-sized town located about forty to fifty kilometers south of Udaipur. Another volunteer would be dropped off at his site even farther south, way beyond the reach of civilization. Our worldly possessions were packed on a back of a truck along with the two of us and off we were on a rather hair-raising trip down a twisting road that settled out of the Aravalli Hills before reaching the bleak, desert like terrain that was to be our home. And I do mean bleak and unforgiving.

We would make many trips to and from our site and Udaipur over the next two years. These sojourns took place on the local mass transit system, busses that surely were constructed by the vehicle maker Henry Ford forced out of business around 1909. Of course, it was always a pleasure to share your motoring experience with locals suffering from motion sickness and with various species of livestock. I always wondered, though, why the goats and chickens got their seat preference before me.

The trip up to Udaipur typically brought doubts whether this sleek motoring machine would make it or whether the duct tape would split, and the engine drop to the road. The trip back down always raised a different concern with visions of hurtling over the side of the mountain, or was it just a hill, to oblivion thousands (hundreds) of feet below. Sure enough, one day the brakes failed, and we hurtled around curves with increasing speed. Everyone was screaming as I frantically fumbled for that "perfect act of contrition" that I had now written out but had trouble locating. No luck, and now I cursed since I could only recall the first line. My prospects for getting to heaven were dim indeed. Our intrepid driver saved the day, however, by ramming the bus into the side of the hill at a brief point where the elevation went up, not down.

Our first trip down the road from hell, however, proved quite uneventful so Randy, my site-mate, and I looked forward to being greeted by a group of excited locals. Surely, I thought, the arrival of the Peace Corps miracle workers would warrant some visible display of anticipation, or at least one lonely greeter. But no, the truck pulled up to a few isolated government buildings that were surrounded by . . . nothing. No sign of life was visible, no town, no welcoming banners, no brass band, in fact, no people at all. The far side of the moon probably looks more inviting. There was just hard packed dirt punctuated by small bushes and an occasional dwarf-like tree or big bush. *This looks exciting*, I thought.

While Randy guarded our worldly possessions, off I went to find civilization. The town of Salumbar was a mile or so away beyond the next rise in the road, depending on whether you took the short cut along a small lake or followed the main highway. It was the major local town that still had a remnant of an old Raj palace, a reminder of its former importance. There was a bank, post office, a restaurant, several tea shops, a gas station, numerous small retail shops, and a variety of government buildings and schools. We were to be housed in the government residences located on the site from which a variety of rural community development activities were administered.

There were accommodations for four or five government workers on site, but none ever chose to live there, preferring to live in town. Of course, it is possible that our presence had driven local real estate values down. All in all, the accommodations were not bad, once we swept out the scorpions, put up some screens, and the electricity arrived. We had been told that electricity was "just now coming" and it was, after about six months. Before bothering to install this amenity, I suspect they waited to see if we would come to our senses and flee back to America. To their dismay, we stayed.

Running water was a luxury not to be enjoyed and one relieved oneself into a hole in a small, unlit room adjacent to our living quarters. You squatted over the hole and then cleansed yourself using your left hand and a small container of water brought along for that purpose. When I explained our Western custom, many locals thought toilet paper very unhygienic. Hitting the head, so to speak, could be an adventure at night, when tipsy, with no moon, and a forgotten torch or what we would call a flashlight. But the rest of the living quarters were adequate, a small office/living room, sleeping quarters big enough for two cots with mosquito netting, and an entrance way that could be used as a kitchen. Good enough, we thought.

On the other hand, we had no idea what the hell we were doing there. I still remember standing with a local farmer as we looked over his wheat crop that had recently broken the surface of the soil. He asked me how it looked. I was surprised the sprouts were green. Why weren't those damn shoots brown, like the "amber" waves of grain in that patriotic song? Or when a local farmer asked me if his soil would be good for these new-fangled, high-yield seeds we were peddling. I picked up a handful of his dirt, scrunched it in my fingers, and threw it up in the air before turning to him with supreme confidence, saying, "Yes, your soil is perfect." How the hell would I know? My only farming experience had been on a 10 × 5-foot garden plot in my back yard while growing up in Worcester. That little experiment resulted in several scrawny radishes.

This lack of confidence was more than just a personal shortcoming. Our primary mission was to help spread the use of those newer, high yield varieties of seed. This was part of what Norman Borlaug and others launched as the so-called "green" revolution. The basic choice farmers faced was simple but fraught with risk. They could throw their usual seed stock into the ground and be relatively assured of a crop, even if this approach resulted in a rather meager yield. On the other hand, they could try this fancy new stuff which was expensive and required careful attention to every detail—planting at the right depth, using fertilizer at the correct times and located the appropriate distance from the seed, and watering at proper intervals. And yet, even if you did all this correctly, you still risked that someone earlier in the seed distribution chain had stolen the good stuff and replaced it with some worthless substitute.

No problem you say, just go for it and encourage the local farmers to engage in a little US-style entrepreneurship. No risk, no reward, right? Not so simple, however. Most farm plots were tiny. Complicating matters furthermore, successes in public health were evidencing unforeseen outcomes. Children were surviving in greater numbers even though rural families yet assumed that many children were necessary to ensure that male offspring were available to support them in old age. The resulting imbalance between progress and perception was overly large families that were to survive on the thin thread of postage stamp size plots situated in what was, at best, a marginal agricultural area. If a poorer farmer tried to be entrepreneurial, and any one of several things that could go wrong did go wrong, the consequences were more than a write-off on this year's taxes. It was devastation for the family. Malnutrition, perhaps starvation, was not out of the question.

Almost unconsciously you chose to work with the better-off farmers who spoke English or at least Hindi (as opposed to the local dialect of Mewari) and those who had the wherewithal to survive disaster. On a micro-level you knew you were exacerbating the kind of inequality that was anathema to crypto-revolutionaries like myself. But the possible guilt associated with failure was simply too overwhelming.

Still, we did have successful demonstration plots. I recall a photo of brilliant, thick waves of "green" wheat growing next to sparser yields from local seeds. A satisfied local farmer is looking at the camera with great pride and satisfaction. Various other projects were entertained to keep us busy. We planted a local garden outside our modest abode to encourage similar efforts locally. Then we built a chicken coop on top of our house to encourage that cottage industry. The garden worked well until thieving animals somehow breached our impregnable security. The chickens laid eggs until they all died while we vacationed somewhere while putting our crack household staff in charge. I even convinced some of my former professors at my alma mater to get their current students to raise money to expand the local school library.

At the end of the day, it was hard to say that we influenced the course of history in India, much less the town of Salumbar and environs. I did, however, run across the somewhat apocryphal "fact" that India went from a grain-importing nation to a grain-exporting nation sometime during our tour, between 1967 and 1969. I certainly like to take credit for this, you can't dispute the numbers. My explanation makes more sense than the conventional wisdom that a severe drought ended during the period of our service due to the return of the monsoons.

Our quality of life, if not survival itself, depended on our faithful staff—Rooknot and Cutchroo (phonetic spelling). Rooknot served as a kind household chief of staff, while Cutchroo, a teenage boy from a local tribe, did the actual work. I guess you could say we had a staff, much like that PBS Masterpiece theater series about the British aristocracy. Our servants were just a bit more rough-edged than their British counterparts.

Their responsibilities involved doing the shopping, cooking, boiling water, identifying which local creatures would kill us, and so on. The boiling water part was crucial. In the local step wells resided the dreaded guinea worm, small cysts that would situate themselves in your body and grow to considerable lengths before erupting through your skin. Your option then was a local hospital, think Marquis De Sade, or the local barber/surgeon who would slowly twist the worm around a stick, hoping it would not break and disappear back under your skin to form a painful abscess. Neither option was appealing. One story is that the current striped barber poll is a stylized version of a worm encircling a stick, a form of medieval ad from the days when step wells and guinea worms existed throughout Europe. There are, of course, competing stories.

Rooknot was a character, always with a mischievous smile. He reminded me of Zorba the Greek from the movie about how a poor Greek villager opens up a visiting Englishman to new experiences. I recall he definitely thought Randy and I needed female companionship, which of course was obvious to anyone noting our twitching and drooling. He kept saying how he could sneak in the women without anyone knowing. But our sense of caution prevailed, barely. Our female deprivation plight was dramatically illustrated when we got a cat (finish the story, pervert, before jumping to any conclusions) an acquisition motivated by the fact that I awoke with a rodent on my chest one night. It took Randy half an hour to peel me off the ceiling.

Each night, we would hear rodents running around our place. Each morning, we would empty the daily catch from our mousetraps. Indeed, a resident cat was the answer. After all, they torture rodents, don't they? In this case, our scheme turned out to be one of our more successful initiatives. We named our feline hunter Billie (pronounced beelee after the Hindi word for cat). No more rats on the tummy. Then one day, a female cat in heat decided to visit. Billie leapt halfway up the screen and began to wail. There was nothing to do but let him out, after which he disappeared for a couple of days. We would hear the cat wailing in the distance followed by silence and then by even more wailing, and more silence. Finally, Billie returned, looking like shit, but seemingly very happy. He slept for about three days straight. *Damn cat*, I thought, *is getting a lot more action than I.* Then again, who didn't?

Fortunately for the gals we trained with in the States, they were stationed well away from us and out of harm's way. That is what we thought at least until we found out that another male group, India-40, was stationed in that area. Females just can't catch a break. As I recall, we all did get together as a group on an occasion or two. When we did, my wit and charm especially overflowed. There was no off switch though the search for one never abated. So, I said to a small gathering of the gals one day, "This damn Peace Corps is misnamed . . . Why, I've been here for six months and haven't gotten a piece yet!" I can still see them bent over while howling with laughter. No offer of relief was forthcoming, though, which naturally was the purpose of my wit in the first instance. The art of nuanced seduction always escaped me. Still, I am grateful for one God-given gift. I have always been good at making women laugh, usually at me.

Rooknot did keep us supplied with local booze, which came in a variety of appealing colors. I think pink was my favorite. We did not ask many questions about its origins, but stories about poisonous additives to the bathtub gin from our own prohibition era kept circling my head. Nevertheless, it remained an irreplaceable anesthetic after long, hot days. During the dry season, the thermometer in our place hit between 108 and 112 on a regular basis. But it was a dry heat as we were constantly informed.

It was lovely most evenings when darkness summoned a cooler breeze off the desert. We could sit on our roof and enjoy quiet time associated with the sunsets of rural India. The pink hues of day's ending would be replaced with a canopy of stars. I remember the serenity in particular, the almost glacial pace of life. From somewhere, we obtained a telescope that enabled us to examine the moon and other celestial bodies. I never felt closer to the world around us. After several drinks of local brew, our final task of the day was to climb down the ladder that we used to get up on the roof in the first place. Descending the ladder without falling and breaking our necks was the trick. Often it was a close-run thing.

One day, I looked out and felt something was missing. I spent that day looking out over the bleak landscape across the highway. Around evening I had my "aha" moment. Someone had cut down one of the few small trees on the horizon and carted away the remains. This was a big change. How different from today when my smart phone connects me to an ever-changing world on a 24-7 basis. I have yet to decide if that is true progress.

Snippets from letters to Lee . . .

I wrote often to Lee, my college sweetheart. I would touch upon what I was thinking and feeling during this period. Life in India was not only about events and challenges but also about living in a different world and in a different way. I found the pace of life seductive and even instructive. At the same time, the daily routine stretched my patience, as it did for all of my fellow volunteers. We were all driven, relatively ambitious, Westerners. We were used to working hard, pushing ourselves. Now, we were isolated, typically alone with ourselves and our thoughts. There was loneliness to be sure, a theme that arises from time to time in a number of these missives. But there also was this struggle to adjust our internal clocks to our new world, a transformation that did not come easily. For me, the water buffalo captured at least part of my new environment perfectly. In one letter to Lee I wrote:

> *Life is really incredibly slow here. As I look out my front door, rickety wooden carts inch their way with painful reluctance along the dust-filled road. At a further distance are a group of water buffalo, which must rank as the ugliest and stupidest animals on earth, who are doing what I suspect comes naturally . . . waiting for death. Their lives, when I think on it, are little more than a perpetual response to momentary stimuli . . . food, water, noise, and other things that catch their attention.*
>
> *In reality, I admire their capacity to wallow in a complete void and lack of awareness bred by centuries of*

dependent servitude. Yet, perhaps my attraction to these beasts stems more from their obvious analogy to the human species. They have adopted many of man's more intractable characteristics . . . dullness, slowness, dependence, and a complete lack of awareness. Yet, they have maintained one inestimable advantage, a debilitating self-indulgence that vitiates their capacity or desire for senseless savagery and pointless domination.

Though not exactly an uplifting message, there were moments of triumph amidst the typical routine of heat and futility. We were, in fact, more ambitious than the water buffalo I so admired. We really did have a bunch of ideas and projects, a few of which resulted in something actually being accomplished.

One such project was the erection of our chicken coop mentioned earlier. We built our monument to poultry on the top of our government housing, so it would be visible to all. It was to be an example to others though I don't recall anyone jumping on the chicken bandwagon. As I recall, we built this edifice entirely with our own hands as a few onlookers watched in amusement while pointing at the crazy Americans. Those who know me have surely succumbed to a fit of uncontrollable laughter by now. Changing a lightbulb typically is a major achievement for a klutz like me. Building a chicken coop, on the other hand, is beyond the pale and a testament to how Peace Corps stretched me.

The high moment of the chicken coop project is described below in another letter to Lee:

> *Well, the miracle of miracles has just occurred. No, it is not the second coming. The fact is that we are now the proud owners of egg laying chickens. That's right! Randy has just suffered a case of apoplexy screaming for me to come up to the roof. There, praise to God, was an egg which one of our chickens had the audacity to lay . . . . . You may say that that I am perhaps exaggerating the importance of this event. Well, perhaps it is true that we do so little right here that we are grasping at straws. Besides, our veracity and claims to expertise had come under question. We had stated on numerous occasions that chickens were capable of laying eggs without cohabitating with their male counterparts (our course in poultry raising was complete with appropriate references to analogous human female functions). This now vindicates our righteousness and enhances our claims to omniscience.*

The physical hardships were real enough. After a cool and pleasant winter, the daily temperatures would rise day after day, week after week. By April, the heat was overwhelming, surrounding us with a debilitating torpor that sapped our energy.

> *Welcome from the world's original blast furnace. Summer is here and the Loo, the hot, dry summer winds have begun to sweep across our developing desert. The*

temperature averages about 110 degrees now, but fortunately it is a dry, more tolerable kind of heat. The only difficulty here is that as soon as you step out into the intense sunlight, the moisture is literally sucked right out of you, leaving your skin with the texture of a dried prune.

As you would imagine, we are not getting out very often. Since the harvests are in there really isn't much to do. As an index of our paucity of work, I've devoured four books and started a fifth (Ulysses) in the past five days. This is the worst time of year. Beyond the heat and the boredom, the incidence of diarrhea and dysentery rises sharply. And a host of unsavory beasts (cobras and scorpions) begin to appear. It is truly the time that tries men's souls, both Indian and American alike.

Despite the daily struggle, the sameness that eroded early idealism, I found reasons to remain positive and upbeat.

It is another typical Rajasthani day here. The temperature under the aegis of a bitterly hot sun is creeping over the 110-degree mark and the sucking dry wind . . . is blowing off the hills and sweeping along the brittle, cracked earth. Like most of the other living creatures here, we simply crawl into some hole for protection until the sun sinks into a bloody demise toward the west . . . life is frustrating, but it is exactly what I expected. It may very well be the difficulty of the experience that gives it value that makes us aware of both our limitations and strengths.

In many ways, though, life is quite satisfying here. There is a great deal of satisfaction in the relationships, the small successes in agriculture, and the increasing awareness of self and other people. And there is progress. Despite some late damage, farmers are impressed and much more of the new wheat will be planted next year along with newer and better seed varieties. A variety of maize (corn) which was used by 30 farmers this year will be sown by as many as 200 in the next season. Farmers are also going to try a new variety of rice we have brought in.

Things are moving, and I am basically satisfied.

Despite the hardships, the heat, the boredom, the loneliness, and some late crisis that I thought might have undermined our outreach efforts, I remained fairly upbeat. My estimate of what we would have called target group penetration (the proportion of targeted farmers who actually considered using the new seed varieties) amazes me all these years later. I am really struck by the discussion of maize and rice, which were not grown in the area to any extent as I recall. But, then again, so much has been lost to memory after four-plus decades.

The feel of the place . . .

You became much more sensitive to the rhythms of existence, the cycles of the moon, repeated patterns of daily lives. Here and now, I never pay attention to things like full moons. There and then, it was a good thing, perhaps even a blessing. At a minimum, it was easier finding the outhouse after a night of local brew if the moon were full and the sky cloudless. Calming patterns were everywhere. We would watch water buffalo wander down the highway. Every once in a while, a bus would roar by and we would begin to count—one, two, three. Around six or seven, the buffalo would suddenly react, long after the bus had moved on. Apparently, it took that long for his brain to be engaged. I thought, *Gee, I have a lot more in common with these creatures than I would have imagined.* We kept somewhat engaged by writing books (well, I wrote one book and I know Randy started one), devouring every piece of literature we could find and desperately savaging every letter and magazine from home.

You often felt like you were trapped in a pulp-fiction Western thriller. I have always liked history, visiting famous sites, reading historical books, and the like. Historian Doris Goodwin, as a little girl growing up in Brooklyn, talks about imagining what it was like living in far gone times. I have always felt a similar pull of the imagination. Walking through parts of Salumbar, I would envision I was actually in Dodge City, circa 1880. I can recall a herd of water buffalo kicking up dirt as they were driven through town by tough looking men riding camels, carbines slung over their shoulders and bandoliers strapped around their chests. One could easily see Matt

Dillon (Gunsmoke) drawing against some desperado or Wyatt Earp lurking waiting to confront the Dalton gang.

So much of what we saw and felt would fit nicely in a time capsule—the women beating clothes by the lake bordering the town, the simple farming tools and techniques used for generations upon generations, the feudal customs that shaped interpersonal interactions. Yet, if you looked closer, change was palpable, subtle transformations both deep and profound. I would look at the generation of elders. They typically spoke Mewari (the local dialect), had grown up during the British Raj and thus were governed for all practical purposes by local nobility, and had a world view that seldom looked beyond their immediate experience. Their children, the adults of that period, typically spoke Hindi, read newspapers, and had a world view that stretched to Delhi and beyond. The young, for the most part, were in school, learning elementary English, and would likely have access to technologies that would broaden their world view significantly. If you looked closely, one's sense of the world, and the individual's place in it, was evolving across generations in dramatic ways.

At the same time, you could sense that so many were trapped in more traditional ways of understanding their world. One attribute that the British had in spades but failed to leave behind was the discipline of the queue. If a dozen Indians met at the entrance of a five-hundred-seat movie theatre, a riot would break out even though it was apparent to all that enough seats were available. I often felt the same about these small farmers who had far more children than they could support on their meager assets. Siring fewer children risked not having anyone to care for them in a society where no public safety net existed. While many more of their children were surviving and reaching adulthood, it was hard to take that risk. India would have to make a profound leap forward if it was to absorb all the kids who would be pushed off the land in the coming decades. It struck me at the time as a Malthusian apocalypse waiting to unfold. The ensuing decades proved that the improbable was more or less possible though not easy.

I recall, in a conversation with a black fellow student during graduate studies back in the States, mentioning the lack of anonymity in India. Wherever you went, particularly outside major cities, you were an object of curiosity. Children would stare and follow you. You were subject to endless and repetitive questions. Sometimes you were made fun of, not surprising given how many mistakes we made, but sometimes you were treated with a deference and respect you did not deserve. But the inescapable reality was that you were always on display, always visible, always the subject of intense scrutiny. He looked at me with a smile and said, "Then you do know what it is like being me."

In India, you were always "on stage" in a continuing play with a set of complex characters and a convoluted plot. In our ordinary lives, we exist more or less unconsciously 90 percent of the time. In my case it is more likely 99.9 percent of the time. Life is a repeated series of well-scripted interactions where the social and interactional rules are second nature. In India, you realize at some point that everything requires thought. You are immersed in a society that is an incredibly complex and chaotic canvass of caste, color, class, religion, language, history, ethnic identity, political disposition, and on and on. You had to continuously calculate with whom you were interacting and what rules and conventions governed those specific interactions. Virtually every social interaction contained at least the possibility of misunderstanding and hurt feelings. It is hard to imagine what it takes out of you to think about what you are doing all of the time.

Obviously, mistakes were all too frequent and sensitivities hurt more than we liked. Over time, the effort to negotiate the labyrinths of this social web wore you down. But it was more than that. There was nowhere to go to "blow off steam," to just relax. You couldn't go drinking with the boys because the boys didn't drink (at least in public). You could not consort with comforting women to soothe the weary spirit since the potential cost was a lot more than a few Rupees; it was the loss of respect along with any effectiveness in your site. You probably could do drugs, but your ticket home would be punched early if caught. As a consequence, you stuffed it in, plodded on, and did your best not to leave with the local's perception of America worse than when you arrived.

Recollections of everyday life are mostly small memories that crowd in, sparkle for a moment, and then are replaced by others.

A group of farmers encouraging me to go ahead and pet that cute baby camel and then laughing as the mother charged while I ran for my life. Fortunately, I could actually run with considerable celerity by this time. I recall being offered sugar cane juice squeezed fresh at harvest time. Nothing is sweeter, trust me. I think of the time I was about to put my hands into the water pot we used to wash our hands when I heard something splash around. I jumped back to the merriment of our household staff who doubled over in laughter. A moment later, they looked in, still smiling at the ridiculous Americans. One look, though, and they yelped in panic. They swept up the pot and rushed out the door midst a great hue and cry. I never got a good explanation. Apparently, though, I escaped something very bad.

I recall our Superman bicycles with unbridled hatred. Month after month I cycled over dirt paths that would suddenly turn to sand. That would send me flying over the handle bars into a heap of hurt on the ground as the damn bike landed on top of me. I was spared even more accidents by the fact that the piece of crap was broken half the time. Years later, my wife could not understand why I did not share her romantic vision of us riding our bicycles at sunset. Personally, I would prefer drinking crushed glass.

I recall wandering through the streets of Salumbar where, over time, our presence evoked less and less curiosity. I had some favorite locals, with whom I would sit in their shops and pass the time of day. It was a good way to get a sense of local life. After the fact, I realized I spent about equal time with a Hindu merchant and a Muslim merchant, instinctively seeking cultural and political balance. Still, as eager as each apparently was to have my company, neither ever invited me into their homes or for dinner. Some degrees of separation were hard to overcome.

I recall doing some fun things, attending local celebrations and refereeing games of basketball at the local high school, which was more like herding cats than calling fouls. On occasion, we played card games with some locals by which I contributed financially to their economy. On days I tried real work, I used to travel to smaller villages outside of Salumbar, the names of which I no longer recall. There, I would chat with farmers as I walked around with a local development officer. It was never totally clear what my role was, but no one seemed to mind my presence. Periodically, I recall filling out some forms outlining all that I (we) had done and all that we intended to do. If only intentions were reality, Salumbar would have become a beacon to the free world.

I especially recall losing copious amounts of weight, even though my appetite for food and drink never slacked in the least. In fact, I grew to love Indian food, even okra, a love that remains with me today. My vision of heaven has evolved over time. Forget about those seventy-seven virgins who theoretically would find me irresistible. My new vision of heaven now consists of unlimited access to a variety of curries containing absolutely no calories whatsoever. During my tour, my weight bottomed out somewhere in the upper 140s, not very substantial given my 6'1" frame. The Peace Corps doctor who checked me out attributed the weight loss, at least in part, to hard work. He obviously never saw me in my village.

Some pictures of me show a rather cadaverous guy with thick, black hair, sporting cool Buddy Holley glasses. No wonder the women were throwing themselves at me, at least in my feverish imagination. The real culprits responsible for my weight loss, once the hard work hypothesis had been discredited, turned out to be an assortment of intestinal parasites with whom I shared my daily sustenance. Looking at pictures taken during my tour, my poor mother thought I was at death's door and came close to contacting our Congressman.

I doubt I look much like that guy anymore. Maybe it's the extra ninety pounds, maybe it is misplacing my hair somewhere, or maybe I should find another pair of cool Buddy Holley glasses. As my first Peace Corps reunion approached, I showed around a group picture taken during our India training days, asking a number of my contemporary colleagues and friends to pick me out. Only two or three did so successfully. Often, when I pointed out the correct choice, the subject of my little experiment would exclaim with incredulity, "That's not you, no way." What really hurt was my wife guessed wrong, and then muttered for weeks afterward something about how cute I was back then and asking what happened.

And there were laughs of course. I just have to share another vignette of every-day life captured in one of my letters to Lee:

> *Randall and I have been enduring the boredom of these last days of April until we are able to take off for the Himalayas on the 1ˢᵗ. Today the temp was 120 degrees, a couple degrees higher than I am accustomed. But there are diversions to keep our corrupted minds occupied . . . we decided to finish off our favorite rat through the discriminate utilization of our rational faculties. We decided, after much thought, on the following plan.*

> *When the rat entered our combined living room, study, and dining room, we would: A) close the door; B) position Randall on the cot within easy striking distance of the door; C) I would flush the rat from behind the combination desk and dining room table (the usual habitat of our prey); D) as the rat scurried to the safety of the other room, Randall would take careful aim and let fly his sneaker (especially secured for the occasion) with precision and accuracy which would inevitably hit me on the toe; E) Randall would fall off the cot in a drunken stupor; F) we would say 'fuck it' and go back to our drinking.*

And after an apparent pause in my letter writing to execute the well-considered plan . . .

> *We just blew it. We had the rat trapped in our combination entrance hall and work room. Randall was*

poised as usual with sneaker while I braved risks far beyond the call of duty to flush the bastard (the rat, not Randall) out from behind its protection. But at the critical moment, my drunken roommate decided he had to relight his half-smoked cigarette (I think he doused it when he took a drink while forgetting to remove the cigarette from his mouth). In his rather uncoordinated state, he only succeeded in burning the tip of his nose, which sent him into some ridiculously grotesque dance of pain. As he hopped around our combination entrance hall–work room, the rat scurried to the safety of our kitchen. Well, you have just witnessed (in a way) one of the great moments in Peace Corps history.

We gave up on our ill-conceived plans. Perhaps if they had been executed while sober, some chance of success might have been feasible. Instead, we conquered the rodent kingdom by bringing in reinforcements, our infamous cat Billie.

Travels in India . . .

I vividly recall third-class trains, particularly during the hot season which also was the marriage season. Half of India seemingly was on the move, so the trains were packed on the insides, with additional scores perched on top of the cars and hanging off the sides. Remember the movie *Dr. Zhivago* when the family was fleeing Moscow after the revolution along with thousands of others? The huge crowd rushed to the train as it pulled in, pushing and shoving their way into a car until a soldier started beating them back when the car was full. That pretty much captured the Indian train experience during marriage season except there was no soldier to beat back the surging crowd. I recall hurtling through a window to get aboard and enjoy the luxury of riding in a packed train in hundred-degree-plus heat while village women threw up next to me, if not on me.

For most of the year there were two kinds of heat: the dry, scorching heat that ran from March to June and the wet and humid heat of the monsoon season that ran through September or October. You thought the first was bad until the second arrived. Every crawling and flying creature imaginable emerged with the rain. After a while, even drinking water from a cup involved challenges. You always covered the cup, with a book or some suitable covering. Without thinking, you raised the cup to your lips, lifted the covering off, looked at the liquid, and only then imbibed. Failure to follow the recommended sequence could result in the ingestion of some unknown insect that would settle in your drink during an unguarded moment. Of course, insects in your drink might prove fortuitous on occasion. When imbibing local booze of questionable origins, the death of a flying pest upon contact with the liquid might be a useful sign of how toxic the booze was.

Two years in India and I never did get to the Taj Mahal. Then again, I never visited many of the historical New England sites until I brought my wife to see them. I did get to one of the hill stations in the foothills of the Himalayas and to Goa, the former Portuguese colony on the west coast of the subcontinent south of Bombay. The hill resort was cool with magnificent views, of course. But my clearest memory was less inspiring. I recall sipping my drink on a veranda looking over the majestic vista before me. My sweet reverie was disturbed, however, by the sight of smallish local men carrying cases of Coke and other drinks up the side of the steep mountain. Apparently, human labor was cheaper than trucking the liquid up to us pampered Westerners. Good to support the local economy and all, but my drinks never quite tasted the same after that. I really felt like the ugly American.

Goa was paradise. Back then, the best places in the world had been discovered by the international hippie community—Nepal, Negril Beach in Jamaica, and Goa, just to name a few. My memory was that the beach was perfect, unspoiled except for a couple of small hotels. The landscape was dominated by local fisherman plying their trade, cool evening breezes, and spectacular sunsets. At noon we would amble down to the small restaurant and tell them what we wanted that night for dinner, then dine rapturously on marvelous cuisine to the beat of the surf just yards away. Or, we might have a lobster lunch for what amounted to something like forty cents as I recall. That is not all, though. It turned out there was a special viewing of the uncorrupted body of St. Francis Xavier during our visit. The occasion was a visit of some papal official. I thought St. Francis looked a bit worn, but he was in decent shape considering he died several centuries ago. I should look so good and I am, technically speaking, still alive.

On the boat back to Bombay, we snuck up to first class, one of the privileges of being a Westerner. There, we met an official representing the Government of Czechoslovakia. For a bit, we sparred about which of us were the real spies, but he agreed that American spies would not need to sneak into the first-class section of the boat. After a few drinks, we became fast friends and he insisted we visit him on our way back to the States. In the months that followed, we exchanged correspondence in which our Czech friend inquired what kind of liquor we enjoyed, what kind of car we wanted, and what type of women we preferred. The last question was easy—women with non-existent standards. Of course, by this time a coat rack in the corner would look sexy to us.

He seemed intent on making our visit memorable or recruiting us as red spies. Unfortunately, we will never know which or how cheaply we might have been bought. All this occurred during the days of what was known as the "Prague Spring," when Alexander Dubcek was experimenting with a liberalization of thought and speech in a nominally Communist regime. Then, one day, we heard that Soviet tanks crushed the hopes of the reformers. We never heard from our friend again.

Our need for Western contact was satisfied by periodic visits to Udaipur. Other volunteers always seemed to be around. We generally stayed at the Chetna hotel, a dump without any charm but within our price range. We ate at Berry's restaurant, which had decent food and looked Western. Occasionally, we saw an English movie that always ran on Sunday mornings. Udaipur was a lovely place with lakes and hills and a rich history. The city stood at the northwest frontier and guarded the country from periodic invasions from the west. Traditionally, Rajasthan warriors were known as fierce fighters. As I looked around, what they were fighting for all those centuries escaped me.

Mysterious India . . .

One local legend involves the area Raj of times past who was called to battle by the big man in Udaipur or perhaps an even bigger man in Jaipur. As in any feudal society, it was his duty to go to war. But he had just married and could not make himself leave his beautiful wife. Several times he left, only to return to ask for another remembrance of her. She would dutifully hand over some clothing or other personal remembrance, all to no avail since he kept returning. Fearing total shame, and in despair, she eventually had her servant bring her severed head to her warrior prince. There would be no more excuses for him to shirk his sacred obligation. Stories like that reminded me of how lucky I am to be born in a time where personal honor is a bit less exacting, like not cheating on your golf score. Still, I wish I learned more about the place in which I spent two years of my life. Perhaps I was too busy surviving.

Part of what remained beyond us might be attributed to a society that, in remote areas at least, had not yet transitioned into a contemporary, so-called rational society.

As I write this letter, it is about 10 PM. The world is silent except for the pained groan of the wind. And I am alone. Randy has gone to Delhi. He has had some form of physical breakdown. To be brief, he has worms, an infected foot, dental problems, nausea spells, general weakness, lesions on his arms, and several other indefinable aches and pains. Chances are, however, he'll survive.

The nights can be somewhat spooky since we are rather isolated. To compound the feeling, I've run across some interesting tales concerning spirits, holy men, and general extrasensory phenomena from rather reliable sources (university- educated men).

One story is about the former princely ruler of a neighboring district. Since this man was educated at Oxford in England, he often entertained foreign friends in a palace built expressly for that purpose, at least until one of his visiting friends died in it. After that, no one was allowed to spend the night, not even the prince. It is reputedly reported that anyone who attempts to sleep in the palace will be physically ejected by the spirit of the dead guest. Stories of communications with dead relatives,

physical cures by holy men, and possession of bodies by
spirits are legion. After a while, it makes one wonder.

Religion and spirituality liberally mixed with town life to provide entertainment for the locals and a respite from the tedium of everyday life. It provided us with welcome distractions as well.

India also involved colorful festivals and sights you would never experience again. A sect of holy men visited the town for a few days. I watched one of them literally rip all his hair out as an exercise in self-mortification. I am well on my way in achieving the same hairless state on top of my head, but in a more natural way, absent the physical pain at least. This colorful, religiously inspired event is described next . . .

Another aspect of Indian culture has been brought to
light this week. It seems that a group of naked Sadhus
(sort of like Saints to those of the Catholic persuasion)
have come to town for a while. When they arrived, the
whole town, it appeared, turned out to greet them. Even
Cutchroo, our 16-year-old cook, took part. Dressed in an
oversized white uniform and wearing a hat which hung
down over his ears, he produced some kind of cacophony
on a drum which some naïve soul had given him under
the ridiculous impression that somehow music would be
forthcoming.

Well, anyways, amid the heavenly strains (?) of the
band, the choking dust, and the milling crowds, these

skinny naked men arrived. I must admit, despite that, the town never looked better. Decorations were abundant. Across every street hung banners, streamers, pictures, and other assorted paraphernalia of assorted colors and shapes.

Another interesting point is their culinary habits. When it is time to eat, they proceed from their temple while thinking of some sign or signal such as a man holding a coconut under his left armpit or something. If they see that sign, they will eat at the nearest house. If they don't, they will fast for another day (they eat only once a day). It really does seem like a tough way to make a living.

On at least one other occasion, I managed to trade words of wisdom with some visiting holy men ...

Have just returned from Salumbar where I had the opportunity to visit and talk with the visiting Jain holy men. These meetings are, I suspect, the very kind of cross cultural contrasts which Peace Corps is famous for brokering ... east and west, mysticism and rationalism, aestheticism and materialism. These confrontations are more awkward than enlightening. Yet, it is probably true that my somewhat affected interest in the Eastern world does create a modicum of good feeling.

India surprised us at every turn. It rooted us out of comfortable Western mind-sets. It helped us place all our understandings in a broader and more flexible framework. It made us tougher and more resilient. It was not for the faint of heart.

Final thoughts . . .

In the end, I suspect we did some good. But like I have heard so many volunteers say, you take away far more than you ever contribute. I was always amused, somewhat at least, by the prevailing rumors circulating among the locals as to why we were there. One explanation is that we were CIA spies, perhaps only believed by the friendly man we were introduced to as the local Communist. I doubt the espionage rumor had much traction. Looking around, what the hell could one spy on in that godforsaken place? The second was that we were there to learn agriculture so that we could be better farmers when we went back to the US. That hypothesis at least enjoyed the virtue of plausibility. Few, it would appear, believed we were there to advance farm production in India.

Old pictures remind me of other memories, small things that bring some joy after all these decades. There is a photo of a band that visited our house and pictures of many government officials with whom we worked, some who were appreciative of our presence and others who tolerated us. One photo that elicited a smile involved Cutchroo milking a goat in the entrance way to our place. His appropriation of the goat's milk clearly was without the permission of the owner, as could be detected from the mischievous smile on his face. Randy and I never inquired too closely on their shenanigans.

As our adventure ended, I recall arguing that PC should not assume that college kids, with a little training, could contribute in technical areas where they had little or no real expertise. At best, it was patronizing to the host country. We had been a wave of volunteers that were sent to satisfy a promise that Lyndon Johnson had made to Indira Gandhi—to send thousands of volunteers to help the country on the road to development or at least get it past the severe drought they were experiencing at the time. By the end of my tour, I wondered if that had been a threat rather than a promise, choose us over the Soviets *or* we will send hordes of poorly trained and incompetent volunteers to mess with your minds. It would be better, I thought, to send fewer volunteers but ones that actually knew what the hell they were doing.

I recall, on the train to Delhi for the last time, many of the other volunteers expressed similar views about the need for more real expertise as opposed to good intentions. We would make sure the top staff understood the realities on the ground, you betcha (as Minnesotans would say). Then, as we did a roundtable debriefing that was part of all such exit processes, one after another talked about their India experience in what I recall as rather glowing terms. So much for searing honesty, I thought. Perhaps my fellow volunteers were right, and I just came across as a whiner, a personal attribute my wife claims I have mastered all too well.

My lingering reservations about our value to India were swept aside, however, when an Indian official gave us certificates thanking us for our contributions in the area of . . . poultry? I think it would have been more convincing if they had gotten the program area right. All was made worthwhile, though, when we received the thanks from a grateful America on a piece of paper signed by President Nixon himself. This was before he was almost impeached of course.

Then, it was over. We were going home. But what kind of home would greet us? For two years, we witnessed what looked like, from afar, the dissolution of American society. There were the assassinations (Robert Kennedy and Martin Luther King), the riots, and the increasingly savage debate over the war in Vietnam. For better or worse, this is what we would face on our return.

The experience, in the end, did change all of us. I think of some of us "kids" and what they did with their lives. From 44-B, our hardy group of male agriculture experts who had never seen a crop before, their subsequent lives could be characterized as promises more than fulfilled. One went on to get an M.B.A. from the Wharton Schools and a Ph. D in economics. His career stretched from being a banker in Paris to an economist with the Federal Reserve in D.C. Another, after getting a master's from Harvard, took a position with the United Nations. He worked with refugees seemingly in all the hot spots over the course of several decades. A third went into the foreign service of the State Department. He was one of the last staff members transferred out of Tehran before the radical students took over the embassy in 1979. A fourth stayed an additional year as a Peace Corps volunteer in India and worked in Africa for several years before starting his own business in the Bay Area. Still another used Peace Corps to rise from a sharecropper's son to become a high official in a national labor union. Yet another got a doctorate from Columbia in Indian Studies. One final example was an excellent musician who earned a doctorate from Stanford in computer sciences and wrote the book on the mathematical foundations of music. He was also one of the earliest employees of Apple Computer.

If you took any random group of college graduates in 1966, you would not come up with such an interesting, accomplished, and eclectic group. Perhaps each of us would have achieved what we did even if we had not served in the Peace Corps. Somehow, I doubt it though. More than personal success, we were, in fact, a band of brothers and sisters with a connection that was forged halfway around the world a lifetime ago, and yet which endures to this day.

We are very fortunate indeed.

CHAPTER 11

TRANSITIONING

I'm a slow walker but I never walk back.

—Abraham Lincoln

Like my Clark experience, India left me a changed man. A hopeful, if uncertain, youth joins the Peace Corps with the best of intentions and brimming with ennobling idealism. After two years of unrelenting heat, frustration, cultural friction, disease, loneliness, technical futility, and romantic disappointment, the young man leaves apparently dispirited and directionless. Appearances easily can deceive, though. Peace Corps proved to be one of those sleeper experiences, a bit painful in the short term and priceless over the long haul.

The really hard things are what makes each of us great, or at least a little better. India was hard, very hard. It tested us, perhaps in a different sense than training did though both had their challenges. India pushed us to the point where our core character solidified and matured. You either grew or, given the challenges, you would bend or even crack. Over the years, a number of volunteers left early, some in not very good shape.

Reflecting on the PC experience . . .

I periodically would dream about my village in India, about going back. I could never quite recall how the villagers responded to my nocturnal return. That was probably a good thing, the image of an angry mob running me out of town with flaming torches (remember those Frankenstein movies) probably would have woken me in a cold sweat. I can almost hear the desperate cry now, "My god, the crazy American is back!"

The Salumbar in my dreams had suburbs. Based on a shot from Google Earth, the Salumbar of today has something close to suburbs. Where the desert greeted my daily examination of the terrain fronting our house, something akin to the classic American-type sprawl lay before me. While utopia may be a stretch, buildings dot what had been a lonely road and green fields have replaced brown dirt unless the Google shots have been Photoshopped. Surely, my old site has changed. How much of contemporary India I would recognize is an intriguing question.

Over the years, my spouse would ask whether I was interested in returning to India or my village. Curious, yes, but I had never felt compelled to return. Perhaps I never quite got over a lingering sense of guilt. Like a lot of volunteers, I could not shake that feeling that I took far more than I gave. We were young, naive, lacking in appreciable skills. What were we thinking back then? Where did our arrogance and hubris extend that we thought we had something to offer? What would I say to those who might possibly recognize me? Yes, I was that tall, skinny kid who stumbled around the fields here looking totally helpless, hopeless, and surely hapless. But at least I left you with a few laughs.

The fortieth reunion of my Peace Corps group, however, proved to be an important epiphany in a way. I had never gone to a reunion before. Well, not quite true, my dear spouse did drag me to her grade school reunion. Yes, that's right, a grade school reunion! I mean, who remembers grade school? I, however, had never been to one of mine, at any level. This one, though, was not to be missed. As soon as we began sharing with one another, my sense of failure did not seem so personal or so unique. More or less, we all harbored a sense of limitation, a harsh introspection born or unrealistic expectations. In the end, we could have done better but we probably did okay.

I had very little contact with members of India 44 over the four decades following our service. After a couple of decades with no contact from anyone, my wife answered the phone one day. She typically performs that service since I have few friends of my own as you can well imagine by now. She continued chatting, so it wasn't someone marketing steak knives or cemetery plots. Suddenly she said, "Oh, Tom will definitely want to talk to you," which surprised me since I never want to talk to anyone.

Most of us have experienced running into someone out of their usual context and, for this reason, have difficulty recognizing them. That is why I ask my wife to wear a name tag whenever she wanders into the kitchen by mistake. This is what happened in this instance, who the hell was on the other end of the line? I faked a conversation while my mind raced to figure out the identity of a vaguely familiar voice. About three minutes into the conversation, it finally hit me. It was David Dell, the India David Dell. On another day I was giving a talk in Milwaukee and a woman approached me asking if I was the Tom Corbett who served in the Peace Corps in India. Though my first reaction was to say, "Not me, I'm innocent," but then I recognized Nancy Simuel from India 44-A and we gave each other a big hug.

By 2009, I had not seen most in our group in forty years. Immediately, it felt more like forty hours since our last time together. Toward the end of the second day, as the reunion was winding down, I looked around the room as people chatted and shared with one another. Sure, body parts dragged and drooped in awkward ways, a few extra pounds could be found on most, and more grey could be found in the hair that remained. But I could easily think back to those bright and shiny faces that gathered some forty-plus years earlier in Milwaukee. Though I am, by nature, a pretty detached guy, someone who skips through life with a joke or two, I couldn't quite ignore the very real emotion that surged through me. "I really do love these guys."

Exiting India in 1969 was an experience in and of itself. I started out with Bill Whitesell and Hap Pedigo. Quickly, we discovered we were not just traveling across physical distances, we were also journeying across time. Reentering civilization affected each of us in idiosyncratic ways, I suspect. For me, I recall the blessing of anonymity. First stop for us was Istanbul, which still felt like Asia. The airline put us up, so we stayed at a fancy hotel overlooking the Bosporus Straights. To this day, I can recall standing on a balcony mesmerized by a romantic vision of this fabled link between Europe and Asia. The Western world I grew up in was now so close I could taste it. But I was not there yet. I realized that I did not even own a pair of shoes, just flip-flops, and was refused entrance to the fancy hotel restaurant due to my untidy appearance. Civilization, at least as I understood it, would have to wait a day or two.

Athens began to feel like the modern civilization that was embedded in my memory but had become a lost world. The first thing I did was buy a pair of shoes. Then I recall getting excited by an escalator, feeling the comfort of walking the streets without attracting attention, and gawking at women in Western dress. We could not have been too anonymous, though. We were hustled by some guys attempting to introduce us to the charms of several young ladies whose interest in us, shockingly enough, was largely pecuniary. I know, I know, hard to believe they were not overwhelmed with our good looks and charm. I must say, the offer was tempting and very, very hard to resist.

The reentry process was surreal in many respects. Literally days earlier, we lived in isolation on the margins of a desert. Now, armed with an open ticket (as long as we kept going in one direction), we felt like jet-setters, at least a little bit. Several times, we got up in the morning and chatted about where we might fly that day. Athens was followed by Rome, and then Geneva, and so on. We began to experience on a grander scale what we sometimes encountered during brief trips to Delhi or Bombay while in India. The contrasts between modernity and feudal, rural India could be like a slap in the face.

I remember splurging on a breakfast at the luxurious Oberoi Hotel in Delhi about a year into my service. I was in heaven. Then, I overheard a Westerner complain about the orange juice not being fresh. No whining, I wanted to scream! Don't you realize how privileged you are and just how utterly arrogant you sound. But now I realized the transition was permanent. I was leaving India behind and I would soon return to my own whining ways absent much guilt.

In each city we ran across attractive women but encountered an unchanging, and bitter, truth. The gals remained as fleet of foot as always while I had slowed down a step. I should have taken up that offer in Athens. Hap headed off to America after Italy, or was it Athens? I recall meeting a lovely gal in Rome, spending a romantic evening with her which ended up at the Spanish Steps, a city landmark. And then nothing, I was as paralyzed as ever. What a schmuck!

In Germany, Bill Whitesell and I made our way to Frankfurt to visit Mike Simonds, the same guy who compared me to a romance novel cover hunk just before his eye issues were discovered. Mike and Bill were fast friends and would become brothers-in-law a few years hence. Mike had undergone urgent eye surgery at the U.S. military hospital there. His journey to Frankfurt went something like this. On the train to Delhi for mustering out, Mike had mentioned a problem with his vision. It seemed minor, but we jumped all over him to mention this *before* cutting loose from Peace Corps. Mike never made it to our final party before we all headed home. He had just been told by an Indian eye doctor that he had a very serious condition but only the Peace Corps doctor could explain all to him. That would be in the morning, the next day! Distraught, Mike wandered about in agony wondering just how painful his final days on earth would be. Surely, he had a terminal disease that would soon ravage his body.

Now, Mike and I were rooming together that night. Unfortunately for him, as it turned out, I did experience some romantic success with an extremely cute gal from 44-B. Miracles do happen. While this lovely lass and I were occupied, Mike finally wandered back to our room. As he tells it, I opened the door, told him to get lost, and slammed it shut again. He next tried Bill who was similarly occupied with the same result. After more hall wandering with increasingly dire death scenarios dancing in his head, Mike returned to our joint room with more determination. He was desperate by this point and was not about to take no for an answer.

Apparently, once I understood his plight, I started doing the right thing, which rather stuns me. Quite frankly, it shocks the shit out of me. All further thoughts of carnal delights were discarded, and I began calling people to find out what might be done for him or at least what fatal affliction was about to strike. As it turns out, Mike was not dying. He had a detached (or detaching) retina and soon he was shipped off to a U.S. military base in Germany where we were to visit him. If he had been smart, he would have used his medical condition to extort some sympathy sex from our female PC colleagues.

When Bill and I caught up with him, he was lying in bed with his head totally immobilized. His mouth still worked, unfortunately, but we managed a pleasant visit despite that before heading off for a trip up the Rhine. According to Mike, as I called people to try to get information on his condition, my female companion that evening told him that she thought my Boston accent and good looks reminded her of John Kennedy. Unbelievably, she thought I was so sexy. Damn, had I stumbled on this scam earlier I would have played that Kennedy card all along since nothing else ever seemed to work!

Paris held some vivid memories. We were there on Bastille Day, sort of the 4th of July in France. I recall walking toward the Arc De Triomphe at night as revelers packed the streets. Bill and I rescued some young American gals from overly amorous Frenchmen, and we spent the night enjoying the sights and sounds of Paris. The morning sun was a hint in the eastern sky when the last café still open kicked us out. I marvel at my stamina in those days, staying awake for the 10:00 pm news (CST) now is an achievement worth celebrating.

These gals could not really believe that I had been celibate for two years which, while not strictly true, was true enough to claim without too much guilt. While my sexual deprivation story struck me as a transparent and disingenuous plea for mercy, they appeared sympathetic to our sorry plight. After all, it was their Christian duty to help. Helping out a sexually deprived male had to be considered one of those corporal works of mercy, no? "Two years?" they squealed in disbelief. "How did you last that long?" And we didn't even have running water for cold showers! In fact, I had a hard time believing it myself. Our appeal to their Christian charitable sensibilities fell short, unfortunately, since they turned out to be Jewish.

Bill peeled off at some point, I cannot recall if it was Paris or London, anxious to get home and back to some girl that was waiting for him though this was not the gal he eventually would marry. I had one more stop to make, Ireland, land of my ancestry on my father's side. My mother, being Polish, would have necessitated back tracking, and thus cost real money at this point. It would also have involved complications like getting a visa to a Communist country when they would naturally conclude that all recent PC volunteers obviously were CIA agents.

Dublin was poor and shabby back then, but it seemed very romantic to me. There were plaques and monuments all over the place commemorating this or that event in the cause of Irish freedom. You know, Billy O'Toole fell off a bar stool on this very spot in 1912 while singing songs of Irish freedom. I must admit, the tug of my Irish roots remained strong, and I had a great time embracing my ethnic origins.

One day I met a lovely young gal from Sweden. We did the sights together before I dropped her off at her hostel in the wee hours of the morning. We engaged in some romantic interplay until she suddenly realized I would be walking out of her life in a few minutes and was not worth the effort. Somehow, I made my way back to my place on foot. As I walked into the hotel at 3:00 AM, I saw a television on in the small room that served as a bar located just off the lobby. Odd, I thought. There, a small group was intently watching something. Who would still be up at this hour, this not being New York? Intrigued, I checked it out. It turned out that Neal Armstrong was about to take that first step for mankind on the moon. I watched history being made in a Dublin hotel bar around three or four in the morning after getting shot down by a gal for the 2,367th time in my life. But who is counting? In a way, she did me a favor. Her sensible decision allowed me to witness man's first step on the moon.

One other night, I sat at the bar and struck up a conversation with an Irishman who was killing time before heading off to see his girlfriend. We bought each other several drinks and then he was off. I thought I could hold my liquor, but he seemed perfectly sober while I desperately tried not to fall off my perch. I truly doubt they would have erected a monument to me, as they had for Billy O'Toole, had I cracked my head open after falling off the bar stool. By now, the bar maid was looking extremely fine to me, as was the coat rack adjacent to the front door. Two years really is a long time. She was spared, however, by my inability to move at the critical moment. That was good. I was spared another amorous flame-out. I had an early morning train reservation which I somehow managed to make. How I managed not to barf my way across the Irish countryside remains a mystery to this day, what a hangover.

My Aer Lingus flight landed at Logan International in Boston. My parents were there, of course. It turns out my father had just been released from the hospital. His lungs were already shot from too many cigarettes and from the foul air of pre-OSHA factory work. My parents kept his condition from me, so I would not worry or cut my travels short. Both of them were to pass too early of lung-related diseases among other problems, the consequences of hard lives and hard choices made in a relaxed regulatory environment. Let no one be fooled on this point, we do sanction outright corporate homicide in this country.

Shortly after my arrival back in Worcester, a fellow volunteer visited me. He was a delightful guy originally from Wyoming. I thought this a wonderful opportunity to recapture one more time those precious memories of India with someone who would know what it was all about. So, I dragged out my several hundred slides to rev up our trip down memory lane, dimming the lights so as not to lose anything in the moment. All went well for a while. As I approached slide 300, however, I noticed that Don was no longer responding, not even issuing the occasional grunt that accompanied every tenth slide or so. Turning on the lights revealed Don in a deep sleep, head plopped on his chest, his face twisted in a look of absolute torture. Since then, I have noticed that I have had that effect on many folks, students in particular. Now that I think on it, perhaps I should have rented those slides to Dick Cheney for interrogation purposes in the war on terror.

The travel bug . . .

Going halfway around the word shattered my provinciality and opened up the world to me. Over the next several decades, I would visit every US state and something over twenty-five foreign countries. I could seduce you with lush descriptions of beautiful scenes, majestic peaks, and stunning seascapes, but most of you have all experiences those things. Better to share a few moments emblematic of why I am now banned from twenty countries around the globe.

The first ouch memory that pops into my head involves the old Yugoslavia where Tito still clung to life. A gloss of Communism remained which held this country together in the late 1970s despite internal ethnic pressures that would soon rip it apart. My wife and I were admiring the city of Zagreb one day from an elevated position, obviously looking like tourists. A man in a suit and carrying a briefcase stopped to chat. On learning we were Americans, he launched into a proud dialogue about the changes under way in his city. Then he pointed to a series of Soviet-looking high-rises. Before he had a chance to go further, Mary blurted out something about how ugly this development was. You can count on honesty to silence a proud monologue. I awaited the arrival of state police to hustle us off to some prison for extreme torture. But no, he recovered and continued on politely.

We were on a boat once going from one country to another along the Adriatic Coast. It was just an overnight trip, but we hit a terrible storm while dining. The boat went up and down with the soup flowing over the side of the bowls. One by one I saw individuals rise and flee out the door. I finished my food as well as Mary's after she too fled the scene. Soon, I was about the only diner left. Curious, I went out on the deck to confront a scene from an old silent movie. People were over the railing spilling out their guts, men were rushing into women's rooms, women into the men's john, it was wherever you could find comfort. Quite a night!

On Corfu once, early in our marriage, we stayed at an inexpensive hotel. Back then we did not have a great deal of money, so we were careful. Mary was extremely careful, only permitting me food on days with no N in the title. We always debated hotel costs. For example, Mary and I would always 'discuss' the number of stars our room should have which dictated the cost. She argued for fewer while I, always a creature of comfort, wanted more. I think this hotel had a half a star which is emblematic of how many marital debates I have won over the years.

Anyways, there was a basin of cold water in which to wash your hands. A shared bathroom was situated down the hall or in the gas station across the street, I forget which. After using this thoughtful service, Mary asked me where I thought she could dump the water. "Wherever you like I suppose," a casual response that was not well thought out. A moment later I saw her fling the basin of water over the open balcony only to be followed by shrieks and screams from below. It just happened that the outdoor restaurant was under our room. Once again, I thought I would be seeing the inside of a local jail as we hid under the bed waiting for an angry mob to break through the door.

There are lots of car stories. Driving a stick shift in the UK always has its moments of sheer terror. You are driving on the wrong side of the road and shifting with your left hand. Not easily done if you are not accustomed to it! Exiting Heathrow once, my wife claims that I scattered several pedestrians as I got my bearings. Driving up winding and death-defying swish back one-car roads also has its moments. For example, we did the road to Hana in Hawaii and up to Monte Verdi in Costa Rico. But heading up the mountainside in the highlands of Scotland had a particular thrill, Mary argued the view from the top was not to be missed. It was the usual one-way road with occasional turnouts to permit two cars to pass one another. Coming in the other direction, however, were a series of large trucks from where I never did discover. Their presence might well have been a population control initiative sponsored by the Scottish government. Each passing was a moment of extreme terror where I saw my car and life plunging several hundred feet down the mountain side. *This would be a gruesome ending*, I thought. My last words would have been, "Damn it, Mary, I told you this was a stupid idea."

By the time we reached the top you had to pry my fingers off the wheel with a crowbar. My promised spectacular view of the Isle of Skye was not there; it was fogged in of course. So, we waited to no avail. Mary was not to be thwarted. She then chimed in that we could always drive back up again in the afternoon for another try. What! I barely made it up the first time. "Go in the damn store and buy a picture post card of the view," I snorted. "We will just tell people it was lovely." She saw my point of view.

On another occasion, our rental car broke down as we drove along a remote Bosnian road toward the Adriatic Sea. We were in the middle of nowhere. After some time, we did manage to start it and limp into a gas station that also was in the middle of nowhere. There, it died once more. We could not communicate with the small group of guys hanging around, and they seemed totally uninterested in helping us. Finally, after spending some time trying to resurrect that perfect Act of Contrition while counting the number of vultures circling above us, I gave over to despair. Clearly, we were doomed!

The indifferent men must have realized we were not going anywhere and slowly ambled over to give a look. Suddenly five guys were under the hood of our car, jabbering and pulling up wires. I wondered for a moment if they were going to steal the engine. But no, soon they motioned me into the car and hand signaled that I should start it up. All was fine. It turns out that I had screwed up the manual choke, which we did not have on American cars even back then. I tried to give them money, but they would not take any. They already had their compensation . . . a story to tell about the imbecilic American who did not know how to operate the choke in his car, payment enough.

Still another time, I can recall driving across the wilds of northern Scotland for what seemed like days. This often took us over the single-lane roads in the remotest parts of this wild and stunningly beautiful country. Traffic was scarce fortunately. But when you did meet a car or truck going in the opposite direction, a fancy bit of vehicular dancing was required to pass one another. Being this far from civilization, you always wondered what might happen if you broke down or had an accident. Help was not a phone call away even if you had cell phones which we did not back then.

In any case, I was most happy to finally arrive at a place where we could rest for the night. I could feel the onset of deep relaxation seeping through my body with a blessed nap just moments away. It was June and this far north the sunlight would last most of the night. But I could always nap. Napping was my strength, always has been. "Wait," my wife said, there is one more thing to see. I am not a violent man but really. After all, who would find her body way out here? And besides, no jury of my male peers would convict me.

It seems there was a craft shop just up the road. A craft shop! Who gives a flying you know what about another freaking craft shop? Hadn't we stopped at every craft shop in the U. K. by this point? And really, wouldn't a talented artist live closer to human comforts and to other people. Okay, maybe not, artists can be crazy. In any case, it is just a few kilometers up the road she assured me. So off we went, kilometer after kilometer. My protests were always met with "I am sure it is right around the next bend." At some point it hit me, how would she even know about this place? Is there some special knowledge that women have that is communicated telepathically? I would not put it past them, they already share special information designed to drive spouses over the edge.

I was about to put my foot down when we came across a small store. "This is it," she screeched. The few kilometers had stretched into many, like forty maybe. And I had to stay awake to drive all the way back. Out she jumps and bounds off into nirvana. I wait, and then I waited some more. Then, I nap as she presumably wandered through the artistic treasures inside. Finally, she emerges looking excited with a small bag. "Look at this," she said with eyes wide with excitement. Inside were a couple of small dishes, maybe ashtrays, with pastoral scenes painted on them. My guess is that the artist was a fourth grader at the local school. I could not even tell if the blobs on the ceramic surface were sheep or cows or maybe just random paint drops. "The place really sucked, didn't it?" I offered. She said nothing on the long ride back while I calculated the spousal points I would place on my side of the marriage ledger where the score was kept. Eventually, even I figured out that these were points no husband ever got to redeem.

That reminds me of one more shopping adventure. At one point, Mary decided to drag me to the southwestern part of the U. S. She wanted us to move to a warmer climate. She actually looked for a job in Arizona as part of this crazy scheme and did get an offer. Anyways, this trip was to seduce me into loving this god-forsaken blast furnace part of the country that is filled with paranoid, gun toting wing-nuts. Right from the trip's start, she talked about a specific leather outlet store in New Mexico. She just could not wait to get there. Finally, we arrive in the area and she was beside herself with excitement. She literally jumped out of the car when it was still rolling and dashed through the front door. I wait and wait and wait. Then I panic. What if she has bought out the entire place?

I thought it prudent to check things out. When I found her, she was crestfallen. She had found nothing in her size or her style or whatever criterion she used. She would take one more swing around the racks. Still bored, I casually looked up to see a small men's section stuffed into one corner of the store. I slowly walked over out of curiosity. As I approached, I could see just one black leather jacket that seemed my style, early fifties biker. I thought there would be no way that it would fit me. But it went on like a glove, a perfect fit. I slowly walked back to Mary, who continued a futile search beset with a countenance of utter despair. "I found mine," I announced with a malicious smile. She did not talk to me for a week. All in all, it was a great trip.

Another time, we approached Dubrovnik, a jewel on the Adriatic. Once again, we hugged a road that ran along the mountain side with deep drops into the sea a few feet away. They never seemed to have guardrails where they needed them, I just assumed this was a population control measure. Anyways, we hit a terrible rainstorm. As I drove all I could see were the rear lights of the car in front of me. If he drove off the cliff, I would be right behind him. Then we stopped, no reason why as far as I could see. Soon, I noticed vague shadows through the driving rain. It looked like people out there on the road. What was going on? This was eerie. Suddenly, out of the gloom to our right appeared a man who started banging on our window. Mary rolled it down, and he started speaking quickly in Yugoslav I suppose. Not that she panicked or anything, but Mary blurts out, "Sorry, I don't speak English." Our intruder then seamlessly switched languages. It turns out he was a doctor who needed to get into Dubrovnik since he was to be the physician on a cruise ship leaving the next day. He informed us that the shadowy men we saw were volunteers who removed large boulders that rolled down on the highway during such storms. Now I was more freaked. We could have been swept off the road to certain death by a huge missile crashing down the mountainside. Eventually, we picked up our journey again and he directed us to a great hotel in this unforgettable city. We had a view of the sea crashing angrily against the rocks below.

Near misses and ouch moments marked much of my life. These travel snafus simply remind me that I am damn lucky to have made it this far. There are those who set out to conquer life and surmount great obstacles. Others merely try to make it to the next day without shooting off their family jewels. I am one of those.

Migrating West.

Someone once told me that I tend to let life come to me, that I don't pursue it with any particular force or sense of direction. I suspect there is a modicum of truth there. Virtually every major decision in my life was casually made or was something that just fell into my lap. In any case, I had heard about this urban affairs master's degree program at the University of Wisconsin–Milwaukee (UW–M) when we trained there for our Peace Corps escapade. Since I kind of knew about it . . . that naturally became the one academic program to which I applied from my exile in the Indian desert. So, in the fall of 1969, it was back to Milwaukee. In retrospect, I should have been more proactive. I thought urban affairs would teach me how to seduce city women, but it was all about politics, economics, and sociology. What a terrible disappointment!

The program might not have been very rigorous, but I learned a lot. It was the end of the 1960s and the energy of that period still could be felt even in a backwater place like Milwaukee. In the Urban Affairs Department we had lots of kids from the east coast, northern New Jersey in fact. It was hard to explain, but there was a pipeline from a couple of colleges there to this program. They brought an eastern edginess to the niceness that was the Midwest which I liked.

The Urban Affairs Department was stimulating for me. It was flexible, rather unstructured, and dealt with real life problems. You would take a smattering of courses in economics, sociology, political science, and so forth. If you were aggressive enough, you could tie into any number of ongoing urban issues at a time when the memories of urban riots and unrest were real. For Milwaukee, open housing was the issue du jour. The city had an eastern or even Chicago feel in that it was divided up into ethnic and racial enclaves that were defined by rather impermeable boundaries. There was clearly a black ghetto on the north side of town, an Hispanic section on the near south side, a Polish section further south, and so on.

Led by Father Groppi, a firebrand priest, the protesters wanted African-Americans to be able to move into Polish and other ethnic white, working-class neighborhoods. The tensions were electric with protests and marches and many shades of fear and hate. The other explosive issue that absorbed my attention during this period was the Vietnam conflict, a holdover issue from the sixties. Many of my urban affairs classmates were left leaning, particularly the ones from the east coast. The faculty also was mostly sympathetic to our leanings. Milwaukee had been somewhat behind other hotbeds of protest like Madison down the road some eighty miles, but it was catching up by this time. We started organizing teach-ins and discussions and other educational and protest actions. Inevitably, our department and the school were shut down at least temporarily.

One of my favorite memories from this period was my roommate at the time named Mike. He was about the most clean-cut kid you could imagine. He had graduated from Holy Cross which was the college I would have attended as a good Catholic boy had not circumstances diverted me to Clark. Well,

Mike was very reluctant to get involved in this protest stuff but maybe my bad example led him astray. When events were at their height, some of us first organized a vote to shut down the Urban Affairs Department and then helped shut down normal university operations. That accomplished, the students tried to disrupt traffic on the main street adjacent to the school. Surely, that act would bring the national government to its knees. A host of law enforcement agencies, along with the National Guard, had been assembled to shut the protest down. It was high noon.

Then I saw Mike standing above the crowd shouting instructions about how to protect yourself when the tear gas cannisters started to explode about us. What! Here was every mother's favorite son suddenly looking like some wild eyed radical. I belly laughed at the sight. About two, maybe three years after these events, I was in Madison working for the State of Wisconsin. An F.B.I. agent sought me out at work one day. My first reaction was that something in my sorry past had caught up with me. I immediately stood up and put my hands behind my back to be handcuffed. But no, he was there to do a background check on Mike who now was being considered for a government position that required a security clearance. No mention was made by me of Mike's storming the barricades moment. I described him for what he was, every mother's favorite son. Apparently, the agent had not come across my own government file before seeking me out.

A group of us were quite passionate about many things back then as the righteous fervor of the sixties remained bright for a while longer. I can remember Bob, Terry, Michelle, Arlen, and so many others. Each was a character in his own right with outsized personalities that are hard to forget. I recall a long conversation with Terry one day. He had been ROTC at Boston College where he also played football as an offensive lineman. Upon graduation he had been commissioned a second lieutenant and sent off to Vietnam. He told me how he had been gung ho on his arrival. After a few months of leading patrols and seeing the total waste of the war, his only priority was the safety of the men in his charge. One day, he said he was leading his squad on patrol. Out of the corner of his eye, he could see something but too late to react. He was shot up quite badly. He still walked with a distinct limp. He had come to loathe those who put our country into the hellish conflict, growling that virtually none of them had ever seen a gun fired in anger.

My biggest societal contribution during this period was the creation of the Bachelors-Aid-Department or BAD. There were several unattached guys who were not averse to allowing the young ladies in the program to cook meals for them. I thought this a great idea but never imagined it could be pulled off. After all, feminism had been added to our list of worthy causes. To my shock, the women lined up with offers to feed us. After a while women were approaching me to find out if their turn had come around again.

I was having trouble rounding up the guys who were complaining about getting too fat. What happened to Betty Friedan? To her credit, my future wife would have nothing to do with this. And once I became familiar with her culinary skills, I appreciated her decision even more.

I was dead set against going to Vietnam. Of course, it was far more than mere cowardice though I am rather fond of keeping all my limbs attached. I had long concluded that our intervention there was insane. I first appeared before my draft board before heading to India. I guess they wanted to check me out to see if I was using the Peace Corps to dodge my military duty. Of course, I had been one of those bleeding hearts who would have volunteered to save humanity, war or no war, but I was glad the Peace Corps was there at that moment. These boards were composed of crusty old men who seemed to look through you with unbelieving eyes. They had heard all the excuses from college shits like me. In the end, they let me go to India.

Now that I was back in the States, my crusty old men were after me again. I was inching toward my twenty-sixth birthday, which would exempt me from the draft but not quickly enough. My notice to take my physical caught up with me in Milwaukee and so off I went. I must admit I was preparing some contingency plans in case they found a sad sack like me fit for service. I did contact an attorney to talk through my situation and started thinking about a conscientious objector plea. Though some elements from my background and past might give me some leverage, it was a long shot at best. So, I also began to think about Canada. Sitting here now, almost five decades later and totally disgusted with the Tea Party drift of American politics, I almost wish I had been forced over the border back then.

Anyways, I showed up for my physical. Many years later I discovered I could have avoided all this by going to Canada and signing up for the draft at an American Consulate which you were permitted to do. Those records got lost in the bureaucracy, but you had complied with the law. Anyways, I showed up. I never tried to trick out the exam by eating five thousand bananas or something to get their readings out of whack. Others attempted to be disruptive or otherwise display their unfitness for active duty. I did none of this. I was still the good boy. I might organize protests, but I did so politely and with respect. I did what I was told, bent over and spread my cheeks when ordered to do so. I was truthful when asked about my medical history. I peed in the cup using my own urine.

The fun began when I got to the written exams to test your cognitive skills and assess your character. The math and verbal part of the intelligence tests were quite easy. I did wonder if I could fail this miserably but assumed that they would be suspicious that a college graduate had an IQ of 45. Today, that might not strike one as odd but back then it would have been a stretch. On the other hand, I did struggle with that part of the test designed to assess your practical knowledge. They had questions like which of the set of tools on the left is most similar to the tool on the right side of the page. What, I had no idea what was going on there. I bet the farm kids aced that stuff. My IQ on this practical crap must have been 35 but that would not get me out. Hell, they probably would have assigned me to the motor pool.

There were efforts to smoke out subversives. They presented a long list of organizations and asked whether we had belonged to any of them. It looked pretty outdated to me with most options striking me as holdovers from the 1930s Spanish Civil War. I probably would have joined one of these had I been alive then. The Abraham Lincoln Brigade was one of those listed, volunteers from other countries who signed on to defend the duly elected Republican Government in Spain. An armed coup had been mounted by the opposition fascists supported by Hitler. Now why would supporting a democratically elected group be on this list? Oh yes, they were for land reforms and measures to help the poor and downtrodden. Helping the less fortunate was clearly and unequivocally un-American for sure back then. Only the Communists did that. Little has changed. Helping the less fortunate today will put you on the Tea Party hit list.

I noticed that one group, the Students for a Democratic Government (SDS.), was not on the list. I had long ceased any connection with them as they spun down the toilet bowl of self-destructive nihilism. But I had belonged for a while in my college days and I was curious about their absence from a list that had not been updated since the days of Harry Truman. At the end I came to an open-ended question that covered all the bases. It asked whether I had belonged to any organizations that advocated for the violent overthrow of the American government or other equally evil things. I assumed this was designed to catch evildoers who had been born after 1950. So, I raised my hand and asked a burly scowling sergeant, "Does SDS qualify under question Q?" His scowl grew even more menacing. "You bet your ass it does, buddy." That was clear enough I thought. I duly wrote in SDS in the space provided and gave it not another thought.

I made it to the end where I was to hand in my now completed paperwork. The door to freedom was steps away. The soldier taking my stuff looked at my name, then at a list in front of him, and then up at me. He also had a scowl. The help that day clearly had not taken any Dale Carnegie courses. "You report to the third floor," he barked. Wait, no one else in line had been told to go to the third floor. They were all exiting to freedom. This did not look good. Could they induct me into the army on the same day as my physical?

I arrived on the third floor and was told to sit and wait. It looked like the high school vice-principal's waiting room where the delinquents were sent to await their punishment. Of course, I surmised this only by rumor having been a good kid throughout my youthful school days. After a decent wait, three men marched in and ordered me to follow them into the grilling room. They introduced themselves. Their titles seemed different, but the word intelligence was involved in each. From what transpired next, the word *intelligence*, I feel, had been misappropriated.

The questioning was exhaustive. They went on about where I had lived, who I knew, what nefarious people I hung out with, whether I was up to no good. They seemed to be taking this way too serious. When they asked me to identify all my sexual partners I considered the possibility that they were trying to develop a list of easy women. If any gal had willingly slept with this schmuck, they must have reasoned, she had no standards whatsoever. I should have made up about fifty names just to impress them and keep them running in circles. In truth, I finally was doing well with members of the fairer sex by this time, clearly making up for my lost youth. My best guess is that women were taking pity on me. Still, I gave them no names. That was none of their damn business, and again, what woman would want it known that she had lowered her standards to the point where she was willing to sleep with a loser like me? Pity is one thing, abandoning all remnants of self-respect quite another.

All in all, I was generally cooperative. Toward the end, in fact, it proved to be great fun. They zeroed in on the core issues. "Okay, buddy, would you fight any and all enemies of the United States?" For these questions I would lean back in my chair and pause as if I were thinking very hard. "Now, I think we had better establish what we mean by the word enemy." I was Clintonesque long before any of us knew Bill Clinton. They would kind of huff and puff and make comments about dropping assholes like me behind enemy lines. But that did not seem likely at the moment, though I was not as certain of my fate in a month or two. As they finally wound to a close, one of them confirmed my current address. When I responded positively, he noted that he was aware of that place and that "there was a lot of good looking ass living in that building." Yeah, these guys were from some intelligence branch for sure. They were scoping out future female victims. I should have walked out as soon as I realized how silly this all was though I must admit to having some fun with them.

I heard nothing for several months and then got a letter saying that I had been found fit to serve in the U.S. military. Apparently, I was not enough of a terrorist threat to escape the draft. *Damn*, I thought, *I should have made up scary stuff during the interview.* But I did get to the calendar year of my twenty-sixth birthday. It was the year of the lottery numbers and mine was 120. If my birthday had fallen toward the end of the year, I would have gotten my draft notice for sure. Then, I would have faced some serious choices. Even so, it was a close-run thing. The anxiety that plagued all young males of that generation was over for me. I could breathe again.

All in all, I enjoyed the Urban Affairs program very much, made great friends, and had the pleasure of getting to know the most unforgettable academic in my experience, and I have known many. Warner "Bud" Bloomberg had received his doctorate in sociology from the University of Chicago. His looks reminded me of Lenin, the famous Bolshevik revolutionary. He was an outsized personality, both intimidating and inspiring us in equal measure. Bud, as he was known, was the only college-level instructor I recall who would reduce students to tears on occasion. As you talked in his class, he bore into you with piercing eyes while the sweat formed on your forehead. But he also could be so kind and generous and supportive. It was just that he didn't suffer fools kindly. I wish I had kept in touch with him after he left for a position in California.

There was a core group of us that partied and protested hard. We might even have learned something along the way but that is uncertain. Unlike my Peace Corps group, which eventually reconnected, my UW-M group did not. I wish we had, I would love to find out what happened to some of them. Funny, I cannot even recall very many of my fellow doctoral students at the University of Wisconsin. That experience virtually had no impact on me.

One of my new friends at UW-M was Mary Rider. I was taking tickets at the Downer Theater at the time and my general popularity soared, even with the women. I had no idea that free movies could be so persuasive. We had one half-assed date and I sort of moved in with her. When I decide something, there is no fooling around. Besides, she didn't charge me any rent. She was funny and smart and never came across as trying to trap me into marriage, which of course was the perfect way to trap a confirmed bachelor like me into marriage.

It was not her cooking that did the job. I recall that her first breakfast was hard-boiled eggs and some kind of bagged meat. She also served the same bagged meat for the main meal along with some side I no longer recall but which also was inedible. These baggies cost a quarter at the time and did not contain much food and certainly no real meat. I was done after two bites and looking for more. She was aghast, responding as if I were Oliver Twist asking for more food in the orphanage. Despite my expensive habits, like eating, she kept me around.

We lived in a small apartment that was owned by an elderly Italian couple who lived in the downstairs flat. In fact, as I recall their last name was Italiano. We tried to be very quiet and discrete hoping that they might never realize that Mary was now living in sin, something they would undoubtedly find offensive. Of course, we fooled no one. One day Mrs. Italiano asked Mary in for a chat. She cautioned her that once the perfume was out of the bottle it could never be put back in. I think this was her take on why would anyone buy the cow if the milk were free. Mrs. Italiano need not have worried. There is one born every minute and I am the one.

We had a good time in Milwaukee. I was gainfully employed at the theater, and she was teaching at a Catholic School on the south side of Milwaukee. When Mary applied for the job, she met with the head Priest who ran the parish and the school. He conspicuously displayed two tall stacks of papers which he claimed were applications for the position. After he was satisfied with her Catholic pedigree, he offered her the position at $5 per hour for the time she was in the classroom and no benefits. Had I mentioned earlier that Catholics were cheap? We were obviously quite poor but happy.

Moving toward adulthood . . .

I was looking for a real job but without much ambition. I did take a trip back to Worcester for an interview with the school system, I think for some kind of student counseling position. I also applied to teach at some community college in New Jersey. I think the young gal who interviewed me was impressed but nothing came of it. I then interviewed for a position as a planner with a War on Poverty community action agency in Newark New Jersey. This interview also went well. I met many of the staff and they all seemed to be either ex-athletes or clearly political hires. They probably needed someone who actually could write grant proposals in the worst way.

I think all these jaunts east had Mary worried. She had fallen for me. There really is no accounting for taste. Between my anti-marriage rhetoric and my long-distance job search, she had convinced herself that we had no future together. But the far-flung job searches were largely prompted by someone pushing me into an interview, my family in the Worcester case and former classmates from UW-M respecting the New Jersey jobs. I wasn't exactly going about this in any systematic way. Not surprisingly, I landed my first real job through total serendipity. Hiring a schmuck like me could hardly be a conscious decision.

A professor from UW-M, not even in my academic department, thought highly of me and had employed me as a research assistant. One day he asked me to accompany him to Madison where he was meeting with several state officials. Hey, I had a lot of free time. I no longer recall what the issues under discussion were, but the topic of my employment woes came up over lunch. One thing led to another and, somehow, I had some paperwork to fill out. I did, and nothing happened. I thought that was that. My career as ticket-taker at the Downer Theater looked safe and permanent and the best I would do in life.

I have told this story elsewhere, but it yet amuses me. I got a call one night from my UW-M contact. "You have a job interview tomorrow for a State job." *Really?* Curious, I asked him for more information. All he had, however, was a time, a location, and a room number. He had no idea what kind of job it was. Since I was not getting hired for jobs that I knew about going into the interviews, my shot at a position about which I knew nothing in advance looked bleak at best. But I hiked over to Madison, the State Capital, the next day and found the correct office building and room.

I walked in completely calm since I had concluded my quest was without hope. They were interviewing for a state civil service position as research-analyst: social services. Now I really relaxed. I knew little about social services and less about research. A three-person panel grilled me for what seemed like days before I was free to go. That was that I assumed. Unlike my other interviews to date, there was absolutely no way I would get this job. Pigs surely would fly first. But then I was called back for a second interview. I had come in fourth on the hiring list and then edged up to third when someone dropped out. I was the final person the hiring supervisor could interview. Again, I felt like I somehow had snuck into this final chat illegally. Maybe the original list had only four candidates and I moved on largely by default.

A few weeks later I got a call from a Shirley Campbell asking me if I were interested in taking this position with the Department of Family Services. I acted cool as if I was thinking the offer over even as I started peeing in my pants with joy. The very next day I got a call from New Jersey with an offer for the planning analyst position I had interviewed for earlier. My guess is that they realized that they did need someone who could do real work. So, by virtue of timing, my first professional job was in Madison after all.

After several months on my new job, I asked Mary to join me in Madison. She immediately found a job heading a study of the career patterns of women in state government. Things were falling into place. I guess that once you are on the downward slide the end is inevitable. As I recall, I eventually proposed to her in the bathroom, always the romantic. Cary Grant had nothing on me.

But it turned out to be one of my better moves. For some totally inexplicable reason, she must have been highly motivated to marry me. I suppose that makes sense. After all, I was still breathing and did have the correct anatomical parts. For me, it just seemed like the obvious thing to do, even I can see a good thing when it beats me over the head. I have found that the big decisions are the easiest. Whether to have pasta or salmon at dinner can be a tortuous choice. But career choices, marital decisions, and big purchases like homes just seem to fall into place without much thought.

She wanted to get married before a scheduled trip to her parent's home at Christmas, but my birth certificate was late in arriving. She started harassing postal workers and civil servants back in Worcester. She called the post office on December 15. A harried worker said something like, "Lady, do you know what day this is? It is our busiest day of the year." But he went off to look, or pretend to, before saying there was no letter for her or us. Then she called the clerk's office in Worcester. It was after hours but she caught some poor schmuck who was late in leaving that day. Again, she convinced this person to find what we needed and mail it that very day. We both can imagine the conversations around the water cooler back then. Boy this desperate broad called yesterday, she must have a live one on the hook and does not want him to wiggle off. In any case, a hand-addressed envelope with the certificate proving I had been born arrived in time. My hopes that bureaucratic inertia would save me were dashed.

Remarkably, she has put up with me for over four decades now. Fortunately, we agreed on the bigger things like whether or not to have children. Neither of us was so inclined. I suspect she did not feel she was cut out to be a mother. And I, as I have said so often, was overwhelmed by the immense responsibility of it all. In some ways, I wanted to keep normative flexibility in life. If you were totally responsible for another human being, you might just be tempted to bend on your core values. I could envision a situation where my values would prompt me to take a stand that would threaten my source of income. But faced with children who were my responsibility, I likely would sell out. It might never happen, but I hated taking the chance.

In addition, I had a very dark view of life in those days. I did not like what I thought the future held and had reservations about bringing a life into a world about which I had significant reservations. In some respects, my early pessimistic vision of the future has come into play since the 1980s. Opportunity for most of our young is now rapidly disappearing while a few at the top garner all the goodies. Beyond that, the U. S. is particularly cruel toward its own children and is getting worse in that regard. Social conservatives insist that fetuses have rights but once born, forget about it. Kids need medical help and the parents cannot afford it, screw them. There is no money. Kids are vulnerable to neglect and abuse, we cannot afford to protect them. Kids are hungry or cannot access a decent education, tough luck. They should have been smart enough to be born into a rich family. I would never raise a child in such a callous and indifferent country.

Despite her deplorable choice in husbands, Mary is smart and accomplished and we got along famously. We still do. In our four-plus decades of marriage, we have seldom argued. It really does help when the woman says jump and the male responds with "How high?" I loved her intelligence and independence. We agreed not to wear engagement or wedding rings, signs of ownership. She kept her own name, I always was confused by that name changing thing, having trouble with names to begin with. And she was a feminist. Yup, my kind of woman.

There were, however, a few adjustments in the beginning. I will mention only one. It was a Monday night in December and she walked in and turned off the television. As I recall the Packers were playing the Bears that night. I am like, "What are you doing?" She explained we were off to buy a Christmas tree. "No, we are not!" "Yes, we are!" She was aghast that I would prefer football over shopping, even for a stupid tree. I was aghast she did not comprehend it was the Packers versus the dreaded Bears. I think she compromised in the end when she saw me break down in tears. That may have been the last time she did.

With regard to her professional life, she had one of those meteoric public service careers. She started out as a limited term (temporary) employee managing that study of women in state government. After accepting an entry-level "real" state position in the Division of Vocational Rehabilitation, she began her upward climb. In a remarkable short period, she became a division administrator in the department that governed employment relations for all of state government. Not too long after that, she assumed the position of Deputy Director for the Wisconsin State Supreme Court, which effectively managed the entire state court system.

Somewhat later, she took a leave to secure her law degree from the University of Wisconsin, from which she graduated with honors. I loved that since it gave me an opportunity to drag out all my sophomoric lawyer jokes—what do you call one hundred lawyers at the bottom of the ocean (a good start). Her career at the court had many challenges and rewards, she was very well respected. My favorite vignette is when the state legislature wanted to kick the Supreme Court out of the capitol building. They would only go if they could get a temple of justice erected on the shore of Lake Mendota. Mary was beside herself since she knew what faced her. How could she find or build something with seven offices of equal size on the same floor, and all with a corner office overlooking the lake. Given their egos, no justice would tolerate anything less than his or her peers got despite what the laws of physics or geometry say. She had fun but was happy when she could retire. Since she left, things have gone downhill as money and partisan politics have turned the court into an ideological free-for-all. You know things are bad when they try to strangle one another.

A lot happened in those few years after college. I survived the transformation from college revolutionary and champion of the downtrodden in far corners of the world to something resembling an adult. Perhaps the revolution was over. But I was far from being one of those adult people in any real sense. I had taken on the appearance of adulthood, at least on the outside. Becoming an adult on the inside would take a bit more time and experiences.

So, let us take a look at what comes next.

India-44 while training in India.
I am 6th from left.

After basketball game in Udaipur.
I am lower left.

Visiting our language instructor's home in Delhi
Hayward, me, and Bill.

Our home in Salumbar with Rooknot, Randy, and Cutchroo.

Salumbar at dusk, like Dodge City in the 1880s.

One of our demonstration plots.

CHAPTER 12

MATURING

When you're curious, you find lots of interesting things to do.
—Walt Disney

From a young boy's perspective, being an adult involved doing adult things. It meant having a real job, being married, maybe owning a home, obtaining the proper educational credentials, and embarking on a legitimate career. I managed to do all those things. In the end, I am not sure any of them convinced me I was an adult. That status yet eludes me most days. For years, I would be in august scholarly meetings at the National Academy of Sciences, or a high-government meeting in the Old Executive Office Building (technically the White House) or be giving the plenary talk at a major conference and would still be waiting for the real adults to send me home. I continued to feel, on occasion, like the clueless kid who roamed over Vernon Hill.

In 1971, I took one step in the right by getting one of those real jobs that adults do. A real job, in my mind, meant becoming self-sufficient. You could pay all the bills and you got benefits like health insurance, sick leave, and a retirement plan. Much like the India recollections, my professional career is documented in my companion publication titled *Confessions of a Wayward Academic.* At the risk of redundancy, I cover some material found there in this work but in much less detail and with more reflection. After all, you may be silly enough to only read this masterpiece.

A real job . . .

I remember my first day on the job as a research analyst with the Department of Health and Social Services (DHSS). I recall it was a foggy September morning and I could barely make out the Wisconsin State Capitol as I made my way to the State Office Building, a fortress-style edifice which looks so intimidating from the outside. It literally screamed power and authority. The nickname for this particular state building was S.O.B, an acronym that most observers thought referred to the occupants and not to the building itself.

Most of us probably start our first real jobs with some apprehension. I was no exception. Years later, when I was playing at being a scholar at the University of Wisconsin, I talked with a *New York Times* reporter about how nervous I was in finding and starting my own first job. Imagine how welfare recipients must feel, I told the reporter, who search for their first jobs without all of my advantages. It was an offhand comment thrown out amidst a more serious discussion. Yet, it somehow made it into his article unlike all the brilliant intellectual insights I also had shared with him. Later, some of my colleagues said that William Julius Wilson, renowned Harvard sociologist, would use that quote in his talks and attribute it to me. William was African-American and had suffered some awkward moments early in his academic career. Thanks to him, the whole country had an insight into my crippling insecurities.

My point is that entering the so-called real world where adults live, and work, is a big transition. This was no paper route or ticket-taker position. A real job was a challenge to my dreaded imposter syndrome. In case you have forgotten this malady convinces you that all the real adults in the room will discover that you are a fraud at any moment. I had long been digging my way out of a deep hole of self-doubt but that initial hole was very deep indeed. The depth of it might possibly be attributable to my mother's persistent carping on my faults and failures which, in her mind, were endless. Perhaps our modest socioeconomic beginnings also played a part. How did a scruffy kid with no apparent talents wind up where he did? Or maybe the disposition toward self-doubt is simply hardwired and I drew the short straw.

Whatever the cause, I walked through the door that morning with less than a full tank of confidence. But the people were nice. As I think back on it, affirmative action had not yet arrived. Everyone in the Research and Analysis section where I worked was white and seemingly all the names were waspish . . . Gale, King,

Campbell, Boyd, Fisher, Ellingson-Waugh, Albert, Nettleton, and so forth. Corbett was at least Irish, sort of. Everyone welcomed me, and it appeared to be a friendly, supportive environment.

The cast of characters were quite talented. I have been fortunate in that respect; I have known good and smart people all along my professional path. Though this was nominally a research and statistics unit, there was little need for any advanced technical skills, at least for most of the time. That was good, since I would have fallen short as would have the others in the unit. Mostly, we did data collection and simple analysis type stuff. No need for advanced experimental design knowledge or a command of econometric techniques. On occasion, though, it would have been nice to know more than I did. Three of us actually took a statistics course one semester to beef up our credentials. It seemed to make a lot more sense this time around than it did back in college. Perhaps that was because the instructor actually could look at the class as he lectured.

Though not technically skilled, the younger staff struck me as very, very smart. The veterans were Joe Gale, Shirley Campbell, and Wayne King. Okay, Joe was a rather uptight bureaucrat, but he did support us when we screwed up. My co-worker, Peter Albert, was a character in his own right. A newly minted social worker, his heart was in the outdoors, not in a bureaucracy. Over time, he climbed some of the world's tallest peaks and named his daughters after his most recent conquest. I am not sure how his daughters felt about that, good thing kids are voiceless for a while at least. Anyways, Peter casually mentioned to a friend of his how we had spent all this money on an automation project with no results so far. The only problem is that his friend was a reporter who sniffed at a possible scandal. We reported this to Joe Gale who did not point fingers. Joe went into damage control and protected Peter. In the end, no article appeared. I learned something from the way he handled it.

Shirley and Wayne were veteran bureaucrats in for the long haul. They were extremely competent. Public service back then was not something evil or despicable. In that era, you could attract good, talented people who were interested in contributing to public policy. There were lesser lights, of course, who put in their time and mostly watched the clock. But they seemed among the minority and could easily be worked around. I found myself among an eclectic group with interesting personalities and diverse interests.

Bill had graduated from Dartmouth and was a dissertation away from a doctorate in political science. He would later get a law degree. Sandi was married to a doctoral candidate in history. She was whip smart and would go onto administrative positions in colleges where her husband found faculty positions. Barbara was quite unique. She also was extremely smart and deeply committed to causes. She was an early feminist who, in her spare time, wrote a regular column on feminist issues for the local paper. Later in her career, I recall hearing that she became a member of the clergy and counseled lesbians. Al was a dissertation away from his doctorate and would remain in state service. He was our computer whizz. He loved tackling technical issues while I liked the big conceptual problems. Others might be mentioned but you get the drift.

Back then, we took pride in innovating and coming up with good ideas to advance the public good. In my short career in state government, we revised the way we carried out the federal quality control system to estimate errors in public assistance systems. We reduced error rates in these programs sharply. In addition, we reshaped the flagship welfare program, the Aid to Families with Dependent Children program, from a creaky, highly complicated system to a smooth, automated one. We lowered overhead costs, reduced discretionary abuses, and made sure that families got everything to which they were entitled. We also started to automate many of the tasks performed by the staff when I argued successfully for the assignment of the first computer terminal to program staff person. I mention all this only in passing here since it is covered in more depth in my policy memoir.

A lot of this progress came about because, as staff, we did not act like passive bureaucrats, at least not some of us. We would look around and see things that needed to be done. We did not wait to be told what to do but just started pushing and prodding to move ideas along. I got pretty damn good at pushing the envelope without getting into trouble, at least not much trouble. I found that I made up for my lack of technical skills with a wonderful talent for seeing possibilities and persuading others to go along with my stupid ideas. In short, I was a good schmoozer or BSer if you prefer. For a long time, I did not think much of this skill, rather feeling jealous of the technical aptitude of others like Al's computer skills. Later, I learned that he envied my ability to write compelling prose. We all desire what we see in others. After a while, I came to realize that technical skills were generally available. On the other hand, the capacity to see opportunities that others could not was a rare ability indeed.

Still, the process by which I eventually recognized some of my comparative advantages as a professional was a lengthy one and not very linear. Readers of my policy memoir will recall the full plate of substantive challenges I tackled. What I lacked in confidence I more than made up in energy, inquisitiveness, and a bit of hutzpah. I must have been an irritating bugger, more like a hyperactive kid in a toy store than an adult earning a living. Okay, I can handle my job but isn't that an interesting thing over there. Oh, and maybe I can help with this other project as well. My ability to multi-task more than made up for any deficits in basic skills and, believe me, those deficits were real.

I always had this awe of what I thought of as real people who got things done, who run the world. It seemed to me they knew secrets that were beyond the ken of us ordinary mortals. Now, I would be allowed to peek behind that curtain, to glimpse perhaps that wizard who performed the magic that made things happen.

Somehow, in those early days, it never fully occurred to me that I might become one of those magicians. Fortunately for me, getting things done was possible within the organizational culture of the day. The bureaucracy was not as top-down. Things were less political and partisan. People throughout the bureaucracy wanted to do things better. Staff was trusted more. Those were halcyon days indeed.

I found that having access to resources and a support staff could work miracles. I would sit at my desk and create some kind of form and then I could send it somewhere and suddenly there were ten thousand copies of this thing. There were systems for distributing my thoughts, words, and ideas to people around the state who actually thought I might know what the hell I was doing. People would call asking for my advice or opinion or response on some matter of importance and then actually listen to what I had to say. You were no longer a child or a student but a man with a title and an office and the appearance of authority. Holy shit, how did that happen?

Madison, being the State Capitol, was where authority started for the state welfare programs of that era. Well, in truth, Madison paid homage to Washington, D.C., but as far as the people actually running the programs, all wisdom and stupidity emanated from the same place . . . Madison. I will never forget the day my supervisor, Shirley Campbell, told me that I should go on the road and train all the public social workers in a new data collection form I had

CONFESSIONS OF A CLUELESS REBEL

designed. I was sufficiently aware of the real world to know that social workers did not like paperwork. They were professionals and loved the autonomy that a professional status conferred on them.

Now I was charged with waltzing in to reduce their complex professional world to a set of simple boxes that were to be filled in on a single sheet of paper. Okay, it is just paperwork you might say. They were not stupid, however. The framework used to summarize their work would inevitably erode the flexibility they brought to their client interactions and their professional position. After all, you get what you measure. I saw that right away, they would as well. They were not stupid. When I voiced my concerns, Shirley looked at me and said, "If they give you any trouble, you just tell them you represent the State and that they have to do it."

Wow, I thought, I represent the State of Wisconsin and I could tell someone what to do. This is too easy. And it was. My co-trainer, Peter, and I barely made it through our first training session with our lives. The hate in their eyes was palpable. At one point, when I thought they might storm the podium, I shifted the blame for everything to my colleague, the only scapegoat available to me. Hey, when the going gets tough, the weak become totally spineless. Both of us managed to survive but we knew that that this "we are from Madison and you have to obey" thing was total bull hockey. You really did have to earn some of your authority.

After that, we got smart as we made our way around the state doing these training sessions. We kept the car running and always made sure we had a direct shot to the door. At the same time, we did get better at what we were doing so the danger of assassination lessened somewhat. I did consider at the time that I might be the first state research analyst assassinated in the line of service. I fantasized about a plague in my honor, or even a statue, somewhere on the grounds of the S.O.B. It would say something about this brave lad sacrificing his life in the quest for better program data. There are some causes for which the ultimate sacrifice is warranted.

On the other hand, I did learn that where you sat sometimes did dictate how smart you were. I was part of a team putting together some data collection form for some purpose or another. The specific project is not terribly important. Toward the end we had to run past our data collection concept past the top boss. By this time, I was beside myself. I had argued vigorously for a certain conceptual approach only to be ignored by the rest of the team. Apparently, I had reached a point where I would defend my position even if I were standing alone, one strong man making a majority and all that bull. Of course, not being that strong I usually went down to defeat.

We get to the review session with "the boss." As the others presented our agreed-upon plan, I sat there sulking, still the whiner. But then I could see that his brow was furrowed just a bit. Something was bothering him. Hope stirred in my breast, perhaps vindication would be mine. Would he support my approach and all these losers would have to bow to my genius? In fact, he did, and began to argue for something very much along the lines I had been arguing all morning, hell, all week. As for my moment of glory, I got nothing. Rather, my team went on to praise our supervisor's insights as if these concepts were being uttered for the first time. "Hey, you morons," I wanted to say but didn't. I am sitting here and was making the same point for the past week or so. They were not morons of course. They were colleagues that I respected a lot. But I was amazed at how easily they simply ignored what I had said and how enthusiastically they embraced the same ideas from someone in a position of authority. Oh, just wait until I had power I thought at the time. Unfortunately, I am still waiting for that power.

Mostly what I learned in those early days was to be honest about what you were and were not and to play to your strengths. On paper, I was a research analyst. But in reality, I was part provocateur and part architect of new ideas and initiatives. Still, I did not have the power or authority to make anything happen. I had to persuade others, hopefully those with real authority, toward my position or point of view. That required convincing arguments of course. But it also demanded that one earn the confidence of others. You learn early on that rational argument was not enough. Reason and logic had to come in an attractive, salable package. And if you were a male with little sex appeal, people had to like and trust you. Apparently, I instinctively had the people skills to go along with a quick mind. I found myself putting together little informal affinity groups so that new ideas could be shared and sold as if they had wider support than they probably did.

Of course, not all new ideas were easily sold. In the early days, my enthusiasm for automating case management of welfare and social service programs met with disinterest or hostility by the powers that be. These were concepts ahead of their time. We were banished to our cubicles for a while, and informed that we really should be doing our actual jobs, the mindless tasks we were being paid to perform. How tedious was that? Finally, though, a savior rose high enough in the bureaucracy to resurrect our project and make it happen. All good things come to those that wait.

What I also recall most from those state days was a strong disconnect between my insides and the outside. My early doubts about whether I belonged were partially dispelled as I rather quickly received a couple of promotions from a research analyst 3 to a research analyst 5. It was more than that. I could tell I was considered a player early on, that I had the confidence of others, including those in power. I would be sent to Washington on official business even as a lowly bureaucrat. Occasionally, I was permitted to sit in on higher level meetings with the Department Secretary. More than once it was remarked that I was a cool customer. I was told that even in tense situations I typically came across as calm and even tempered. During this period, I had a number of job offers from consulting firms and other states, a very rare occurrence for a nominally low-level civil servant. Were all these people smoking funny cigarettes?

Inside, I was anything but confident or calm. Still, the surprises kept coming. My colleague Sandra and her husband shocked me one day. Mary and I socialized with her and Steven and we did agree to serve as godparents to one of their children. Then they approached us about being named legally as the designated people who would take charge of their daughter if anything tragic would happen to both of them. I was stunned. What were they thinking? Why in the world would they even contemplate such a move? I did not want children myself, felt totally ill-equipped for parenthood, and had little confidence in myself as a real, functioning adult. It would be better to select someone for this role by throwing a dart at a random page in the phone book. When the shock wore off, it hit me that maybe it was not as absurd as it appeared at first blush. From their perspective, Mary and I must have struck them as smart, employed, funny, laid-back, enjoying a solid marriage, and generally having it all together. What other people see and how you view yourself can be worlds apart. I don't know much about their extended family, but we looked sufficiently better to put up with any grief that would come from awarding their children to someone on the outside. Go figure!

Casual decisions . . .

To my mind, adults were supposed to be thoughtful and analytical. I could be surprisingly impulsive and risk-taking. My wife and I had been together for a couple of years when I finally got around to proposing, in the bathroom as I mentioned earlier. I don't recall giving the marital decision a lot of thought. One day I got up and decided it might be a good idea. I had just had a blood sample taken for some other purpose, so it seemed efficient to use the sample for this as well. I now forget why that was needed. Anyways, I had already decided to get a vasectomy. After all, there would be no children and better to take the possibility off the table than to sire an offspring by mistake. I might as well take care of all this stuff at once.

When I called to make an appointment for the big cut, all went well until my marital status came up . . . I had not yet taken the plunge. After what seemed like five minutes of silence, it was strongly suggested I be psychologically examined. They had to sort out those who were into self-mutilation from those who were capable of making serious, adult-like decisions. Of course, I understood. No doubt, a young man could easily make an impulsive decision that he would regret upon meeting the love of his life. I thought my decision rooted in deeper stuff but that was something the person on the other end of the line could not possibly know.

Off I went to see if I were as crazy as others had argued. I did all the ink blot tests, the random word associations, the picture interpretation stuff and the pencil and paper tests. The psychologist then probed for my reasons by asking a few open-ended questions. My favorite was "if you could be any animal, what would it be?"

"A sloth," I replied and saw the one and only reaction I would get. I explained that I liked the pace with which they approached life. Then I cringed internally. This was no time to get cute or funny. What I saw as witty might be interpreted as a sure sign of deep seated neurosis if not a full-blown pathology.

As we wound things up, I mentioned that I thought we were testing the wrong group. People who decide not to have children are, at worst, hurting themselves. Those who decide to have children are taking on society's most demanding job. Yet, we act as if parenting is an inborn skill for which all are endowed with the proper attributes and dispositions. That is an outrageously fatuous premise. In my experience, only a minority of parents are really good at the job. Others might be brought up to snuff with training and support. To me, it seems foolish to take a hands-off posture and just hope for the best.

As things turned out, Mary and I had gotten married between the time I had set the appointment and the actual moment of snipping and cutting. She had to come in and sign that she agreed to the procedure. I am sure the good doctor thought he was dealing with a couple of loonies whose marriage would not last forty weeks, never mind the forty-plus years it has. I guess it is hard to tell at the beginning. I doubt the Vegas betting line was favorable for me managing a long-term marriage. Friends of mine were incredulous at the news. You, getting married, and then uncontrolled laughter! I must have talked the good line about the evils of commitment back then. I was astounded that people both listened to what I said and gave it credence. Still, I must have been convincing since no one apparently had me down as good marriage material. Go figure!

Mary independently decided to have her tubes tied . . . talk about making sure no offspring would spring forth. Besides, at the outset neither of us fully bought into this monogamy forever stuff. That made marriage sound like a life sentence without the possibility of parole. I was grilled by her doctor about why I would not get a vasectomy, which I already had. However, if I admitted to it, they would not proceed with her procedure. So, I lied for her and came across as looking like a total chauvinist and narcissist. Let her go under the knife, I could not be bothered! I hung tough, though, despite the fact I am a terrible liar.

Mary and I went down to the Madison City Hall one day. We asked the clerk if there was a judge who would marry us without being offended if Mary kept her own name and if we wrote our own vows. We didn't want all that obey stuff in there, at least Mary didn't intend to obey me. They thought for a moment and said that Judge P. Charles Jones would do it if anyone would. We wandered down to his office and chatted with him. He was great. His only requirement was that we had words that told him that we knew we were getting married. For a moment I thought there may be a loophole here but no go.

On D-Day, disaster day, I awoke early and sat down to create the wording for our ceremony. I procrastinated on everything. Below are the words and sentiments I typed out that fateful morning:

> *We affirm that the basis of this marriage is a search, a search for what two people can be for one another, and a search for what they can be together and as individuals, in this fragile and tenuous world.*
>
> *We affirm that we will not relax with what the stereotypes of marriage demand but direct our energies toward what it can become.*
>
> *We affirm that we shall not possess one another, but rather allow each to grow, to aspire, to interact, and to fulfill whenever possible the potentials we each possess.*
>
> *We affirm that we shall share on an equal basis the greatest trials and the most trivial demands that life will afford us.*
>
> *We affirm, simply, that we are what we are and will not exact from each other anything beyond our individual capacity for giving, our individual capacity for understanding, but that we shall ask each other to simply live out with honesty the evolving definition of this union.*
>
> *We reaffirm our commitments to seek out a living understanding of what it is to exist in a social fabric of humanness, and justice, and freedom, and the simple concern that each human being must have for another.*

December 22. 1972

Apparently, the good judge found in this gobbledygook good enough to convince him that we did, indeed, want to get married. Damn, my attempt at obfuscation failed so he proceeded to legalize the nefarious deed. The thing is, we had never told anyone we were getting married, neither friends nor family. We had two co-workers to serve as witnesses and two other friends who took pictures, period. The real kicker was that circumstances worked out so that our so-called wedding day occurred on the same day we were scheduled to visit Mary's family in the Twin Cities. I now look back on this with wonder. What was I thinking? In any case, after the ceremony we embarked on the four-and-a-half-hour trip to St. Paul and her family home. On that day, I would meet the entire family. Were they in for a surprise!

I had met the parents once before at their lake cottage up in northern Minnesota. Then, however, I was one of several guys though her mother figured out that Mary had set her sights on nailing me. Upon arriving at her parent's home, we sat around for a while chatting before Mary found some clever way of indicating that we had gotten married that morning. There was a moment of silence, even uncertainty. It then hit me, a little late of course. What will they think? Will they erupt in outrage? Will they throw me out on my ear? Does Mr. Rider own any weapons? I really did not know these people.

I did not have anything to worry about. After Russ (Mr. Rider) figured out what was going on, he arose from his chair. For a moment, it did occur to me that he was heading for a gun collection and that I might better be looking for an escape route. Not to worry, though, he brought out a check. "Upon accepting this check," he intoned, "there is a no-return policy." I looked, and it was for $500. Not bad in 1972 but not a munificent sum either. Perhaps I should have negotiated for more. Really, if you are that desperate to get rid of her, it is going to cost you more, much more! How many cows and goats can you throw in to seal the deal? Okay, I am embellishing here but not much.

Then he started with the jokes, "Well, I guess you won't need extra blankets tonight." I blushed. He thought this was a real wedding night in the usual sense. Oh my god, this was mortifying. Just shoot me! This whole venture had not been thought out very well. I knew that Mary's mother had figured out that we had been living together. Mary and I had this arrangement where we would say wrong number if her parents called and I answered the phone or if my parents called and she answered the phone. Then one day the phone rang at some ungodly hour of the morning. Groggily, I answered. Without thinking I said, "Just a moment," and handed the phone over to her. Then my brain unfroze, and I looked around for a knife to slash my wrists. When Mary and her mother talked later, her mother's only request was to keep the secret of our sinful lifestyle from her dad.

In truth, I got along great with her folks. Her mother tried to keep me fed, knowing that Mary had no domestic skills. She had this perverted philosophy that as long as Mary did well in school she would not get stuck with women's chores, a feminist before her time. But now that Mary had a live one she was not so sure she had done the right thing. Perhaps there was still time to show her daughter how to be a good, supportive wife by example. I was showered with affection and food and all manner of good things whenever I showed up in St. Paul. The car would be loaded down with food stuffs for the lean days that would follow our return to Madison. I did not have the heart to tell Mary's mother that it really was too late. That horse had left the barn. Good thing there are restaurants. Mary's dad was great. We would sit for hours as he regaled me with stories of his early life. Apparently, I was a good listener. Others in the family were stunned that he would talk to me so much since he was very reserved and extremely quiet with others. We just clicked for some reason.

With my folks the road was rocky, particularly with my mother. When I told Mary that I would send a letter to my folks telling them of the marriage, she was aghast. I was forced to call them with the news. I tried preparing poor Mary for the day she would meet them to no avail. She had grown up in a normal family. She thought my family would be like hers, you now…normal. The first word's she heard as we walked off the plane was my aunt turning to my mother and saying, "See, Jane, she is not pregnant." That was the only reason they could come up with for the sudden marriage. Within two days, my mother had Mary sobbing in the bedroom. She was not prepared for someone who was both controlling and insecure. Neither was I, ever.

Despite a few bumps, we were off on a very successful marriage. As noted earlier, I really cannot recall many fights or arguments over four-plus decades. We agree on the big things and somehow compromise on all the rest. Despite my negative attitudes toward marriage, there are worse forms of commitment. Perhaps the secret is to go into it with realistic expectations. If you expect wine and roses for the rest of your life, no one can provide you with such bliss over the long haul. What you can find is a life partner to share things and build a path to the future. I was fortunate indeed.

Of course, there were those special moments. I recall the time, some two decades into our marriage, that Mary surprised me during our anniversary. It fell a few days before Christmas, but we usually found a way to have a romantic, celebratory dinner at a nice restaurant. This particular fete was during her school days when she was working to upgrade her credentials with a law degree. Okay, I will admit she was a bit stressed, having just completed her grueling exams. I gave her an exquisite piece of jewelry signifying what she meant to me. She, in return, gave me a small package. I opened it eagerly since it just had to be a Rolex watch. It took me a minute or so to figure what was in inside. Then I started laughing.

It was a nose trimmer but, in her defense, a high-tech one. I think she realized her *faux pas* immediately, turning a bright shade of red. After years of being lectured that gifts were supposed to be luxurious and personal, she had gotten me an item devoted to nasal hygiene. She started stammering and stuttering with an explanation. I tried to say something about the bloom being off the rose, but I could not stop laughing long enough. Since then I have told this story often. Even her girlfriends, who always back up the female in any gender dispute, bail on her over this one. But I always tell her it was the best gift she ever gave me. I cannot recall a single other anniversary gift, not a single one, but that nose trimmer is etched indelibly into my memory and heart forever.

It was my turn one Christmas. I had made several mistakes early on by buying practical gifts. Okay, lesson learned. Still, one day time was running out. I was in panic mode. I hate shopping, really hate shopping. I always feel out of my element and just want it over. But then something hit my eye. There were sewing machines beckoning to me. Mary's mother sewed. Her sister-in-law sewed. I thought, don't all women want to sew? Bad thought! Still, I marched in and bought just about the best one available, top of the line.

Mary was intrigued by the big box. She was beside herself with curiosity by Christmas Eve. This was not a piece of jewelry or clothing. This was different. What had Mr. Wonderful bought her? She tore through the packaging and ripped open the box like a kid.

When she looked inside her face went blank while her mother and sister-in-law shouted my praises. As Mary looked at this infernal sewing machine she had that "deer in the headlight" look. I could just see what was going through her head, a sewing machine? A sewing machine! This total moron bought me a sewing machine? I knew immediately it was going to be a cold Christmas.

The worst part of it all was that there were a series of lessons that went with the gift. I had to accompany her to them, the only male in the room. Mary would freeze up during the lessons, and I would explain what the instructor was saying. The final humiliation was when we tried to make a dress together. We got a pattern and cut out one half of the dress material. Then we decided that we had been robbed. Where was the other half of the pattern? When we ran into these domestic conundrums, we always called her mother. It was another question met by silence as her poor mom tried to figure out how a daughter with so much education could know so little. Finally, her mother quietly said, "You turn the pattern over, dear." Within a week, we found an underpaid woman who needed such a machine. She tried to ask us how much we wanted for it. "All we ask is that you get it out of our sight." That was more than enough payment for us.

But back to the early days and fulfilling the rites of passage toward adulthood! Not long after surviving my marriage and trip to St. Paul, we were playing monopoly with friends. They were searching for their first house. They mentioned seeing one they thought was cute but located in the wrong area given where they worked. I casually mentioned something about maybe we should think about contacting their realtor to discuss getting a home of our own. It was all highly theoretical in my mind. But within a few days a plump, eager agent was knocking on our door. I made sure she understood that we were in no rush. We would take our time and feel out what we wanted in a home. I believe we even prepared a list of sixty or so non-negotiable attributes a home must possess.

It was a dark, rainy evening in late February when we headed over to this place. After a cursory tour during which I could think of remarkably few questions to ask, we returned to our apartment. I sat down and looked over at Mary. "What do you think?" She merely shrugged in response. "Oh, what the hell," I said. "Let's buy the damn thing!" I don't recall for sure, but I believe our agent peed in her pants. The next day at work, my fellow bureaucratic inmates started asking all these questions like what color is it? Does it have a roof? And other things much more technical that I realized every other guy in the world would know about except me. I sat there mute thinking . . . what did I do? Just why is mercy-killing illegal?

So now I am a home owner. That made it official. I have a real job. I am married. I own a home even though I am uncertain whether it has a roof or running water. I am now a full-fledged adult. Yet, nothing had changed. I was still this clueless kid. Down the road I would get a doctorate. I felt no different afterward. None of life's major transitions amounted to crap as far as I was concerned. I was still a kid trying to fool everyone that I knew what he hell I was doing. I didn't.

You know, everyone says you will learn to love to do home ownership crap. That is crap. I went out and bought all those "do it yourself" books and the appropriate tools. Maybe I tried a few things, but I quickly learned that you have to know who you are. If your skill is using a phone, USE IT! Call someone who knows what the hell they are doing. There is a hilarious episode of *Two-And-A-Half Men* where Alan refuses to "call the guy" to fix the dish receiver on the roof despite everyone telling him to "call the guy." Of course, Alan falls off the roof and winds up in a partial body cast. It did not take me that long to learn this invaluable lesson. Always call the guy! That is why the guy is there. I am smarter than I look.

Another serendipitous event happened in 1975 that again turned my life in a different direction, eventually sending me on a path to the final key to adulthood…a career rather than merely a job. A professor at UW-Madison needed to get state support for a research proposal on assessing the role of front-line discretion in the making of welfare decisions. The source of federal funds he was seeking required that state government make the official application, not the university. Even though the distance between state government and the university was only a mile, they were universes apart. No senior state official thought an egghead from the university could possibly contribute anything to the proper management of welfare. They found a lowly functionary (me) and told me to work with this clown.

I did, spending a fair amount of time working to make the application something my employer could support. Off it went and I forgot all about it. Then, one day, the phone rang. It was the professor, saying he got the grant and wondered if I would consider moving to the university to manage this complex undertaking on a day-to-day basis. As with all great decisions in my life, I thought it over for six or seven seconds and responded with a "Sure, why not?" It really was that casual. Fortunately, it was a good thing. He was smart as an academic but clueless about how government worked.

Though Irv was a professor in the School of Social Work, the study was to be run through something called the Institute for Research on Poverty (IRP). IRP was, at the time, the only academic-based national research center funded by the federal government to assess the causes and cures of poverty. It had been created as part of President Johnson's War-On-Poverty. Years later, when I testified before a U.S. Congressional committee chaired by Senator Daniel Patrick Moynihan, the welfare expert in the Senate, he mused that the Poverty Institute was one of the best legacies of Johnson's so-called poverty war. Of course, Pat was known to engage in a bit of hyperbole from time to time. And he did have a fondness for the spirits as we Irish say.

This decision to leave civil service for a mere temporary job at the university reflected the schizoid nature of my personality writ large. I was insecure yet jumped at a chance to take on a new challenge in an environment I knew would be demanding in the extreme. Not only that but I made this decision on the fly and without even asking any questions about the position. Here I was giving up a civil service position with all that security for a something that was temporary and might well be beyond my skill set. I pretty much took a leap of faith.

My only real regret at the time was that I was heavily involved in union negotiations with the State of Wisconsin. I have no idea how I became the official representative for the Research and Analyst bargaining unit. Though pro-union by default growing up in an ethnic, working-class household, I did worry that unions could be rigid when flexibility was required to get the job done. They were sticklers for things like hours on the job, not going beyond your job description, and seniority. I instinctively ignored things like official position titles, rules, and bureaucratic rigidities when I focused on a task or project. For me, it was all about getting stuff done. It was not a great fit, the union culture and me, but I made the most of it.

It was a very contentious set of negotiations that dragged on for months. I loved it when we sat around singing Solidarity Forever and The International. There was a sense of brotherhood and sisterhood that was irreplaceable. As tensions rose, we flew out to D.C. to strategize with Jerry Wurf, the head of the largest public employee union. Eventually he came to Wisconsin for head-to-head meetings with the governor. As head of the researchers, the smallest and least powerful of the bargaining units, I had an inside seat to it all. It was great watching how power politics played itself out. But then the university offer came along, and I had to bow out before it was all over. I must admit, I would have liked to play that one out to the end.

A career . . .

A career would offer something a mere job would not, a more definitive purpose and trajectory on the professional sphere. The academy might just offer what I needed in that regard. Two years later, as the study wound down, I looked around and concluded that this academic life sure beat out working for a living. But I needed what is considered the union card for the academy, a Ph.D. I promptly enrolled in the doctoral program in social welfare (i.e., social work). I was fortunate to study under some of the giants doing poverty research, including Irwin Garfinkle (now at Columbia), Sheldon Danziger (later Michigan and the Russell Sage Foundation), Michael Sosin, (later at the University of Chicago when he passed away), among others.

It turns out that I would never leave IRP except for a one-year stint in Washington where, on leave from the university, I worked on Clinton's first welfare reform bill. I did eventually accept a couple of faculty appointments within the University mostly because others pushed them. They proved to be disasters. The first appointment was in the Department of Government Affairs. I never figured out what they did and had no contact with them. The second appointment was in social work. This was arranged while I was in Washington on leave from the university working on Clinton's welfare bill. The best I can figure out, UW administrators thought it would be cheaper to have me on the faculty since I was teaching so much. That school never figured me out and I stepped down from teaching and administration at IRP before my tenure decision arrived.

For all practical purposes, though, my real career remained centered at the Poverty Institute where I served as associate director and acting director for the last decade or so of my academic career. The Poverty Institute was my dream home. It was a nationally known think tank and research entity with an impeccable reputation. I could pick the issues I wanted to work on and had access to the best and brightest minds doing social policy. It was like playing in a candy store, which is where all kids faking at being adults love to play.

They had a big party for me when I stepped down from teaching and administration (I did project work until recently). In my remarks at this 'getting out of Dodge' gathering, I reflected on the good fortune associated with my more or less accidental academic career. I paid special tribute to the lessons learned from my hardworking parents who labored in real jobs. That lesson was simple and direct—never take a job that involves heavy lifting. What did I do for most of my career? I flew around the country to work on incredibly difficult and fascinating social issues with the smartest and most talented people available. What amazed me most of all is that they paid me to do this. As one of my cousins always says, is this a great country or what?

I never forgot the laborers who carried caseloads of drinks up the mountainside to my hill station resort when I was on vacation during my Peace Corps service. I never forgot the emaciated looking farmers holding body and soul together by pulling small yields from the parched soil of Rajasthan. I never even forgot the hopeless futures facing the young Native American's on the isolated reservations of South Dakota. I never forgot those poor kids in Worcester whom, at a tender age, were already starved for affection and dreams. Consequently, I was never totally sympathetic to the whining from privileged faculty at a research university like UW–Madison. Clark Kerr, one-time president of the University of California system once described the modern university as "a bunch of academic entrepreneurs held together by silly disputes over parking and office space." I thought I was a master whiner but some of these folk in the academy put me to shame. My experiences taught me just how damn lucky I was, a lesson I hope never to forget.

Working on welfare and poverty issues over the past several decades proved stimulating, even provocative, and more than a little frustrating. These were what we call "wicked" social problems where goals were contentious, underlying theory and values were conflicted, and solutions were debated forever. Welfare reform definitely was not a topic for the faint of heart. I was on the speed dial of many media folk around the country. When in my public role, I always tried to maintain an objective and dispassionate tone. I always strove for neutrality in a content area where opinions were deeply held and quite emotional. I recall one day a top Wisconsin official thanked me for supporting a controversial idea that the Republican governor was pushing at the time, and which was being savaged in the press. I chuckled, noting that I call them as I see them. In the case of welfare reform, I only felt I was approaching the truth when no one agreed with what I was saying. By that measure, I must have been very close to truth's "holy" grail.

Doing policy work, even as an academic, had moments of drama. A couple of examples must suffice. The "Learnfare" concept was an early effort to link welfare to appropriate behavior on the part of recipients. As such, it was at the forefront of the emerging social contract approach to welfare design and management. Not surprisingly, it was hugely controversial. I had written about Learnfare and thus was asked to testify before a Congressional Committee in Washington, a city that had become a second home in those days. Though I thought testifying was a bad idea, the IRP director at the time gave me a stirring speech about my duty as a scientist, about academic freedom, and all manner of related rubbish. My fear was more mundane—that all our remaining contracts with the state of Wisconsin would be terminated, which at a minimum would have thrown a lot of graduate students out of work.

I was lobbied fiercely, even on the plane out to Washington. A former Republican legislator from Wisconsin who then held a high Food Stamp position in DC looked me right in the eye and said, "Tom, you know what happens to people who try to stand in the middle of the track?" Yeah, I know, the train runs right over them. For one of the few times in my life, I really prepared my remarks. After the testimony, a Thompson appointee came up to me and said, "Well, Tom, those remarks were fair. The child support research contract is coming up for review next week, and I think you will like the outcome." To this day, I cannot tell if my testimony was totally truthful or whether I slanted things for political purposes. I certainly did not do so consciously.

One thing was certain, life was interesting back then. On another occasion, then Wisconsin Governor Thompson yelled at me from the podium at a public meeting being hosted by a Chicago-based foundation. This was years after he personally put a crony on a review panel to make sure IRP did not get a contract to do a federally mandated evaluation of one of his nationally touted reforms. In the convoluted world of welfare, as it turned out, even a governor's personal attack might prove beneficial. As his tirade ended, the president of the host foundation walked up behind me and whispered in my ear, "Tom, in our eyes your stock has just gone up."

At the end of the day, there was always something both comforting and frightening in the fact that I could be my own man. Perhaps with the exception of my year in D.C., I was always in a position where I could come to my own conclusions about what was right and about how I should conduct my professional life. I tried not to be an ideologue, nor partisan, nor predictable. Searching for my own personal truth remained a precious opportunity, and burden, for me.

Similar in some respects to my PC experience was the year I spent in Washington, D.C., working on President Clinton's first, well only, welfare reform bill. It came about as casually as everything else in my life. The Institute Director at the time Bob Hauser sent a message to all IRP affiliates asking who might be interested in spending some time at the Office of the Assistant Secretary of Planning and Evaluation (ASPE). This was the place that oversaw IRP's work and provided the federal core funding for the Institute's work. As with most of the adventures overviewed in this chapter, I describe this episode much more fully in my policy memoir titled *Confessions of a Wayward Academic*. Initially, I discarded Hauser's message without much thought. Who would want to spend time in D.C.? But I softened during the course of the day and eventually broached the subject to my wife. Since she worked for the Wisconsin Supreme Court, she would remain in Madison while I sauntered off to save the Republic. I thought she might have misgivings, but she seemed delighted to be getting rid of me.

I did have a moment of dismay when I got a call saying that everything was set. How soon could I join them as they set about to reform the nation's welfare system? I mumbled something about needing to finish out my semester's teaching obligations. They understood but told me not to tarry too long if I were not to miss the boat. Oh my, this would be like a young man missing the war. When I arrived at ASPE, I was worried that the planning process might be well along and that I had missed out on the fun part. Not to worry, they had barely started. Plenty of fun remained for me.

My time at ASPE was intense and full of high drama. But there were funny moments as well. Not long after I arrived, several of us were assigned to make a formal presentation to a group of what might be called trade groups (national organizations that represented specific agendas or populations or issues). It was a big deal to the Administration since they wanted to keep these groups "in the choir" so to speak as the president moved forward with a few controversial ideas on welfare reform. We met with the Domestic Policy Council at the White House to go over our presentations. I did my bit and the Chair of the Council approved it but said it was too long and needed to be cut back. Without missing a beat, I responded, "No problem, I'll just cut out every other word." Ah, the look on her face was priceless.

Washington types are way too serious. It is a place where everyone claims to have just talked to God. The presentation, it turned out, went well for me but for a different reason. I had written an article just before leaving Madison. It was included in *FOCUS*, a publication of the Institute that had pretty wide circulation among many policy wonks in DC. The piece was called "Child Poverty: Progress or Paralysis" and contained what I thought were some interesting insights coupled with a little humor. It turned out to be a sensation in DC and people wanted to meet the author. The folk at the General Accounting Office had me over for a talk and later told me they used that piece for years when Congressional folk wanted a background piece on poverty and welfare. I had my 15 minutes of fame. Go figure.

Sometimes the grand and the trivial combine to bring us the best moments. There were these early morning meetings where the planning powers that be gathered to make big decisions. Unfortunately, Washington is not geared for big decision-making, and it turned out that few would be made in these meetings. One day we were talking about teen pregnancy and what to do with this scourge. A well-known D.C. economist offered the following . . . why don't we condition access to Pell Grants (help for college costs for low-income students) on teen girls avoiding pregnancy? It was a classic incentive strategy to alter behavior. After a few moments of silence, a woman from the Department of Labor spoke up saying that "Sure, Betty and Bob are going at it in the backseat of the car and Betty says, no, no, stop, I will lose access to my Pell Grant in two years." We went on to the next idea.

In the end, we did not end welfare as we know it. The Clinton team was too internally divided to make quick decisions. By the time a plan emerged, it was too late The Republicans took over Congress and pushed harder reform ideas. Clinton, after vetoing a couple of Republican Bills, signed on to one in 1996 and cash welfare for poor families with children ended as an entitlement. It was like most of the policy windmills toward which I tilted my lance. I seldom righted many wrongs largely because it was not always easy to distinguish right from wrong. But that in itself made it a great way to spend my time. If it were easy it would have been done by now and there would have been no fun left.

All in all, it was an enormously satisfying, if exhausting, career. Admittedly, I was never a conventional academic, nor did I aspire to be. I evolved into a policy wonk, the proverbial itinerant policy tinkerer who wandered among the most complex of public challenges seeking solutions or at least having a good time. As noted, that odyssey is detailed in the companion memoir titled *Confessions of a Wayward Academic*, a great read. You really don't want to wait for the motion picture. All in all, the real world always was much more fascinating to me than publishing technical pieces in peer-reviewed journals to be read by a handful of colleagues. That struck me as little more than intellectual incest. I preferred to write for broader audiences and for real-life impacts. On that score, I am well satisfied.

I would humbly submit, though, that I was pretty damn good teacher and inspired more than a few students over the years. I found that you never knew what kind of impact you were having on the kids you taught. Once in a while, I taught undergrads and recall a young gal who complained mightily how hard my course was and how she was going to have a breakdown from all her studying, etc. She complained so much I actually stored her name in my memory in case I ran across it in the newspapers under student tragedies, or more likely, she returned to the campus sporting a semi-automatic weapon.

Years later, an economist at Johns Hopkins University approached me at a conference and asked if I remembered a certain former student. It was her! Oh my god, she sent this guy to track me down and exact revenge. I had no idea that Burt Barnow was a hit man disguised as an academic. And yet, I still admitted to remembering her. My colleague smiled rather than punching me. "She is my stepdaughter, and she still talks about you as the best professor she had at UW." This reaffirmed my sense that you just never know what kind of effect you are having on people.

In the end, it was all great fun. I had the pleasure of working with the best and brightest from academia, think tanks, the philanthropic community, top evaluation firms, and government officials at all levels. I gave perhaps hundreds of talks all over the country and in Canada. A colleague came up with an estimate once when she was introducing me at a conference, which unfortunately I cannot recall. But I gasped at the number myself. I've had my writings entered into the Congressional Record, served on a National Academy of Sciences expert panel and, most importantly (to me at least), had the respect of both my academic colleagues and policy practitioners at the local, state, and federal levels.

It all could be exhausting, though, as I juggled the teaching of courses, helped administer a poverty research center, raised money, managed multiple projects simultaneously, and traveled continuously to give talks and consult. In the old days, BPP or before Power Point, I used to carry around a huge file of transparencies that I would continuously update. When I got on the plane to fly somewhere to give a talk, I would pull out the file and start sifting and winnowing and reordering. By the time the plane landed I would have my prepared talk, sort of. I never really knew what I would say until it was time to say it. Colleagues would comment that they were preparing for a talk they were giving in three weeks. Three *weeks*, give me a break! I felt ahead of the game if I was ready three hours before the talk.

I suppose I began running out of steam at some point, too many mornings of getting to the office at 5:30 or 6:00 AM, too many flights (particularly through O'Hare on Friday evening), to many hotel rooms, and too many battles. After a cardiac scare and lecture from the top heart doc at University Hospital, I gradually cut back but continued to do project work until rather recently. I left the policy field, and many unresolved problems, to the young and the restless. I now have an opportunity to read for fun. With some exaggeration, my spouse often has noted that she never saw me with a book that did not have a colon in the title. You know, books like *Poverty: The Curse of the Working Class*.

Most importantly, I now have an excess of life's most precious commodities...time. This newfound luxury has provided an opportunity to write all those books that have been on the back burner all these years. I now can put to paper a lifetime of accumulated nonsense stored somewhere in the recesses of what passes as a brain for me. I am sure the world can hardly wait.

CHAPTER 13

RECOVERING

There is no path to happiness. Happiness is the path.
—Buddha

Life is multidimensional. Perhaps a simple physics example helps illustrate this obvious point. White light hits a prism and breaks into its many constituent colors. A single beam goes in and multiple colors spray out. What does this tell us more broadly? Well, too often we see the surface of a life, the white aggregate, yet cannot comprehend all the constituent parts. We see an individual at a point in time and mistake the momentary presentation for the whole person. We see someone in a public role and assume we are witnessing their totality. At one level, we know our understandings are simplistic, yet it is hard to get beyond what we easily see, what our cursory impressions present to us.

Images of me taken over time would provide an incomplete and even distorting picture. Early on you would see a rather timid boy, rambunctious at times, but very obedient and largely explained by the enveloping culture and times. Fast forward a bit and you notice change. There were signs of searching and questioning, a reaching out for an individual philosophy and unique sense of purpose. Inch forward a bit more and you sense a man slowly emerging from a cocoon of self-doubt to make a small imprint on the world. You might detect rebellion against the norms and constraints of time and place. Moving further on, you begin to see a struggle between finding a place in the world and engaging in a nihilistic descent into self-destruction. Approaching my dotage, you found someone at peace with himself but still a bit irritated at the world around him. Now, you find a cranky old man really irritated at the world around him and pissed that people could really vote for an idiot like Donald Trump. I was all of these and yet none defined me.

This work has been a collage of memories mostly from the early years. It was spawned largely by questions everyone asks toward the end of life's trajectory. How did I get here and what the hell happened during the journey? While a good portion of the adult part of my journey is found in *Confessions of a Wandering Academic*, snippets of the early years are also found in *The Other Side of the World*, and *Return to the Other Side of the World* where I focus in more detail on my Peace Corps experiences. This effort, at least the first several chapters, examines what I think of as the foundational narrative of my life trajectory. How did the most ordinary kid on the block take a path less trodden and even become just a little more than ordinary? How did he separate himself from his peers?

Nothing surprised me more in my adult years than the fact that people paid attention to me. After all, I was the kid who was labelled slow in grammar school and proved so insecure socially that he could barely ask girls out on a date. So many snippets come to mind about an adult who was at odds with what his childhood seemed to promise. Students I taught at the University of Wisconsin would write to me later on thanking me for changing their lives or helping them figure out who they were. I would walk into a room of movers and shakers, whether in Washington D.C. or some state capitol and people would listen to me as if I had some wisdom to impart. I would regularly get calls from the New York Times and other media outlets from across the country and wax eloquent as the welfare debate raged across the headlines. When USA Today, the preferred daily news venue for those usefully occupied in the bathroom, wanted a social policy or welfare expert, they tapped me.

I slowly began looking at myself differently, becoming more proactive in academic and public situations. A colleague of mine, a well-respected economist, and I were talking about scholars we knew who had strong reputations in their field. They held tenure so were safe. They had already earned the respect of their peers. Yet, they seemed overly cautious, almost afraid of getting out of their comfort zone. While my colleague and I respect the desire to ground opinion in evidence and to remain faithful to the cautious cannons of science, this reticence to speak out almost bordered on the pathological. What were they afraid of, criticism or debate or being exposed as being human? I learned early on you cannot please everyone nor can you be right all the time. I myself missed perfection by a mere 90 percentage points.

My transformation from pathetic to purposeful did not happen easily. It took me decades to fully shed the remnants of my imposter syndrome. By now, you should know for how long I felt like a dumb shit from Vernon Hill whom the adults had erroneously permitted to play with the big kids. I would be chucked out of the room when the mistake had been discovered. These feelings persisted long after others saw me as a player in policy and academic circles. They are still with me to some extent as I write these words. Public speaking, or offering my so-called expert opinions, reminded me of those pitiful moments of my youth when I asked a girl for a date. I always braced for laughter and ridicule.

Over time, I became more at ease with sharing my self-imagined profundity. I spoke out as if I knew something even when I did not know much at all. Slowly, I sensed that I had interesting, even stimulating, things to say even when they struck me as banal. As words poured forth from me, my sense of confidence would vanish on occasion. Halfway through my statement, that awful fear I was uttering gibberish might surface. No doubt in my mind, security was certain to be summoned and out the door it would be for me. "And don't come back," would be the last words ringing in my ears.

Such an embarrassing exit never happened, or at least I have repressed the memories. Even as a lowly state employee sent to

Washington when higher-ups should have gone, I realized I often would be the one making astute and incisive points. People would be turning to me for input and guidance. It took a long time to accept this unlikely reality was not an accident, a dream, or a drug-induced hallucination. Early caution slowly yielded to greater confidence and occasional acceptance of my place in the policy and academic worlds.

All kinds of people from high in public service or the academy would listen, say approving things, and invite me to speak or consult or play with the big kids again and again. The edifice of insecurity and self-doubt had been built high and solid. Like first loves, the hurts of childhood stay with you in a bright and hard fashion. When you are criticized constantly at home, see yourself as a failure in school and on the playing field, and seemingly strike out with the ladies on a daily basis, it is impossible not to look in the mirror without perceiving that latent smidgeon of self-doubt if not a distinct sense of self-loathing.

Ironically, and a bit tragically, I started losing traction just as I began to realize that I was not the dumbest kid on the block or the slowest adult in the room. It was an odd conjunction of progress and failure. I saw the possibilities of adult success just as my ethnic curse that had stalked me for years slowly took over. An inherent addiction to alcohol finally caught me and slowly began to consume me. The whole process was a bit like seeing the peak of the mountain you had been climbing only to lose your footing and sliding back down the slope. As I saw fleeting images of myself as a competent, successful adult, I started to tread water and go under. All too quickly a rip tide of fear and doubt swept me out to near oblivion. It was not to be a pretty sight.

The darker hues of the prism...

One day, right around my 40th birthday in 1984, I sat immobile at our kitchen table. I was exhausted, not from exercise or hard work or long hours of intellectual labor. I was totally worn out by battling a reality that had taken over my life. I was an alcoholic. I knew it. My wife knew it. Most of the people around me knew it by this time or had high suspicions. Probably most people in Mongolia knew it. Yet, I would struggle day after day to hide bottles of booze, sneak drinks, and worry whether or not I was fooling people around me.

You look in their eyes. What are you seeing? Is it pity, disgust, sadness, or the blessed signs of ignorance? And as long as they don't confront you, you play your little game that you have kept your dark secret intact for one more day. The sad thing is that too many people never had the courage to say what I had become. It would have been more compassionate to tell me I had become a disgusting drunk. But almost no one did. I certainly did not have the courage to tell myself, not completely at least, not until that moment perhaps. Not even my internist, who mentioned his suspicions to Mary, said anything directly to me.

Now, I am not one to blame addiction on psychological scars. I was not a drunk because my mother criticized me, because I failed my dad's expectations, or thought I did at least, or because my dreams for fame and glory were falling just a tad short. No, I eventually developed a different theory, one that saved me in the end. I concluded that most substance-abuse addictions are basically chemical dispositions built right into some of us. My body simply processes alcohol differently than a non-alcoholic's body. Still, it is likely that the disease can be triggered, sustained, and exacerbated by environmental stresses and tensions. Chemistry is not necessarily destiny, but it is a damn good start to one's destiny. That is my story and I am sticking with it.

My little bit of reading on the topic allowed me to stumble across the following theory and I just love theories. The narrative I embraced is based on evolution and natural selection. At its core, it is really a quite simple notion. Alcohol, in one form or another, had been around for thousands of years. Some innovative ancestor stumbled upon yeast and the right fruits or vegetables and had this eureka moment, probably in the same way that Sir Alexander Fleming came across the wonders of Penicillin by accident. Though antibiotics proved just a bit more useful than booze for mankind, both are used in a similar way. Both antibiotics and alcohol are employed as an ameliorative to control infections and disease, in one case real and in the other imaginary.

Alcohol first flourished in today's mid-east and areas adjacent to the Mediterranean Sea. After all, there were lots of grapes there and grains and sunshine and innovative people. As the story goes, booze was embraced with great gusto. What was different across people was their ability to process the drug. Some had a body chemistry that facilitated the development of an addiction by virtue of the way alcohol was broken down and absorbed by their body. Others did not. For some, booze was a palliative, for others a toxin that impaired performance if not worse.

Think about that for a moment. If you faced dangers from wild beasts or hostile tribes or bad ass members of your own tribe, your odds of surviving were diminished if you were drunk all the time. If you died prematurely because you were too hammered to outrun the mastodon, there would be less opportunity to spread your seed. Besides, young maidens were probably smart enough to select a guy as a viable mate with a reasonable chance of bringing home supper that night. A drunk hunter is not a good hunter. Some things never change. And even if courtship were a bit more primitive, the maidens could probably outrun you if you were staggering around in circles waving your club to bludgeon them into submission.

Over a short time period, you don't notice large effects. Over a longer time period, selective survival and breeding permits the non-addicted members of the communities to dominate. So, after centuries and centuries where the drop-down drunks died off early, Italians and Greeks and even the French could sit around drinking wine like water and not suffer much in the way of consequences. How? Only the non-addicted members of the original ethnic clans survived in great numbers. But remember that these evolutionary trends occur extremely slowly as did the migration of technology in ancient times. You did not jump on a superhighway and speed north to peddle your new booze making discovery up in Finland.

Slowly, very slowly, the ability of cultures to create alcohol and get blitzed every night moved away from the Mideast, through southern Europe and eventually to the far northern countries. Climate change also played a role. That means that those ethnic tribes up in Scandinavia had less time to weed out the biologically addicted. Besides, even drop-dead drunks probably were surviving longer in more recent times since survival was not so dependent on agility and responsiveness. Even the losers were spreading their seed around with abandon, probably more so since they were buzzed all the time. The bottom line, the rates of alcoholism are much higher in northern European countries and places like Ireland. The more recent the exposure to alcohol, the less likely selection would eliminate those disposed to its deleterious effects.

Native Americans were exposed to alcohol in a big way when European settlers moved into their neighborhood, talk about property values plummeting. If our ancestors could not kill them off with disease and guns, perhaps alcoholism would finish the job. It almost worked and the rate among Native Americans is depressingly high. I am not Native American. But I am Irish and

Polish. Frankly, I don't know if the Poles are disposed to demon rum, but my Celtic ancestors are, in spades. I probably was doomed from the moment I stuck my head into the world at 5:55 AM on May 20, 1944. There are probably many problems with this theory, but I do not care. It makes sense to me and, much more importantly, has helped to keep me sober for over three decades. I would believe in the laying on of healing hands if it actually seemed to work.

My parents and their friends drank daily and consumed copious amounts of alcohol. I would see my mother early in the morning drinking a beer, smoking cigarettes, and talking on the phone. Neither of my parents demonstrated much personality change when they imbibed in excess, from what I recall. At a minimum, they seemed to get more social, voluble, and animated. My mother worked in bars where customers bought her drinks. My dad sat in bars after work on a daily basis before heading home to the nightly battles with my mother. They would get together with friends to play cards or just socialize and consume even greater quantities of booze. It was part of the ethnic-working class culture, something woven into the fabric of everyday life. You ate, you drank, fought, you laughed, you drank some more, and you fought some more. Perhaps they even made love though that strikes me as improbable.

I still recall the time I had turned 21 and joined my dad at his favorite bar after work for the first time. It was not as if I was an alcoholic virgin. Unlike my sexual inexperience, I drank a decent amount in college but not nearly enough to impair my functioning as a student. I knew from the start it was a mistake to try to keep up with my dad. But I was committed to not failing him in this endeavor as well. Maybe I could not be a great athlete but at least I could drink like one. Finally, he said it was time to go, not a moment too soon. Great, my head had started swimming some time ago. We stood up and a wave of panic swarmed over me. Shit, I am going to fall on my ass right here. How embarrassing would that be? But I aimed at the door and made it through into the bracing outside air. It was a close-run thing, but I had passed the test.

Alcoholism can take one of several routes. In my case, it crept up on me over many years. There were signs, many signs, some starting early on. I could hold my liquor better than most of my peers. I thought myself as having more wit, more insights, more eloquence, and surely more attractiveness if I had a little buzz on. If you consider yourself ugly as shit, booze really helps. As I eased into adulthood, it wasn't that I thought people disliked me or that women found me totally repulsive, I just didn't feel that comfortable in my own skin. When I looked in the mirror, I saw a young man with below average looks and a bit of social awkwardness. Everything seemed to get a bit better, a bit easier, with just a little booze.

Toward the end of my college years I began to experience occasional panic attacks. If you have not had them it is difficult to understand how disabling they can be. The problem was, I never quite knew when one might hit. There did not appear to be a pattern. What I deduced from these attacks was that alcohol might serve as an analgesic, a killer of pain and a reducer of anxiety. It could, I thought, get me over the rough spots. It seemed to work, not always, but enough to permit me to draw an erroneous lesson. Alcohol was my Penicillin, my drug to ease uncertainty and doubt, to enhance the illusion of competence and acceptance. I was making a classic rookie mistake. I was dragging the causal arrow in the wrong direction. Over time, unfortunately, you need more medicine to counter the negative symptoms. But I did not have these thoughts together as I sat at that kitchen table exhausted. I just knew I was tired beyond thinking. Finally, I picked up the phone.

I cannot recall now how or where I heard about this treatment program. It was an intensive, outpatient therapeutic intervention for people battling addiction of one form or another. It was new, probably had not even started when I finally decided to reach out. It could well be they were advertising as a startup program and someone told me about it. Either way, I would be getting in on the ground floor. I would have been in the first group except for a scheduling issue, I was in the second group to go through the program. I suspect most comparable, existing treatment programs were either in-patient stays of several weeks or long term individual therapy.

At one point I tried the individual therapy thing. I thought doing something might get certain people off my back, like my wife. A colleague at the University gave me a name of a psychiatrist whom he thought I would like. The Docs credentials were little more than he was a poker partner of my colleague. Perhaps not the best basis for making such a choice but I obviously was not serious so what the hell. When I met the good doctor, I was startled. He looked just like Rasputin, the Russian holy man and all-around whack job who held sway over the Czar and Czarina just before the Bolsheviks took over. Rasputin had a good thing going until some Russian nobles recognized the danger he posed to the established order and knocked him off with several gallons of poison, seventeen bullets, and a drowning beneath the ice of a freezing Moscow river. He died hard.

Anyways, I would see him (my shrink, not Rasputin) once or week or so and we would spar. I suspect he was trying to find some deep-seated psychological scars that would explain why I was a drunk. He did scare me by saying if I kept on going as I was I would be dead in a few years or maybe he said a few weeks. But, after thinking on the matter, that did not seem like such a bad thing. Life pretty much sucked by this time. After weeks and weeks of our jousting, he got frustrated with me. He said at one session that he had never run into a cleverer patient who intellectualized as much as I did. I took it as a complement, but I doubt he meant it as such. At some point, our enjoyable battles of wit came to an end. I did not have my handy theory yet, but I knew this crap was useless.

Not all that long after, he popped up in the newspapers. He was accused of sexually abusing female patients and using his position of authority as a therapist in an inappropriate and unethical manner. After hearings and what not, he lost his MD license for a period and had to undergo therapy himself with a court appointed psychotherapist. It all sounded like a plan until it was later revealed that the therapist assigned to counsel him later was found to be abusing his own female patients. That was good for a laugh. I wondered aloud if they traded seduction secrets during their sessions.

Anyways, Rasputin did not cure me, and I continued to spiral downhill. This had been a twenty-year slide or so, very gradual at first and then picking up speed during the end game. It was a constant struggle, the final two years in particular. I don't know if you can ever define or recognize the bottom that people talk about. I did not crash the car or physically harm anyone other than myself. And yet, any pretense that I was a functioning human being was lost by 1983 and 1984. I had past beyond the walking wounded state to become one of the crawling wounded. On some days, I was the immobile wounded verging on death, or so it felt like.

I had become a pathetic basket case. I would stay at home many days, only occasionally going into the University. An academic position was not a helpful place for me to be during the darkest days since my movements were not constantly monitored or even casually monitored for that matter. Each time I entered the so-called real world, I had to exercise a colossal effort of will. I would try so hard to look normal, to hide the booze on my breath, to get sufficiently drunk to feel safe from unknown demons and yet not so drunk that I would fall over on my face. For a while, perhaps way longer than they should have, my calibrations of tolerable alcohol intake worked but that could not last forever. I knew in my heart that my days of fooling people were long over. I was not hacking it. I had become a maintenance drinker where the buzz never ended.

Everything was spinning out of control. For a while, my Rasputin look-a-like therapist had me on some kind of anti-depressant medication. That was a joke absent the mirth. The interaction of the meds and alcohol had the effect of causing my blood pressure to plummet when I stood up. The effect was not immediate. So, I would stand up, a feat in itself toward the end, and walk across the room before passing out. My head would bounce off the carpet if lucky, a table if unlucky. Often, I would get to the bathroom before heading to the floor. Then I might pin ball off the wash basin and the toilet. One day, after a more conventional blackout, I came to with the flesh on the underside of my right arm torn away at the elbow. I have no idea how this happened though it took a plastic surgeon and several layers of stitching to put me back together.

Several other stitching up jobs were needed over time but this was the only one to leave a permanent, commemorative scar. It is my badge of dishonor to my years of insanity. My call to the outpatient program probably came just in time. I was called into the Director's office at the Institute where I was struggling to survive. Everyone liked me a lot and they were quite concerned. We had one of those 'come to Jesus' talk. Fortunately, I now could admit that I had a problem and that I had just taken step one to address it. I informed them that days earlier I had arranged to enter a program. Perhaps they were skeptical, but I got the benefit of the doubt. My wife also was about to throw in the towel, so she told me later.

No question, I was on the verge of something catastrophic. I had fierce nightmares, waking up thrashing on the floor. Many times, I had to crawl down the stairs in our house since I was too shaky to walk down upright. Every day was a torture with the personal demons around me 24/7. So many times, I would come to prone on the floor or woken by my wife returning from work. Worse for me, the unstructured life in academia permitted me to get away with much that would never be tolerated in a real job but even they had run out of patience. It is impossible to believe I could have gone on much longer.

The thing was, would the program help? Would anything help? I had heard the stories about alcoholics struggling mightily with demon rum to no avail. The old joke about a guy not having a drinking problem because he had quit dozens of times in the past was no longer funny to me. At the same time, not having booze in my life scared me to death. How would I deal with the anxiety and panic attacks that had made my life an increasing misery? I felt like I was in a vice, a trap with no escape. Many a day, I saw my life continuing to spiral downward to complete destitution and then death, perhaps even at my own hand. Of course, being a committed coward made suicide a bit of a problem. Yet, the image of becoming one of those homeless guys begging for change on the street haunted me as a real possibility.

In any case, I did pick up the phone that day. Sure, they would love to talk to me and help if they could. But first I would have to go through an assessment, a triage, to determine if I was appropriate for their kind of program. Oh, oh, I would have to get by someone who was used to dealing with bullshit, even when flung around by a master bull shitter like me. For some reason, I really did not want to go into an in-patient program. Somewhere inside I knew it would be better for me, but that would be an admission of just how sick I was. Way to go, you hopeless idiot. Keep your head buried where the sun doesn't shine. My triage interview was a close-run thing. This program was run by a major local hospital and they had an excellent staff. Their gatekeeper really wanted to put me into an inpatient alternative. I danced and wiggled and did everything I could to stay out of that. Somehow, my charms worked, or I wore him out. At the time, though, I wasn't so sure it was much of a victory.

A funny thing happened. Even before my first day, I started to feel better. I can yet recall my last drink about three days before my first session. I was still woozy but somehow a bit confident when we started. Within days I had hope that this might actually work. By the end of the four weeks of intensive sessions I pretty much knew my life had turned around. At the end of several more weeks of follow-up sessions I had little doubt. Why hadn't I done something years earlier?

My salvation proved simple in the end. I first realized that all the things I had thought were peculiar to me were part and parcel of being a drunk. They were universal experiences. Second, I fell into my theory, the selection and evolution narrative described earlier. It made total sense to me. I found the theory in a book they recommended but did not mandate. Academics love books and I probably was the only patient to read the damn thing and fully embrace these concepts. Third, based on that theory, I could fully buy into the disease model of alcoholism. There was a chemical basis to my addiction, not a failure of will. Fourth, I realized that I had my classic causal path going in the wrong direction. Alcohol did not diminish my feelings of anxiety and panic, it exacerbated them. Finally, I discovered that the world is infinitely better without booze. Let me repeat that, the world is infinitely better without booze.

Some of the others in my therapy group had struggled in the usual way. They had stopped and started on their drug or drugs of choice several times. Sobriety did not come easily or without continuing support. Their stories concerned me, so I initially accepted the counsel to go to AA meetings. For the first time in years I felt whole and good and I did not want to risk that sense of peace. So, I did go to a number of AA meetings for several months including a few sessions in Canada during a trip north. But I never did get into the higher power thing, the making amends, the giving over as if personal fault was involved. I never did get a sponsor or go through the steps. Still, I enjoyed the meetings. They affirmed my intuition that my struggle with booze was very familiar and predictable. In the end, though, AA was nice but not necessary for me.

It was so simple. It was biology. I simply could not drink, period. The nasty things I worried about like anxiety, insecurity, and panic attacks all went away. The explanation, in the end, was so simple that I kept kicking myself for months. Alcohol exacerbated my symptoms and did not cure them. Get the basic things right, like the direction of the damn causal arrow, and all else falls into place. And did things fall into place, immediately and irretrievably.

I slowly returned to work at the University over the remainder of that year. After the program I rediscovered the world. Everything was fresh and bright and worth experiencing again. There was no struggle and no daily battles with desire and temptation. I had learned all the rules about not putting oneself in harm's way. Don't go into places were alcohol was served. Don't hang around with people who drink. Don't walk within 100 yards of a bar. Check out cough medicines for the alcohol content so you can avoid the dangerous ones. The list went on and on. I seldom paid attention to any of those rules. It just didn't matter. In the end, none of that mattered.

The bottom line was simple. If I drank again I would spiral into advanced alcoholism faster than the Cubs can fall into the cellar of their league. And besides, now I was enjoying life. On the few times I was mildly tempted to fall off the wagon, I always had a quick fix. I would recall what a miserable wretch I had been for so long. And by that, I mean a really miserable wretch, not like my normal miserable self that I display to others. It was never any contest. I did worry for a while whether I might not be as funny or witty or as charming as I had been in my early years. Soon, any fears there were dispelled. Wit and charm are not byproducts of any alcoholic drink known to man. As my poor friends have found out, all three of them (that is all I can afford to lease from rent-a-friend), there is no off switch. Believe me! They have desperately looked for it.

That summer turned into fall and winter and then 1984 became 1985. I emerged back into the world healthy again. I wonder how long it took people to trust whether I was really 'cured.' How long did they look for telltale signs of slippage? At some point I began losing any sense that I had been a walking disaster. That old Tom disappeared. Occasionally, I might simply tell others, or people would catch on to the fact that I never consumed alcohol, or they might catch some clue in something that I said. On rare occasions, someone would *sotte voce* ask if "I was a friend of Bill." That was the secret tell that you had been a member of AA, Bill Wilson being one of the founders of the movement. For years after, I would occasionally have dreams, nightmares really, that I had started drinking again. Guilt and paranoia would overwhelm me. When I awoke, it took me several minutes to realize it was not real. Since 1984, I only know of one sip of alcohol when I ordered what I thought was a fruit drink. One sip convinced me it was more than that.

My big fear at the time was that I might have killed off too many brain cells. I read articles about the ravages of alcohol on the brain. Then I would sit down and calculate how much I must have consumed over two decades of excess intake. A frisson of fear would course through me that I had only a few dozen cells left. I was somewhat mollified that I could perform the autonomic tasks of life like breathing without help. Perhaps all was not lost. Time would tell. Based on the next three-plus decades, a sufficient number of brain cells remained.

There is little left to remind me of those days. This is the first time I have explored through the written word what had to be the darkest moments of my life, perhaps except for my early efforts to manage life's tasks as outlined in the first chapter. Alas, the scars from those failures remain vivid to me. When I became a college level teacher so many students looked to me for guidance and even inspiration. Even now, many years after the fact, I receive an occasional contact thanking me for the wisdom and direction I shared. What if they had known where I had been just a few years before I walked into a classroom. Would I have still been someone to emulate, to go to for advice? I had never thought of myself as being a source of wisdom but what do I know. The magic apparently works from time to time.

Over the years I repeatedly said two things to my students. One is that the real world is highly over rated. They always struck me as being overly eager to get out there. Most therefore ignored my wise counsel. The second is that life is a long journey. Never get too concerned with the bumps and pitfalls you come across from time to time. Keep your focus on the long view. There will be time and opportunity to get back on track. Just figure out where you want to go and what you want to be.

Brighter hues from the prism…

I went from despair and suicidal thoughts to a new life in a relatively short time. If you read my professional memoir, you will wonder how I made it look as if there were few or no bumps in my colorful policy wonk career. It just goes to show you what you can do if you get to wield the pen or laptop. However, if you were paying attention you would have noticed some gaps in my many public triumphs in the earlier part of the 1980s. One clue is that it took me like a decade to finish my doctorate. There were other reasons for this but being a drop-dead drunk for a while did not exactly help.

From the mid-1980s on, however, my professional life really was like playing in a candy store. The joy expressed in my policy memoir is no exaggeration. I did travel around the country working with the best and brightest on some of societies' most vexing and difficult issues. Not only that, I operated out of an academic environment where I had no real boss nor bureaucratic rigidities (not quite true but true enough) with which to deal. I could free-wheel it to my heart's content. I also enjoyed passing on my passion and insights about social policy to a generation of young students. And guess what, they paid me money for doing all of this. Hell, I probably would have done it for free if I did not have to worry about starving to death.

I had secured myself a special niche. I was in academia but not encumbered by the culture of academia. That culture, in the extreme, could place even well-intentioned persons in a straightjacket. The typical goals were narrow and provincial. If you wanted to be a success, particularly in the traditional disciplines, you needed to perform in certain prescribed ways. You had to choose theory over application, narrowness over breadth, limited over general audiences, peer-reviewed journal articles over venues that might be read and used in the real world, and personal credit over collaborative endeavors. You can violate these strictures on occasion, but don't make a habit of it.

If, by chance, you harbored any interest in the real world, the safe strategy was to play the game long enough to get tenure and establish your career. After that, you could do what you wanted though there were some prices to pay even then. Because of my circuitous route into academia and the speed bumps I encountered due to demon rum and a limited attention span, I would encounter the tenure gauntlet rather late in life. There was absolutely no way I was going to waste the best years of my professional life pleasing a small group of academic peers. There were too many policy mountains to climb.

Once sober, I rather quickly burst upon the national stage in a much more dramatic fashion. First, though, I had to finish up that pesky dissertation requirement which had been lying around untouched for about a decade. As I began to pick up speed in my usual multi-tasking style, it probably became apparent to the Social Work faculty that I was moving even further away from completing the degree. I never had any doubt about how I was viewed by most everyone associated with the Poverty Institute. Irv Garfinkel, former Director and Social Work Professor had called me the smartest student to come through the program in his estimation. My Prelim answers had been a raging success. I had established a relationship between the Institute and the State of Wisconsin that was bearing many research and policy development opportunities. I had played a seminal supportive role in several large-scale Institute projects.

However, I was doing absolutely nothing to complete my doctorate. My Committee, some of them anyways, became more concerned about my drift toward oblivion than I was. At some point, several of the faculty got together and hatched a plan to give me a doctorate by hook or by crook. Sheldon Danziger, then Director of IRP, probably as the main instigator. He caught me in the hallway one day some two or three years after I had achieved sobriety. He put his concerns to me simply. Time to kick me out of the program. He suggested that I put together a few of my papers and present this collection to my Committee before they all expired of old age. It sounded like a scam to me but hey, I grew up in Worcester Mass. Scams were a part of life. However, he convinced me it was a legitimate approach. He, himself, had used this approach to secure his doctorate in economics from the Massachusetts Institute of Technology. In any case, Sheldon was a man whose advice was not to be ignored. He would go on to lead the policy school at Michigan and then to head the prestigious Russell Sage Foundation in New York.

I was dubious, but I decided to humor Sheldon and give it a shot. I took off some time to put this contrived work together.

Sheldon had suggested three papers, which was the MIT norm. I got carried away and selected seven I believe. I instinctively fell back on a timeworn strategy. If you cannot baffle them with brilliance, then numb them with unending BS. I believe my original tome stretched to over 500 pages. The day of my defense arrives. Though I had been skeptical of this scheme from the get go, I assumed the deck of cards had been stacked. If I have a strength, it is an ability to read people. I looked around the room on that day and immediately could tell that all was not well.

The problem is that the co-conspirators associated with this end-run of a conventional thesis had not lined up all the ducks in advance. One member of my Committee had moved from Wisconsin to the University of Chicago. They clearly had not prepped him in on the scam before his arrival for my defense. My Chair, and the man who brought me to the University in the beginning some thirteen years earlier, probably was uncomfortable with the scam as well. Irv and I were great friends and I saved two of his large research projects from disaster, so he owed me a lot. However, he was a traditionalist when it came to the academy. I suspect he had to be brought along on this scheme kicking and screaming. I know he always thought of me as extremely bright but misguided. I did not buy into the academic culture which he rather worshipped. It was shades of my father all over again, another male authority figure that I had let down.

In any case, their decision was Solomon-like. I had passed but needed some revisions. I suspect there was at least one vote for starting over and writing a real dissertation, perhaps two out of the five. My initial reaction was puzzlement and even a bit of anger. This was their damn idea; can't they get their act straight. Hell, I had wasted valuable time putting this piece of crap together. In truth, I also thought that the so-called MIT model was lacking in some respects. It needed something to bring the papers together. It needed a story line. Have I ever mentioned that I love creating story lines?

No one ever mentioned that this was needed at the beginning. As far as I can recall, I got no advice whatsoever on how to do this type of thesis. No matter, developing a coherent story line was in my wheelhouse. I simply set about writing an overview piece. I pounded out a long introduction and a shorter postscript to make the whole thing thematic. Of course, it wasn't really thematic since the papers dealt with widely different topics, my interests had always been catholic in the sense of being universal or eclectic. Thankfully, I am touched with the Celtic muse. Through words, I could make the selling refrigerators to Eskimos sound compelling.

Now the damn thing was well over 600 ages and I feared I might have to employ three bound volumes to bind the tome together. I seriously doubt that any of my Committee read the thing, either the original version or the expanded one. But the core members of my Committee were determined to make me a member of their club. Everyone signed the necessary documents and now I was a Ph.D. Those devoted to kicking me out of the program must really have applied pressure to the one or two who believed that academic standards were worth protecting. As I recall, the only existing copy of this priceless masterpiece is the one required copy for the University Library. I know I never kept one.

Perhaps I should have tested my theory that I had gotten a pity vote by submitting a similar sized document written in Sanskrit just to see if anyone had even glanced at it. On the other hand, I might just be a bit too hard on myself. After all, this Committee was a group feared and avoided by most normal Doctoral Candidates. They were known as the hard and demanding ones. I should take some solace from the fact that they wanted me in their club. The other explanations are that they wanted me out of the doctoral program since I was taking up space or were moved to extreme pity as social work types. Only the first of these is plausible.

It is not as if the degree made any difference to who I was or what I did. I had already begun my teaching career in Social Work. The list of projects and issues that came to be my candy story of personal policy issues to confront was filling in rapidly now that I could walk without falling down. There was one consequence to my casual manner of exiting the program. Most students go through the Doctoral experience as a rite of passage. When you come out the other side of this ordeal, you feel as if you are elevated to a new status. At least, this is how it is supposed to work. This transformative experience helps the student assume the norms, values, and culture of the academy. It is the same as any ritual that confers adulthood on a young person or valued membership in a closed society. The rite of passage is to be of sufficient moment that you know you are now different. I never experienced any such passage. My transitions were so seamless that I was still the same old guy. I did not feel one whit smarter nor one whit different in any way. Unfortunately, I was the same old guy who felt a little bit like a con artist who had just made off with the family jewels.

One day in the 1990s I was walking with Sheldon Danziger who, by this time, had moved on to the University of Michigan to head a policy and research unit there. Since I no longer saw him on a regular basis I was moved to thank him at long last for what I yet saw as a favor he had done for me years earlier. This was unfinished business in my mind so to speak. For all his accomplishments, he struck me as shy and seemed embarrassed by my thanks. He murmured something about no need to thank him. He went on to say that there were few other U.W. graduates from my era whose papers and articles he used in his classes. Despite his modesty I was thankful to him. I know I would never have moved on if it were not for his initiative and scheming. Sheldon, along with Irv Piliavin and Irv Garfinkel will always have a special place in my thoughts.

Bright lights from the prism…

The past three decades seem like a blur. From the pit of despair, I climbed to the summit of where I wanted to be. I wound up teaching several different social policy courses to undergraduate and graduate students. I worked with the Wisconsin Legislature on developing new approaches to welfare. I also worked with colleagues and the state officials to introduce radical changes to the child support system that would have national impacts. I got involved in several contentious research and policy issues such as the welfare migration debate or did poor families move to Wisconsin for higher welfare benefits. I brought a team of nationally recognized colleagues into Kenosha County to put together the first successful integrated welfare and workforce development system. It became a national and international model. I started working on how we could refine and exploit social indicators as a way to gauge social conditions and manage public interventions. I collaborated on a national effort to revise the official poverty measure. I developed the peer assistance model for bringing top state welfare officials together to collaborate on reform and to better envision the future for their programs. I worked with Karen Bogenschneider on models and theories for bringing research into the policy making process and with Jennifer Noyes on theories and protocols for integrating human service systems. The list goes on.

Though Wisconsin was a laboratory of social welfare innovation and reform at the time, it became too provincial to encompass all my growing interests. In the midst of all this I went to Washington for a year on a kind of intergovernmental transfer thing to work on President Clinton's welfare reform concept. Older readers will remember the phrase 'ending welfare as we know it.' It was a campaign slogan that drew big applause but proved intractable in the doing given the deep divides within the Democratic Party at the time. I had been to D.C. many times in the past, but that year extended my contacts and reputation throughout that city. From a base in the Department of Health and Human Services I worked with officials from Labor, Treasury, Agriculture, Commerce, and several other executive agencies. In addition, I interacted with all the trade and advocacy groups including the Center for Law and Social Policy, the Center for Budget and Policy Priorities, Child Trends, the National Governors Association. The American Public Human Services Association, the National Council of State Legislators, the Brookings Institution and so many others. It is a big town.

Even after my year battling to end welfare as we know it and failing, I would return so often that some D.C. insiders were skeptical that I ever left. Howard Rolston, a top official in the U.S. Department Health and Human Services turned to me in a meeting one day. "Are you sure you returned to Wisconsin," he queried. "I still see you more often than I do my own staff." Another time I ran into Alan Werner, a top researcher at ABT Associated, one of the top three national social policy evaluation firms. He also did a lot of work in D.C. I had arrived at the event late and ran into Alan in the door way of the meeting conference room. The session had just broken up for lunch. As participants streamed in and out, most stopped to say hello, many of the women giving me warm hugs. Finally, he looked at me with wonder. "Do you know everyone in this town," he inquired with some admiration. I guess I did. For someone who less than a decade earlier was virtually a panic-stricken hermit hiding in his house, this was a miracle.

We had failed to end welfare as we knew it but that was no particular problem for me. In truth, there were so many other policy windmills at which to tilt my lance. There were always mountains to climb and dragons to slay. Are there any more labored metaphors to use? Clearly, one of my favorite counters in my metaphorical policy candy store was my work with states across the Midwest and elsewhere across the country. It was another concept I stumbled upon almost by accident. I structured one of the many Washington meetings in such a way that the panelists interacted with each other rather than talk to an audience, which were mostly federal officials in this instance. The consequent dialogue was quite unique, and I stored that experience in my head.

Later, as national welfare reform approached, I realized that more welfare policy making would shift to the states and local government. Perhaps they would need a venue and platform to create a new vision of social assistance for poor families with children at least. So, I created WELPAN, the Welfare Peer Assistance Network. I brought together the top state human services officials from the seven Midwest states where a good deal of welfare innovation was taking place. Starting in 1996, when the old Aid to Families with Dependent Children's program was dismantled and replaced with the Temporary Assistance to Needy Families alternative, this group would meet quarterly to confront the challenges of reform and to envision a next generation of human services.

For me, WELPAN was a ring side seat into a dialogue among the best state human service managers and planners in the country. It was also an opportunity for me to help guide their thinking. I came to realize that I had two particular gifts. The first was a talent for the blarney bequeathed upon me by my father and by the many sons of Eire who excelled at the literary arts. In short, I could express myself well. The second was an ability to do innovative or lateral thinking. I could absorb diverse input and integrate them in ways that few others might, see connections not obvious to others.

Those strengths were useful in the academy and among my academic peers for sure. But they were also very critical when working with policy makers like the members of WELPAN. At the height of the post-national reform welfare debate, there were three such Peer Assistance Networks encompassing well over one-third of all the states. In any case, I would listen to the dialogue among the members, distill the essence of the ideas being shared, and then push the discussion in new directions. That plus my natural roguish humor made these venues very popular. It also gave me an insider's view of policy trends outside the claustrophobic worlds of academia and Washington. I loved it.

I cannot cover all the brighter lights that burst through the prism in the latter part of my professional career. Those details are recorded elsewhere as you know by now. Still, I would be remiss in not pointing out my pride in playing a part in continuing the Wisconsin Idea. This cherished concept dates back to the late 1800s and basically integrates the work of scholarship to public policy. This mission burst upon the scene during the Progressive Era of the Early 1900s. Wisconsin scholars were instrumental in developing Social Security and other parts of the New Deal in the 1930s. Each generation of new scholars from Wisconsin added to the legacy including playing a critical role in launching the War on Poverty in the 1960s.

The University of Wisconsin was a natural site on which to locate a University based entity devoted to Poverty research. The Institute was founded in 1966, and today remains the only such federally sponsored site remaining. Over the decades, the Institute faced several crises. In the 1980s Reagan almost put it out of business but Senator William Proxmire, a politician known for his antipathy to political pork saved it. In the 1990s, it again almost lost federal funding when a reviewer of the applications for the continuation of a national federal poverty harbored negative feelings toward IRP. I was Associate Director by this time and had worked tirelessly on behalf of the Institute, spending much time on the road giving talks and participating in conferences and workshops to keep the Institute visible. I think it worked just a little since the Department of Health and Human Services kept IRP alive while the main funding went to a University of Chicago-Northwestern Consortium. By no means do I assume full credit for this narrow escape.

Today, several other federally-sponsored poverty research centers have come and gone but IRP keeps on going. When the close association between IRP and the State of Wisconsin fell on hard times during the Tommy Thompson administration, it looked as if that unique state and university partnership might dissolve and disappear. Eventually, though, I began working with Jennifer Noyes who headed Thompson's highly regarded welfare replacement program known as W-2. Despite the mutual suspicions on both sides at the start we slowly rebuilt a working relationship. Today, the two organizations now share data and conduct numerous studies and analyses for the benefit of both parties.

I began to slow down in the early 2000s, but I did not stop. I realized I was going at a breakneck pace. I often taught full time, helped manage a national research unit, ran several projects, consulted with state and national policy makers, was on the speed dial of reporters across the country, and maintained a heavy commitment of talks and panel discussions. There were too many Friday nights at O'Hare airport waiting for connecting flights to Madison with all the other disgruntled travelers driven to the brink of desperation. There were too many flights where I was putting my presentation together on the way to give a talk and then putting my next class lecture together on the return flight. I wondered what had happened to that boy on Vernon Hill who had plenty of time for imagining new worlds and great adventures.

I did begin to dial it back. I stepped down as Associate Director and from teaching. I loved both, but it was time. I continued to work with WELPAN for a number of years and did get heavily involved in the issue of reforming human service systems. In searching for better ways to design and deliver human services I crisscrossed the country and beyond to work with those seeking a better way. Jennifer Noyes and I published several articles on this topic in *FOCUS*, we still get calls from local sites who yet stumble on those pieces. I pulled our best thoughts together in a volume titled *The Boat Captain's Conundrum,* which covers many of my intellectual pursuits. I recently reviewed an academic paper for a peer-reviewed journal. The authors, at my suggestion, read *Conundrum* and praised it highly in private comments. My colleague Karen Bogenschneider and I published a book exploring ways to bring rigorous evidence to the policy making process. It is called *Evidence-Based Policymaking: Insights from Policy-Minded Researchers and Results-Minded Policymakers.* The publisher has asked us to do a second addition.

Earlier, I noted the retirement party for me though I was hardly retiring at the time. Academic types never do. Though it was more a shift in direction than anything else, it remained a milestone of sorts. On that day I would flash back to some moment earlier in life. I was the insecure kid struggling to fit in on Ames Street. I was the below average student being assigned to the slow class at a decrepit, working class grammar school. I was painfully shy young man almost paralyzed by the thought of seeking a date. I was the young revolutionary using his rhetorical and writing skills to motivate others to righteous anger. I was the young professional waiting for the adults in the room to wake up and throw him out. I was the drunk who thought there was absolutely no hope left. And I was the smartest guy, or damn close to it, in many of those academic and policy rooms where I spent the final decades of my professional life. Ultimately, I was a rebel who did things my own way. One life, one light, many and varied hues.

In May of 2015, I helped organize an IRP workshop called Poverty 101. We brought in over 25 college-level professors who teach courses on poverty and inequality. We exposed them to leading experts affiliated with IRP so that they can broaden their substantive knowledge and enhance their teaching materials and skills. It is a way of paying forward, of helping the next generation deal with one of societies' most intractable problems. Hopefully, they will go back to their colleges and universities with a bit more passion and commitment. It has always struck me that this is the core of the Wisconsin idea.

Sharing with others what might be a bit new and different and perhaps challenging has always been a particular passion of mine, whether the audience is students, policy makers, or academic peers. Understanding, expressing, and motivating others are the joys of my life. I am so glad I made it to the point where I could indulge those passions on a national scale. And they paid me to do this. As my cousin's husband always said, "Is this a great country or what?"

My wife Mary and I traveling the world in the early years

Bob Haveman and I run Poverty 101 Seminar for
college level instructors from around the country.

UW Colleague Jennifer Noyes who helped me restore IRP's relationship with the State of Wisconsin and then worked with me on WELPAN and human services integration

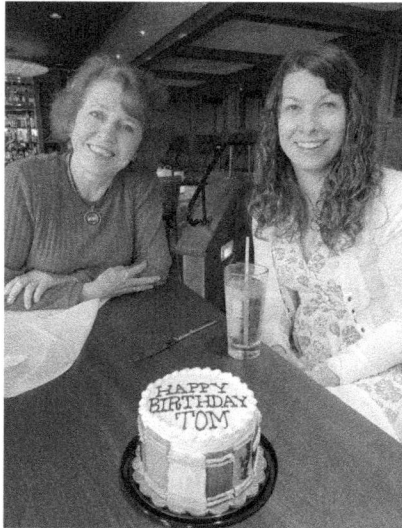

Another academic collaborator Karen Bogenschneidet (left) and her grad student

Me with Mary, my folks, and Aunt Ag and Uncle Bill.

India 44 Volunteers at India Embassy in Washington, 2011

CHAPTER 14

MUSING

The highest forms of understanding we can achieve
are laughter and human compassion.
—Richard Feynman

If you are old enough, you will recall a television show called 'This Is Your Life.' The host would surprise some unwitting, though celebrated, member of the audience with the infamous words… *this is your life*. After looking shocked, the guinea pig for the evening, always dressed immaculately and always present in the audience, would be escorted up to the stage. There, he or she would be showered with moments from their luminous past like the time they were arrested for felonious assault or trying to seduce the under-aged baby-sitter by getting her drunk.

Then, the unforgettable people from the celebrity's past would be paraded out, like their favorite prison guard, to say a few endearing words about the evenings star. "Tom never tried to escape, not even once. He was always so polite to everyone even during the weekly beatings." The show's premise strained our credulity even back then when we were more trusting. How is it possible that these chosen luminaries always were in the audience on the designated night for a show known for such high-jinks? Of course, it is possible that famous people took special stupid pills back then or was it the audience taking the drug? Most likely, this was a precursor of future reality shows in which much of the emotion is staged.

Anyways, the show inspired my dad to put together a photo album organized around the same theme. "Tommy Corbett, This Is Your Life." I must note that I was always Tommy and he was always Tom though his given name was Jeremiah. For a while it was 'big' Tom and 'little' Tom until little Tom (me) spurted past big Tom in height. Then, I became Tommy. Surely, there was reason to be concerned about the confusion. Not even my father wanted to be confused with me. Anyways, in the album were photographs of me and mine from the miracle of my birth in 1944 through 1969 when I finished up my Peace Corps service. Thus, the album essentially covers the first quarter-century of my life, serving as a good vehicle for one final tour of that long-ago era.

My dad had come a long way as a parent from those early days when I probably was more of an inconvenience than anything else. By now he seemed rather proud of me. As the 1960s ended I had already graduated from college with honors, served two years in India, and managed to stay out of the slammer. In addition, I had

CONFESSIONS OF A CLUELESS REBEL

not knocked up any girls mostly due to the absence of opportunity and an abundance of guilt. He would have been decidedly less proud of me if he had known just what a sad sack I was in the female seduction department. I was not a chip off the old block in so many areas.

It was always hard for me to assess my mother's real feelings. Unfortunately, she remained paralyzed by what other people might think. This kept her hyper-vigilant focus on my real and imagined transgressions with respect to what 'everyone' thought was proper conduct and appearance. She always worried that I was screwing up. My father worried less about what people thought. He probably did worry just a bit that I might join the Communist Party or some such foolishness which, even I admit, would have been most difficult to explain away. By my Peace Corps days, I sensed real affection for me on his part. Don't get me wrong. There was no hugging and no expressions of love or any such crap. He was an Irishman after all and that touchy-feely stuff was strictly verboten. Despite my lack of athletic prowess and artistic skills and female seduction talents, he might well have detected some of himself in me.

While I did not inherit much of his dark Celtic good looks, I did absorb his whimsical sense of humor and his gift of gab. He was funny about social gatherings, much as I am. Later in life, he would resist going to parties and such. This was particularly true as his health deteriorated. Once he got there, however, he would enthrall any gathering with his wit and storytelling. I too have to get myself up for social gatherings but often can schmooze with the best of them once there. I am grateful for the small portion of blarney he passed on to me.

My sense was he, of all the extended family, probably had the most liberal views. He was no social liberal by any means, but he had a basic sense of decency and fairness which I must have absorbed. I have searched my memory hard for other sources for my non-traditional views as a young man about civil rights and social justice. I even joined one-world government entity, or tried to, in the mid to late 1950s. Being irredeemably naïve and trusting, it probably never occurred to me that it might be a Communist front organization. Such musings often get me to thinking about my larger family and friends from early on. Surely, they played some part in what I became. My dad's labor of love is always a great place to start.

Scraps of feelings...

I came across the scrapbook along with an old box of photos. The box had once contained Riviera pears. Now it contains a host of totally unorganized snapshots, many now faded with time. Most are unlabeled. A surprising number contain people and places that now are totally unfamiliar to me. Some of these shots capture my adult life, enshrining people and events I recall vividly. It is the old and faded shots, the ones tarnished by time and neglect, that pull me in. They are the ones that contain worn sentiments that stay just beyond reach. They feel more like lost thoughts of some distant life belonging to another. These are the moments in time where the river of people and events had been frozen in place if only for an instant.

I don't move through the pictures in any particular order. My life's album is chronological, but I find myself jumping from page to page, moving from the album to the box of unsorted pictures and then back to the album. I pause over a picture of my dad and his brother Tim. It is probably from the early half of the 1940s though Tim is not wearing his World War II Marine Corps uniform. They both are in suits, both very handsome, both with slightly roguish smiles as if they just shared a private joke. I suspect my dad was by far the more mischievous and adventurous of the two, at least that is what I gleaned from their adult demeanors. According to him, they somehow ended up in the same class in grammar school. But he was kept back one year by the nuns because, he argued, they could not tell the brothers apart and thus did not know whom to blame when bad stuff happened. Apparently, bad stuff happened quite often when they were present. My best guess is that dad was the prankster and routinely placed blame on his look-alike brother. The nuns would quickly put an end to that.

In another, the two brothers are with their dad. This time Tim is in his uniform, the year on the back says 1943, the year before I was born. The site looks to me like the old mental hospital off Shrewsbury and Plantation Streets. I had heard those stories of my grandfather. Apparently, he would drift off at times into state of melancholy and withdraw from the world. I noted earlier the faintest memories of being taken to the facility at which he spent his final years, but I must have been a tyke at the time. I have no memory of meeting him before his death but that might be my failure of recollection. As I look at these pictures, I wonder what my grandad thought about my existence, if anything. Was he even aware of me when I entered the world? Would he too have been a good storyteller, a man of wit and charm? Was he the source of the gift for bone dry humor, awful puns, and weak jokes that my father and I burdened others with throughout our lives? It is a secret that will necessarily remain uncovered.

I come across a few faded pictures of my mother's dad. Though he survived into the late 1950s, he remained an equally remote figure. He always seemed ancient and grizzled, and a bit eccentric with his preference for eating the fat off the ham he loved so dearly. One picture has him sitting on the front porch of my Aunt Mary's house. That is also my final memory of him, sitting on that porch all day long. I don't even know if he spoke English well enough for a conversation, I certainly do not recall conversing with him, not once.

He always struck me as solid and soft at the same time. He seemed so large and foreboding when I was a child. He labored amidst the fire and molten steel of the big mill that loomed at the bottom of Vernon Hill. A lot of the Polish and Lithuanian and

Swedish men who migrated to this country found work there. As a kid, you could look into the open structures from the street. You could see what looked like red-hot rivers right out of hell flowing to places where I guess they were molded into the foundations of skyscrapers or the architecture of trucks and trains and other things that moved America. I wondered what kind of men worked in such places and then it would hit me, my grandfather did. But I never got to talk to him about that. So sad.

There is a picture of several kids playing ball between three-deckers on Ames Street. It is a tiny area that separates our old three-decker from the adjacent one next door. Back then, it rivaled Fenway Park and seemed just fine for our hard-fought games which, over time, would range into the larger back yard or into the street. It was much later that we finally migrated the long block to an expansive city park and the formal playing fields. It is amazing how we kept ourselves amused absent all the digital toys of today's world. We had endless other kids and our imaginations to create all the distractions needed in a world where even TV was a sometime thing. We would have many years left before our heroes and our villains would be consumed by the complex nuances of reality.

There is a photo of my folks with my mom's sister and her husband at a place called Singapore Sam's. It looks like a picture that would have been taken by someone working for the establishment, souvenirs for visitors. The year is 1951, I would be 7 years old. It seems so typical of the times. My family and their wide circle of friends did enjoy endless good times. Often, I was dumped with neighbors, other family members, or brought to the weekend poker games to sleep on the pile of coats until it was time to be bundled up for the trip home. It never felt like a deprivation since everyone else seemed to enjoy the same life style. You simply did not expect anything else. No one would play classical music to me or try to give me a head start by teaching me the alphabet as a small tot. If they did, I surely have no memory of such. But I did inherit that wild imagination, surely a precious gift.

I see a shot of Nana, my dad's mother who caught me sharing views of my privates with the little girl upstairs. She overlooked that transgression to give me tons of warmth and comfort when I was a little monster. In this photo, she is with her daughter Winnie, the youngest of her children and my cousin Billie who was born in 1953. Nana was tough and sweet. Even I realized as I grew older that Winnie had a lonely life. There were rumors, though, that she took up with a guy after Nana passed. I was happy to hear it, others were scandalized.

I suspect that Nana did not have the easiest of lives. She probably had to raise five kids pretty much on her own. How did she do it before welfare and social services? I have no idea what her husband, my grand dad, did for work when he was not institutionalized. Nor do I have any idea for how long he was able to cope with life. I cannot imagine the uncertainties they faced, the fears. They lived through the great depression, the great wars. They migrated to this country with nothing. My God, I am looking upon the faces of heroes.

I come across one of my parents where they actually look happy with one another. From their apparent ages this probably predates me and possibly their marriage. A funny thing about that marriage thing, there are no wedding pictures at all. It was never talked about. I don't recall seeing similar pictures for my dad's sister and husband. In fact, when my wife asked my uncle about their marriage, he said something about it not being a topic for discussion. Maybe they all eloped or worse. Did they live in sin all their lives? It is hard to imagine what secrets might lie in the family closet other than the addled boy my parents raised. That was no secret at all.

Photos capturing others in the extended family are found throughout. My mother's youngest sister and her husband were a good-looking couple. George was quite an athlete and played in what were considered semi-pro leagues in the 1930s and early 40s. The big manufacturing companies actually fielded teams with the ball players getting the best jobs and other perks. They likely earned something for each game played. George worked and played for Norton Company which I think made a lot of big machinery for other firms. He made a name for himself as a talented left-handed pitcher.

They had three boys, the older two of which truly were hellions. My cousin told me that no one wanted to babysit for these brats when they were little. It was so bad that my aunt and uncle had to drop them off at a local orphanage since no one could be persuaded to look after the little dears. Even I must have looked good by comparison. Everything is, after all, relative. Tragedy would strike when the oldest boy died in the service while stationed in France. The truck he was driving malfunctioned and crashed. I yet remember coming home and the woman who lived on the second floor catching me as I was walking upstairs. She had been tasked with telling me the news, looking quite uncomfortable as she did so. It was a long drive to my aunt's house on the other side of town.

The second son, Paul, was a gifted athlete like his dad. We were the same age and sometimes played ball either together or as opponents for our respective junior high teams. He made it pretty far up the California Angels organization but not all the way to the big leagues. He stayed in California after his playing days ended so we lost touch. The sibling rivalry between my mother and her two sisters was fierce, extending to which of the children were worth saving. Only my aunt's youngest son, Bobby, garnered much support with the rest of us being deemed beyond any hope. No wonder my mother was so worried about my apparent lack of skills and social graces.

There is a picture of my mother's mother holding a baby. I wish I knew the year. She was a real matriarch, holding the family together and ruling things with an iron fist. If there were marital elopements in the family, it was probably because she disapproved of what were considered mixed-marriages at the time. All the partners of her daughters and sons were white and Catholic but not from the same ethnic tribe. She wanted her children to marry good Polish boys and girls. But the oldest daughter and my mother married Irishman while the youngest daughter married a Lithuanian. I don't know why Lithuanians were not considered suitable mates. Hell, it was right next door to Poland, but I guess the connection was not close enough. The nice son married a lovely Italian gal and went to live among the Italians while the bad son married someone about whom I know very little. She seemed very nice and I am quite sure she was French by background. Five chances and not a single one found a suitable Polish mate. There must have been a lot of yelling in that house in those early days.

The bad son was Johnnie. Apparently, he was in trouble from the time he escaped his crib. Rumor had it that he broke-out with a stolen kitchen knife at eight months and went on the lam. As far as I know, he lived by his wits as a con man and never had a legitimate job in his life. But he still managed to marry and raise several kids who all turned out to be respectable, law abiding, citizens. It was not that Johnnie was really evil. Like me, he was averse to real work and never found a legitimate way to avoid it. I did see him and his family on occasion when he was not in jail. And my mother loved him dearly since I think she always had a bit of larceny in her own heart. I recall we visited him and his family at least once. He pulled out a huge cardboard box full of ties and told me to take as many as I wanted. Just what a kid wants, too bad he was not stealing electronics that week.

My favorite story about Johnny goes as follows. Apparently, he would often hitchhike the road between Worcester and Providence. It was not a long distance but long enough to ply his trade. Back then, people were more trusting, and rides were not difficult to secure. He would engage the kind stranger who picked him up in conversation. Eventually he would bring up the fact that he knew where 'hot' TVs or other valuable items could be gotten on the relative cheap. New Englanders were always on the lookout for the deal. It is in the local DNA. They would drive 50 miles to get something a buck cheaper. When he roped a sucker in, he would have them drive to a certain address. Upon securing the money, he promised his mark that he would be right back with the merchandise. Of course, that was the last the mark would see of Johnnie, or his money. My uncle was long gone.

Unfortunately for Johnny, some guys routinely make the same trip quite often. One of his marks saw him hitchhiking again and offered him a ride. Really, this was bound to happen given the frequency with which he pulled this scam. Johnny, to his regret, did not recognize the man, too many marks to recall. As he spun his well-worn tale of bargain deals at a fraction of the cost, the guy appeared quite interested. Johnny was probably still talking when the guy pulled up to a Providence police station and turned him in to the arms of the law. I think they always kept his favorite cell warm and cozy for him. Still, my mother did love him and would even visit him in jail. She did worry when he would turn up at the bars and night clubs where she worked. Johnny was always on the clock and she feared he would scam her friends who were well warned in advance to keep their hands on their wallets.

Walter was the good brother even if he did run off to the Italian tribe with his lovely wife, Laura. I must admit, their three-decker made our place look rather luxurious. It was situated across from a decrepit looking factory and right next to the railroad tracks. But they probably got a break on the rent since Laura's parents owned the building. Their family name was Gorretti. I liked going there because they had a bocce court, two in fact, in their yard right next to the fence that separated them from the tracks. In case you don't know, bocce is an Italian game that plays like curling but with round balls and no ice. It is generally warm in Italy.

You start by throwing a small ball down the other end of the court. Then each team has so many throws trying to get their larger balls closer to the small ball or dislodge their opponent's balls that had been situated near the small ball through dastardly talented throws. When I explained the rules to my spouse, she thought dislodging a guy's balls sounded like great sport indeed. At the end of each round, the team with the closest big ball to the target ball gets points, one point for each ball closer than any of the opponent's balls. Got it! It may sound simple but there is quite a bit of skill and strategy involved. Word of advice, don't play the game for money with any Italian over the age of 70. They will clean you out.

I would spend hours playing bocce with their one child, Walter Jr. Unlike me, he was a really nice kid, very sweet. Though about my age, he did not seem to develop normally. His walking gait was a bit off and I never sensed that his overall social skills were quite within the bell curve. I never did find out if my suspicions were correct since he left us far too early. Wally and I were approaching our teens. I recall spending a day with him one week and the next I heard he had been taken to a specialty children's hospital in Boston. Then he was gone, and I never found out why other than it was some terminal childhood disease or a deadly virus. My fiercest memory of the event was watching total grief on his mother's face. I recall hearing her say something at the gravesite about joining him soon. I thought I must have misunderstood until she died within months of burying her son. She was such a lovely person and Wally was a kind and gentle soul.

I came across a photo of my father's brother and his family. There is Louise, his wife and the three kids...Timmy, Paula, and Billie. Timmy was probably a year or so older than I, with Paula a couple of years younger and Billie about nine years younger. They lived off of Main Street in Worcester, not far from Clark University where Louise worked as a secretary and could keep an eye on my comings and goings while I was in college. She always knew my grades before I did. Early on in life, we spent a lot of time together on holidays and for birthdays. But Tim came down with stomach cancer at a rather early age and tragically passed. That must have been hard on my dad, but he never talked about it. Emotions were not his strong suit. I never did see him cry or even come close. It is an Irish thing I suspect. The get-togethers were rare after that.

Paula became a school teacher and had a family of her own though the marriage did not last. Timmy and Billie were the only other male Corbett's and thus capable of continuing the family name. While Timmy did marry, it did not last either and there were no children. Billie never married and, as far as we know, had no children. I recall my father once mentioning that it looked like the Corbett name had come to an end. I don't know if he was lamenting the fact or just stating the obvious. I felt that old sense of failure again, I had disappointed him one more time. I never verbalized my consciously decision not to have children, I wonder if he suspected as much.

My cousin Billy was an interesting case. Even as a young kid he loved listening to police scanners. I am not sure what the attraction was but becoming a police officer evolved into his life's passion. These were difficult positions to get at the time. I am sure affirmative action (both minorities and women) were reducing the number of slots for white males. He never flagged on this commitment however. He first became some kind of patrolman's aide who did very routine police work like take information on traffic accidents and other tasks that did not require carrying a weapon or arresting people. Every year he would try to make it on the official force and every year came up short. He was running out of time when the magic finally worked. The last time I saw him I was in the Worcester City Hall around the time of my Dad's death in 1987. We met by accident and he was wearing his uniform. He looked totally happy. It is good when you get to be what you are meant to do.

There are several pics of Ag and Bill, my dad's sister and her husband. They were my surrogate parents when I was young. I spent hours at their house as a child until they moved away to the north side of town and a house of their own. I cried when that happened and managed to get out there as often as I could. Damn, I seemed to cry a lot as a kid. Not so much anymore. They were wonderful people and would have been superb parents. Unfortunately, they had no children of their own.

I was the first of several surrogate children for them. Another was Amy, a neighbor girl younger than I who became a very successful owner of a realty company on Cape Cod. My father's oldest sister was named May. She died before I was born, in childbirth or soon after. She had twins, a boy and a girl. They were both very attractive. The girl was also Agnes. She went into the convent but left after a couple of years. Her leaving may have had something to do with a strain of Lupus Disease from which she suffered at the time. In any case, she moved in with Ag and Bill since the twins never got along with their stepmother. My aunt and uncle looked after her until she passed at a tragically early age. This was my third cousin who died young. I was beginning to wonder.

Her brother was a Tom as well. He was really tall, dark, and handsome. Clearly, he got the looks in the extended family while I got the shaft. He was several years older than I, but he did take me to movies on occasion. I idolized him. He was everything I wished to be, a good athlete, popular with girls, and charming with a winning smile. But his life stalled after high school. He went into the Air Force and spent time in Italy. Upon returning, he met and married a really beautiful Lithuanian girl with blond hair, blue eyes, and lovely features. It seemed like a perfect match. But reality fell short of perfection.

After several children, also beautiful, they struggled financially. My uncle Bill tried to get him a job in sales with Nabisco, where he was the regional sales manager. But for all Tommy's charms, there was something wrong and he lost that position. It turns out that he also was afflicted with the Irish curse, a fondness for drink. He did manage to keep a job as a bus driver for many years, but his marriage and his life eventually spun out of control. In truth, I don't know what happened to him in the end, but I suspect it was not pretty. More than once I realized that could well have been me. So much early promise lost.

Larger circles...

Now I come across a picture of my mother with her best friends from her waitressing days. She rather loved that work. It was hard but there was a lot of drinking and laughter and friendships. Early on she worked at a place called Jim's Inn, a nightclub where they also had acts on weekends at least. Later, she went to work at a local establishment called the Ivy Café, more of a neighborhood place like Cheers where everyone knows your name.

Several of her fellow waitresses were also good friends. When they weren't laughing and drinking on the job they got together at their place of employment to continue the laughs and drinking on their own time. A few were on the hefty side. My dad would often remark that they could form the line backing crew for Notre Dame. I noticed he never said that within earshot of them. Have I ever mentioned that he was a was a wise man? I can recall being dragged to Jim's Inn, where they all met, on Sundays up until I became a teenager. They also got together at each other's homes for the poker games that they loved. They did manage to laugh a lot even if their day-to-day lives were rather difficult financially and their life dreams never quite panned out. When longer-term ambitions remain out of reach, the short-term laughter seems more essential.

There were quite a few pictures taken at various beaches. There is this skinny young kid and then a skinny teenager in a lot of them. Oh, that was me. The miracle is that I was skinny. Going to the beach constituted vacations for the working class. There were no cruises, no expensive spas, no European vacations. You went to the shore, rented a room in a boarding type house near the beach where the shared bathroom was probably down the hall. But it was near the sand and surf and boardwalk. You spent all day in the sun and then strolled among the amusements playing various games to win some silly prize and stuff your mouth with cotton candy or other delicacies. Within hours, white skin first became crimson, shed off, and eventually evolved into a golden brown. In recent years, I have had a good deal of basal cell and other forms of skin cancer carved out of my body as a result of those youthful indiscretions.

I now wonder where the amusement lies in baking in the sun from early morning to late in the day. The splashing through the surf provided some diversion as did the game playing on the sand. You could play forms of touch football and catch in the soft sand but that was hard. Run around in that powdery stuff for half an hour and you were hurting big time with your legs turning to jelly. Better to look for the hard sand left when the tide was going out. When the waters receded, what remained was compact and firm. That was excellent for quick movements with bare feet unless you stepped on a broken shell, which would result in much yelping as you hopped around on one leg. My favorite was to dig the outline of a tennis court in the hard sand. Then you used a rubber ball to play a tennis-like game using your hand as a racket.

Walking along the shore was also a favorite past time. Somehow, I would manage to amuse myself for hours on end. I particularly loved the little birds scurrying along the edge of the water seeking edible detritus washed up by each wave. On occasion, I would find sea shells or other treasures in the sand. Perhaps I would come across a sand castle being erected or, on occasion, would build one myself. There were endless adventures by the shore. But mostly it was the simple magic of the sea itself, the endless waves and cool breezes in the evening. It was the sand that would stick to your hair and skin, the parched feeling of scented dry husk would take over your body. I never ceased to be enthralled by the rhythm of waves washing ashore, it was hypnotic. Such sensory reflections stayed with me the rest of my life. My wife later remarked I was like a lemming to the sea, always drawn irresistibly to salt water.

It was not like we went to five-star resorts of course. Early on, we would go to Nantasket Beach south of Boston. It could not have been more than 70 miles from home yet seemed like the other side of the world. I recall the last few miles where a road curved through a largely residential area. At each curve I would peer ahead expectantly. I knew that around one would loom a large public bath house. I suspect it had not been used for years but was still there. It marked the first landmark telling us we had reached the promised-land. Next were the smells. Nantasket was at the beginning of a long peninsula where good clamming could be found. When the tide was out, there was an unmistakable, pungent scent. Forever after, I would be vaguely disappointed when beaches did not emit some similar odor.

Nantasket did not have a boardwalk per se. It had a restraining wall that held back the ocean with sand routinely dumped to keep the shoreline away from the wall. Across the main road that ran out to Hull Massachusetts located at the tip of the peninsula was Paragon Park. This had all the rides and games that any kid would want. It was probably small and dingy by today's standards, but I thought it the magical kingdom. Who needed Disney Land or World or whatever? There was a roller coaster and another ride where you got into a boat and took a trip that simulated some coaster thrills absent the danger. At the end you plunged down into a small reservoir of water sending plumes of spray onto spectators who crept too close.

Many years later I brought my wife down there as a part of a sentimental tour. It is the price that a woman must pay to land a winner like me. I was crushed when we arrived. The ocean now came right up to the restraining wall and Paragon Park was being torn down. It was being torn down for crying out loud. How could this not be a preserved national landmark? I had played here as a kid. But I had to accept it, my childhood beach was no more. I suspect the land was more valuable now to residential developers. And so it goes.

In later years we would go to Wildwood, New Jersey, which was located south of Atlantic City. It is not clear which was the poor cousin, Wildwood or Atlantic City though probably the former after gambling revived the latter. Compared to Nantasket,

Wildwood was upper class though still a largely working class get-away for the Philly crowd when the working class could yet afford to get away for vacations. The sandy beach went on for miles, as did a real boardwalk with all the sights and sounds and smells associated with these fun strips of sensory overload. Nantasket seemed cramped and old by comparison.

I could amuse myself forever on the boardwalk. It was called such since you would be walking over, guess what, wooden boards. Each day would start with a great breakfast and then hours on the beach. That would be followed by strolls along the boardwalk to try the games, eat cotton candy and similar crap, or just gawk at the endless delights. As I entered my teens, the gawking was directed at the young teen girls who remained beyond my reach but who disrobed just to torture me. One game involved rolling a ball down an alley and up to several cylindrical holes. It was called Skeet ball or something close to that. The higher and smaller the hole, the more the shot was worth. Higher scores earned you coupons. Earn enough and you could win a stuff doll or something equally inane. I would play for hours. If lucky, I would spend a fortune, for me at least, for a prize worth a buck or two. But it was the thrill of the chase after all, was it not?

There are also numerous shots of guys I grew up with, played ball with, wasted enormous amounts of my youth with. I wonder if the kids of today spend nearly as much time on the playgrounds and basketball courts as we did. I doubt it. Between structured activities, video games, and social media not enough hours remain in the day. It is hard to say which is better. Should you spend hours trying to master athletic skills at which you have no comparative advantage whatsoever or hours interacting with digitally created worlds and on-line companions? We won't know the answer for quite some time.

A very educated woman recently remarked that her two and one-half year-old daughter can make her way around a tablet with far more ease that she can. I could barely talk at that age. It is true! My mother was so concerned about my slow development that she took me to a doctor. I don't recall that visit but I guess I will have to up my count of doctor visits by one. I think the next time I saw a doctor was when my tonsils needed excising and then when my appendix burst almost a decade after that. As a mute two-year old, I think the professional diagnosis was that I was just slow, which made sense to all who knew me. Most of those who know me now would love to see me struck with a similar affliction…the blessings of a mute Corbett.

Of course, there was the time my mother asked me to pull down a venetian blind which reminds me of another way we tortured our good teachers in high school. When we were asked what the Phoenicians were famous for we would all yell out in unison, venetian blinds. Not very original but we thought it hilarious at the time! Anyways, I pulled and the whole contraption came down on my head, blood gushing from one eye. I am sure my folks had a heart attack thinking I had gouged my eye out, but the wound just missed the eyeball. It had to look ghastly at first with all the blood. Best of all, I got stitches, always a war wound of significance among the neighborhood kids.

Athletic achievements...

The whole sports thing was pretty sad. In my immediate cohort, at least during my younger years, I was a somewhat of a tweener. I was a year or two younger than my peers and too old for the group that came after me. It always felt like I was playing catch up, either in understanding girls and the basics of seduction or competing on the courts and playfields. I forever thought everyone else was ahead of me and I would never catch up. Later, I would hang around with guys my age but who really were good athletes. Several played varsity sports in high school. That was a sure-fire remedy for an inferiority complex.

Still, there were moments to remember. In Junior High School I became the starting pitcher when the ace of the staff quit for some reason I no longer can recall. We were 1-2 when I took over and came within a whisker of sweeping the final three games. I vividly recall the one game I lost. I had pitched very well, and we were only down one run in the bottom of the ninth. We had the bases loaded with no outs and our power hitters were coming up. I was already basking in the sure victory to come when I saw each one of our sluggers go down, not even getting the ball out of the infield. My perfect record was lost. In another game I had a no-hitter going into the last inning. I got the first man out but then lost it, two outs away from glory.

One of my wins came against the school on which my very athletic cousin played, the one who came pretty close to making it to the big leagues with the Angels. They were leading the league. His dad, my uncle, was umpiring. I guess conflicts of interest were not taken seriously then. It was Worcester after all. Back then, he called balls and strikes as well as the bases, so he stood right behind the pitcher. The budget was rather pinched.

This is the uncle who had been a well-known pitcher locally in his day. Everyone called him 'lefty' Kadis since he was a southpaw and his last name was Kadis. Clever, no! In any case, he could not resist giving me a running commentary on my pitching technique. Every time his son came up to bat I would get so nervous I could not get the ball over the plate. At least he didn't get a hit off me. We won the game, but it was a high scoring affair and I needed late-inning relief. My big moment came in clearing the bases with a hit. So, this was one time I felt pretty good about things. You would think I would have made it to second on a bases-clearing hit but I only got to first. Did I mention that I was slow?

I do wonder if I might have gone further as a pitcher. True, I did not have a blazing fast ball, but I was crafty. I had a better than average curve and several delivery motions, overhand, sidearm, a submarine type thing. The batter seldom knew what this maniac on the mound would do next. Of course, I would sometimes fool myself even. I was going through all my gyrations on the mound and as I came down with the pitch I realized the catcher was standing upright motioning out to the outfielders about where they should be positioned. I stopped mid pitch and the ball trickled out of my hand to land ten feet in front of the mound. It was a balk of course and more proof that I was not destined for sports stardom, not that such proof was scarce by any means.

There was a team baseball picture that included me from the late 1950s. It was for a Babe Ruth league team for young teens 13-15. I do tower over the other players with the exception of my good friend Ralph. He was tall, gawky and rather homely but a wonderful young man. We had played on the same teams since Little League and I spent much time at his house, his dad was one of my couches for a while. Ralph went on to the Coast Guard Academy and a career as an officer in that branch of the service. The photo in question appeared in the Worcester Telegram and Gazette and is dated 1959. The attached short story is that we had won the league championship with a perfect record. I have no recollection of ever being on a winning team. My Junior High team had a .500 record and my little league team was terrible despite my heroic play. But the paper would not lie. I was a champion, go figure!

On another occasion in junior high, I recall pulling off the hidden ball trick, a baseball rarity. Davie, the sports hero of the neighborhood, was playing third base. I went over to him for a 'consult' and handed him the ball. For this to work, I could not be on the mound, so I leaned over on my way back as if I were lacing up my shoe. And it did work! Despite some glimmer of talent and a few minor achievements I ended any formal sports when I entered high school. All agreed this was probably a good thing for the future of all mankind.

Golf was another minor obsession back then. My uncle Bill gave me a set of clubs that were so old the so-called irons had wooden shafts. I think they were made by 'Old Tom Morris' at St. Andrews, the home of golf. Still, we would walk all the way to Pakachoag Golf Course, a nine-hole venue that keeps being overlooked as a site for the U.S. Open. Go figure! We would pay our buck and whack at the ball all day. Later on, we branched out to real courses and even went to Cape Cod to play. It is not that we needed tougher challenges. We sucked on whatever course we played. We would cheat on each other like mad, "no, my ball really did hit a tree and roll back onto the fairway."

But it was fun. The strangest thing about my times on the links is that so many people over the years, even those who give lessons, would complement my swing. Unfortunately, that did not translate into hitting the ball anywhere close to where I was aiming. One time I recall a tee shot that went 90 degrees to the right of where I was aiming, straight through the door of the clubhouse. Lucky, I didn't kill some poor schmuck paying his green fees. Now give me some credit here…that takes talent. And to make matters worse, my wife has a hole in one and I don't. Talk about proof that there is no god, what more do you need?

There are photos of people and places that now fade from memory. A few catch my attention. Ronnie Senosk was a friend from those days who has remained in my life, a rather rare event. Most keep moving and drop off the radar screen to avoid me, often volunteering for the federal witness protection program. There are several photos of his wedding and his parents. I spent much time at his house even though they lived in one of the Worcester suburbs. He was one of those better athletes with whom I hung around, averaging like 25 points per game in high school basketball. Anyways, we did catch up with one another as adults around the time his dad passed away, I just happened to be in the area by coincidence. Later, when I spent time in D.C. working on national welfare reform, he spent time at the Pentagon as a Lt. Colonel in the Army Reserves. We would play golf at the War College, just about the weirdest course on earth. One hole had you driving down a narrow fairway with parking lots on either side. I mean, really, is this not an invitation to a night in the brig after denting some General's car with an errant shot.

But I digress. Ronnie's wife, Mary, is one of the sweetest gals I know. Absolutely everyone thinks she is a saint for putting up with him. Funny what people remember! She recalls wise advice I gave to her before they got married. I had invited the two of them to a party at Clark. During the evening I apparently went on and on to her that she should forget about marrying this lug. She was still young, I apparently told her. She should explore the world, it was far too early to get tied down. Of course, I don't recall giving her this sage advice at all, but she never forgot the experience. And I must admit, it does sound totally like my BS from that time!

It really is a good thing no one listens to me. If they did, the species might be on the way to extinction by now. I was not a big fan of marriage. My advice to her turned out to be ill-advised. Mary was a woman who was cut out for marriage and motherhood. She and Ronnie raised a quite large family very successfully. Again, you do have to know who you are and want you want. And, for heaven's sake, don't listen to morons like me.

Random stuff...

Something falls out of my "This Is Your Life" album. It is a letter I wrote to my Uncle Bill and Aunt Ag almost seventy years ago. It is written on Hotel Paramount stationary so that clearly is where we were staying on this jaunt to the Big Apple. The stationary itself claims that every room has a bath, radio, and circulating ice water. I wonder if it had hot water as well. I noted in my letter that the room cost $11 dollars per night, a princely sum no doubt in those days. Why anyone saved this missive is a mystery, it is not exactly great literature. I talk about bad weather, what floor we are on, and the tall buildings. Stop the presses on that one. There were tall buildings in New York City? I bet no one knew. There is no hint of any future as a best-selling author here. I suspect the literary lure of this masterpiece is found in a PS at the end.

PS: Show this to all the relatives. We also got locked out of our room when nobody was with us, but the laundry woman came up and opened the door for us. She is a nice lady.

Was I confused on the pronoun here or was I too embarrassed to admit that getting locked out of the room was my own doing. That does sound like me. It must have seemed prudent to share fault for this misadventure, but I am pretty damn sure this is another Tommy misadventure when my folks were off enjoying themselves. Actually, it is shocking to realize that my parents took me to the big city in the first place. I must have been a drag on their buzz. My best guess is that no one wanted to put up with a monster like me or they hoped I might wander off and get lost. I wonder if they ever considered dropping me off at the same orphanage at which my two wild cousins often were dumped? Hmm, maybe they locked me out of the room on purpose. That never occurred to me before now.

Anyways, there are pictures from high school as well, parties with classmates. Wow, did we look clean cut and nerdy. I cannot imagine any deviant behavior from this group. A couple of them even went on to the Priesthood. A very ascetic young man named Richard was in several of the pictures. He was with a girlfriend of all things. My surprise partly comes from the fact that he was way more committed to a religious vocation than I ever was. The last I heard, he was a high ranking official in the Vatican. And partly it comes from signs that he very likely was gay. I cannot imagine the agony and anxiety back then of knowing you were different. If others discovered your sexual preference, your life would become a living hell. I cannot recall any of my peers, not a single one, who came out in those years. This was a topic none of us would broach back then. But now, I would be immensely curious about what he felt and thought during his high school years.

Many of the names escape me now. There is one young man among some of the prom and party pictures. He was from Chile and his parents sent him to St. Johns for his education. My vague memory is that they were part of the elite, though not likely at the very top. How else could they afford to send him abroad? I suppose a good grounding in English and Catholicism was considered good for his future. But I also recall him saying that hid parents feared a leftist takeover. This was right after the Castro takeover in Cuba and fear must have spread through many South American oligarchies. His parents were likely keeping him out of harm's way. I was rather apolitical at the time. If anything, I would have commiserated with his fears of godless Communism. So, we became pretty friends during his time in the U.S. It would not be all that long before I would start my journey leftward. Perhaps I would not have been so sympathetic to him at the end of that journey but who knows.

As I look over the faces, I wonder where they are now. I yet get the publications from the St. Johns Alumni group talking about the great things they are doing for the next generation, for the community, and for the faith. I suspect that most have stayed within the culture in which they were raised. I do get the sense that so many third and fourth and fifth generation kids now attend the school. Of course, you now see black and brown faces mixed within the vanilla flavor that dominated in my day. For years I gave to St. Johns. I was truly thankful for my academic preparation. I suspect it had a lot to do with the competitiveness of the place. You were up against the next generation of Catholic leaders for sure.

Yet, I became uncertain about my support in recent years. There was too much talk about continuing the Catholic culture and its values. I kept saying to myself, I don't believe in those values and that perspective. They are too exclusionary and narrow. The few nuns left in the various orders seem okay today, but the male hierarchy seems straight from Himmler's finishing school. They seem more concerned with abortion and gay marriage and birth control and the institutional preservation of the church than poverty or social justice or charity. Women are still treated by the Church as second-class citizens in a world where so much progress had been made regarding gender equality.

I am no longer a man of St. Johns. I no longer want young people to be grounded in those ancient, crusty values. Of course, then a man like Pope Francis comes along and suddenly I recall what drew me to Christ's message and to the seminary so long ago. Back then there was a Catholicism of inclusion and love and justice, the version represented by Dorothy Day and the Berrigan brothers. It did not represent the church as a whole, but it was there. I can recall vividly Maryknoll priests standing with migrant workers and the oppressed. I can recall Maryknoll nuns losing their lives to the economic elite while serving the poor in areas of Central America. Perhaps if that spirit can be found once again, I might be more sympathetic.

My father, as was his wont as I grew up, volunteered for the men's club that helped St. Johns in various ways. I think it was called the Pioneer's Club after the school's nickname. By this time, his wilder days were pretty far behind him and he really was getting into my life. Surprisingly, he rose to become the President of this organization. I say it was surprising since he was a working man among professionals. He clearly would have been the undereducated one in the group. This was yet another sign of his potential never fulfilled.

As President, he got to be friends with our headmaster, the camp warden who loved to torture us during the cold lunch breaks as we ate in the school yard while snowflakes turned our hair white. Slowly, I picked up small tidbits that the good brother would dress in civilian clothes and frequent the night club where my mother served drinks. He and my dad might hang out on occasion. Probably, as head man, he had more freedom. But it did make me wonder if they were not quite as cloistered and self-sacrificing as we students suspected. And yet, I never heard one whisper of scandal that involved him or any of the others.

Today, you see stories daily about kids battling drugs, ennui, promiscuity, pregnancy, and violence. Some simmer with rage and lash out in the most violent ways like shooting up their schools with AR-15s. The pressures on them and their parents seem enormous and unrelenting. But as I look over the pictures of my youth I am reminded that we did live in a 'leave it to Beaver' kind of world. Sure, some wider acquaintances might talk about getting drunk or scoring with some girl, but I never knew just how truthful such adolescent boasts were. You could get into a fight, but it never went beyond fists.

My closest friends seemed innocent beyond words. No one ever got drunk that I recall. I never heard of anyone using drugs or 'knocking up' a girl or disrespecting their parents. People still talked about jail bait (girls under 18) and 'doing the right thing' if a girl did get in the family way. I still recall vividly that one of my classmates at St. Johns had a vehicular accident where he struck a woman who died. It was an accident, but he was in a state of shock for weeks afterward. That incident seemed horrendous to the rest of us and we treated him with great care.

I did have one brush with the law as I recall. St. Johns had moved to the suburbs in my senior year and I would drive a few guys back and forth to school using my dad's car. One day, the guys in the back seat yelled out the window at a student driver as we passed the Ann Spragna Driving School training vehicle. The poor student driver behind the wheel almost lost control and weaved across lanes for several moments. At the next light I saw the instructor writing down my license number. Oh shit, I thought! But this is Worcester, I quickly realized. If you were connected and white and Catholic and from St. Johns, most things were fixable. I remember being told by a State Trooper back then that all the traffic citations he had written one day had been 'fixed' or discarded since every miscreant had connections save one. He tore up the last ticket himself since he felt sorry for such a friendless soul. Anyways, when the police called to ask me to come in for a "chat," I called on my good friend's father who was a cop. All was taken care of; don't you just love corruption. Today, if a black kid was in the same situation, a swat team would be sent to take him down and odds are the kid would wind up riddled with 127 bullets. Sadly, that is not much of an exaggeration.

There was another near miss one snowy New Year's Eve. I recall having others in my car, presumably we were off to a party in my father's car, the usual piece of junk. What I remember best about this mode of transportation is that the driver-side door would not open. Anyways, we were on side streets and came over a hill to see, for some unknown reason, a police car just sitting in the middle of the upcoming intersection. I applied the brakes, but we simply kept sliding right toward the patrol car. It was all in slow motion, my car out of control and the impending crash approaching. I can still see the expression of horror on the cop's face as I finally slid to a stop a foot away from where he sat. He was sure he had some drunken teens on his hands. He was even more sure when he asked me to step out of the car and I told him I couldn't. It did not look good at that moment. But I did explain the car malfunction, slid out the other door, and passed a sobriety test. We were really good kids.

Of course, an all-boys school will be full of ongoing taunts and one-upmanship. You had to be quick-witted and cool if you were not to be eaten alive by the other guys. It was a dog-eat-dog, Darwinian culture where the weak fell by the wayside. But that was all part of the process of forging character and making you a man. After all, you were expected to go forth and be soldiers for Christ battling heathens like the Lutherans or worse, the Baptists. I must admit, while I survived quite well, I felt vulnerable back then. My tough skin that would weather attacks from Governors and the like had not fully developed yet.

I continue turning the pages. There are several pictures of me with my Seminary friends. Funny, I cannot even recall their names any more, at least not with certainty, though I believe both of my roommates were named Peter. In one, the three of us stand there in our white shirts and black ties, the uniform of the first two years. We would dream of the day when we would be able to wear the cassocks of upper classmen. To us, that signaled we had made it. I doubt that any of the fellows made it all the way, but I have no way of knowing for sure. There are other pictures of family parties, waiting with my mother and aunt for a bus that would take me to Illinois and my new life as a Priest in training. There are pictures of weddings and other events that mark various kinds of life adventures.

Putting the album down…

The final shot was taken at Logan airport. It is 1969. I had just flown in from Ireland, my final stop on my trip home from India. I am giving my mother a hug. There is no indication she is hugging me back. Still, I will assume she is happy to see me. I have a touch of a smile on my face. Am I glad to see my folks, glad to be back in the U.S. or merely bemused at all the promise and uncertainty before me. Here I am, college trained, Peace Corps tested, and not at all sure what is in store for me.

Then again, isn't that what life is all about, the not knowing. I feel fortunate that I never settled for what I was. I broke away from the conventional life imposed by the working class, ethnic, Catholic culture of my youth. In college, I toyed with being swept up in the anger and irrationality of the times but remained attached to sanity and mainstream society. As I aged, I did not settle for security but remained free to seek out new ideas and challenges to stimulate my active imagination. Now, toward the end of things, I can look back on a life with a satisfied smile yet wonder if something exciting is yet around the corner. I am definitely looking forward to a time when a buxom Swedish nurse attends to my needs as an elderly fool in assisted living…even more foolish than I am at present.

There is a great scene from the movie, the *Last Hurrah*, where the old Irish politician who served as Boston mayor and then governor for many years is finally dying. The inspiration for the protagonist presumably is a real-life politician named James Michael Curley. In public life, the movie character fought against the WASP elite on behalf of his working class, ethnic supporters. Spencer Tracey plays Frank Skeffington in the movie version. His friends and a few political enemies visit as Frank apparently lies in a coma, about to pass. An old opponent muses, "Well, one thing for sure, if he had it to do over again he would do things differently." Frank opens his eyes for one last observation on life before passing, "The hell I would." I could not have said it better myself.

Frank Skeffington was a rebel. I like to think that I was one myself. One difference between the Skeffington character and myself? He knew what he was doing. I was totally clueless. Then again, perhaps that is what made it all so much fun.

Clueless Rebel and spouse in his dotage

CHAPTER 15

ENDING

*Memories of our lives, of our works, and
our deeds will continue in others.*

—Rosa Parks

Each life is much like those individual snowflakes at which I marveled as a young boy. In the aggregate, the flakes became a vast universe as my imagination thrust me through the infinite reaches of space. At that macro level, all seemed homogenous, white and blurred as the multitude of specks rushed by to nowhere in particular. But, on closer examination, one might see that each flake was unique and beautiful and perfect in its own way. If there is one epiphany that we all stumble upon at some point, it is that everything depends on perspective. What you see and what is real might be quite different. We may never get to know the latter.

Most people have surface similarities and dissimilarities. We observe what we are allowed to see or maybe what is inescapable on casual glance. At some level, though, we know that is insufficient.

Perhaps the iceberg is a more appropriate analogy. There is the portion of reality lying above the water and which is easily seen. Then, there is the immense mass of frozen water lying beneath the surface which we cannot easily view. It is here that the bulk of the structure's mass resides and much of its uniqueness as well. To see the rest, you have to look much deeper than we typically do. Some risk is involved.

I recall back in my urban affairs master's program back in Milwaukee. We spent much time talking among ourselves, often about politics and values and how to make sense of a world that was spinning out of control. It was the very end of the 1960s and earliest days of the 1970s. We had just witnessed assassinations, urban conflict, rebelliousness, and a seemingly endless war that made little sense to most of us. Still, I kept being surprised. I would get to know young men and women whom I dismissed as too conservative or mainstream or conventional to be of much interest to me. But when I took the time to listen, they often proved fascinating indeed. They were deeper and more complex than I ever imagined.

We all have nooks and nuances that would surprise others, secrets that would amaze, and foibles to make others smile if not guffaw outright. Each of us is more complex and more intricately constructed than imagined. We just have to take the time to tell our story and for others to listen. And yet, what I have shared in these pages just scratches the surface. No journey is over, not until the fat lady sings at least. Every one's story is yet unfolding.

Opportunity . . .

It turns out I got lucky or maybe I had more insight and determination than I normally acknowledge. I emerged as an independent and marginally successful man. I found a niche in life where I could do what I wanted to do on my terms. I built my own philosophy of life and an ethical infrastructure that made sense to me. I have no regrets, no reservations no second-guessing. Okay, it still bugs me a bit that Hugh Hefner never tapped me as his successor.

I feel so fortunate to have been born and raised in my times. When I tumbled into this world in 1944, it was a different world indeed. War raged around the world, the continent of Europe remained under Nazi oppression. Hitler was alive, as was FDR, as was Stalin and Mussolini and Franco and Mao. Apartheid reigned in much of America. Japanese-Americans on the west coast were confined in America's version of concentration camps at the same time some of their children died fighting in Europe for the same country that imprisoned their parents and loved ones. Homosexuality was a crime. Alan Turing, the British genius who helped launch the computer revolution and still had time to save untold allied lives by breaking the German's enigma code, was later imprisoned for his sexual preferences.

If I had a vote at that moment I am sure I would have crawled back into my mother's womb. The world did not look like a good bet at the time. Few rational men would have given even money that the future was worth the gamble of taking a chance on it. Of course, no one asked me as I plunged into my future. According to eyewitness reports I developed very slowly. Both the ability to talk and walk came to me quite late, then again Einstein reportedly developed quite late in childhood. Moreover, I was a pain in the butt to all around me. Apparently, I threw temper tantrums, often in very public places. I still vaguely recall lying down in store aisles screaming my head off when denied my wishes. I strongly suspect that if a broader vote were taken in those first years, my preference to return to where I came from would have been affirmed by a voice vote with no dissents.

But I came of age during the 1960s . . . the wild, raging nonsense that was the sixties. Though I had very little in the way of mentors or financial resources as a kid, my generation did have great opportunities. The American dream meant something in those times, at least for white citizens. America had not yet begun to congeal into an oligarchic economic hierarchy where the path to success would become increasingly difficult for most. That lessening of optimism and opportunity would not begin until the Reagan revolution in the 1980s. We could take chances, dream dreams, go off to the Peace Corps, take jobs for the good that they might do and not merely the financial advantages they bestowed. Life was raucous and open to us.

I recently chatted with several neighbors who served as Peace Corps volunteers between in 1967 and 1972. We shared our good fortunes about the times in which we came of age. We all agreed that we did not obsess about a career, did not agonize over which courses to take starting in the third grade. Our parents did not consider suicide if we were not selected into a premier, private grammar school. We graduated from college and graduate school without mountains of debt that would narrow future choices. We could think about ideas and issues and life in the broadest sense. If you were smart and energetic, the world was yours. How great was that!

I think back to what I was by the end of the 1960s. I was pretty unrecognizable from the high school kid who entered that decade in 1959. Principles such as social justice, equality, and peace were now part of my fabric. More than that, I was often quite angry. I hated that my country waged war so easily and supported some of the most repressive, totalitarian governments in the world. I hated that so many fellow citizens fought against basic equality, throwing their passions in favor of continued hate and exclusion. I despised the fact that so many seemed unable to fully participate in what we saw as an economic bounty that ought to have been more broadly shared. Why could we not do better?

At the same time, I recognized that many of my elders would look upon my youthful exuberance with bemused tolerance. Once he matures, buys a house, starts paying taxes, and has a child, surely then he will ossify into Republican, if not conservative, orthodoxy. Like death and taxes, responsibility accentuates self-interest and overweening narcissism. Tommy surely will come around as so many have before him. I had my doubts that would happen but could not be sure. I was comforted by a belief that my generation, full of idealistic visions of a better society, would soon rise to positions of power and influence. When we did, utopia could not be far behind. It sounded like a plan to me. Too bad plans don't always work out.

To a small extent, the conventional wisdom had a point. My anger did subside as I became more involved in career and adult things. Part of my moderation came from becoming a policy wonk. To be effective in that role, I had to move from advocate to educator. I had to work with people on all sides of an issue. If a reporter contacted me, and they did at least weekly during the height of welfare reform, I typically assumed an academic posture. I always tried to do the "on the one hand and on the other hand" thing to cover all legitimate sides of an issue. If they chose to select one ideological or partisan side, that was their prerogative. I had done my task of providing full and balanced information.

Several times I wrote articles that really attempted to bridge the ideological divides that separated people. One piece titled "Child

Poverty: Progress or Paralysis" introduced the notions of truncated perceptions. Simply put, all sides in most arguments about welfare reform were both right and wrong. The welfare population was heterogeneous and not homogenous. Thus, various explanatory theories and strategic solutions to the welfare challenge all had some merit. Each typically focused on part of the population, part of the problem, and thus represented part of the ultimate solution. The secret to progress was for all sides to recognize this simple fact and work with one another, not against each other.

The piece was wildly popular and was used by the U. S. General Accountability Office (the GAO) for many years. At conferences and meetings, people would seek me out because they wanted to talk to the "onion" man. Of course, one article does not change the world. Politicians were still dragged in partisan, conflict-oriented, directions but I found myself arguing persuasively for rationality and compromise. One of my favorite one-liners in later years was that one generation's solution was the next generation's scandal. We ricocheted from solution to solution because each addressed only part of the challenge. I felt comforted when I would be accused of being a running dog of the left and a running dog of the right on the same day.

Anger . . .

Now I am in those golden years. With occasional exceptions, I am no longer working on practical solutions to specific policy challenges. Rather, I am looking hard at what my country is becoming in a larger sense. As I do so, I am becoming angry again. I next restate several points I first made toward the end of *Confessions of a Wandering Academic*. For that I do not apologize, redundancy is sometimes a very good thing.

Technically, I have entered my eighth decade. That sounds real old but only means that I am in my seventies. What I feel inside is very similar to what I felt in my late teens and early twenties, during those tumultuous days of change and questioning. It could be that, as a spectator rather than player in the current policy wars, I can once again give vent to my values and emotions. I now read the *New York Times* and find myself once again roiling with emotions not felt since the 1960s. I am deeply troubled that we have concentrations of income and wealth seldom seen before in this country. The Gini-coefficient, a measure of inequality used by economists, now shows income and wealth disparities in America close to those found in banana Republics that we used to laugh at not long ago.

The economic elite now command as much of the income and wealth distribution now as they did just before the economy collapsed in 1929. A tiny fraction at the top of the distribution (one-tenth of one percent), control 23.5 percent of all the wealth in the U.S., while the top 1 percent commands at least 35 percent. On the other hand, half of all Americans have negative net assets and our median wealth figure puts us way down the list of our peer nations. Yet, too many of those at the top of the income distribution see fit to spend their fortunes turning the policy levers further in their favor. I sit back and stare with wonder. Is there no end to such avarice and greed? Besides, it all seems self-defeating in the end. Who will buy what they have to peddle when they have all the money?

What I find particularly troubling is that our easy strategies for dealing with declining economic opportunities (stagnating incomes for most families along with growing inequality) appear exhausted. We have already delayed marriage, had fewer children, thrown our spouses and partners into the labor market, saved less and borrowed more (using household equity as personal ATMs), and added more advanced credentials after our names. And our children often delay establishing their own households (good luck in kicking them out of the nest). And still, economic outcomes grow more unequal. Throw into that mix global warming and a few other societal challenges and you want to scream. Carbon dioxide levels are at highs that portend environmental disasters we can barely envision. Where has our sanity and compassion gone? If I were popping out of the womb today, I might look around and come to the same conclusion I would have made in 1944. This place sucks the big one.

We laugh at young people who talk about finding themselves. And there is often something about this at which to laugh. Searching for one's self is often a shallow excuse to idle away time indulging in sex, drugs, and rock and roll which, come to think of it, has its merits. Seriously, there probably is a core justification for this exercise in self-examination. There is a personal space, if we can find it, where we would feel most comfortable and probably would be the most productive. The trick is to identify what that is. The challenge is to make it happen. In the end, I came damn close to finding my special place, close enough to be mighty satisfied.

I suspect I have come full circle. As I emerged from the cocoon of my childhood and began to think on my own I was full of passion and commitment. Now, as I slowly slide into dotage, that same sense of outrage is back with me. What I became back in my youth is who I am and who I will be. I still laugh a lot at life and in life. But at the end of the day I do care, I care a lot. Rebelliousness can be a good thing, particularly if it is warranted.

Peace . . .

Have I stumbled across any big lessons over the course of seven decades? Well, I doubt I have uncovered any insights that have not been fully explored by others or already expressed in excruciating detail. Besides, any lessons learned apply only to me. I do not know the secrets of the universe or the meaning of life. Perhaps, as the mathematics of string theory apparently suggest, there are an infinite number of parallel universes out there. Perhaps all that we experience is a fancy holograph, more mirage that substance. Maybe the universe we can measure is only a speck in some larger entity whose existence will remain beyond our reach during my lifetime. It is marvelous to contemplate such things and marvel that we have come this far as a species where we can imagine the unimaginable. Such considerations calm me in a way. My pitiful existence is put into perspective.

Two images come back to me from my early years which, in a way, frame the range of my inner struggles. In one, I am sitting with a comely lass, a Clark classmate. Her name is now long gone in the mists of time. We are sitting in a car talking, though I recall that some light sensual play took place while unfulfilled dreams of deeper eroticism played in the recesses of my libido. Her body was exceptionally inviting as I recall. Alas, we mostly talked. I did waste a lot of time talking with these lovely women, didn't I?

Anyways, what I most recall is that I enthralled her with a summary of my life philosophy at the time. *"You are born at some point in time and sometime down the road you die. There is not much of substance or meaning in between those two points except for what we choose to assign to our lives, all those matters of nonsense and trivia which we select to fill in our allotted tenure on earth. I choose to fill up my years doing things that will bring the least harm to others and, from time to time, bring to those around me a few laughs."* It was a simple philosophy, pessimistic if not cynical yet very heartfelt at the time. It also was a line that promised very few evenings of sexual bliss. I always thwarted my erotic hopes with brutal honesty.

A few years later, after returning from Peace Corps, I was sitting with friends from the Urban Affairs program at UW-M. Again, I was regaling people with my philosophy on all things large and small as I was moved often to do. Perhaps I was yet looking for some line that, at long last, might finally bring me sexual success. As I now think on it, I wonder how I got any party invites at all. At one point that night, probably at about 3:00 AM, I swept my arm in an upward arc. I was trying to illustrate the fact that change was happening at an exponential rate all around us. As a species, we would be entering a transformational era, one that would alter qualitatively life as we know it. What would happen was unknowable but could be as significant as the transition from ape to homo-sapiens. I recall stopping at the height of my arc and thinking, "Who the hell is this blazing optimist?" When did I, the Black Bart of the soul, suddenly become so hopeful?

I suppose that my life has bounced between these extremes. Sometimes I look around and despair at the irrationality and narrowness I see. Other times, I can still sense change and hope and promise. It matters not that I cannot see to the other side of any transformational era in which we might be participating. It does not even matter that I could not resolve most of the thorny policy questions I tackled during my professional career. As long as I have my imagination, conundrums to ponder, and my ability to express myself, I will be content.

As I bring this work to a close, I am drawn back to a comment Lee made in an e-mail after we had reconnected. She argued that I had become a complete version of the man she saw in my unformed youth. From afar, she saw the same intelligence, wit, sensitivity, passion, and commitment that made me special to her back then. But now, in her mind, I had the balance and confidence to shape those attributes into a coherent and pleasing whole. I seldom take compliments well, but I will give her the benefit of the doubt here. After all, she knew me better than anyone other than my spouse and probably could be more objective than most.

I do feel blessed. There were moments when my fortunes might well have gone in a different and a much more tragic direction. In the end, though, all worked out despite a woeful lack of skills and a few haphazard life decisions. Perhaps there is a lesson that life bestows on those curious enough to seek out such things. You can be held captive, even tortured. You can be fed constant propaganda, even by those close to you. You can suffer defeat and humiliation and all sorts of degradations. However, if you examine life around you with raw honesty and incisive logic touched with heavy doses of imagination, you will remain free. Seek your own philosophy and your own path. Never settle. It was fun being a clueless rebel. And like I told that long-ago nameless co-ed, I did fill up my allotted time on earth with interesting experiences. But mostly, and of this I am most proud, I left everyone with a few laughs.

Beyond that, I never came up with any final answers to life's bigger questions. That is a matter of little consequence, however. In the end, it is the quest that brings us pleasure, not the achievement. It is the journey, not the end. *Carpe diem!*

CPSIA information can be obtained
at www.ICGtesting.com
Printed in the USA
LVHW111918031218
599057LV00003B/217/P

9 781948 000208